LEAVE NO TRACE

LEAVE NO TRACE

BY RANDEE DAWN

SF & FANTASY
ARC MANOR
ROCKVILLE, MARYLAND

SHAHID MAHMUD
PUBLISHER

www.caeziksf.com

Leave No Trace copyright © 2025 by Randee Dawn. All rights reserved. This book may not be copied or reproduced, in whole or in part, by any means, electronic, mechanical, or otherwise without written permission except short excerpts in a review, critical analysis, or academic work.

This is a work of fiction.

Cover art by Dany V.

ISBN: 978-1-64710-161-9

First Edition. First Printing. September 2025.
1 2 3 4 5 6 7 8 9 10

An imprint of Arc Manor Inc.

www.CaezikSF.com

For Julia, who's always helped me find the way.

Contents

Part One 1
Going Offguard 3
Burt Fuckin' Badass Reynolds 12
A Girl Named Jim 18
Welcome to Camp Furey 26
King of the Forest 38
Mostways Ready 46
Impossible Birch Trees 57
Down the Rabbit Hole 64
See the Pieces, Make 'Em Complete 68
The War Comes Home 72
Changing the Rules 76
We Live Here Now 83
Betwixt and Between 90
Living in a Box 94
What Needs Protecting 98
What Can Be Sacrificed 104
No Unnecessary Deaths 110
The Bear Chooses You 119
Rebalancing the Scales 124
The Truth of a Blue Knit Scarf 128

Part 2 131
Forest Dreams 133
An Unholy Mess 143
For All That Bodes Well 148

The Country of the Young	154
A Dark, Worn-Up Place	165
The Unseen	171
The Places That I Hide	176
Fixer, Finder, Healer	182
The Invitation	187
Bear Necessities	195
A Wild Test	198
Where Is the Exit	201
Chateau Artio	209
Shoot When the Target Presents	215
The Mercy Kill	220
Natural Magic	224
The Way Is Clear	230
Start Where You End	233
Glossary	239
Acknowledgements	240

PART ONE

*"Nae endings w'out need
Nae beginnings w'out purpose"
— the Ghillie Dhu*

Going Offguard

"Daddy was fulla it," Jim always said.
Fulla what? I always said back. Knowing. Wanting him to say it.
Shit! Jim always shouted, so loud I thought everybody left in the world could hear. But wasn't nobody around to hear him xcept me and the trees. *He's fulla shit!*
And I laughed and laughed, sounds comin' outta me like fireworks.
Jim never did.

Morning's when you get stuff done in the woods, Daddy says. Get up before the sun, when even the Oscar owls are sleepy and the Harry hares are hiding and everybody else is in dreamyland. Sneak behind the back of the world so you can prepare. Do the thing nobody else is doing and nobody ever sees you coming.

Offguard, Jim xplained it once. You catch 'em Offguard. Offguard's not a place, xactly. Offguard's what happens when you go faster than the others. Whoever the others are. Get organized before they do. Then you're ten steps ahead and you know the lay of the land.

I am always ten steps ahead. That's 'cause I'm faster than anyone else in the forest. It's one true I know about myself, one thing I know for certain on days when I feel like I don't know anything else: I am the fastest.

Okay, xcept for maybe Artie.

We have a job starting later this morning and Daddy definitely wants me up and at-'em soon as he's ready but I'm not waiting for him, I got my own place to be. Hard sometimes to get a minute on my own. Always chopping and hunting and peeling and cooking and hauling and—it doesn't end. Was easier when Jim was here.

Jim, who isn't here now. Jim, who left me behind. But thinking of Jim too much puts bees in my head and I don't want to waste time being mad at him so I look up at the cabin's ceiling and see where the roof beams join and cross and I find a little knothole I know about and I put all my Jim thoughts in there. Then I close my eyes and when I open them I'm me again.

I hurry hurry out of bed and creep out of the loft slow slow and leave Daddy behind making *zzz*'s. Got to be quiet. If I wake him he might find things for me to do. If I wake him he might think I'm trying to run away, like Jim did.

I wouldn't, though. Got noplace to go. But doesn't mean I don't think about it.

I'm out in the forest with the trees and the sky and it's just black and blue shadows outside the cabin, the old Sun still gone nighty-night. For a minute I look back at the cabin and hear the *zzz*'s and I stick my tongue out far as it'll go.

See, Daddy, you don't know everything 'bout me.

Turning round I take a sniff of the night-morning air. Heavy but cold. Wet. Snow's a day off, prolly. Two. So yeah. Coming but not yet. Early, tho. Only September. Prolly.

Time to go Offguard. Got my pack and bow and arrow and cap and boots hanging off my belt and two apples and the book. I start a light jog, silent. Blink and you'd miss me—I'm just a bit of skin and hair and cloth. My toes pad over dead things like I'm hardly even here. Never liked shoes, not even boots, noisy stiff things. Xcept mocs but usually I don't even wear mocs. Be too cold for barefeet soon. Winter comes fast and hard 'round here.

There's a small clearing in the tall tall trees about a thousand jogsteps away and I stop. Listen. I can kinda hear Jim if I go still enough.

We could leave now, he said to me once right in this very spot. It was a hot day and we were supposed to be checking the snares but we were throwing round his baseball. *He'll never catch us. We can go home.*

We are home, I said back.

Dummy, he said. *There's a whole wide world out there an' you think this's the whole deal.*

I slugged him in the arm. 'Course I did. Been here a long time. Don't remember much else. *Daddy says people are sick.*

Daddy's the one who's sick. He made a face. Jim always acted like he knew more than I did but there's no way he could. We both got here the same day. Daddy gave us both the grape soda. But I trusted him. Even if he was a stupidhead for always trying to find the way out. We both knew there wasn't one.

And we didn't go. Least not that day. Least not me.

Jim never wanted to stay here. But Daddy said we had to. People got sick and the world was going crazypants and he saved us by bringing us here. He said. So of course I believed.

Sometimes I do think about what it would feel like to leave. To put my feet (with shoes on them) on that black hard road and keep walking until there were more people and houses and cars and dogs barking in the yards. I'm *this close* to asking Daddy 'bout it. He once said grown age was eighteen and I'm almost there.

Next time the snow melts, I'll be eighteen. Then I'll ask. He might try to hit me but I'll risk it. I am fast.

But could I go without Daddy? He knows most everything. Only stuff I know is right here right now.

I get out of my head and back into the trees. Thinking 'bout Jim makes me dumb, I don't pay attention. But if I go too long not thinking about him he sneaks back into my head anyway and that makes me sad. He's all over the forest to me. Over at Blueberry Cliff where we hunted or the Great Meadow where we ran around or in the forest clearings when it was fogmisty on the ground and he would say it's like living in a cloud. He's in all those places.

I bite my tongue 'til it hurts and there's salt in my mouth and that wakes me up and puts Jim away for now.

Gil! That's why I'm out here early. If Gil's 'round we'll have some time before I have to work. Make Daddy wake up on his ownsome and make his own coffee and have to come find me. Anyway, if I want to see Gil I have to try now—if I don't I prolly won't see him for a week. More. So I take a deep breath and put my hands up and whisper the abracadabras he taught me: *Tha an t-slighe soilleir,* which he says means *the way is clear* and then the trees go soft and wavy and hum to me and I read them like a map.

I lower my hands and breathe another minute. Saying the words makes my head hurt some. Like I thought and thought so hard my brain got sweaty. So I have to rest. After a minute, two minutes I look up at the map. It's just waiting for me. And I go:

1) Over a chewed-up log.
2) Scrambly up the sweet long grassy hill.
3) Touch the top of the stunty little tree, for luck.
4) All 'round the flowers (I only step between) with a look over my shoulder. I know I'm getting close when the bluebells show up. There's so many it's like the sky is napping on the ground.
5) Leap over the pine needle path, not onto it, nobody knows I was here if I do it that way.
6) And I'm here at the cliff base.

Climbing up the rock face is tough and can get noisy so I take it easy and slow like Daddy showed me. One hand one toe one hand one toe always three touches on the rock at once. Go careful, go quiet. Be part of the forest so nobody and nothing xpects you're there xcept maybe an early-riser Rocky raccoon or Paul porcupine. When Daddy brought me and Jim to the cabin 'bout ten summers back I started giving all the animals names. Game I made up and Jim helped. So all the snakes are Susie and all the mountain lions are Leo.

Only one Artie, though. She's different.

I go up and up hand and foot, foot and hand. I am the cliff. I am the rock.

Like I'm supposed to be here, part of the growing things. I *am* supposed to be here, in the forest. Didn't know that for a long time. This is my place. This is why I get a little scared sick in my belly when I think of the Wide World Jim talked about. Here's where I'm fast and quiet and the trees hum to me and the caves sing to me and I understand everything.

I am the forest.

My toes are strong and they grab hold of the jagged gray rock like fingers. They wrap 'round the outcrops and I can push hard down on them and I don't even go "ow" anymore if I hit a sharp bit 'cause my feet are tough like shoes on the bottom. I stop once to get my breath but then finally I'm at the top and it's one more push with my hard little toes and I'm up and over, flat on the ridge, face down in the dirt and grass.

I take a deep smell of the earth and it's like I'm smelling the skin of the world. It's rich and dark and there's metal and wood all bundled up in there with the bugs and the grass and everything's okay. Same as last time I was up here, maybe three days back. I can smell when things change in the dirt, 'cause when things change it means I gotta be ready to change too. Daddy always says the ones who survive in the forest are the ones who adapt. You have to be like a mirror. You become whatever, whoever you see in that mirror right that minute. And when that minute's over you go back to who you really are.

If you can remember.

Jim didn't adapt, Daddy says. That's why he's not here anymore.

We don't have mirrors in the cabin. Instead we have lakes that hold still when the wind stops blowing. And there are mirrors at the hot shower place Daddy took me to a couple of times so I have a little idea what I look like but I don't see my face regular. I don't know if I remember who I was once. I'm just me, today.

Okay, maybe I know some. I was a second grader way back when. I was a Brownie. I liked science stuff when it was about animals. I could tell an ocelot from a lynx and I knew elephants had ears shaped like the place they were from. I was in a school with boys and girls and some who weren't either and just wanted to be called "they" and homework and touchdesks that changed when you poked with a finger. But those things I remember are only bits and pieces, like flat rocks I bounce on to get from one side of a creek to the other. They don't mean anything. They're what was. 'Course if I was still a Girl Scout now I'd have all the badges they made for hunting 'cause that's what I do really good. That's another true thing: I am great with a bow and arrow and I can skin and dress a deer fast as Jim used to.

Leap!

I'm up on my feet making a big Harry hare jump and then I'm down in a crouch again and looking round. The treemap is still humming and the bluebells are thick on all sides of my ankles but I like to 'valuate things. I catch a bit of piney sap and a musky whiff that makes me think animals were here jumping on each other. There's a breeze, soft and full of morning and it's tickling my cheeks, slipping into my hair like fingers.

My memory jumps to another flat rock. To Mom. She combed my hair with her hands, her pointy thin fingers making braids. Once my hair was long and flowy and she could do it up faster than I could think and I'd be like *ow ow it hurts* but it didn't really it just surprised me. Now my hair's short like Jim's was.

When Daddy started taking me to work he cut it all off and told me to burn the long tail in the fire and that was the end. My eyes stung watching it go. But Daddy made me understand why I had to be somebody else when we went on jobs. How I had to *adapt*.

I'm humming a little bit. Gil likes it when I hum. Likes it best when I sing. I don't sing much. I only know a couple songs. But sometimes there's just a tune in my head and then I put in words. Mostly the words are lists, things I must remember to do or that I did and if I hum them to myself I remember 'em better. But you don't want to be too loud in the forest. You might get heard. So I am humming about climbing my cliff and smelling my ground and how the sun is just now starting to put the colors into the trees. About getting to see Gil.

Wind goes still and the fingers fall from my hair and Mom slips away again.

Now I have the measure of the place. I get tall and blink, then stride round the flowers—Gil says they're called harebells sometimes—and I am the fastest softest quietest thing in the forest.

A too-whoo-whoot sound lifts over everything and I turn to one side so my chin hits my shoulder. There they are: seven tall bright birch trees. They're huddling together in this C shape that Daddy called a "stand." The trees are so beautiful; they're straight and true and like they were just made yesterday even though they're tall as any trees around. Their white bark glows.

And smack in the middle, standing on the softest patch of pine needles you ever dreamed up is Gil.

"Wean." He smiles and thin blades of grass tumble from his hat like rain. "Knew ye'd come."

Prolly been five years since I met the Ghillie Dhu. That's what he is. He doesn't have a name, xactly, so he told me to call him Gil, that first time we met. Sometimes he shows up as a girl and then he's Gillie. Two in one. Gil's more fun than Gillie; she usually is about telling me what to do or what not to do, but whether Gil's being a boy or a girl he looks pretty much the same, like a person the forest grew.

He's my only friend.

"Come, wean," he says to me and holds out his hand. His words roll around like he's got a pebble in his mouth and make me think of songs. "Set."

I put down my bow and arrow—*nae weapons* he told me that first time—and my fingers curl round his and then I'm *inside* his clean bright pine needly place. We're both still in the forest, and I can see everything going on out there but once I'm *inside* nobody can see me. Us. Leastways I don't think so, unless Gil wants them to. He can do things people like me and Daddy and Jim can't and I'm still not totally sure but I don't think he's *people* xactly, but I don't ask. Maybe he'd be mad and go away if I asked the wrong thing.

I hold out one of the apples from my backpack.

"Thanking ye," he says, whisking it from my hand, and sits down next to me in the needles. He eyeballs that apple like it's the first one he ever saw. He smooths his hands over it and a little shiver runs through him. I always bring an apple, if we have apples. They keep a long time but they're rare 'round here. It's the first and only thing I ever gave him he really wanted. He brings the apple up to his nose and takes a long, deep smell and the colors on his face dance and shift and his eyes—they're almost all black, just a little white on the outsides—shine out at me. "'Tis a beauty. Like y'self."

Gil's 'bout as tall as me when he's standing. That's always been true: Whatever age I am he's my height, tho' I don't know what age he is. He never changes. Got a grass hat that folds over his head like a roof and his jacket's made of springy soft moss and grooved lined bark. His pants are like solid mud that bend when he moves. His skin shifts color, depending on the light and what he's thinking about. Sometimes he's brown and green, sometimes orange and yellow, sometimes sunny white, sometimes night black. Colors of the forest. But he's always got this light all 'round him.

Took me a while to understand Gil. He doesn't talk like people, but he doesn't look like people either, so it makes sense. He's the only person I talk to regular, xcept Daddy. When Gil calls me a *wean*, instead of my name, he means a little girl. *Wee one*, it means. "I'm not wee anymore," I say.

"Nae," he says. "But to me ye are, seems."

I have to see Gil alone 'cause he won't come round when Daddy's near. Just for me, I guess. He shows up whenever he feels like it, but only when I'm by myself. Today's different, though. I'm here right now 'cause Gil came into a dream in my head. Last night he froze up the other stuff I was dreaming about and stepped right into everything.

Come, he said to me. *Come in the morn. We have of which to speak.*

I lean back on my hands as he nibbles at the apple, then opens his jaws and chomps out a great big bite. Juice runs down his face and vanishes before it drips on the moss.

"Can't stay long," I say. "We're working."

He sets down the half-eaten apple and stares at it. Pats it. Looks up at me. "Aye," he says. "Ye will be taking some visitors a-huntin'."

"Aye," I say back with a smile, trying to ape his voice, but I always sound silly. "They want a deer."

"That's nae all," he says. "They want more." *Mair*, it sounds like. His face goes green-brown. "They want Artio."

There are other bears in the forest. But Artie—Gil said she was really named Artio but I like Artie better—is the only one I've ever seen. She's a whole lot bigger than most and full of unxpected things and I wonder if she's got her own abracadabras. Sometimes I walk in the forest and I see her deep in the trees and she's looking at me hard. I know what to do when I see a bear. I know how to not get eaten. But Artie never seems to want to come after me. She just looks.

No way Gil is gonna let them take Artie. He knows we gotta hunt, time to time, but there are limits.

"She's not easy to find," I say. "I bet they won't get her."

"They will ask ye to help," he says.

"Well," I say, poking at the needles. "That's our job."

"But ye will *nae* find her, ye ken?" he snaps. "She's nae for them."

I sit up straight and look him in the eye. He's never ordery with me. That's what Gillie does. But first time I met Gil he did stop me from getting a deer I wanted. *Ye came to hunt*, he said to me then. Five winters back. *But ken that isnae how 'tis done in this part of the forest.*

What isn't done? I asked him then. He was impossible, standing there all bright green in the middle of our snowy winter. But there he was. I was littler and I believed everything about him.

Death, he told me. *Willful an' unnecessary death.*

As the Ghillie Dhu, Gil is in charge in certain parts of the forest. He shows up with his stand of birches, these amazing glowy trees that move on their own. He watches, he takes care of things. He shoos off animals that are in danger if he can. But this is the first time he's asked me for something so partic'lar, something about a job. First time he has instructions for me.

"Okay," I say and it's easy because I'm sure we won't see her. I don't know how to feel about Artie. Her watching is not like what a bear is supposed to do. Bears are supposed to be afraid of people and when they're not, people just have to stand their ground or get crouched and low and hope for the best. She's strange. I wouldn't mind her gone but I don't want to be the one to do it. "But Daddy—"

"Artio's in *yer* care," says Gil and it's almost like he's angry. He's so serious I look careful to make sure he's not really Gillie this time. "Ye will *nae* go after that creature. An ye will stop her being harmed, it comes to that, so ye will. Ye will do this for me."

Gil saved me once. So I owe him. I promise. "But the deer—"

He sighs. "Ye know how I feel."

Willful an' unnecessary death. He doesn't care if we kill so we can eat. Everybody has to eat, even Gil. He just doesn't like the jobs, when people come in so they can take pictures and horns and heads. Sometimes I swear he's spooked deer we were tracking, would be easy shots, and the clients get mad at us though nobody knows why xcept maybe me. Gil doesn't xplain.

"But you won't stop us." Actually, I don't know if he could stop us xcept to scare any prey away again. I only know I don't want him to be mad at me.

He shakes his head and grass rains off it. "Nae," he says. "I dinnae want anythin' to do with *those* folk." He lifts the apple again and smells it and takes another big bite. "Other thing," he says after chewing and swallowing. His voice is small and slow and he waits for me to look into his eyes. "Ye must listen, for 'tis a hard thing I share."

I sit up straight and feel like I'm falling into those black holes.

"There 'tis one who will come in this hunting party, one that disnae like my kind," he says. "His blood boils. He's full o'angry bits an cannae be trusted."

"Why?"

More grass falls. "'Tis a long story for a very other day. But. In the world beyond these trees, beyond the ocean, battle wages 'tween his folk and my folk."

I tilt my head. "A battle? Which folk am I?"

The colors on his face shift. "In some ways ye are more like my kind. But I am all *sìthean*, and there's no way 'round it all. An' this one who comes, he fears and hates and harms we *sìthiche*."

It's a new word for me and sounds like *shee*.

"Who started the fight?"

He stares into the trees beyond his birches and doesn't say anything for a long time. "'Tis a war, more like. I ken not all of the story. Nae enough time today to tell more. Know only that he isnae ye's friend. Ye need not know more. An 'tis why I will stay clear 'til he departs."

I can hardly move. Ordery and now talking about the Outside—the real Outside, outside the trees—this is all new to me from Gil. He never's like this. I know it must be important but I get that sick feeling in my belly whenever I think about what's past the trees. When part of me is so excited about what might be there and part of me thinks I would be eaten up the minute I left the forest.

"The center cannot hold," I say, remembering a line from a book we have in the cabin.

"Aye," he says and we both go quiet. "Nae anymore. So. Ye ken?"

"I ken," I say, but I don't. Not really.

Gil brightens and he's the friend I've always known. He reaches over to the backpack and upends it. The book slides out and falls between us. "Well, wean?"

Business is done. Now he's hoping for something else. I open the book, which he stares at like it's another apple. He's heard the whole thing prolly five times by now. Every time I finish he wants to start over. I say there are more books to read but he doesn't care. He can't read our words so he says it's up to me to tell him the tales of the Hundred Aker Woods. He says he likes them because they have animals and there are trees. Since he likes them, I like them.

I look up and there's a smile on his brown-gold face. His white teeth shine and his eyes are deep dark pools. He takes my hand and gives it a squeeze and my chest gets tight. Then he lies back in the soft brown needles and stretches like a cat. His eyes go closed and he points a finger in the air. "Now, wean. Speak ye's words to me. How is the Eeyore this morn?"

I begin, and we both tumble into a hole in the world that takes us to familiar places and windy days and jars of hunny. I keep reading and traveling until I hear it: a high whoot-whistle that soars over the cliff and into my ear. It's Daddy's call, our signal.

I keep reading. Daddy can wait.

The whistle comes again and I stop, but I don't move. Gil is watching me now. "Ye will go," he says.

"I don't want to." I want to stay right here, doing just this. And I can't decide if someone whose blood boils is scary or something I really want to see. Don't I ever get to decide?

Daddy's voice comes to me from a distance, a low growl that sounds like a puma getting ready to pounce. "Don't make me wait," he calls to me. "I know you're up there. I hear your voice."

That freezes me up. He can't know I'm talking to anybody. Gil's eyes meet mine, and he nods.

"Coming!" I shout so loud Gil flinches, but he holds open the invisible door to his trees and waves at me. I slam the book closed and stuff it in my pack.

Gil smiles, offers a hand. I touch his fingers and back out of the shelter.

Time to go to work.

Burt Fuckin' Badass Reynolds

When T.J. Furey is nineteen years, six months, and fourteen days old, he gets stoned in his hotel suite and watches *Deliverance* on one of the classic movie streams. Unlike most people who watch the film, he does not come away having learned any of its lessons, the two key ones of which are *don't go into the woods unprepared* and *don't screw with the locals*.

Stephanie Holliday, who is watching him watch the movie while pretending to read a book on the other side of the couch, sees the change unfold. T.J. sits back against the room's leather sofa and takes another toke. "Burt Reynolds," he mutters. "Burt Fuckin' Reynolds. Burt Fuckin' Badass Reynolds."

Stef supposes she can see why. In the movie, the classic film star is White Man Incarnate. Or at least what White Man Incarnate was back when her grandparents were kids. Virile, tough as nails, loaded with a bow and arrow. She calls up Reynolds's bio on the Cloud and scans to see what T.J.'s plugged into, nodding. The movie Burt is before the mustache and the naked magazine spread and a hairpiece that settled on his head like a badger that died of heatstroke. Movie Burt could handle a broken leg while riding the rapids and still come up swinging. He wasn't a joke then.

Over the last few days, Stef has seen how quickly a person can go from being on the top of the world to being a joke. It pains her, and she knows that is not how T.J. sees his life playing out. She knows this without having to hear him say it; they've been best friends most of their lives.

T.J. leans back and howls like a wild animal. Then he turns to one of the roadies and snaps his fingers a few times. "Toss me the rest of those cookies, Bud."

The roadie isn't called Bud; it's Kwame. Stef has made sure to know the names of all the crew and roadies, since it's just good sense to know who you're hitting the road with for months at a time. But T.J. never remembers anybody's name until it's important to him.

"Toss yer own cookies," T.J.'s manager Tony Garcia growls, but sends the pack of Mallowmars over in a neat arc. T.J. scrabbles for the soft, sweet wonders and stuffs three into his mouth.

Stef likes watching T.J. move. First of all, he's a seriously beautiful young man. She's observed him for years, watching as he went from a string bean of a boy with a persistent acne rash to a clear-faced, doe-eyed, sturdy young man with a carefully curated flop of bright blond hair that tumbles over one eye and makes the girls sigh and press their legs together tight. He's pale as the underbelly of a fish, and white boys aren't usually Stef's thing. But T.J. exists in a universe of his own, like he's from some better world and just got lost here on Earth for a while. Get to know him a little while, like Stef has, and the truth comes out—he's far from perfect. In fact, he's her imperfect jerkface soulmate of a foster brother and they're tight as if they were blood. That is, if you can sometimes have hot and sweaty thoughts about your blood, which you're not supposed to.

For his part, T.J. is lost in the fog of the smoke and his own spinning brain and only barely aware of others in the room. The suite is full of people who've been lingering and sponging off him for days now. They range from the roadies, Tony, and the guys from the band up to another six or seven hangers-on from the label, groupies, and journalists. Stef half turns in her seat, one spiraled dreadlock dangling over her glasses, and counts. Right now, there are sixteen people in this room and she knows perhaps a third of them. None of them are paying her any attention; she's not the star attraction. She just writes the songs.

Passed out on the floor, head on a pillow, lies their guitarist Daryl Wu, gangly legs making everybody nearly trip over him as they pass, a slick curl of drool waterfalling onto his digitally tattooed hand. The pool of spit is covering up this week's semiperm inking: a line from one of T.J.'s hit songs. Daryl knows where his bread is buttered. Drummer Ian Altschul perches on the couch's edge between T.J. and Stef, sitting ramrod straight and absolutely still, platinum hair standing up in twelve different spears—the more spears, the more anxious and argumentative he is—and balancing the shared joint between two fingers like he's David Bowie or some other space oddity. The others are pasted around the rest of the suite like ink spots: dressed in black, continually sliding from the snacks in the fridge to the drinks at the minibar to the toilet and back again.

And then there's Tony, who wears his expensive fitted suit like a uniform, jet-black hair carefully pasted back, always on high alert. Like he's still out there on the battlefield, fighting mysterious forces no one else can see. He's actively doing much of what Stef is pretending not to: monitoring T.J., the man whose situation has kept them trapped in here for the last few days. The two-bedroom bungalow at the Chateau Marmont has been their prison ever since the headlines broke a week ago, and while Stef can't speak for anybody else, she's getting serious cabin fever.

Of course, they can leave anytime they like. Step out into that monotonous California sunshine for some Vitamin D and keep on keeping on. But nobody in the band or crew will depart unless T.J. goes first, and T.J. isn't going anywhere. It's T.J.'s face that's been plastered on the cover of every virtual tabloid CloudPage around the world and in the vids of millions of wannabe newsmakers, and he won't risk a paparazzi ambush. Some of the others might be staying out of inertia, or loyalty to his cause, or because he is their meal ticket. Doesn't matter, really—they stay.

In his high flying state, T.J. is magnanimous and adores them all.

Most days, they aren't alone. The room gets regular visitors—the pot doc comes like clockwork, always making the same stale joke about room service. The record label PR lady Tiffanee pokes her fluffed head in the room once a day, seven p.m. sharp, coughing ostentatiously to remind everyone that smoking in a nonsmoking room will rack up extra charges. Charges that Stef knows the label will absorb for now, but will ultimately get hoovered out of T.J.'s royalty checks down the road. *The back end*, they'd explained it when she and T.J. first signed contracts, and at the time T.J. snickered that of course it comes out the back end, all his earnings just pour out of his ass. Everybody in the room—his lawyers, the label heads, the marketing goofballs—laughed, but it was a brittle candy sound.

That's a sound T.J. never made before they got discovered. Before the songs took off. But Stef's gotten used to hearing that noise a lot over the past couple of years. And every time she hears it, she thinks of lollipops cracking against your teeth when you get sick of sucking out all the sweet and just want to crunch the life out of the thing.

How many licks does it take before we get to the center of T.J. Furey and want to hear him pop?

Stef dreams of blowing this clam stand with him, going down through the service entrance after they scramble their GPS chip signal, smartglasses on tight and blackout hoodies pulled up. That way even if the papweasels take their pictures they won't register on cameras. But they both know T.J. would be spotted eventually. Whatever he does, wherever he goes, they know where he is. Everyone is a snitch in this town; paparazzi have a network of DigiCoin informants who'll call the hotlines and say yes, indeed, T.J. Furey is sitting at the bar/having a slice/dipping his toe in the pool/buying toothpaste in their establishment and please come over right now.

Or one of the informants might just turn on the camera in his enhanced contact lenses and film it for themselves. Stream it to the On Demand PayCloud, make a couple thou without taking two steps left or right.

Naw, it's easier to hide out and dodge the questions, dodge the embarrassment. Smoke a lot of pot and try to forget about Mandy Kowalski, that thirty-seven-year-old waitress out of East Fucking Jesus Nowhere, who popped up in the middle of T.J.'s current tour to announce she was having his baby. When that happened last week, Stef felt like they'd all woken up in the middle of that Michael Jackson song Gramma liked.

The one about the kid not being his baby. Or son. Or something.

Whole idea is disgusting, T.J. tells Stef later that evening. Like he'd even consider poking some old bat who has more years on her than his mom.

"You protest too much," Stef shoots back. "Methinks."

Every night around midnight the room clears out—hangers-on, friends, crew, even the rest of the band go to their respective rooms or homes or alleys. Stef remains, and they both prefer it that way. They go out on his patio and leave the sliding glass door open, clear out the day's fug of smoke and body odor, and stare out at the jewel-bright city beyond.

"Methinks?" T.J. snickers. "You're starting to sound like your books, Peps."

"She's not a bad looking lady, that Mandy. Your mom's not bad lookin' either, come to think of it."

T.J. makes a swipe at her, but she's already dodged aside. She's always been fast on her feet; Stef was tops on the high school baseball team, back when they both had normal lives. That's another reason for having her around: In addition to her ability to assemble some pretty terrific tunes, Stef isn't afraid to tell T.J. what time it is. Knowing somebody since you were practically in footie pajamas gives you special privileges. "Last I checked, my mom is your mom, yanno," he says.

Stef grins with a Cheshire cat smile, imagining that her gleaming teeth are the only feature of hers he can make out as night closes in. They do have a funny history. T.J.'s mom and pop died when he was ten in a crazy FreeCar crash that wasn't ever supposed to happen. Landed him a nice trust fund after the lawsuits settled. The Fureys and the Hollidays had been pals since college, and when nobody on the Furey side stepped up to take care of the kid, the Hollidays arranged things so T.J. came to live with them.

"Admit it, though," says Stef.

"Admit what?"

"That you'd've had her if offered."

"Mandy Kowalski?"

"Sure as hell don't mean our mom."

T.J. laughs. Stef sensed he would. She can read people; she's spent a lot of time observing. She studies people all the time in books, in school, in the world, backstage. Helps with her writing, makes it easier to come up with the words T.J. will eventually sing on stage—the ones that get the girls' hormones spiking and let them know what an orgasm will feel like eventually. Stef thinks for some of his fans it isn't even imagination—she's seen their faces during the shows. It's like this special power T.J. has—sure, there are other PoppyStars who give the girls nice dreams, but he's got it a little stronger than anybody else does. Always has.

"Maybe I would've," he says. "Probably."

The thing is, Stef's pretty sure they never met Mandy Kowalski. All the faces they meet on the road run together in her head, so it's not impossible, but in the end there's no way that lady is carrying T.J.'s kid. Just not possible. Still, the lawyers keep saying it's gonna be awful hard to prove something didn't happen until they can compel a DNA test, and in the meantime the headlines are killing ticket buys. So on the advice of the firm of Adler, Mohegan, and Said LLC, T.J. is laying low. Being a ghost. Number of comments made to the press: zero.

"So this is what the Hotel California is like," Stef says. "I guess we can check out whenever, but … etcetera, etcetera."

They are silent a good couple of beats.

T.J.'s fingers are scratching on the balcony railing anxiously. He needs to do something. The tour is off for now. They tried to keep it going after news broke, but when the press turned on him, the crowds started getting rowdy and someone threw a bottle at the stage midway through a show—so, time to hit the pause button. Tony put it out there that T.J. lost his voice. Exhaustion an issue. They postponed dates. Life is now on hold.

"Burt Fuckin' Reynolds," he mutters.

Then he whips around. Stef jumps back, heart thudding. "What?"

"*Deliverance*," he says.

"Soo-wee," she whispers in relief. "You still stuck on that movie?"

"We could go," he says. "To the woods."

Stef screws up her face. "You want to go *camping*?"

"Whole other world there," he says, staring into the city with soft eyes. A few horn honks drift their way. "No news. No headlines. You can disappear, maybe never come back."

"We talking about the same thing here? Is this a camping trip or early retirement?"

He waves his hand at her and his smoldering joint leaves tiny dragon trails. "Picture it," he says, bouncing on the balls of his feet. That flop of hair jostles with every beat. "Us five. Me, you, Tones, Daryl, Ian. In the woods. Hunting. Bag us a deer."

The idea makes her uncomfortable on a few levels. "Get eaten by a mountain lion more likely," she says. "Or a bear."

"Yeah!" he pumps a fist into the sky. "A bear! We'll go bear hunting! Come on, Peps."

He's serious. She can tell because he's being cute, using that nickname. T.J.'s been Salty and she's been Pepper ever since they first met up in school. Got called a lot worse over the years, so once they hit high school they decided to own it. Corny as hell, but who cared: They were a team. It was the name of their publishing company, too—Salty Pepper.

"We can live it like that movie, without the bad parts," says T.J. "Nobody'll find us. They got dead zones in the woods can't track nothing. I'll even use a bow and arrow. No guns."

Stef folds her arms. She was in Girl Scouts; she did the summer vacation in the woods—including that weekend they got dropped off and had to find their way back through ten miles of forest *without* checking their GPS even once. Not T.J., though. "Didn't you quit Cub Scouts when they told you about a five-mile hike?"

He waves his hands. "Not like that. We can do it our way. Gonna be Burt Fuckin' Reynolds, kill ourselves a bear."

"You are *still* high."

"No shit." T.J. can't help but laugh. "But this is the best good idea I've had in weeks."

A Girl Named Jim

Crunch crunch go the leaves under Daddy's feet. Under mine it's only *swish swish*. He hasn't made me put on my boots yet so it's almost like I'm not even here. But I sometimes feel his eyes on me. Watching. 'Valuating. I pretend I don't see.

Over our heads the tree branches are scraping and waving and poking at the sky and the whole forest is easier to see through. The leaves are mostly gone by now and all that's left are the forever-ever-greens and pines that keep watch and don't change and are always ready for you to go climbing up and hide.

Here's some things to hide from:
1. Pete pumas
2. Artie
3. Blizzards
4. Mad Daddy

But there are other reasons to scale the trees:
1. Eggs in nests
2. Seeing far away to know where you're going (I don't need that anymore but I pretend for Daddy sometimes 'cause he can't know about my abracadabras).
3. Waving. Jim always waved at anybody he saw off in the distance. *Somebody might wave back*, he said to me when I why-ed him.

Walking from our cabin to the meeting spot is almost three days, Daddy says. I don't even count steps when we go that far. We always go to far off spots to meet people 'cause Daddy says they shouldn't find out where we live.

Never let predators follow you home, he told me a whole long while ago. *Take 'em where you can hide or bring 'em into the water and let 'em drown. Once they know where you sleep you're never safe again.*

What about people? I asked him.

People are the ultimate predators, he said and his eyebrows got low and he looked at me, serious.

Daddy doesn't say much these days. Used to be, we came here and he had all the words. When Jim was with us, Daddy was *fulla* a lot more than he is now, both shit and shine-o-la. Took me some time, but 'ventually I got to figuring out when he was fulla shit and when he was being true. For the shit times, when he went on and on about how bad people were and the world was in a handbasket and nobody had the guts to do what needed doing I nodded and shut my head. Let it go over me all cool and clear like when I jump into the stream for a bath. Water in my ears, glug, glug. Water in my nose. Water in my eyes. La la la.

When he was being true, though, I opened up to hear it all. Telling us about the forest it'd be like Daddy swallowed a flashlight. Was like brightness poured out of every inch of him. His bushy black hair went this way and his long smoky beard went that way and he waved his arms and his eyes went wide and he told me all the shiny things I could never guess on my own. His eyes got wide and even darker than Gil's and you felt like you could fall into them. If he said something I remembered it.

I'd be dead out here without him. On Day One. Maybe Day Two. All of us would've been deader if we hadn't come to the forest. Daddy said so.

Some of the things he told me over the years:

1. How to start a fire with special stones.
2. How to pick stuff off trees and bushes and put it right in your mouth for good eating.
3. What stuff never to put near your mouth.
4. How to make your own bow and arrows. And shoot 'em.
5. How come the Outside was unsafe now.
6. How to string a snare, hide it so animals don't see it until it's too late.
7. Not to talk to strangers ever in the woods unless Daddy said it was okay. (I didn't listen to him when I met Gil, though.)
8. Fishing with your hands.
9. How to pop a shoulder back in the joint after you fall out of a tree. (It hurt and I cried but then it was better.)

Daddy has all kinds of magic even if he doesn't use abracadabra words. I don't think he's finished showing me everything yet. He does all kinds of other stuff that isn't magic, too. He can throw a rock farther than anybody, least he could until Jim got big. Can take a deer down from up on our ridge, skin it and make the meat last for a week, maybe two. Can hide himself so smart in the trees he's like a big old branch.

But since Jim left, he doesn't have so many words anymore. And when we walk or when we sit or when we eat or when we run the noises we make mostly aren't words, just grunts and chews and cracks and breathing. I eat my quiet with my dinner and think about being mad at Jim. 'Cause Jim left without taking me along.

I take Jim with *me*, though. Soon as I came down that ridge yesterday I was Jim. I wear Jim's clothes and his hat and I have his haircut and when we hunt, Daddy calls me *Jim*. It was his idea at first but 'ventually I signed on. When Daddy went back to tracking for campers, maybe two weeks after Jim vanished, he said he would need a new assistant. But he couldn't take a girl.

I why-ed him.

'Cause people are dangerous, he said. *They come in here with big ideas and think they know everything 'cause they read about it in a book. People from the world have a sickness I try to keep you from every day. Sickness called civilization. Nothing good ever came from being too civilized.*

This didn't mean anything to me.

People who don't know you are gonna think you're weak. They're going to see a small person and a girl to boot and they're not going to think you can track, he xplained. *They're going to look at you and maybe want to touch you and hurt you. They might seem nice at first but before you know it they will jump you.*

He told me this after we were here five winters. I was prolly thirteen.

I can jump too, I said.

Naw, chicken. Jump you like you see the animals do to each other.

I knew what it meant when the animals were on top of each other. Either they were mating and making more animals or they were fighting and probably making less animals. But people aren't xactly the same as that, Daddy told me round the time we had this talk. He said I should watch the animals that weren't fighting closer. This book Daddy gave me way back was called *Our Bodies Our Selves for the New Millennium* and had a lot of drawings of people doing things and body parts and lists and I read it a couple times but a lot of it didn't make any sense. In the book they didn't call it mating. They called it sex.

That's one word for it, he said. *But you're too young. I'll tell you more when you're not too young.*

I figured that was all right. And I'd wanted to get back to the point. *But if you can't take a girl hunting—*

You'll be a boy, he said. *You'll be—my son.*

I didn't know why being a small person but a boy was better for people we might take tracking but I didn't care much. It meant I could pretend while we were working. I could pretend to be—

Jim. You'll be Jim.

That got me quiet for a while. *I want another name*, I said.

He rubbed his chin a while and stared up at the sky. *Nope*, he said finally. *Jim it is.*

I didn't know how to fight him. Once Daddy got an idea in his mind it was hard to take it back out. Early on he called me *Jim* and I wouldn't answer. Then he came over and sometimes bring the strop. And he never used it on me but I thought he might. So I started being Jim. I even didn't mind it after a while.

If Gil could be Gillie, I could be Jim. Sometimes it was like having him back. I was smarter when I pretended to be him.

So now when we track, I am Jim. And he is Daddy Samuel. And that is that.

Daddy's been watching me all day and not in a friendly way. Pretty sure he wants to ask me something but he's holding it back until we stop for the day outside this cave we visit every summer. We get the fire in the pit going and cook our food and it's all soft and silent for a few minutes while he eats.

Lexi, I hear. *Lexi.*

'Course I'm not really hearing my name. Just sounds that way. The cave we're sitting in front of is a special place for 100s of reasons, and one is that it sings. Way back in the cave is a deep crack and when the wind sighs through it—this warm, funny little breeze that sometimes smells like bread—it feels like it's singing to me. Singing my name.

Leeeexxxxi, I hear again.

Daddy mutters something under his breath I can't make out but I kinda know what he's thinking. Every summer we wall up over that crack and every year our patches fall back down again. Daddy calls it our Sissy Fuss task. *He was a man cursed to roll a rock uphill only to watch it fall down again*, said Daddy once.

At least we're not rolling rocks uphill.

Anyway, we were last here when it was hot out and when we left that crack was all blocked up. Now it's singing. So it's open again.

Daddy mutters some more. I keep eating. Then the singing stops and the night starts crawling in and Daddy gets to what's on his mind.

"Who were you talking to today?" he says, just out of nowhere.

But he can't get me Offguard. I can smell when he's feeling ornery. Comes in handy. "When?" I ask. Him keeping both eyes on me all day was no fun at all, so I decide to ornery him right back.

"You know when," he says. "You ain't said more'n two words to me all day. Don't sass."

I wait a minute, poke the fire. Feel my gut turning over. When Jim was with us Daddy hardly had much to say to me ever. Just told me to do things. He wasn't mean; I never got the strop with Daddy, but it was like I was an extra bit he couldn't trim off. Was pretty clear once I got old enough to see it how Jim was the one he spent most of his time on, gave most of his training to. But since Jim's gone, I'm the only one he has to keep in line and it's like having a rope 'round my neck.

"Nobody," I say finally. "Just readin' to myself."

"And what you want to do that for?"

The lie twists in me. I don't like lying. But I also know I can't ever say anything bout Gil to Daddy. "Forest's too quiet sometimes. Got to fill it up a little."

He studies me and it's like I feel his stare burning into my head. "You know the rules."

Rules. There's lots of rules. But I know the one he means right now. We're not supposed to be here, not supposed to xist. Leave no trace, he always says. "But we're going to see people now," I say. "We see people all the time. Who cares?"

"I care," he says. "Up to me who you see and don't see."

I look up and meet his eyes and they burn me some more and I hold in place. "Not forever," I say and grit my teeth.

Just in time, 'cause then he cuffs me on the side of the head. He does that, he thinks you're being out of line. But he's not too mad, I can tell, since it's not hard enough to knock me down. "You want to say something, girl?"

"I'm Jim," I say, rubbing my head. "There's no girl here."

He's waiting for me.

"No," I say, 'cause I don't want to have that talk right now. The talk where I maybe suggest I'm old enough to leave the woods if I want. He always said eighteen. I'm almost there. But then I do have a question for him. "Yes."

"G'wan."

"Is there a war happening Outside?"

He goes quiet a long while, then laughs. "There's always a fight goin' on somewhere." He turns and looks at me. "How d'you mean?"

"I mean," and I try to remember what Gil told me earlier, "is it a big fight between people like us and—sick people?"

He's looking at me funny now. "That something your friend from the trees told ya?"

After Gil saved me from the snowstorm years ago and I came home after three days and should be dead, after Daddy finished hugging me I told him everything. About Gil and the stand and the trees. Daddy went very white and his lips went really thin and he told me that I must have hallucinated it. Made it up. There was no such thing as men in grass hats living near birch trees. I said there was. Gil was true. I knew it.

He stood really straight and I didn't know who he was just then. He was 'valuating me, like I 'valuate the open spaces, case there's a danger. *If I thought you'd caught the sickness,* he'd said then in a quiet voice, *I'd have to take steps. Don't make me take steps.*

Daddy thinks anything abracadabra magic is a sickness. It's why he brought us here. He said everybody was getting 'fected and changing 'cause of it. In that second where he said he'd take steps, I connected Gil with magic for the first time. My head had hurt a little 'cause I didn't know and maybe I was 'fected and sick. But Daddy saying he might have to take steps made me scared. Scared like I never was about him before.

So, tell me again, he insisted.

I swallowed down all the Gil stories I knew and lied. *Just kidding,* I said. *That was a dream I had. I made a snow fort and hid.*

For three days.

I nodded. *I learned a lot from you.*

That seemed to be okay. He didn't think I had the sickness anymore. And I never told about the abracadabras.

But he asks me about it sometimes still. When I'm not ready. He says things like, *How is your friend from the trees doing?* and I have to remember Gil is a secret and say I don't know what he means. Or Daddy might ask me how I know the way to one place or t'other so well and I will have to say it was 'cause I learned how to read a compass and follow the trees. I can't say I have special words that make the trees hum to me and tires out my brain.

I don't know what Daddy means when he says he'll take steps, but the way he looked at me when I was thirteen and fresh home from being missing for a bunch of days—I thought maybe he wanted to hurt me. I don't want to find out. Never have tried talking about Gil in front of him since. Almost five winters I've been hiding Gil, and it's not easy. But if I didn't have Gil I might die anyway. It's hard out here, nobody to talk to.

Now he's looking at me the same way he did when I came back from the snowstorm, making that face with the thin lips and white skin.

"I mean," I say, "what's so bad about Outside anyway? People keep coming in and we take 'em hunting and they don't seem sick."

"They hide it," he says. "It's not a sick like you get rashes or a fever or you swell up. It's something that started a little before I took you and Jim away. News reports from far away talking about strange happenings. Places in the air or the ground that started glowing. Some people who lived near 'em started acting funny. Could do things people ain't supposed to be able to do. Some folks called it talent. Some said it was magic. Some said it was sickness, pure and simple. So did I. When you start hearing about people who can hold their breath underwater for twenty minutes and not die, or make walls fold themselves, you have to wonder. You have to wonder. Your mother—"

I lean forward, eager. He never talks about Mom.

"Your mother, remember how after she had the baby she could talk to him without saying words? And he could talk back to her in his head even though he was only a couple months old?"

I did, a bit. But I was too little to think it was different. I thought all moms were like that with their babies.

"That was one kind of sickness," he says. "Human beings aren't supposed to do that. Then your mother tried talking to *me* like that one time and I—" He pauses. "I took steps. Didn't want to. Had to be done. Then I grabbed you and Jim before you two showed up sick like her and we ran off."

Inside my stomach gets all funny and it's like my back is cold. "What kind of steps?" I ask.

"Stop talking," he says. "This is a finished topic."

My head's hurting. Did Gil give me the sickness? Did he teach me words so now I'm sick 'cause I can read the trees if I want? I don't feel sick, xcept right after I say the words.

Then I think of the other thing Gil said.

"You know Artie?" I ask. Daddy looks at me. "Is Artie sick? Do animals get sick?"

He's still looking at me.

"You know, the big black bear we see sometimes. Is she—"

"I know which one."

"Well, she's kind of a special bear, don't you think?"

"Not to my mind."

"Oh," I say. "Well, I think she's kind of a special bear. We shouldn't look for her."

"If animals start getting sick," he sighs, "I don't know what we'll do. She's just a bear, chicken."

"But a really big bear."

He tugs at his beard and that's a good sign. It means he's thinking about whether there's true in what I say. "Well," he says. "Don't worry so much. She's probably hibernating by now."

I feel better. But I also feel like I dodged something bad with him. More questions I have, the more I worry that Daddy might start thinking about *taking steps* with me.

"But," he adds, "you never know what you're gonna find in the woods."

Daddy brought us here when I was eight. I came with my Brownie uniform on, 'cause nobody warned me about it first. Just me and Jim—he was eleven then—but not mom and not the baby. Daddy picked us up from school with his big old brown truck packed full of boxes and bags and water bottles and handed us grape soda. We drank it too fast and burped and then we took long naps without dreams and woke up with the trees all around.

Our arms hurt. We had deep cuts way up, under our pits. Band-Aids over, don't touch, don't want 'fection, Daddy said.

He took out our trackers, Jim told me later. *So we're invisible now.*

Liked that idea. Back home everybody had an Eye-GeePeeEss in them; you got it when you were born. It was The Law. But we were special thanks to Daddy. Being invisible is a superpower, even if he'd call it a sickness.

Jim said he thought we were in Colorado. He did calculations and figured how long we were out sleeping and guessed we were in the rockiest of mountains but I never did find out for sure if he was right. The trees were just here and we were just here. The place where we were. Don't need a name.

Here was supposed to be for a visit. That's what Daddy said first. Jim and me were going on this xtra long spring vacation, and Mom couldn't come 'cause she had the baby. So it was just us three. The Scooby Gang, that's what Daddy said we were.

Daddy packed the truck xtra serious tight with so many supplies and boxes I couldn't figure out how we'd get through it all in three weeks. But he didn't xplain, not shit or shine-o-la. He just drove us to the cabin, unpacked everything and then drove off and left us behind in that leaky place that smelled like old underpants. Jim and me climbed up into the cabin's loft with our sleeping bags and stretched out end to end, our toes almost touching.

That was a cold night. I was too scared to even get up and pee.

Daddy was back in the morning but the truck wasn't. He said this was our new home. We had to live here now, he said, 'cause there'd been a popalypse back home. A real big sickness came out of nowhere and everybody was acting crazypants in the streets. We were safe because we left in time. He used his tight serious voice that scared me. He said he'd taken steps and that mommy and the baby were gone. We saw any new people, they could get us sick, he said. So we had to be quiet and not see anybody for a long time.

I couldn't breathe, I cried so hard.

Daddy gave me my stuffed dog Marches and that helped a bit.

Jim put his arm around me and didn't say nothing. Didn't make any sound. But that night I heard him sniffing and coughing in his sleeping bag.

I hugged Marches and faked I was asleep that night. And when I reached out with my toes, I could touch Jim's on the other side of the loft.

That's how things started out for us.

Welcome to Camp Furey

Former Special Army Emissary Second Lieutenant Anthony Garcia is *awake* for the first time in years. If only he could catch his breath.

That first taste of Rocky Mountain air is bracing, smooth, and clear as water. He's glad to have the wretched *thup thup* of the helicopter out of his head—the noise-canceling headphones he wore for the entire flight out from Eagle Airport were for shit—and he pauses at the copter's doorway, drinking in the still, fresh outdoors.

But he has to breathe deeply and long, because this is not the fat air he's become accustomed to in Los Angeles. Or even the fog on the frontline plains of Northern France, heightened with ions and smoke left behind from plasma bursts. This is some thin-ass air and it's going to take a minute to adjust. He breathes deeply again.

Was that a scream?

Tony shivers. He's sure the sound he just heard was only the rattle of a loose memory, but sometimes it can be hard to tell.

"Oi," says T.J., and gives him a gentle shove from behind. "Make a path."

Tony jumps into the dry brown grass and grimaces. The ground is as hard as concrete, the landing juddering up his battle-weakened knees. The others clamber down behind him, blinking like newborns. Daryl yawns, stretching widely before shrugging on his backpack; Ian nearly turns turtle when he tries heaving his own on, though it only weighs about ten pounds. Stef has hers down by her legs, and she's applying—is that lipstick?

He rolls his eyes. These children know nothing about what it's like to shoulder a sixty-pounder across hostile terrain, knowing it contains everything you'll ever need to save your life. Including the ability to end it, if the enemy gets hold of you. Tony recalls the first time he put on a bulky backpack. Surprising how that thing can weigh you down. Sometimes, it's better to ride light.

But he regards his small platoon without sympathy. Soft. Weak. Untrained. They're accustomed to letting someone else do the heavy lifting for them. Usually, that means Tony. Good for 'em to shoulder their own burdens for once. He considers hopping back in the chopper and letting them figure out the next two weeks without him, then sees T.J. light up his latest blunt.

Nope. Got too much invested here. Need to keep eyes on.

The wide open meadow they've landed in is filled with sharp brown grasses and outlined in spiky evergreens and bare-branch trees. The only color he can make out except for that dark green is a strange profusion of flowers—little blue hanging ones and tiny yellow daisy-types. He narrows his gaze. This time of year shouldn't be hardly any flowers out here. And he's seen that combination before: bluebells and primrose.

He drank more primrose tea over in France than he ever thought he could. Gallons of it, served up every day for the whole troop. Made the enemy visible, sharper. Easier to take out.

Not a good sign, soldier, he thinks, an old combination of fear, dread, and longing rising in his gut. *Should cut and run now.*

Then Tony imagines trying to explain this to T.J., the punk kid who pays the bills. *You wanna leave 'cause of some stupid flowers?* He can hear the whine. *Gimme a better reason, man.*

That's where Tony would fail. These kids know nothing. And they know nothing because he tells them nothing. Lets them know nothing. He finds anybody on tour talking about what's going on overseas, he sends them packing.

Probably won't make any difference, he thinks, considering the flowers once more. He pats the pocket of his cargo pants. *And if it does, there are remedies.*

A skunky scent wafts Tony's way, and T.J.'s standing there with his pack dangling off a bulked-up shoulder, the smoke between his teeth. "Earth to Tony, man. Come in, Tones."

"For real?" Stef is chiding T.J. about his blunt, lipstick tube poised in her hand. Tony realizes it's actually crimson lip protectant. "This air's got me high by itself, Salty Dog."

"It's a Rocky Mountain high." T.J. giggles.

"Somebody had to say it," noted Stef

Tony regards them both. T.J.'ll do fine, and if not, Tony'll make him do fine. He's like a kid brother, about ten years younger than Tony is. But Stef has no point being here—yeah, Tony had a superior officer who was a female, but most of 'em don't handle the great outdoors or things like hunting with any skill or grace. They'd rather kick back with a glass of wine and a book. But these two are a package deal; he's known that from the start.

Fact is, the pair of them changed his life just a few years back, after he spotted a video on the FreeCloud of T.J. and Stef performing at a school talent show. By then Tony wasn't doing much else but nursing his discharge and his knees and staring at screens all day, trying to figure out what he wanted to do with the next part of his life. Was he going to honor his promise to the enemy? Or was he going to keep hunting them down until they had no more hold over him?

'Course, that kind of thinking got him sent home in the end. So he used his know-how and contacts to locate the high schoolers in their small nothing Maryland suburb. He mostly wanted T.J.; Stef was just playing guitar in the video while her best pal charmed the crowd with a song she'd written—but T.J. said from Minute One they were a team. Whatever else T.J.'s been soft on the last couple of years, he's always been solid about that fact. Whither he goest, so does Stef.

Tony understood, and it was still a good deal. Plus, having Stef on hand has kept T.J. mostly on track—he's always concerned about what she thinks, even more than he cares about what Tony thinks. But Tony's not very rock 'n' roll or Popper or whatever the kids call it today. He's not even all that much of a music fan, and Stef delights in tripping him up by mashing classfunk or classmetal bands together and acting like he should know who they are—Iron Chic, or Bootsy Metallica. She's gotten him more than once.

He knows he looks more like the guy who blocks the back door of concerts than any music manager out there. Built like a wrestler, he's still got the neck of a football player, though he's getting a paunch these days since he can't work his legs like he used to. He doesn't talk about his overseas service, not his Equatorial War deployment or his stint in the Oz Dreaming Fracas, and certainly not with the ongoing Celtic Sanctions. But they know, just from looking at him, that he's not one of them.

Tony's fine with that.

Stef finishes with her lip whatever it was and puts away a small makeup kit, and he can see her struggling with the air, making rabbit breaths. "Take it easy," he says in a low voice. "You'll adjust."

She gets interested in her backpack and heaves it on without comment. He admires the exposed small of her back for a moment, then turns to the group.

"We're settin' down about two, three klicks that away." Tony points west. "Setup finished last night 'round midnight, should be all coordinated at our arrival time, which is at 14:00. We're back here in twelve days at this here spot, 09:00 and no later unless there's an emergency and we have to set off the beacon. Capiche?"

T.J. offers a mock salute.

They head west in a loose line. Tony offers pointers along the way: direction, temperature—late September is warm enough in Denver but out in the woods at night will be the ass-end of cold.

"Do *not* go out after dark without carrying a moonbeam," he intones, marching with purpose and determination while everyone else struggles. "That's a flashlight to you civilians. Do *not* go out for a little stroll without a buddy. You *will* get lost."

"He thinks we'd forget to wipe our asses if he didn't remind us," growls Daryl behind her.

"That's just you." T.J. chuckles.

Daryl laughs back but it is a thin thing. Tony is sure he only makes nice because T.J. writes their checks. He's sarcastic as hell and lazy and always leering in Stef's direction. That's partly her fault, putting herself in the middle of all of these men all the time. Wearing too-small shirts that show off her body. Tony doesn't say anything: He's not her dad. He'll protect her as an asset, but otherwise he'll let Stef fight her own battles.

It takes him less than ten minutes of the hike to get why the mountains are named Rocky. Jagged points and scattered stones litter the trail to camp; he catches the band members tripping more than once, and Ian nearly faceplants twice. Still, even Tony finds it hard to keep an eye on the road ahead; he's become hyperaware of his surroundings, alert and watchful of the alien landscape.

Not that there is much to look at. September is the tail end of fall around here, with winter coming along quick. Back East the leaves are still waiting to turn into fire auburn and flame gold, but here the already-empty branches are like naked spears. The grass comes in every shade of faded green and sapped brown. At least pine trees with their broad spreading arms offer some green, sending a sharp tangy scent out on the wind. The only indication that anything will ever grow here again.

What startles Tony most is the absence of animal life. He hasn't heard any bird cries or abrupt shuffling in the undergrowth. Part of his interest in coming here is to explore a living, breathing forest—one with enough critters to make hunting interesting—and absent even the barest of signs, the world feels like a wasteland.

This place is asleep, he thinks. *We're walking through its dreams. Or we're just being watched.*

That frisson of fear trills through him again, and this time he doesn't shrug it off so easy. Could the enemy be here, too? Last he checked the front line was thousands of miles away and holding steady. But what if they jump the pond?

'Course, if that did happen, Tony could handle it. He would report to his former CO, and they'd need him then. They'd realize he was right all along. They'd have his number on speed dial.

Grinning, he glances up at the hikers and spots Stef scribbling in her tiny notebook. Probably writing some lyrics. She nearly trips again and catches her glasses before they fall off her nose.

"Cocksucker." T.J.'s voice cuts through the silence.

"Dick." That's Ian.

A pause. "Elephantitus of the goolies." That's Daryl.

Stef sighs and Tony stays eyes forward. They are such boys, still. Not that Tony doesn't swear and drink and toke with the rest of them, but he is the outsider here as much as the girl. He's older, seen more of the world, knows its uglier side.

Stef, meanwhile, is not even part of the actual band, has different private parts, different hair, different skin. Her sole purpose for being with them on a regular basis is this: She's T.J.'s songwriter. She could be in college right now—she got into three good schools Tony encouraged her to attend—and could be hitting frat parties and protests and kicking ass on the chess team or whatever it was people did at college, but Stef deferred her admissions.

It's an adventure, she told Tony after shutting down his latest attempt to get her to stay in school before she and T.J. signed on with him. *Who doesn't want an adventure?*

Hard to argue with that.

But being with half men, half boys can be wearing on the soul, particularly in a place like this.

"C'mon, Stef," T.J. needles. "Your turn."

"You guys," she says, glancing over her shoulder. T.J. waves the blunt at her. "Seriously, Teej?" She frowns. "Ever heard of a forest fire?"

"Only you can prevent forest fires," chuckles Ian. "Smokey Bear."

"Smokey." Daryl giggles back. "She's smokey all right. Burnt, even."

Stef stiffens and lengthens her strides. Tony shoots Daryl a glance and the guy rolls his eyes. It isn't worth more of a fight, not over the blunt, not over the comment. Fighting all the time, on every slight, gets exhausting. It's part of the exchange: To hang with talent you have to put up with some seriously juvenile bullshit. He's sure she'll get Daryl back, later. Find some ants, put them in his sleeping bag, that kind of thing.

"I think you hurt her feelings," says Ian.

Blessed forest quiet falls all around them once more. Ahead, tree branches arc high over their heads as they step away from the meadow and into the forest proper. They are swallowed up by the trees, shaded from the sun. Tony's sunglasses slowly lose their tint.

The moment of silence lasts about forty-five seconds.

"Elephantitus of the goolies? That's pathetic," says T.J.

"That's all I got, man."

Ian sighs. "No effort at all. You're losing it. 'Fuckwad.'"

"Jesus," mutters Tony. Being on the road leads to dozens of time-wasting games, from "What's That Smell?" to "Alphabeticus Vulgarius," but the obscenities are really getting on his nerves. "Have some damn respect."

"For what?" Daryl holds his hands wide. "There ain't nothin' here."

"For the place," Stef speaks up. "Just for the …. Never mind."

Daryl grunts. "This place is complete shit. You know that, right?"

"Then why the hell did you come?" T.J.'s voice whipsaws.

That puts the quiet into him.

Finally, Tony thinks.

T.J. pulls up alongside Stef, who's bent forward under the weight of the backpack. "This place is gonna rock," he says with cheery confidence.

Ian boots a stone to the side. "Already does."

Stef chuckles.

"Gonads." Daryl is back at it.

"Hellfire," says Ian.

Tony rolls his eyes and thinks, *Imbeciles.*

Tony hears the camp before he sees it. Huge, thudding bass beats ripple through the trees and brush, pounding in a manner that at first makes him question whether earthquakes are possible in Colorado. But now, as he nears the freshly made clearing, a melody line threads in and he nods with recognition.

It's exactly what he knew the boss wanted: A song Stef wrote, complete with T.J.'s thin warble layered on top, blasting through the forest. It's one of those Forever Remixes popular these days, where DJs battle to see who can craft the lengthiest, yet still artistically sustainable extension of a popular song. If Tony's right, this one—"Laughing Out Loud" is the title—might go on another forty-three minutes or so.

What T.J. wants, T.J. gets. Even if he doesn't specifically ask for it. That's part of the job.

The rest of the band catches on seconds after Stef and Tony do, and there is much stoned rejoicing and goofy dancing on their way into camp. Daryl hops up on a broken boulder and begins strumming on air guitar, and Ian does a little narrow-shouldered dance like he's one of the Peanuts characters. T.J. races ahead like a gazelle, one hand cupped to his ear, occasionally grinning backward over his shoulder at Stef.

His cap is askew, and Tony can't help but smile back at his sweet, idiotic expression. He gets it in these seconds why millions of teens of every sexual orientation and gender configuration want him; T.J. radiates in-betweenness. Child and adult, boy and girl, devil and angel. Apparently, he's been like this ever since he hit puberty—and it only heightens when he sings.

What drew Tony to T.J. and Stef in that FreeCloud video had less to do with the song than the audience's reaction. At one point the camera panned around to catch the crowd's faces, settling for a few seconds on the rapt, edge-of-your-seat reactions Tony's only seen in a few popidol archive films before—Elvis, Beatles, more recently Matcha Papa. And that Irish band that went global about twenty-five years back, the one with the bassist who never seems to get old, they had it in spades, too. But in all of those archives, screaming often overwhelmed the music. In T.J.'s video, there was almost no screaming. The audience squeaked and squealed but remained seated. Their faces were serene and absorbed—even as their bodies bounced up and down in their seats. They'd claw at their cheeks and hair and their eyes might go wide, but not in the typical exaggerated concert reaction.

At first he thought he recognized the look; it seemed a little *adult* for kids, though. But then he looked closer. It wasn't arousal, not exactly. It was ... well, he'd once gone to a yoga class with an ex-girlfriend and at the end, when everyone else was saying "namaste," he was noticing this slightly vacant look everyone wore. Like they'd all just had a very satisfying ... something. He couldn't figure it out beyond that, and with T.J.'s crowd, it seems to only happen in person—live. Recordings don't affect folks the same way. But watching that video was all he needed. Those few seconds told him that if he could land that singer, he'd never see a negative bank balance again.

So far, he's been very right.

T.J. lurches out of nowhere and catches up Stef's hands, twirling her around. She nearly loses her footing thanks to her backpack, but laughs anyway. "You're goony," she says. "And loony."

"And swoony," he tosses back, crossing his eyes. "That's us, Peps!" He releases her and races forward.

What's funny, though, is how T.J.'s singing doesn't seem to do anything for Stef. You'd think, best buddies since they were kids, she writing the songs, sitting next to him day after day—they'd be all over each other. But she just has the normal reaction to his singing her songs—she's appreciative, even joyous. Not about going all serene. Maybe that's 'cause they're almost like brother and sister. Often, Tony thinks Stef and T.J. reside in a kingdom where the usual rules do not apply.

Everybody thinks they're an item, and everybody's wrong. Stef's parents, who by the time Tony came into the picture were T.J.'s legal guardians, explained that they were extremely conservative about sexual relationships. It was something they and the Fureys had agreed on: You don't put your pecker into some rando's cootch unless you do the ring and the church thing. That was Tony's phrasing, not theirs. T.J. isn't exactly religious, but he got it burned into him that Jesus has to bless his sexual congress. Many other house rules failed to stick—drinking, smoking, carousing—but the whole sex thing seems totally fenced off in his head. That's how Tony knows that lady from Michigan is definitely not carrying T.J.'s baby.

Though he'd defend him either way. T.J. is the territory.

Stef looks over her shoulder at Tony, who's folded his thick forearms over his chest. "This your doing?" she asks.

"Not as dumb as you look," he says, striding forward and grabbing the space between her neck and shoulder, propelling her forward. "C'mon, already."

There's a small break in the trees a few more yards ahead, and there the forest halts, widening into a broad circle. Tony pauses at the opening as the others surge around him like water meeting an obstacle, and nods again. It's exactly what they had mapped out back in LA.

T.J. may have come from a modest suburban backwater, but it didn't take him—or, for that matter, Tony—long to become accustomed to the magical ability conferred by the phrase "your wish is my command." T.J. sketches out what he wants on paper napkins, and instantly minions spring into action, like Mickey's brooms in *Fantasia*.

For this particular getaway, T.J. has gotten his wish. Tony strides into the clearing, passing stumps of freshly felled trees as he takes it all in. A semicircle of tents describes the clearing, fifteen-foot-high beige canvas constructions held in place by wooden poles that raise the roofs into gently peaking slopes. Atop the center peak of each tent flies a small black flag emblazoned with T.J.'s initials. Each tent has its door flaps tied back, allowing for brief glimpses at the interior. In the center of the partial circle crackles a firepit, lively flames licking skyward; the pit is ringed with an eclectic seating arrangement of a rocking chair, a bean bag, a prop throne, and an Eames recliner with ottoman.

Four of the tents are larger than the exterior two that bookend them, and outside each of the big tents a wooden stake rises from the ground with a band member's name carved into a sign. One of the smaller tents has smoke pouring out of an opening in the roof, and Tony can just now make out the rich aromas of melting cheddar and crispy bacon wafting their way. The final tent, standing at some distance on the far north end of the campsite, is unmarked. Doesn't take Tony long to remember what it's for—though he detects no smells in particular coming from it. Yet.

"This is camping?" Stef asks Tony as she drifts toward the tent with her name. It's about as big as T.J.'s hotel suite at the Chateau.

"Glamping," Tony says with a gritted smile. He'd have gone modest, low-key if it was just him camping, but he had orders. "I just work here."

"But you don't disapprove," she says, not waiting for a reaction.

"Tastes differ." *And I know how to follow orders*, he adds to himself.

"Not bad." She gives him a rare grin before disappearing inside.

Tony smiles. The whole thing with the woman from Michigan has changed his relationship to T.J., and in some ways to Stef. He knows they looked at him with disdain when life was peaches and cream—he was just there to sponge off of them, ride their success—which wasn't entirely true but certainly not untrue. But when the shit hit the fan, Tony knew just how to step up. He will do whatever it takes to protect his asset, even if that means protecting the asset from himself. They seem to recognize how hard he's working to do that now.

Tony knows about being protected from yourself. After he made his one genuine fuckup in the field—by identifying a little too closely with the enemy—his superiors could have had him drummed out. Instead, they showed him the error of his ways, had him remedy his mistake, and took him in for a chemically induced reeducation. Problem solved.

Except after his tour was over, his request to re-up was denied.

Cue the sad trombone music.

Fortunately, back home, Tony found a few targets worthy of protection from the elements. And for when things get hairy, he still totes around one of the portable PEP guns—pulsed energy projectile—that they used overseas. Just motioning to it usually turns the beat around whenever there's trouble; the compact beast of a weapon strikes fear in the heart of anything that breathes, more or less.

Always be prepared to discharge your weapon when the target presents, he says often. Sometimes it's metaphorical, sometimes it's literal.

So Tony has obliged T.J.'s request for the most glamorous outdoor trip possible, in large part because the more cossetted his asset, the less chance of failure or danger to life and limb and the longer he can ride this money train he's locked himself into. If anything, or anyone, considers altering the status quo regarding one T.J. Furey, Tony is Minion No. 1 springing into action.

Tony lets his pack slip off inside his tent and tosses it to one side, checking every angle. It's expansive and charming in here, with fresh grassy sod rolled out like a carpet and a full-size bed draped with mosquito netting. The rest of the space is filled with a storage chest, a sink with a basin and pedal to pump filtered water—there's a thousand-gallon tank set up just behind the kitchen tent—and a full-length mirror and armoire in which his clothing has already been neatly hung, one-inch spaces between every hanger. Next to the armoire sits a set of speakers he can use with a music chip, linked by a set of wires to solar cells outside. Directly in the center of the tent's inner peak hangs an inverted Tiffany chandelier lamp that sends a warm glow against the canvas walls.

Okay, Stef, he thinks. *Time to write a whole new set of Cloud-busting hits to pay for this thing.*

Then he starts laughing. The girl was right, staying out of school. This ride is an adventure. And a pretty hilarious one sometimes, too.

They gather around the firepit a half hour after arriving, steaming bowls of macaroni and cheese in truffle oil flaked with bits of applewood-smoked bacon set on small tables before them. It's T.J.'s favorite dish—he even named it TJM&C—which means Tony has had it a lot in recent months. He takes the firmest, least attractive of the chairs on offer and forks some of the hot children's food into his mouth, barely tasting it.

After he's had a few bites, he sets the utensil aside and puts on his big voice, which usually gets a workout each morning on the tour bus. Yeah, he's T.J.'s manager, but he's got a lot of other line items in his job description.

"Welcome to Camp Furey," he announces, and there is a round of light applause. T.J., poised on the throne, twirls his fork like a scepter, a benign smile crossing his face.

Tony points. "Down there you got your mess tent. Inside is Martinique, who's here full-time. Three squares a day and a dessert/snack bar open 24/7. He also knows not to fraternize."

"Where's the actual bar?" asks Ian with a hopeful lilt.

"Ain't one," says Tony. "This's a dry camp. I know y'all brought yer own stashes and you'll do what y'gotta, but T.J.'s wallet won't be paying for you to get shit-faced for the next two weeks."

"Fuck." Ian sets his meal down. "That was the whole point of coming."

"Go home, then," T.J. hisses at him. "Y'can start walking right now."

Ian glares at him, but Tony's sure he'll back down. On the one hand, they need real musicians in this band. Daryl and Ian are hired hands Tony hoped would become mentors, friends. But they've got more talent than brains—and there's no real heart in what they play, only experience. You can't buy magic, at least not legally. But on the flip side, if Ian leaves, he'll be walking out on a lot more than a camping trip. Same for Daryl. Tony'll make sure they both have bigger problems than unemployment—he can get them blackballed with just a few casual whispers in the right ears.

Fact is, T.J. did want a bar. It was one of the only things Tony told him "no" about. On the flight over they had to revisit the about fifty reasons why it was a shit idea, including insurance. *One of those idiots gets drunk and falls in a fire or lost while wandering in the woods to piss, that's a big liability*, said Tony. *You want your money going to defend that?*

Second fact: The only hospital in the area is an hour chopper flight out of here, and there's no chopper getting here in less than two hours, even after they set off the emergency beacon. So Tony compromised, and there's a modest bottle of Johnnie Walker awaiting every one of them in their tent lockers. Let 'em ration, if they can.

When Ian glances away, Tony points out the latrine off to one side and explains it uses cold compost. "So it won't smell too bad or need cleanin', not for the short time you bunch are here," he says.

"They haven't seen what Daryl can do to a toilet," quips Stef. "Not pretty."

Daryl makes a leering, kissy face at her and waggles his finger up under his bowl of mac. She smiles broadly back at him with narrowed eyes.

"Fire," says Tony, gesturing. The three-foot pit encircled by stones gives off an assembly of flames that dart skyward like the center of a furious eye. "That's on you all to keep goin' during the day. We got six months of fresh wood over by the latrine, just haul it back here when you want it lit, let it die down when y'don't. If it goes out overnight, Martinique'll coax it back up again every morning before chow."

"That's a hell of a lot of wood for two weeks," says Stef. "Does it just go to rot after we leave?"

"We cut down twelve trees to make this space," says Tony. Stef winces. "Might as well use it."

"We done yet?" Ian slumps forward. "I gotta check the Cloud."

Tony chuckles. "Web don't reach out here, y'goober. I told you back home. No regular satellite, no Tooths—black, blue, or orange—and no fuckin' Cloud. Signal's too thin to penetrate and nothin's wired out here. Yer GPS arm trackers might work about 30 percent of the time, depending on elevation and triangulation and weather conditions and satellite placement. Anyhow, I got the impression that bein' unplugged was part of the point of coming. Right, T.J.?"

T.J.'s own smile is less enthused this time.

Stef nods at him. "You do not want to spend your whole time goggling at tabloid headers," she says. "No shame in ghosting everybody. If you want to get away, you gotta get all the way away."

He grins a little. "No way."

"Yes way." She grins back. "I dig the whole thing."

As does Tony. A full twelve days in which he doesn't have to think about the business, or the candy-colored shallow pool that is celebrity life, or touring, is the first true vacation he's had in years. All he has to do here is mind T.J. and enjoy the great outdoors. And go hunting. He's looking forward to shooting something again, though this time with a bow and arrow. T.J. just has to learn to trust it, let the forest happen to him.

Plus, there's the bonus of watching Daryl and Ian squirm from being unplugged, though that doesn't mean they'll have to sit on their asses. They'll get the remainder of this day to rest up and then Tony's going to start them on wilderness training and how to shoot a compound bow. Nobody but T.J. has to participate, and he's halfway sure Daryl and Ian will develop head colds or other reasons to dodge the hunt once it happens. But he suspects Stef will be on board, at least to pick up new skills. She's the kind of egghead who gets worried when she's not learning something new.

End of day two, Tony reminds them now, is where things get interesting. Hired trackers will show up right around dinner, spend the night, then take everyone who is going hunting out before daybreak. They'll rough it in ultralight tents carried in their backpacks until they find a deer or a week goes by, whichever comes first.

"Or a bear," says T.J.

Tony shoots him a look. "You take a deer down first. Then we talk."

"So who is this tracker guy, anyhow?" he asks, waving for another bowl of the TJM&C.

Tony chomps on an apple; he usually has one handy. "Old man o' the woods, from what I hear," he says. "Knows the area around here like the back of both hands, every skill rolled into one. He'll find you quarry."

"A *bear*," T.J. repeats, and a small whine comes into his voice. "I don't want a shitty deer."

Tony chews thoughtfully. "He'll do what he can. Bears hibernate; if they've gone to ground that's the end of that story. Nobody here can do magic, Tom, and don't ask 'em to."

T.J. opens his mouth, then shuts it. Tony uses T.J.'s born name when he's losing patience. Nobody calls him Thomas or Tom—even his foster mom doesn't say Thomas James when infuriated.

"How'd you find Mr. Hermit?" Stef asks.

"Didn't say he was a hermit," Tony says in a clipped tone. "Didn't say I found him. Doesn't have a business, no CloudPage, nothin'. Used what we did down in Rennes: Spoke to the locals. They told me a guy for hire sometimes shows up at a particular campground, certain day, certain time. Sometimes has a boy with him he's training up. Two experts for the price of one."

Stef leans forward, her face bright, interested. "What's he charge?"

"None of your beeswax, nosy," he says, then dials it back. "Supplies, mostly. He'll get all this"—he waves his arm around the campsite—"when we go."

"That explains the wood," she murmurs. "So he lives out here all the time?" She's pushing her luck, and he's about to start ignoring her again.

"Who the fuck cares?" asks Tony, tossing his core into the fire, where it pops and sizzles. "Maybe."

"Then he is a hermit," she says.

"He's got a kid with him," says T.J. "Nobody's a hermit with their kid around."

"I'll come with you for the big hunt," says Tony. "It'll be cool."

T.J. stands from the throne seat and smacks his fist into his open palm. "Fuck yeah," he says. "This is the best trip ever." He blinks at Tony. "I'm gonna get you a bear claw."

Tony laughs. "That'll make my fuckin' year," he says. "While you're at it, make sure that phone of yours takes pictures. We'll show the paps what you're really made of."

"And probably piss off PETA," mutters Stef.

"Fuck 'em," says T.J. His cheeks are flushed, his eyes flashing. He is once again the boy who gets what he wants. "This is my ride."

King of the Forest

Stef brings the leather glove to her face and inhales deeply. It smells of grass, of summer, of the past.

"You goin' on a date with that mitt, or just catching a ball?" T.J. taunts from deep within the meadow.

She lowers her hand and adjusts her glasses, then drives her fist into the palm of the glove. "Right," she shouts. "Over here!" As if he's going to throw it somewhere else. They're alone in the field, and it feels to her like they're alone in the universe. "Wing it!"

T.J. stands a couple dozen yards away—just a bit of shadow amid the pale, dry, chest-high grasses. He hefts the ball, juggles it from hand to hand, and arcs back in a graceful, familiar bend. It launches dead-on and smacks into her glove satisfyingly, sending up dust and pollen.

While Stef was usually the pitcher and T.J. the catcher on their Little and Mid-League coed intramural SmartBall teams, they were able to change up with ease if necessary. He only knows the game as well as he does because he can trust her to be there and catch whatever he throws; she's only as passionate about the sport as she is because he's usually been the one ready to throw, straight and true.

SmartBalls help. The little tracker inside isn't legal for the actual game but makes practice more efficient. They've got it on its lowest setting so it's practically like playing with the real thing. Old-fashioned real balls are hard to come by these days, but one time when they were kids they discovered one in some boxes T.J.'s mom left him. They threw it around a little, but it was starting to come apart, so they did a dissection, picking open the casing. Inside they found a ton of yarn surrounding a stiff cork interior. It was like digging to the center of the Earth, with themselves as explorers.

Daryl and Ian opted not to come to the field—*good riddance*, she thinks. They've barely left their tents since dinner last night and have turned up their noses at any instruction from Tony on fire building or wilderness first aid or whatever. They did perk up when the compound bows came out, but Daryl smacked his inner arm with the string and hopped around hollering about workers' comp, then stalked off. Ian slipped away soon after. Mostly they've sat around like dead weights, alternately going through the stash like it's the last they'll ever have and eating everything Martinique can cook up.

Not for the first time Stef wishes the pair of them had stayed at home, but then it would be just her and T.J. and Tony, and that configuration isn't something she's comfortable with. It would feel like a sleepover with dad chaperoning, a little more intimate than she wants to consider. Anyway, that particular topic is a bright light she can't gaze into the center of yet. If she puts too much thought on how T.J. has been on her mind lately, in ways he never was before, things may get awkward between them. And once it's awkward between them they'll have to talk and—nope. All she wants right now is her pitcher, the man who sings her words, her best friend.

"Back atcha!" Stef shouts, releasing the ball. T.J. dashes to the treeline, clocking instinctively what has to be done next. Then the ball is in his hand and he sends it back to her, a missile on a trajectory home.

The memory of meeting T.J. sits at the front of her mind, but they've told it to other people in shared conversations so often she pictures it from both his side and hers, and sometimes can't recall the difference. Their parents had been friends for ages and probably tried to introduce them once or twice when they were babies, but it must not have stuck since she has no superearly memories of playing with him. But then came third grade. T.J. ran up behind her on the playground, roughly tweaking the nubbins of her tightly bound hair—and escaped toward the jungle gym as if nothing had happened.

It was a dare, he told her later, and at that age T.J. turned down no dares, especially not from playground miscreant Mickey Rosencrantz. Apparently Mickey said, *Go tell me what it feels like. I bet it's greasy.*

Stef was very proud of her hairdo on that day; it was a tidy configuration of neat squares, each with its own beribboned bun. It had taken her mom a lot of hours to do over the weekend, and she'd had to be patient, sitting up straight and not wobbling her head the whole time. When T.J. came along, she was doing something unimportant—probably drawing with SmartChalk on the solar panel sidewalk, standing up to admire her handiwork before sending it Cloudward. Then some fingers out of nowhere were grabbing at her head and pulling one of those minibuns loose.

Was softer than I expected, he said later. *And you smelled like chocolate on the beach.*

That's cocoa butter, goofball, she teased him.

It was cute later, kind of. But in that moment she was furious. White people always wanted to pat her on the head for some reason. Stared at her 'do like it wasn't part of her body. She had one friend with a kickin' strawberry Afro, and he'd been told more than once that he was *good luck*, like he wasn't a person but had magic powers. In his *hair*, apparently. Sometimes the well-meaning folks were the worst to deal with, 'cause you didn't see it coming.

The day of the hair tug, T.J. managed to get all the way to the metal bars and was hoisting himself aloft when she yanked on the back of his shirt so hard a sleeve tore. He tumbled back against the padded ground, and she took a stance over him, glowering. Thought about letting a long stream of spit dangle down to his forehead. See how *he* liked getting mauled for no reason.

Y'all think that's funny? she asked. *Who told you you get to touch me?*

T.J. gabbled nothing words. When he freed his tongue, he croaked, *Mickey*.

She shot her gaze around until her eyes landed on the instigator. *Stay there, you.*

T.J. did as he was told, watching from the ground as she strode up behind Mickey, who had his back to her, and kicked him in his ass. When he whirled around she reached over and gave his shaggy hair a hard yank.

Mickey stood there, too stunned to react.

Then she was looming over T.J. again. *I know you*, she said. *Your parents are friends with my parents. You've got a little yappy dog and your mom smokes cigars. And I know where you live.*

Stef had made it her job the summer before to know everything about everyone in her cul-de-sac. Being ferociously well informed gave her a leg up on strangers. Good to be prepared, she always thought. So sometimes you could see them coming.

You didn't answer me, she said.

What was ... what was the question? His voice was as small as a pebble. And his gray-blue eyes were like glass marbles.

You think it's funny, touching my hair?

He shook his head.

You think you wanna do it again?

Again, a head shake.

You think you wanna touch anything *on me without my say-so?*

Another head shake. He closed his eyes, clearly waiting for something horrible to happen. She thought of the spit again. But spit was disgusting. Messy. You saved the spit for someone who really did wrong. This little monkey bar king seemed sorry. And he had those funny eyes. When he opened them, she had her hand extended over his body. He took it, let her haul him up.

She pointed at the piece of hair he'd yanked on. *My momma made that. That's a Bantu knot. Or it* was.

Now it's not, he said. *Not knot.*

She blinked at him. *That's good. I like that.* Then she was laughing, a hiccupping, full-throated sound.

T.J. laughed, too. The sound ran through her like a warm-water bath, and she felt tickled inside. It was the first—but not the last—time his voice would touch her that way.

SmartBall or not, ease with throwing and catching or not, T.J. is out of practice. His pitch goes high and wide, missing Stef entirely and arcing directly at the treeline.

"I got it," she shouts, dashing after it but skids to a halt.

At the edge of the trees stand a bearded man and a skinny teenage boy in a baseball cap. The boy raises a hand, not to wave, but to show he has the ball.

T.J. closes the gap with Stef. "Looks like we've got company," he says.

Stef trots closer to the pair and holds up her mitt. "Here," she says, gesturing.

The boy glances up at the bearded man, who nods. Then he tosses the ball underhand so high it nearly vanishes against the clouding sky, white against white. Stef takes position and it falls neatly into her glove.

"That was terrible," she calls to the pair. "Come here, lemme show you how it's done."

"We don't know who they are," hisses T.J.

She eyeballs him. "Sure you wanna go with that, Sherlock?"

Realization dawns on his face, then disappointment. These are their mighty guides. The ones who're going to find him living things to shoot. The bearded old man of the forest and his son who can't even throw a baseball overhand. T.J.'s jaw tightens. "C'mon," he barks at Stef. "Let's go back to camp."

"In a minute," she says, striding forward. "Really," she tells the guides. "It's okay."

The boy starts to dart forward, but the man catches his shoulder and yanks him back. They have a brief, heated conversation that ends when the boy wrests his shoulder away and backs into the field a few steps before whirling and heading in their direction. He moves strangely in the grass, weaving from side to side. It's like watching a gazelle and a panther all at once, clearly in motion but barely causing the grass to ripple as he changes direction. He halts a few steps in front of Stef and shakes her hand, muttering something. She can't quite make out the kid's features; they're hidden by the brim of his hat.

Kid, thinks Stef. *This "kid" isn't much younger than us old farts.*

"Jim, you say?" Stef echoes what she thinks the boy said, and he nods. "Jim, meet your boss for the next couple of days. This is T.J., King of the Forest."

T.J. rolls his eyes. "Not really."

Jim tilts his cap back a bit and gives them both a direct, steady gaze. He has fine features, a narrow nose, and angled jawline. Stef catches a flash of green eye when the light angles just so. His clothes look like they're a size too big, rolled up on the wrists and ankles but still hanging free. There's an earthy, musky scent to him—he's currently in that space between needing and requiring a bath—but the smell doesn't bother her too much. It's no worse than T.J.'s bedroom back at home with its funky, lived-in scent. Instead, she's left thinking of that handshake and the hard callused palm that just held hers. It left behind a small but detectable vibration that's now running through her system.

Stef puts her hand in her pocket.

"So," says T.J., glancing between them. "We gonna play ball or what?"

Thick, warm scents reach Stef long before they return to camp and set her stomach growling. Martinique has been coming through with all the delights of home, and she's not disappointed to discover that tonight's chow is fresh spaghetti and meatballs and crusty, steaming rosemary bread slices slathered in butter and roasted garlic. The man is a marvel with a cookstove.

It's all comfort food, and Stef likes it. It's good to know what's coming next when your lives are full of curveballs like strange women who claim you knocked them up. Given her druthers Stef would prefer more variety like curries and that Ethiopian sourdough you tear off and roll your food into, but she doesn't speak up much when it comes to the menu. It's easier to like what T.J. likes, do what he does. Pick your battles. And anyway, it's what you do when you care for someone—you want to see them happy. What you want comes second. Or third. Or never.

Truth is, thanks to the money, they're able to reshape their strange world into whatever comforting shapes they might like. Sometimes Stef feels they haven't sold their talents at all, just their boring anonymity. Like selling themselves. It's a fair trade—let the world have those outer shells, and they'll keep their inner selves happy with small, selfish things. She'll have hot peppers and injera on her downtime. When she actually gets some.

Harder to curate, despite the money, have been the people around them. You can hire whoever you like, but you don't buy their friendship or loyalty, as she's noticed with Daryl and Ian. They're both reliably useless, and in Daryl's case there's a streak of mendacity she doesn't like. She'd prefer to see them both ditched after the tour. The tech exists for T.J. to have hit the road solo—they could be piping in hologrammed backup musicians for a rental fee—but T.J. balked at the idea. He preferred the old-school method of warm bodies on the road.

Then there's Tony, who's a whole other kettle of fishy things. T.J. has glommed on to their manager-cum-fixer as if he were a long-lost relation. He trusts Tony with his life, and in return, if Tony says "jump," T.J. leaps as high as he knows how. Stef gets it—Tony radiates competency and authority, but something about him makes her nervous. There's a shoe that hasn't dropped about him, and she wonders what it'll sound like when it hits the floor. She also knows her place in Tony's universe: She's an add-on, tolerated to keep his main investment happy. Still, she admires his focus—Tony is a one-man army. And he's not hard to look at either, all those sleek muscles and just-this-side-of-tan skin. He's another kind of comfort food.

But T.J. is not comforted now. Throughout dinner he seethes while settled on his throne. At one point he leans over to Stef as everyone else digs into their pasta and hisses, "What the hell was Tony thinking with those two?"

Stef cuts her eyes over to the newcomers, who are very invested in their meals. She hasn't formed any particular opinion except to think that the smaller one looks like a stiff wind could blow him over. "The dad looks like he's an escapee from the ZZ Top retirement home," she whispers.

T.J. snickers and turns back to his food.

Fact is, she has no expectations at all from the trackers. For one thing, she's only recently decided she's even coming on the hunt—the idea of staying back alone is bad, staying back with Daryl and Ian worse. But T.J.'s looking at the father and son like there's no way in this universe they're going to be able to turn him into Burt Fuckin' Reynolds. And he really seems to need that.

Funny thing, Stef realizes. Once you get to the top of whatever mountain you've been climbing, all you think of is the next mountain. How it has to be bigger, tougher. T.J.'s on top of the world as a musician and has everything he could possibly want—but lately he's been eyeballing another mountain. He wants to be a he-man. A hero. And she's not sure where that's coming from.

She gives their trackers a closer inspection and agrees: They are an odd pair. Beardo's eyes have a glassy, fixed look to them, an empty place where you think life should spark. Between those dead eyes and the tangled, thick beard, he puts unease and fear into Stef's soul. Like if he found you inconvenient, he'd have no problem erasing you from his equation. Then there's Jim, shifty and skittish as a deer, and she can't get a bead on him. There's something about him that's both young and old at the same time. He's quiet and closed off. She tries engaging him, but he's more of an eating type than a talking type. He goes through three servings of spaghetti like he only just discovered the dish exists. When he gets the garlic bread he holds it up to his nose and winces but then returns to it like a cautious dog, hoovers it up and asks for more.

When Jim catches Stef staring he pulls his jacket tighter and his hat down over his ears, like he wants to roll up into a ball.

After dinner Daryl breaks out the blunt and passes it around. Beardo waves it away on his and Jim's behalfs, but just about everyone else takes a toke. Good to have the weed after a nice meal like that. Settles your brain so your stomach can do the work. T.J. takes the cigarette back from Stef and draws down on it once more.

Tony tosses a fresh log on the fire. "I see some of you already met our guides. Samuel and Jim know more about this forest than you or I know about anything else in our entire lives, so I'm gonna advise you to listen good and do exactly what they tell you, no more, no less. I'm comin' on this great hunt, but I am not in charge when it comes to these woods, right?"

Tony fixes his gaze on T.J., who waggles his head in an approximation of assent.

Stef can't imagine a situation Tony is involved in where he doesn't believe he's in charge, but she doesn't comment.

"Samuel, you like to say a few words?" Tony asks.

A long, drawn-out silence as the man stares into the flames. The light flickers in his flat eyes, and Stef holds her breath.

"You're here to kill," says Samuel, voice gentler than Stef expected, deep and sonorous. "We're here to help you kill. But make no mistake, where we're goin' is nothing like what you've set yourself up for here."

He glances around. "We've got days of long walking, cold nights in the tents, and a whole lot of waitin' around an' bein' quiet. Deer don't show up if yer yappin'. Or listenin' to music. I ain't planning to take the lot of you on a long hike; I'm plannin' to help you track and take down some game. This cozy little setup y'have here is pretty, but pretty don't work well out there. I'm not yer daddy or yer mommy, and I'll keep ya safe but I might not keep ya comfortable. If y'don't think y'can hold yer own for the next bunch of days, don't come."

"That's me out," says Daryl, giggling through his high.

"Me too!" Ian coughs. "Think I'm getting a cold anyway."

"You two are useless assholes," T.J. barks at them.

"Watch it," says Samuel.

"Or what?" T.J. snaps. "You gonna stop me, Gandalf?"

There's a flash next to Stef, and before she can even register what's happening, T.J. is prostrate on the ground, grabbing at his ear, and Tony has jumped to the other side of the fire circle, holding Samuel's head in a wrestler's grip, the man's free hand locked behind his back.

Stef falls on her knees next to T.J., whose ear has gone scarlet. "Can't hear," he says. "Like I'm under water." She helps him to his feet, watching Samuel and Tony struggle—and then gets the full tableau. Jim is standing, equipped with a bow stretched with what looks like a homemade arrow nocked and pointed right at Tony's heart. Jim's face is a mask of concentration; his hat has blown off, and longish, curly hair shifts in the night breeze.

"Tony," says Stef in a low voice. "Please. Let him go." She glances at Jim, holding out her hands. "How about everybody take it down a few notches?"

Samuel nods tightly inside Tony's big arm, and Jim lowers the bow and arrow. Tony relaxes his grip and backs away, hands raised. "We understand each other, Sam?" Tony asks him.

"Reckon we do now," says Samuel in a tight voice. He slides his gaze at T.J. "Sorry 'bout that. Not fond of foul words. Be respectful in the woods."

But you abide smoking weed and killing things, thinks Stef, her rage sudden and unexpected. How dare he touch T.J.?

T.J. spits in the dirt. "We're done here," he barks, still holding his ear. "You're fired."

"Fine and dandy," says Sam. Jim begins zipping up his coat. "Thanks for the grub."

"T.J.," says Tony, cocking a finger. "A minute." He walks off to the tents, and after tossing the remaining bit of weed into the fire, T.J. jogs after, giving the trackers a wide berth. But from where she sits, Stef can see and hear everything.

"Are you fucking kidding me with this?" T.J. says the moment they are away from the fire. He zips his coat, shivering. "He hit me! We should sue!"

"He slapped you upside the head," says Tony. "And I'm not saying you *deserved* it, but you deserved it. Quit being such a spoiled brat. Like he said: Have some damned respect. You're in his house now. That's what he was tryin' to tell you."

"I'm *paying* him," says T.J.

"Don't mean you *own* the man," says Tony. "Now, I grabbed him 'cause if anybody's gonna whup you it'll be me. He knows that now. But do not disrespect these people. They're the only reason this trip is gonna work. And if they walk, you wanna know how many deer you're gonna bag? Zero. You wanna hit that emergency beacon and go home tomorrow, back to the Chateau Marmont Prison?"

T.J. steams and finally huffs out his answer. "No. Fine."

"Good. Now go back there and do what you gotta. From what I can see from here, he and the kid are packing up."

Stef glances at Jim, who has picked up his hat but not returned it to his head yet. Something tugs at her, but she hears T.J. and turns back to the discussion.

"That's no kid," says T.J. "He looks little but that's a lie."

Tony grabs his shoulders and turns T.J. around. Samuel is staring at him like a bug.

"Guess the word 'please' is going to have to happen," says T.J., squirming under the gaze, slouching back to the fire. Stef elbows his leg as he passes. "And sorry," he adds. Another elbow. "Please stay."

"That's my boy," says Tony. "Now. Let's tell 'em what we got for dessert."

Mostways Ready

I get wakey before sunup. All times of year. It's the best way since it's Old Sun that tells me if morning's a scavenging thing or a cleaning thing or a bathing thing. If I'm lucky, sometimes it's a resting thing. But if the sun gets up before you do, it's not a hunting thing.

Today's a walking thing. Off to Blueberry Cliff.

At least, once everybody else is up. I feel like it's not sun but it's not night either, it's in-between times. Above me the tent fabric's rippling like water. Starting to kick up out there so today'll be windy and warm. Gets like that before a big storm. If there's snow on the ground we call it a snow eater but since there's no snow on the ground the wind's going hungry today.

Prolly. Too soon to tell.

I run my tongue over the roof of my mouth. Still some chocolate ice cream taste there. Ice cream's impossible out here but last night they made it happen. Was like a dream, one I had when I was a little girl. Before we went to nighty-night I asked Daddy how come they can make ice cream happen out here and was it magic and he said they don't do magic it's just 'cause they have more money than sense. He said you can make anything happen but happiness when you have money.

I don't know, I was pretty happy last night.

Someone else is up. Moving, outside our tent. Daddy's going zzz again so it's not him. He sleeps hard, that's why I can sneak out when I have to for hunting or Gil times. Though he did wake that one time with Jim.

Another little cracking sound. Not from where the toilet is, that's on the other side of the big clearout—boy did they take down a lot of trees. Whole place smells like wood. So whoever's up and rustling outside isn't going for the toilet tent. An inside toilet! Almost like the little room outside our cabin but not as smelly. I don't care what Daddy says, this place is magic. But I remember what Gil said and I'm trying to figure out which client has blood boiling so I can beware. Might be a couple of them. The men here get mad real fast.

Not the woman. She's interesting. Makes me think of Gil a little.

Anyway, that rustling's moving near our tent but not xactly here. Big enough for a bear. Artie? That would be bad. I roll out my bed and slide on a sweater and then my coat 'cause I remember I have to be Jim and if I don't have much on it's pretty clear I'm not a Jim. No shoes. Feet are icy but I don't wanna be heard. I want to see. I get low and grab my knife and step out the tent opening. They gave us this place after the tussle at the fire last night, said we could sleep here, boys could sleep together and the big man—Tony I think—could sleep in the same tent as the little one. Tee Jay, they call him. I coulda slept by the fire, do that all the time. But they gave us this place, so Daddy said we wouldn't say no.

I drew my bow last night. Didn't even think about it. Daddy was held by that Tony and he was getting choked. Coulda killed him. Never saw anybody take another person with hands only. Jim could snuff out a squirrel or strangle a rabbit caught in a snare with just a few knuckles but a person who could make Daddy stand still was the toughest person I ever met.

So okay, Tony is interesting too. He might be the one Gil warned me about.

I didn't think that at the time. I just saw death pawing our way and did what I had to to stop it. Like a muscle twitch. Something in me bounced. I got hot in my chest and there was a roar in my ears. I made out every inch of that man's face from the thick hair on his head to his veins pulsing like rivers. For a second I thought about how I'd feel if he grabbed me like that and part of me was scared but part of me got warm all over, like the hot I felt in my chest was free to go anywhere.

True thing.

Then my bow started shaking and the lady punched out her hand and said *wait* and I came back.

Outside my tent right now, there's nobody. Can't see what moved where or if there's anything worth seeing. Definitely no Artie. She wouldn't hide from me. But somebody was out there being careful like I would be careful. They were sneaking. They were trying to be invisible.

"*Tha an t-slighe soilleir,*" I whisper though this time there are no trees to hum. Instead the ground vibrates under my feet and the rocks bounce around and the little patchy grass quivers and the air ripples. My head doesn't get too tired 'cause it's just a short little distance and the way I figure, it hurts me more to say the words when the way is far. I wait for the ache to go and then I'm following the tremors forward and to the right. They stop just outside one of the tents. The lady's. Stef's.

So maybe it was just Stef, walking back inside her tent. Maybe she wanted fresh air. Maybe she knows where I can get more ice cream before breakfast.

I slip out into the morning, feet *swish swish* on the cleared-out dirt. I make no sound while I slip up to her tent opening and pull it back just a little, just enough—

"Out," I hear her say and I nearly drop it, figuring she's seen me but then I catch that smell from last night, the cigarette smell that's sweet and made everybody laugh. "I'm not kidding," she goes on.

Some mumbling. Deep voice. Can't hear it clear so I pull the flap a little more. There's someone else in her tent, someone with long dark hair all stringy over his shoulders, and he's leaning over one side of Stef's bed. I can't see her but she's small under her sheets, all balled up and tight.

"You get until 'three' and then I am gonna yell up a—"

He reaches out and does something that makes her stop talking and I'm inside the tent, that muscle twitchy thing going off in me, my chest getting warm. I don't think, I'm just doing it and I'm up behind him and I grab a big handful of his hair and pull hard, then put the point of my knife up at the soft part of his jaw. He stumbles back with a "yawp" sound and starts to twist but I push the point a bit and there's a bead of blood there. For a second I feel like Tony, I grabbed someone and I made them stop in place.

But I have a knife. He has nothing.

I'm breathing hard and there's a roar in my ears again. I look up and Stef is up on her knees in the bed, holding her hand out flat like last night, shaking her head. She has a book in her other hand and she's got it in the air behind her head like the baseball from yesterday and she's talking.

"... Right, okay, that's good enough, Jim," she's saying, which I can finally hear when the roar dies down. I look at her and she nods.

"Get down on your knees," I whisper tough-like at the guy. "Hands up." When he does that, that's when I pull my knife back and stand behind him, holding his hair like it's a tether. It's Daryl, the one from last night who just smoked and smoked and hardly said anything but stared at Stef a whole lot.

Stef puts her book down and looks from him to me and back again.

"You're done," she hisses at him. "You get that, don't you?"

He spits on the floor. "You want it," he says. "You been looking at me funny for days."

"That's disgust, you pig," she says. "Here's what's gonna happen. I'm not going to tell Tony, because this is T.J.'s week and Tony will kill you and T.J. will spit on your grave and that would really fuck up the whole trip. But you better find a way to not be here when we get back, 'cause if you are then I *will* tell him. And I'll have Jim here to back me up."

"Bitch," he hisses at her and punches me in my side; a hot bolt of pain shoots up and down my body and I let him go, stumbling.

A book comes out of nowhere and clobbers him in the face. Stef's aim is good.

He stands, rubbing his eye. "That's gonna bruise, you—"

I glare at him, holding up the knife.

"Another thing you have to deal with, then," she says, getting out of bed. She's got on a long flowy gown and fuzzy socks and again she makes me think of Gil, who is also fuzzy and flowy and has skin of all kinds of colors. "Hey," she looks at me. "You won't say anything, will you."

I shake my head. "Don't have to."

"Good." She looks at Daryl. "Once more, with feeling: You have until 'three,' and—"

He turns and storms out of the tent.

Stef looks at me and I look at her and I don't know what to say. "Okay?" I ask.

"Yeah," she says, falling back against the bed. "No. Yeah. Look, I can take care of myself."

I put the knife back in the sheath and what comes out of me is a surprise. "I can help."

"Ain't no help for that boy," she sighs.

"What'd he want?"

Her look goes cool and she crosses her arms. "Don't think I know you well enough for that."

It's weird between us then. I prolly should leave. But I can't not ask. "Think there's leftover ice cream?" I wonder.

That makes her chuckle. "Yeah," she says. "Bet there is."

People confuse me.

I don't see too many, so that's prolly why. When it comes to people, here's what I mostly don't get:

1) They say one thing and they do something else.
2) Sometimes they don't say anything and I'm supposed to know what they mean.
3) They have all kinds of words they use that don't make sense but they think I should know what they are.
4) They do a lot of washing.

I didn't see anybody but Jim and Daddy for a long time but that changed some after Jim left. First Daddy would leave me alone a couple of days, even a week at a time. Said I was old enough, knew where everything was and he'd be back. He had to work. But when I got another birthday older Daddy changed things again.

"Come with me," he said one morning and we started walking away from home.

We have the only cabin in the woods. It has a big main room with a bed Daddy sleeps on and doesn't smell like old underwear anymore. There's a loft up a ladder where we keep things in boxes and I sleep in my sleeper bag. Jim used to sleep up there with me, and now I have all the room. It's not much fun. That's the whole place—a bed, table, four chairs, big black metal stove, sink, and cabinets—xcept for under the bed, a trap door with Daddy's storage. Daddy calls it a root cellar but there aren't roots, just all our backup supplies. Canned sauces and jams and pickled vegetables in glass jars and sacks of apples, potatoes, onions. We grow some of what we eat but Daddy's paid mostly in supplies by clients so we have some interesting xtra things like powdered lemonade drink and hard cookies. That's our cabin. That's our territory.

'Less Daddy's with me I don't go more than a half day's walk away 'cause:

1) I have to be back before bedtime every night.
2) I might run into people and get sick.
3) If I get hurt Daddy has to know where to look for me.
4) Daddy said so and that's the end of the discussion.

Xcept once I did go more than a half day away. Once I just kept walking, past the Great Meadow, ended up at our swimming lake. Didn't plan, just went. Took me most of three days to get there. And I got scared. Saw all that water and all those mountains and couldn't move another step, like something was tied 'round me and holding me back.

I caught some fish and turned 'round and went back to the cabin. Didn't want to, but didn't have any place else to go. I stopped off for a bit and picked up some supplies at our cave—we keep supplies and some cots inside it and the outside has this special cammyflage so nobody knows it's there—and went home. Daddy was madder than anything and grabbed the strop, and I figured it was my turn to get hit but I didn't care. I stuck out my lip and said *I just felt like it* and why couldn't I do some things if I felt like it.

Didn't say I wanted out. Didn't say I was running anyplace. I know that's the fast way to the strop, and maybe to see what happens when Daddy takes steps. So I showed him what I got at the cave. Pretended that was my plan all the time. *We needed peanut butter*, I said and I was pretty sure that was true.

He had a look on his face like he wasn't too sure if I was shit or shine-o-la and put down the jar and stormed out of the cabin for an hour. When he came back he told me: *You're mostways ready.*

Ready for what? I asked.

Ready for whatever comes next. For being grown up.

So when am I all ways?

When I say so, he said. *Do not do this again.*

And he hung the strop up.

Soon after that Daddy started taking me to meet clients. It's a long way to find them, more steps than I can count. Mostly if we leave after breakfast first thing we get there by afternoon next day.

That first day he took me I wasn't Jim yet tho I did have short hair. We got to the edge of the woods inside a big clearing where the trees were so tall it looked shady in the middle of the day. There were a couple of shacks and picnic tables and a tall pole in the middle with a striped and starred flag whipping around the top. Daddy stopped at the clearing edge and put his big hands on my shoulders. Turned me round.

Look at me, he said, and xplained the plan again: Go inside the building near where we were standing and take a hot shower. I got two silver coins to pay for the water and he said it would only last five minutes so move fast. Then I was supposed to put on my Jim clothes and come out and hide in the bushes until he hooted for me.

Nobody looked at me when I went into the girl showers and then the water was gushing all over me and I rubbed our little bite of soap and I was gasping it was so wonderful. Delicious like food and comfy like a blanket and then the five minutes were up and I was staring at the showerhead, hoping for just one more gush. But I had no more coins so I shuffled into the changing area.

It was packed. Maybe 10 women in there with me, most in towels and some wearing nothing but floppy shoes attached to their toes. They stared in mirrors and brushed their teeth and talked and splashed water and put on makeup. I kept my eyes on the ground. Kept thinking if I didn't see nobody, nobody would see me. But I looked up sometimes to see if any of them acted sick. Daddy hadn't said anything about sickness in the showers. Mostly what I saw that morning was bare feet and toes painted with bright colors. One set of toe colors shifted like Gil's face when the foot they were attached to moved. Everything was brand-new and shiny—sneakers and hiking boots and slippers. It was all sharp and clean and not me.

The room felt like it was getting smaller around me so I backed up and turned 'round and faced a strange but familiar face. She had suspicious eyes and faint freckles and wet hair that stood up in sections. It was the strangest face I'd ever seen and it was mine.

Next to me a girl who was maybe my age fussed with her hair in a long braid. She had on a pink lacy top that ended about an inch before her jeans started and I was sad that she'd grown out of her clothes. She had big hooped earrings that made twinkling sounds when she moved and was slipping on fabric bracelets. Someone called a name—Jessie—and she whipped her head 'round and I saw the tops of her ears had jewelry on them too. She was chewing something. She was beautiful.

Caught myself staring so I went back to feet. Daddy was waiting so I jumped into my old beat up Jim clothes, jammed on a baseball cap and slipped into the trees. I watched Daddy take a seat at a picnic table. He got up once or twice and walked 'round then walked back into the trees and came out again a minute later like he just arrived. Two hours passed and I slapped at mosquitoes and it wasn't boring at all. I just watched the people go this way and that way and talk to each other and sometimes I made up stories, like I saw Jessie with an older woman and I imagined her saying, *Mom my shirt's too short can I get another* and mom saying back *of course when we get home I will buy you 10 shirts* and then they walked off. I sang to myself all quiet, my little list songs I made up so I would remember things. The people were like reading a book, but happening in front of my face.

Finally a man sat down across from Daddy. He had silver hair and a backpack that was almost as big as he was. A twin of the first man but younger with black hair plopped on the bench too, a half-folded map dragging on the ground. They spread the map on the table. Daddy ran his fingers over it a minute later and then they were laughing.

These woods are deep and hard to walk around if you don't know your way but you are in luck today, I imagined Daddy saying. *I am the best tracker you will find and I can make sure your trip is the best ever.*

Well we are lucky fellows, I thought the silver-haired man might say. *How much do you charge?*

I will take all your leftover food and supplies, but there is a bonus: I have my son Jim with me and I will not charge you extra for him, Daddy could say back.

Deal! the other man would say.

The father was Ray Allston and his son was Paul. They talked a lot about *the market* and a place called Chicago. Ray had the idea to *rough it* in the woods for five days but the *goddamned map* kept leading them astray and Daddy was a *godsend* even if his quiet son Jim was *a laggard*.

Thing is, having people nearby was like hitting me in the head with a branch. I couldn't talk much. Words kept sticking in my throat. Daddy didn't seem to mind me acting dumb and pretty soon Ray and Paul stopped seeing me unless they needed something grabbed. They hardly talked to Daddy either; it was like they were having conversations with the air. They weren't there to hunt, just hike and sleep wild and take nice pictures to put up in the clouds—whatever that meant—and maybe catch a trout for supper.

I made them nice fishing poles since they didn't have any and they started calling me "Huck Finn" who was a boy in a book we used to have at the cabin. They had a good time and caught four cutthroat trout for dinner and we ate well. Daddy gave them nothing but his own brain knowings and a little muscle here and there. I carried wood and made fires and found bait.

On the final night Ray broke open a bag of small soft white squares. They stuck them on the ends of sticks they had me sharpen and toasted them on the fire, then mashed the cooked pieces between brown crackers with a little square of chocolate.

Ess mores, said Paul, handing me one. *Gotta have ess mores when you're camping.*

I ate one and it was like my head might explode, it was so sweet. I was bouncy for hours later and my stomach made noises all night.

Next day we walked them back to the shower site, and Ray handed over his backpack full of extra food and things to Daddy. He tossed me the leftover bag of marshmallows. *Here, kid*, he said. *Put some meat on your bones.*

I looked at him in the face for the first time in days. He had brown eyes and brown hair and smooth, white teeth. When I eat sweet things I think of that face.

He ruffled my hair and the baseball cap went sideways. *Don't eat 'em all at once.*

Then Ray and Paul were gone.

That went pretty well, I think, said Daddy. *Yeah?*

I couldn't say anything. I had four marshmallows jammed in my mouth.

Stef and me stuff ourselves with leftover ice cream by the fire while the rest of the forest wakes up around us. There's never zero noise in the woods, if you know how to listen, but I pay attention to how it comes alive—if the birds arrive first, or the bugs, or the wind or the trees shifting and talking to each other. I hear the conversation they have in part, 'cause I know if it ever stops that trouble is on the way.

While we eat Stef doesn't talk about what just happened in the tent so I decide I'm not going to either. But she keeps looking at me like I'm some puzzle she wants to put the last piece on.

"How old're you?" she asks me.

"Most way to eighteen," I say.

"You seem younger," she says. "And you seem older."

I shrug. The ice cream is what's most interesting to me. They even have little chocolate bits you put on that make it crunch on top of the melty part.

"How come you were up so early?"

"I get up when the sun does," I say. "If you go hunting you get up early."

"And you hunt a lot?"

I shrug again. I look at her and try to guess if she has an abracadabra like I do. Gil seems to think we all do, but we usually never know it. He says knowing the way is mine and my having the right words helps it come out. He says it'll hurt my head less if I use it more but I can't 'cause Daddy can't see it. He would call it a sickness, but I'm starting to think it's a talent. Or a sense. Like smelling or tasting. "What do you do?" I ask.

She puts her spoon down. "You're direct."

"Don't have to talk," I said.

"I write words down and T.J. sings 'em."

"That a talent?"

She thinks about it. "Guess so. What's yours?"

I wondered if she knows for sure that I have one. Then I wonder if maybe she knows Gil. "Don't think I know you well enough for that," I say, 'cause I remember what it felt like when she said it to me earlier and it sounds smart.

That makes her chuckle. "Touché, touché." She scrapes the edges of her bowl and slowly licks off the spoon. The inside of her mouth is pink like mine and like everybody else I know but she's still one of Gil's colors on the outside. I never have been. I don't know if I've ever seen anybody like her before. I bet she's got an advantage in the woods 'cause she blends in a whole lot better than I do. Born with cammyflage, that's what she's got.

She looks at me a long time, head tilts to the side. "You really know how to find a bear out here?"

My eyes get wide. There's only one bear out here these days and I do not want to find her. "Deer," I say. "Just deer."

She chuckles. "Well, I know somebody who won't be happy to hear that. T.J. wants him a bear and won't be happy if he doesn't bag one."

"We shouldn't look for Artie," I say and then think I'm already talking too much. I say things with her out loud I'm supposed to only think.

Stef snorts. "Artie," she says, giving me a funny look.

"It's just a name. For a bear I sometimes see," I say.

She stands up and laughs, heading to the kitchen tent. "Your bear sounds like an old Jewish comedian."

I watch her walk away; she's got a good strong walk with a little back and forth sway like she's a sapling tree. So maybe she's stronger than the others but fact is I know they're all soft. Soft like our beds last night. Daddy and me, we're wire, we're rope, we're tough and you can't pull us apart so easy. These ones will go all to pieces first time they have to pee without their little outhouse tent. Xcept maybe Tony. The one whose blood probably boils. Not wire at all. He's chain and nails and metal.

I get washed and brushed and dry everything off on the fluffy towel they have in the toilet tent and all there is to do is wait, so I go to the firepit and there's Tony, backpack propped up and ready to go. I look this way and that way but there's no place really for me to be, so I put on my Jim walk and tuck my hat down a little more and go sit over there, too. Not close, not far, just far enough from him.

"Mornin'," he says, raising a mug of coffee to his lips. He's tan, I didn't see that last night, all toasty brownish orange, and his pale eyes are like sky-colored ghosts in his head. He's all suited up for the day, long pants and white long-sleeved shirt covered by a vest with like a hundred pockets. He could leave now. We could leave now, if we wanted. Just go.

Part of me wants to say *let me show you this deep hole in the ground and I will push you into it so you don't scare Gil*. And part of me wants to say *show me how you did that thing with Daddy last night* because then I would learn something. And because then he would be touching me.

I don't say anything. Best not to talk if I don't have to.

I don't abide foul words. Nearly laughed at that last night. Can't think of a day Daddy doesn't swear up a storm. Still don't know why he went after T.J., but I don't ask everything. T.J. seems a little like Jim was, so maybe that's it. I know Daddy and Jim were not happy with each other when Jim left.

"—leave soon?" Tony is talking to me. I lift my head, tilt it a bit. He sighs. "Just wondering if you think we'll hit the road soon."

I shrug.

"So where are we headed today? East? North? South? I know not West, that's the mountains."

Again, I shrug.

"Do you know *anything* about this particular trip, Jim?" he asks, leaning forward. "Is there any reason why you're here if you don't?"

My cheeks are getting red; he's acting like I don't know anything. I want to pick up my bow again and aim it at his neck and say *this is the only reason I need* but the bow and my arrows are in the tent. "I can track," I say finally in as low a voice as I dare.

"It speaks!" he cries, sitting up and splashing some coffee. "So, what else don't we know about you, Jim?"

Everything. "We're not finding a bear."

He starts to say something, then retreats. "We're not, are we?"

I shake my head. "She's special. She's not for you."

"I see," he says, and touches a full pocket on the side of his pants for a second. "How come?"

I don't say anything. I'm already too close.

"She does special tricks?" Tony asks. "Glows in the dark? Only eats poppies for dinner? What?"

I still don't say anything but he's getting close and something in what I don't say makes Tony get all tight and frozen. He sits like that a moment, then smiles at me and there's nothing good in that smile. Nothing at all. "Is she … magic, Jim?"

I see what I did and my throat closes. These new people. They're not like our other clients. They poke a hole in me and words come out. "Magic is a sickness," I say and it's a small strangled thing coming out my mouth.

Tony takes a long drink of coffee and gives me a long sideways glance. He knows something's up.

I have to be better at being Jim.

Over the years Daddy and me did tracking for lots of kinds of clients. Pretty quick I learned I can go eye to eye with them and not burn up complete. But I try never to talk much. That's okay 'cause if I don't talk mostly they do and I can listen not only to what they say but how they say it. It makes them less strange to me, and it makes me less strange to them. I need to know how to act. In case.

Mostly it's men who come out here. Men with sons. Men with work friends. Men with bosses. They bring beer and we soak the cans in the stream every night when we camp so they stay cold and they stay up late getting drunk and the next day they can barely take aim. So there's not a lot of hunting they do and Daddy ends up taking down the quarry but lets them take the pictures. Or the head. They usually really, really want the head.

Sometimes there's a woman. Hardly ever though. When she comes, she's usually somebody's something. Wife. Daughter. Girlfriend. Once five women came together and said it was about some kind of shower but it didn't rain at all the whole time. Daddy sent me home day after they hired him. Did the tracking solo that time. But when there are women I watch them closest of all. I am one, or sort of like one, but they are harder for me to read. And sometimes I mess up.

One time I stared so long and hard at this girl who was 'bout my age her dad told Daddy, *Think y'all's son has a crush on my Cindy.*

Daddy played it cool. *Kids that age*, he said. Later on, he told me, *Don't be so weird.* I didn't know xactly what he meant.

Truth: I think women see through me. They don't know I'm a girl, xactly, but they stare right back like something's off about me and they can't put their finger on it. They're 'valuating, taking stock all the time like they want to figure me out or fix me. And the men just keep talking, talking.

Men are easy. Their eyes slide right off me 'cause I'm not important. *You're not a threat 'cause you're small for a man, and you're not going to kiss 'em, so they can ignore you*, said Daddy one time. *Guys have to sort everybody out before they can rest easy. If it ain't about fucking or fighting, they don't care.*

So when it's all guys I hunker down in my big clothes and hat and listen to them at the fire. They say words Daddy never lets me use, and their voices are low like friendly growls and they put me right to sleep.

During the day, though, Daddy and me are in charge. We take clients down back paths, threading through the brush and up ledges and rises until we find a waterfall or pool. They jump in to cool off and we head back. Xcept me. I stay on land, 'cause I always have to be Jim. Out of clothes, everybody'd know I'm not Jim at all.

But mostly clients are here to hunt. Early on we only walked people with arrows—that's how I got so good with the bow myself—and once Daddy gave a client a free day in trade for his gear, so that's how I got my first equipment. I make my own arrows now, though. These days most people come with guns so 'ventually Daddy gave in and took them on, too. He stares at their licenses like he knows what to look for and says he'll help 'em bag whatever they come for: elk, moose, deer. I don't come on all those trips. If Daddy doesn't whistle for me after landing a client I scoot back to the cabin or the cave—the cave's good in the summertime 'cause it's not so hot in there—until he returns. Lots of times Daddy comes back with spare meat, since clients can't take home all they shoot, and we dry and salt it and chew for weeks and weeks.

That's how it's been, all these summers and falls and springs and winters. Guide. Hike. Live in the cabin or the cave. Jim's clothes mostly stopped smelling like him a long time ago; now they smell mostly like me. And now they're not so big anymore. Sometimes I wonder when we'll get to walk away from the cabin and keep going, all the way to the Outside. Daddy doesn't say, though.

Guess I'm still only mostways there.

Impossible Birch Trees

Everyone's on T.J. time; Stef's used to that. But T.J. isn't up at seven. Or eight. Or nine. At half-past nine Stef gets Jim to chase her around T.J.'s tent, and they make so much noise laughing that it wakes him up, which was absolutely the point.

Soon as Stef hears him rustling around she bursts into his tent and tackles him on the bed, saying it's about fucking time he gets moving. "Jeez, deer as a *species* will have gone extinct if you wait longer," she tells him as he dallies over what shirts to pack.

"What's your rush?" he snaps at her.

"What's your delay?" she snaps back. "You turning chicken, Old Salty?"

That gets him moving.

Now, as they pass through the deep trees, Samuel bushwhacking a trail at the head of their line, there's not much chatter. Everyone's still simmering at the late start. Slowly, Stef feels herself relaxing into the quiet and soon senses she's hearing better, hearing more. There's the constant plod of their collective feet, of course, but above and beyond that is the quiet. Not silence—there are too many shifts and creaks and sighs and buzzes—but quiet. A place in order, where life unfolds without being scheduled or organized or told what to do. It's much better than Alphabeticus Vulgarius.

She's particularly drawn to the twisting, burled tree trunks. She might not know the varieties other than a birch or an oak, but these ancient giants hold her attention. They remind her of old men and women, snarling and smiling at those who dare to intrude. She smiles back, wanting to be on their good side, and takes out her notepad, scribbling a few lines. Wonders if T.J. might consider sitting down with the travel guitar they packed to hash out some of the lines when they take a break.

"Teej," she says softly, the first words any of them have spoken since leaving camp. "Teej."

No response. She leans forward and realizes he's out of it. Ears completely plugged, music playing. Lost in his own inner soundtrack. Stef rolls her eyes. Come all this way, learn how to shoot a bow and arrow, and then ignore the song of the forest. Sometimes she wonders just what it is she's supposed to find so fascinating about him. Some days it's like he got stuck at fourteen and she's overtaken him.

Time passes slowly, and she feels enveloped by the world around her. Stef tunes into the complex forest music, which no longer feels quiet in her ears, and as the trees thicken and blot out the sky, more of its sounds reach out to her like tendrils seeking purchase: the shush of the branches, the crack of the trunks, the scraping of boughs, the flap of bird wings, the scamper of tiny feet in the brush, everyone escaping the big mammals plowing through their neighborhood. Samuel hacks through the underbrush and twigs, making room for them to pass, and the sounds of him clearing a path add to the music. A sneeze, a cough, a deep breath. It all folds together and Stef hears it like she hears a song—not necessarily musical, but as one aspect of a great machine, wheels turning and cogs fitting into place. A machine entirely made of nature, not forged elements. It is as if she has stepped into a great clock tower and can see one small part of how the world's pieces fit together. She's glad to have left her makeup back at camp and brought instead their small travel guitar. Out here, she wants to be natural. Listening. Being. She hopes to be completely herself—not simply half of a pair.

Eventually they take a toilet break and on returning, Tony speaks quietly with T.J. while Stef drops back to walk alongside Jim. "So what happens in winter?" she asks.

Jim gazes at her, a mix of curiosity and wariness in his face. He's got cheekbones most girls would crave, and his eyes are more hazel than green right now. Their color seems to shift and bend depending on the light. "Winter?"

"Yeah. Snow. Ice. That season."

"Too cold," he says. "Don't take people out much."

"But you're out here in the woods—all the time?" She's fascinated by this setup. Sure, during her Scouting days they had some challenges, but there was always the safety net of their internal trackers or the knowledge that if something truly bad happened, they could be spirited away. She'd read books on living in the woods, maybe even picked up a few tips here and there. But this was a very different level of challenge. She doubts she'd have the mettle for it.

Yet thinking about it reminds her how a while back there was a push for this kind of living. A bunch of folks decided to live off the grid, skip paying their taxes. Thought they'd be safe in the wilds of the world, at least safer than in the crumbling suburbs and overpriced cities. But most of those types came home in a month or two, tail between their legs. Once the world became a more dangerous place, people seemed to want to clump back together again. Safety in numbers.

"Sure," he says. "All the time."

"Where do you go to school?"

"Daddy taught me. I don't need school anymore."

"So—do you like it out here?"

"'Course."

"But if you wanted to leave, you could, right?"

He shrugs. "Maybe." He looks at her. "You and T.J. married?"

She laughs. "Just friends. My mom and dad helped raise him when his parents died."

"So like brother-sister."

"Kinda, sure."

"Are you with him all the time?"

She stares out in the woods. Why does every question have two answers? "I go where T.J. goes," she says, knowing that sounds pathetic.

They walk in step for a while. Stef knows she should thank Jim for showing up earlier this morning. But opening that can of worms is not a place she wants to go. First off, she doesn't like the great white hunter showing up to save her poor Black ass. She'd've done fine if he hadn't gotten there. Probably. Daryl's mean but not naturally vicious. She met him about a year ago when he laid down tracks in T.J.'s recording studio outside LA, before he was grafted onto T.J.'s touring band, and one late night they had too much tequila and ended up without their clothes on in a soundproofed room. It wasn't a bad scene, but Daryl was sloppy drunk and couldn't get it up for very long even with some help, so they never got around to the textbook definition of sex. What they did get up to was pretty satisfying for her at least, and she left him passed out in the room overnight and hoped he'd forget altogether.

Then he joined the touring act and she had a sinking sensation that he did it largely because he was hoping for some easy, nondrunken sex, but Stef doesn't get involved with coworkers. Too messy, and besides T.J. is *right here*. Daryl has spent the past months trying to corner her, half of the time with verbal jabs and the other half by staring at her. This morning was a disturbing departure on his part, but she was more surprised than shaken. Stef's pretty certain it wasn't just the drink that night in the studio that kept his pecker from saluting for very long.

But she can't exactly bring up the subject with Jim.

Then she gets an idea. "You asked—earlier—you asked what I did," she says.

"You write words down and T.J. sings them," he parrots back.

"Yeah." She nods. "People pay us a lot of money to hear them. People buy tickets to hear T.J. sing them. Did your dad tell you about that?"

"Is it a talent, too?"

He's not being mean, but the phrase is so dismissive a flare of anger lights in her. "Can you do it?"

"Maybe." Then he starts humming, and in a minute comes up with a song that's not a song, it's just a story that doesn't rhyme about what happened that morning. Like a list, or a memory. It's not good or bad, it's just—different. It's not what she does.

When he finishes, she takes over. Starts up one of the tunes she's most pleased about—one that isn't just about puppy love and longing, one that's about the deeper corners of the heart where things can't be spoken and it's about the light in a person's eyes that guides you to them. It was a deep cut on the last album and never even came close to being released as a single. But Stef has always liked those tunes best. The fans who know those songs are the ones who're paying attention.

She doesn't sing loud or long, just enough for Jim to know what she's made of. And when she finishes, the look on his face is enough. "*That* is a song," she says.

He pokes his eyes with dirty fingers. "That's nice," he says. "That's really nice."

She nods at him. That'll show him. "So yes, it *is* a talent."

"And that's your job."

She laughs softly. It's refreshing to be with someone who knows absolutely nothing about the shallow depths of the career she and her best friend have chosen. "It's not just a job," she says. "It's an adventure."

While everyone lounges around the fire after dinner, tired from their day's long march, Stef unzips the cover from her travel guitar.

Tony shakes his head. "Who brings a guitar on a deer hunt?"

"Bear," T.J. corrects.

Stef ignores them. She's working on new lines from a song and doesn't want to let the thread snap. A few gentle strums waft across the campsite like smoke from the fire, and she tries to match the chords with the words she'd come up with during the day. The process fuels her soul, fills her up in a different way than the fish and potatoes they had for dinner.

Curious, T.J. removes his earbuds and shifts her way. "Whatcha got there, Peps?"

Stef slides over her notebook of lyrics, tapping on the phrases she came up with during the hike. "Just ... musing," she says. "Got it in you?"

"Hmph." T.J. combs his hair from his face. "Challenge accepted."

They start small. Quiet. Not exactly hesitant, but like walking across an icy pond, unsure of where to tread. After a minute or two, T.J.'s voice locks into place. His thin warble goes in and out, improvising. She keeps up with his changes, offering her own notes and tones and shifts.

In time they unbend from one another, and Stef eyes their tiny, rapt audience. Dollar signs shine in Tony's eyes, like they always do when T.J.'s singing.

No earplugs tonight? she wants to ask him—he always has his ears plugged with something when they make music. She'd asked him once why, and he'd only muttered *war injury*. But Tony's not the only one paying attention—the cranky old fart Samuel is twirling his beard in a finger, trying to pretend he's not interested, yet humming along.

Sliding out of her new track, Stef picks up one of the first tunes she'd ever taught herself on the guitar from this oldrock Irish band whose bassist she's crushed on since she was a kid. T.J. grins, knowing of her mild obsession with the band, and puts a lilt into his voice as he picks up the lyrics. They grow louder and more confident, moving from that tune to even older ones from the early part of the last century. That gets Samuel's attention for sure, and suddenly he's singing along word for word on this ancient Hank Williams tune. T.J.'s feeling it, charm oozing from his bright eyes, his voice, his entire body—even though they're only sitting on fallen logs around a campfire, millions of miles from a stadium gig. Stef has missed hearing him live, and he's clearly missed the stage. It lifts him up in a way the weed never can.

But Stef is mostly interested in Jim. Not just because she's about 100 percent positive this is the first live music he's ever heard, but because she wants to see how T.J.'s voice affects a complete newbie. Something funny happens to people who listen to T.J., something she's never seen with other musicians. The crowds start out screaming, then slide into a kind of soft hypnosis, waving their phone lights high, singing or humming along—but with a dreamy, lost expression on their faces. Like they'd just gotten straddled by an angel and were ascending to a heavenly climax. Stef has seen this happen from her side of the stage, hundreds of young people—and some as old as her parents—biting their lips, crossing their legs, acting like T.J. was touching them personally, intimately.

Stef doesn't feel it back. Oh, she loves T.J.'s voice. It's not the greatest instrument she's ever heard, but it has a character and depth amid its thinness that makes her feel like she's listening to someone from another world. But it doesn't *dose* her. Maybe she's immune to exposure from T.J. after all these years. Lord knows, his behavior can make a person immune if you know him too well. But she rarely sees how he affects people who've never heard him before.

After a few minutes, Tony stands, flicking dirt and debris from his trousers. Samuel gets to cleaning up the leftovers from dinner and gives Jim a nudge to help him out. But Jim doesn't move. He's sitting straight, arms around his raised knees. He doesn't clap between songs, doesn't even blink when his father nudges him a little harder.

Tony shakes his head at Samuel. "I'll help out," he says. "Let the kid enjoy the music."

Stef half smiles at that. She turns back to Jim, who has his finger over his lips as if to indicate silence. He's looking beyond T.J. now, and Stef turns to see what's so interesting—but all she spots are more pine trees, bare trunks, and a pretty collection of birch trees all clumped together that she hadn't noticed earlier. Shrugging, she picks up the music again and Jim falls back into the spell.

By the time she wraps things up a few minutes later, Jim's face is beet red. He scrambles up without a word and joins his father, who orders him to pick up fresh wood for the fire. She wants to know what he felt. If he felt it. What it felt like to *feel* T.J.'s voice.

"Good stuff, Peps." T.J.'s voice is rough. "Even out here, you got it."

Stef sighs. "Thanks, Old Salty."

She'd have to wait until later to quiz Jim.

Deep in the night, Stef is wakened by a rustle outside of her tent and goes on full alert. Her fingers brush a fork she lifted from dinner. She knows it's not Daryl; he could never muster the gumption needed to stalk her several miles into the woods, then hang out until everybody went to sleep. But someone else *is* up.

A tent zips, followed by a soft shuffling in the leaves. She tries to remember the layout: T.J.'s tent is right next to hers, and Tony's next to his, so it has to be either Samuel or Jim, and she's curiously excited at the prospect that it might be the latter. She carefully unzips her own tent and pops out her head. No one's moving. Slipping on her doused headlamp and sliding into her coat, she emerges into a world that's darker and colder than anything she's ever seen or felt. Shifting cloud cover blots out the stars and the moon right now; it's as if someone has set a blanket over the forest the way people cover up a birdcage for the night. All she can make out are darker shades of dark, the old trees she admired earlier now poised like monsters, ready to strike.

Yet while the sounds are different from earlier that day, the forest is not sleeping. A high buzz made up of insect song and random movement, night creatures living, eating, dying, threads through the trees. Dark movement near Jim's and Samuel's tent catches Stef's eyes, and she shuffles after the figure, remembering too late that she only has fuzzy woolen socks on her feet.

Lines from the song she and T.J. were creating after dinner drift into her mind, keeping her focused and calm. She realizes it's fairly certain that's Jim out there going walkabout—and that'll give her a chance to quiz him on the performance. See what's going on beneath that filthy baseball cap and slouched posture. She follows, figuring he's probably just off taking a whiz, and decides if she hears him making water in the bushes she'll waylay him on the way back to the tent for a chat. It's not just about his reaction to the song, though. There's something up with Jim that she can't put her finger on. She presses the side of grandmother's old antique watch. It brightens for a second to reveal that midnight's just passed, then darkens again.

The shushing is gone. She cranes forward, listening for the sound of piss falling. Instead she picks up muted voices. Stef takes careful steps up to a small rise, beyond which a glow pulses—a soft, faint yellow-white reflected by that stand of birch trees she saw earlier. But she sees no one and instead hears two voices speaking low and quiet. Silence falls.

Stef swallows, then finds the courage to peep over the edge of the ridge again.

A face greets her: dark-brown skin cut through by forest-green patches, with chartreuse eyes glowing bright.

Stef yelps, stumbles backward, and falls down hard. *Dreaming, I'm dreaming—*

The face disappears, and a whole person jumps over the rise. They stand tall and set their hands on their hips, tilting their head. The person is covered in moss, mud, and sticks that all form some kind of rude clothing. "Nae to worry 'bout," they call over their shoulder. "Only tha wee gel."

The newcomer crouches to where Stef has frozen against the ground. "Don't suppose ye have an' apple with ye?"

"She won't!" Jim's voice calls over the rise. "She's supposed to be *sleeping*."

"Pity." The creature tilts their head this way and that. "Are ye sleeping?"

"N-no," says Stef. "Don't think so."

"Well, then." The person stands and offers a hand. Stef accepts it and is helped to her feet so quickly she realizes whoever this is could probably fling Stef across the forest without breaking a sweat. "May as well come tha whole way. Up with ye." The creature bounds over the rise once more.

Stef hesitates. She's not sleeping, she's not dreaming. But if she went back to her tent right now she could burrow into her sleeping bag and convince herself this was all a dream. She could hit rewind, probably. Forget it all.

A hand extends again, wrist dripping with leaves and moss. "Well, and?"

Stef reaches back. She almost flies over the rise, stumbling in front of the stand of white birches she noticed earlier in the evening—and gets her second impossible surprise of the night. Standing just outside a semicircle of satiny-white trees, bare feet resting on a pile of pine needles, stands Jim.

Jim without a hat.

Jim wearing just long johns.

Jim with curves.

"I have questions—" Stef begins, but the words are mere croaks. She's starting to shiver.

"No doubt ye do," says the creature, taking up Stef's and "Jim's" hands. With a gentle tug, they all slip into the warm, glowing stand of impossible birch trees … and disappear.

Down the Rabbit Hole

Ten minutes later, some things are clearer. That doesn't mean they make more sense.

Stef's head is spinning. She's alternately darting her gaze between the forest newcomer and the former "Jim," and it's like her eyes won't focus.

"So, if I understand correctly—" Stef halts there because no, she doesn't understand a thing. She's got her hand out again like when she was trying to keep Tony from crushing Samuel's windpipe and Jim from shooting Tony with an arrow, only this time it's like she's trying to keep insanity at bay. "*If* I understand correctly," she tries again, turning unsteadily to the new person wearing pieces of the forest, "*you're* a Ghillie Dhu, whatever that means. You keep watch in the forest. And …" her voice grows steadier. "While you're Gillie right now, sometimes you're Gil."

Gillie tosses her hair proudly and tips her bark cap forward. Grass tumbles across her shoulders. "Ye has the right of it, so ye do!"

Stef turns slowly. The former Jim has her arms crossed and hunches like she still thinks she has something to hide. "And *you're* actually Lexi, but sometimes you're 'Jim.'" Her voice is tight as she tries taking in the woman who she'd thought was a teenage boy.

I knew it, she thinks. *I was getting there. I was close.*

Pink rises in Lexi's cheeks as she nods.

"Let me cope with you later." She points at Lexi, sticking with one impossibility at a time. Without thinking, she removes her coat; it's oddly warm inside this little curve of trees.

Gillie extends a cupped leaf that holds a clear, steaming liquid. "G'wan."

Lexi gives Stef a small nod, so she sips it down. Half of her expects to grow or shrink like Alice. *I'm sure down a rabbit hole already,* she thinks. The tea is sweet but otherwise plain. Nothing happens to Stef physically—but Gillie abruptly appears sharper and clearer.

"That's some magic potion," says Stef. "I might be dreaming after all."

"No dream," says Lexi. "Primrose tea." She blinks at Gillie. "Is it magic?"

Gillie's chuckle is the sound of leaves whispering in the trees. "Ye never have asked, wean," she says, gesturing so they all take seats on the pine needles. "'Tis nae a word we use, muchtimes."

Wee one, thinks Stef. She's only heard Scots on Cloud videos and never met one before. Few can travel beyond the Isles anymore, thanks to the Gaelic-Caledonian sequestering and the New Troubles over there—but she's fond of their music and the galloping, blurred way they speak. There are lots of Cloud videos, if someone is interested enough. Gillie sounds like someone who comes from a deep, ancient part of the Scottish world. Like she should be reading Robert Burns's poetry.

"What is it?" asks Lexi. "If it's not magic?"

Gillie slides a wary look at Stef. "An' is she safe?"

Lexi glances between them. "Oh! Well. Stef, you okay with this?"

"What am I supposed to be okay about?" The tea has made her pliable, the warmth soothing, but she's fighting it. Things that shouldn't exist—shouldn't exist for a reason. It doesn't matter how nice it is in here; she's keeping her guard up.

Gillie glances around the stand and closes her eyes briefly. It begins to snow in their small, glowing space. Flakes float onto their heads, noses, hands. "This," says Gillie. "Ye may say 'magic,' but we know it as the *unseen*."

Stef stares at six points of a tiny crystal on her wrist that melts into a single tiny drop of water. Reality hits and she jumps to her feet. The snow ceases to fall. "What—what are you?"

"As I say, I'm the Ghillie Dhu," says Gillie. "An' I come from elsewhere to watch and protect."

"She's from The Green Place," says Lexi. "A place that goes on forever. Least, she says it does."

Stef feels unsettled. The primrose tea is sloshing around inside her. A strange ... someone just handed her a leaf of liquid and she *drank it*. Was it drugged? "Magic. Unseen." She's shaking her head. Magic is Las Vegas. A show of tricks and disappearing scarves and pigeons in cages. It's all sleight of hand and mirrors—there is no real magic in the world. "Bullshit."

Except—there's a rattle in her mind. Buzz on DeepCloud channels has rumbled for ages about magical things. Of people who do much more than disappear scarves or hide pigeons. But those stories originate overseas. From people who sound a lot like Gillie. And from other people who talk about personal magic like it's a virus or infection. Stef doesn't give much credence to those subsections of the Clouds—everybody's got a conspiracy to peddle—but she's heard the rumors.

Gillie shoots an anxious look at Lexi, who looks confused. "You haven't met a Ghillie Dhu before?" she asks.

Stef blinks quickly. " 'Course not. I never even *heard* of a Ghillie Dhu until tonight." She gives Gillie a long, hard look. "You're—not a person. Are you."

"Nae," says Gillie. "We say *sìthiche*. Ye might say fae or—"

"Fairy," says Stef. "Holy shit." Her legs want to move but the very concept lights a fire in her heart. *No, no, not real.* And yet. She worries the empty leaf cup in her hands, shredding it. "No wings on you. And you're kind of big. For a fairy."

"Nae, and suppose so," says Gillie, smiling throughout. "But, 'tis truth." She looks at Lexi. "As I say, wean, this is a special place ye live in. With me an' Artio an' all."

"Artio?" asks Stef. "Wait—"

"The Jewish comedian bear," Lexi whispers behind her hand, then shrugs. "I figured Gillie went to every forest. That everyone knew her."

Stef blinks.

"Ye ken little of the Outside," says Gillie.

"Aye," admits Lexi.

Stef swallows. "Just how long have you lived out here, J—Lexi?"

Lexi's mouth turns this way and that. "Last I remember Outside was when I was in second grade."

Stef breathes deeply and sits down again. This fact is almost tougher to absorb than the appearance of a make-believe creature. Alleged make-believe creature. "But—*why?*"

Lexi—Stef's still having issues with not thinking of her as Jim, a fact that probably shouldn't matter but does—screws up her face. It's as if no one has asked her this before. "Daddy said people were acting strange, the way people weren't supposed to act, so he took us here and here we stay," she says.

Strange. Like a virus, thinks Stef. *Like an infection.*

"An' d'ye feel sick?" Gillie asks.

Lexi's face lights up. "Oh, yes! I am incredibly sick, Gillie. And I don't care, if this is what sick feels like." She looks at Stef. "I have unseen! I find the way. I have my abracadabras, and they show me the way."

Stef turns all the words around in her head, eyes jumping from one creature to the other.

Gillie leans forward, skin shifting from brown to orange and green. "Her Da calls *unseen* a sickness. Many of ye's kind dae."

How tight is that leash Tony keeps us on? Stef wonders. *Do we know ... anything?*

Gillie flashes her white teeth again. "But. I didnae come here to discuss unseen. Came to thank ye for yer music."

The change in topic is like being jerked backward. "The ... music?"

"She's here tonight because of your songs," says Lexi. "See, she was gonna stay away when you all came with us to hunt, but then you and T.J. started singing." She blinks at the Ghillie Dhu. "I never knew you loved music so much."

"Ye rarely ask much about myself, wean," says Gillie. "Perhaps ye should."

Lexi stares at her hands, abashed. "I like you better as Gil."

She laughs. "Ye love Gil, 'tis so," she says. "But this is only me now." She looks at Stef. "The singer is more my interest. Folk I know should like to meet him somewhen."

"Oh." Stef makes a face. "He gets that a lot."

Gillie chuckles. "Yer songs are special, too. The music and the maker in tandem have unseen that's rarely about nowawhens."

"'Unseen' again," says Stef. "You're saying there's magic—unseen—in the *music*?"

Gillie toggles her head back and forth in half nod, half negation. She leans forward, fingers brushing against Stef's watch. "Nae; unseen is somethin' ye's kind are born with."

"My kind?" Stef bristles.

"Humans, lass," says Gillie, meeting her gaze without blinking. "Y'see, we folk wear it 'round us like a cloak, but ye's kind live with it sleeping inside, an' it needs to be coaxed into waking. Those wise to its ways are powerful indeed. When ye cease breathin'—it flies free. Finds a new home. Unseen is always with us, just needs a place to live."

It sounds to Stef like Gillie's talking about a soul, but she can't bring herself to make the suggestion aloud. It's too absurd. "I don't think I get you."

Gillie nods at grandma's watch. "Aye, I see. What d'ye call this device?"

"My watch? It's old but not magic." She takes it off and shows how to turn the dial to wind it, then presses the side to light up the face.

In a breath, Gillie has it and holds it up to her ear.

"Hey," says Stef, waggling her fingers. "Give it back."

Gillie ignores her. "For what is it?"

"Tells the time," Lexi says. Behind her hand again she whispers again to Stef, "Remember, she's not from around here."

"Y'don't say."

"The Green Place is behind her trees. I've never been, though."

"Aye," says Gillie. "I go where tha trees take me. But sometimes, I'm called." She takes the watch into one fist and squeezes. A crunch follows. Stef jerks forward, tries to grab it out of her hand, but the *sìthean* holds her back effortlessly. "Nae, nae," she says, and opens her palm. The watch has burst open and the wheels, springs, drum, and back have all separated.

Stef can't speak.

Her grandmother's watch is dead.

See the Pieces, Make 'Em Complete

"Gillie," says Lexi, stunned. "What'd you do that for?"

The *sìthean* pulls a piece of linen from inside her bark clothing and lays it out on the needles, setting the watch and its parts on it. Her fingers are a blur as she arranges each piece in order of size and sits back. Nothing is cracked or broken—just separated from the whole. "There."

"'There' what?" Stef's anger bubbles out. "You've ruined it."

"Have I?" she asks. "Make it well, so."

Make it well, thinks Stef, despairing. Her grandmother died a year ago. This is all she has left from her. She makes balls of her fists and looks hard at the *sìthean*.

"Ye can try to hit me—or ye can repair it," says Gillie.

A cool trill runs up her spine; this is so far outside of Stef's understanding that she has no idea how to react. Part of her is curious; the other part wants to flee. She looks down at the ruined watch and the tips of her fingers tingle.

Ye can do this thing. Gillie's mouth hasn't moved, but Stef hears her in her head.

Stef has never fixed a watch in her life. She's never even examined the innards of one. She thinks of the baseball she disassembled with T.J. that one time, but this is far more complex. Gingerly, Stef touches the watch casing, turning it around once, twice. One part vibrates like a tiny heart and she picks it up. Places it inside. Another shimmers and she selects that one. It's as if the watch is speaking to her, telling her how it should come together. She chooses piece after piece, pressing the pad of her finger on top of the tiniest ones she cannot lift, and they all fall neatly into place, one after the other. She feels warm and focused, and the rest of the world drops away in this moment as she puts all the pieces back together and clips the back on with a final flourish. Flipping it over, she sees the second hand traveling in its normal direction and quickly winds it again, resetting the time to make up for the three minutes she's just spent assembling a watch she had never seen opened before.

Abruptly exhausted, she holds up her hands, which are as numb as if she'd been sitting on them for an hour. She shakes them, wincing at the pinpricks of circulation returning.

Lexi's eyes are wide. "You did that without any abracadabra!"

"Aye," says Gillie, smiling. "Yer own unseen. See tha pieces, make a thing complete. What ye already dae w' words, ye can dae with things, ken?"

The *sithean* is on to something. The fervor Stef just experienced assembling the watch approximated how she felt while composing a tune—a momentary loss of time and absolute focus. She's even written so much for so long that at times her fingers have gone numb, too.

"Gillie knows these things," says Lexi. "She can see what's inside us, what we can do." She looks between the two of them. "She taught me how to find the way wherever I go. I just say words and the trees hum at me."

Sickness, thinks Stef. *Magic. Unseen. Different ways of looking at the same thing. And it's inside us. Like a virus.*

T.J.'s singing. That thing he does to the girls. Something that developed about ten years ago. And ten years ago, or thereabouts, Samuel brought Lexi to the forest to escape sickness. *See the pieces,* she thinks. *Make them complete.*

"T.J. has it, too," says Stef.

"Aye," says Gillie. "He has it twice over when the songs are yers. Why d'ye think I braved comin' out tonight?" She turns to Lexi. "D'ye ken if *yer* brother had unseen?"

Lexi's head shoots up. "What does Jim have to do with this?"

"Wait, wait," says Stef. "You have a brother?" Another piece comes to her and she lets it glide into what she already knows.

"Did," says Lexi, so quietly it's almost not a word.

"He's—"

"Jim ran away," says Lexi. "Daddy brought him here too and he ran away and he didn't take me. He didn't have to … he wasn't … sick."

"An' yet," says Gillie. "Yer father would rid himself of unseen things in the world. He takes steps, does he not?"

Lexi pokes at her eyes and stares at the ground. Stef can almost feel her misery as she approaches some kind of answer. "Jim ran off."

"Aye, wean, if ye will have it so." Gillie sighs, then looks at Stef. "Ye also travel with a one who *takes steps*."

Stef has to blink a moment to understand. "Tony?" she whispers.

"Ye knows the true thing, if ye look inside," says Gillie softly. "Before he traveled with ye, Anthony Garcia was an enemy of our kind. Made some amends, not near enough. An' now he is still, make no mistake."

Anthony Garcia. Gillie knows the full name of their gatekeeper. The man with their Cloud passwords, spare keys to their apartments, their trust and reliance.

He has full access to the backstage of their lives. But do they really know him? What Tony did in his pre–T.J. history is gray and misty. It had to do with the parts of the world that are hidden from her now—places the old maps call Great Britain or Ireland.

"He was in the army," said Stef. "He was a soldier."

"Aye," says Gillie. Her voice is tight and holds a tremble. "A good one, at that."

Trouble "across the pond" has been part of the backdrop of Stef's life, but it lives in a deep, unexplored territory. She knows what most people do—sanctions have been in place with various Celtic countries and territories since she was in middle school with T.J. They learned bits and pieces in history class, but neither of them have ever paid much attention to the news. She thinks she knows that it's been a decade or so since the British and Irish isles have been cut off from mainland Europe's union. That there's a collection of peacekeeper forces barricading the English Channel. But what they're barricading—what they're keeping out, or in—is unclear to Stef. That's where Tony served, but what he did there she doesn't know, and he won't talk about it much.

War injury, he'd said once.

What she does know is that he's always got one of his weapons from that conflict handy. It's not a gun, not exactly—those aren't useful in the current conflicts. Today, the hot item for fighting overseas is an electromagnetic pulse coupled with plasma ray guns—complicated machinery that requires a fingerprint ID to operate. A "PEP" gun, or a "Peppie." They work on sound frequencies, and the only reason Stef knows even this much is that Ian and Daryl are forever discussing this stuff after watching videos on the DeepCloud. Whatever requires such specific, sophisticated weaponry is not her world. As with any conflict, all she knows is invaders are showing up from strange places, and they are not friendly.

Final pieces slide into place. *I'm talking to one of those invaders right now*, Stef realizes. "Jesus." She scrambles to her feet, grabbing her coat. "You're one of *them*." She pushes through an invisible barrier until she's outside the stand. The night air hits her like a scythe.

"Wait, Stephanie." The laughter is gone from Gillie's voice. "Hold."

"You did this to me." Stef turns to yell at Gillie and Lexi—but she doesn't see them. She's alone in the woods, with just the glow of satiny-white birches behind her. *The tea*, she thinks. *It's the tea.* A chill steals over her. If she's been—in Samuel's parlance—infected by unseen, and it's something people to go war over, she's been conscripted into a fight she wants no part of. "Where *are* you?"

A space between the trees parts and Gillie slips out, followed by Lexi. "Never far," says Gillie. "We cannae be seen in the trees, so."

Stef shakes her head. "Take it back. Take back my … unseen."

Lexi frowns. "She can't. She can't take back what she doesn't give. It's *in* you, Stef. It's part of you! She just woke it up."

"And I wouldnae if I could," says Gillie, giving Lexi a proud smile. " 'Twas inside ye afore I came tonight. A seed. Just as Lexi is a keen tracker but wisnae as a bairn. Ye have the unseen inside, but it flowers w'us around. When we come through. An' more o' us are comin' through nowawhens. As we must."

That is the strangest and most unsettling thing Stef has heard this night so far.

"Why would you leave The Green Place?" asks Lexi. "It goes forever."

"Nae so much now." Gillie sets her free hand on Lexi's shoulder. She gestures at the trees. " 'Tis a split, y'see. On one side is this world, tha other, The Green Place as Lexi calls it. 'Twas a forever-going-on place, once. But … now, our world grows smaller. We ken not why. So we must leave. Go somewheres—to yer world. But we're not so wanted by everyone. They fight to end us." She pauses. "An' then some o' us must fight back."

"Great. Fine. Whatever." Stef's teeth are chattering. "Not my fight."

Gillie shakes her head, raining grass. " 'Twill be in time." She cocks her head. "Shh. A noise comes, methinks—"

Stef waves her off. "Whatever. Not interested. Look, I'm going back to bed. I'm gonna pretend none of this happened." She doubts that's possible, but with time and denial anything can seem like a bad dream.

"Stef, please—" Lexi tries shushing her, but she won't be quieted. Gillie has gone hyperalert, glaring at the rise they recently all climbed over.

She points at Lexi. "You wanna keep being a boy, be my guest. You wanna believe in fairies, you go ahead. Your secrets are safe. But I am done." She's shivering, in part from cold and in part from an odd excitement that threads through her terror. She turns to the rise and sees a strange metallic glint.

"Stef," says Lexi, leaping after her. "Wait—"

Just then, a concussive *thump* punches through the trees—and all three of them are knocked to the ground by an unseen force.

The War Comes Home

Stef's gullet heaves and she vomits bile and partially digested potatoes into the dirt, blinking away tears. "What the—" She gasps, discovering Lexi is also down on her knees, wiping at her mouth. The sour stench of upended dinner wafts Stef's way, layered with a burning, crackling scent.

At first she thinks Gillie is gone; the space the creature occupied between herself and Lexi is empty, but a second later she sees the *sìthean* curled into a ball on the leafy ground, shuddering silently. Her ever-shifting skin has frozen into a single color, a mix of red clay and golden yellow, and as Stef watches the grass and mud and wood clothing that she has worn first crumbles into chunks, then disintegrates into dust around her reddish-brown body. The hat of grass goes last, and a tangle of dark curled hair tumbles out.

Lexi stumbles over, covering Gillie's nakedness with her coat. The stand of birches behind them flickers and dims until it is as dark and featureless as every other tree in the forest. Remembering her headlamp, Stef reaches to switch it on, but it's dead. She presses the side of her repaired watch and the light it gives off is brighter than she ever saw before; it illuminates almost as broadly as the stand once did. Now she can see Lexi's face and the burning light in her eyes that might be fear, might be anger. Or both.

The whole experience takes seconds.

Brush along the rise crashes open and Tony pushes through, grappling with the PEP gun he brought back from the war, its wide barrel glowing with heat. "Goddamnit," he growls, toggling a switch on the side. His voice is high, excited, quavering. "Fucking thing's stuck." The latch slips into place and he takes aim at Gillie. "Get the fuck away from it, Jim. Lemme finish this."

Lexi snarls at him, hugging Gillie closer.

Stef has never seen Tony like this, so amped up and ... well, *soldiery* that he can't even see that Jim is not really Jim anymore. Her mind's awhirl again, but the anger and fear she'd been feeling toward Gillie a moment ago have shifted. Now it's aimed at Tony. She can't just let him *shoot* Gillie like an injured animal. That doesn't even take a second to think about.

With a shout, Stef launches herself at Tony, grabbing at his gun hand. She wants to knock him aside with her shoulder, but his body is a concrete wall, and she bounces off him, tumbling to the forest floor again. A thin, magenta plasma beam shoots from the PEP and severs a thick branch a few feet away. The wood thumps to the ground, leaving behind a scent of campfire.

"Crazy bitch," Tony barks. "Do you two have any idea what's going on here? Or are you as stupid as you look?"

He crouches by Lexi, who has stretched her body across Gillie's. "This is not a person," he tells her. "This is a thing. It might be cute and it might have neat tricks, but this is the end of the world if you let it live. Trust me. I saw it on the battlefield."

"Leave," growls Lexi. "Now."

"Not on your life. These things are like rats. Gotta keep 'em contained. Jesus, so far as I know we don't have 'em in North America yet. This might be the first one. And if they start taking over here like they did overseas, it'll be all-out war."

Lexi's voice is thick, her cheeks wet with tears. "I don't care."

"Yeah, well, you'll care when *we're* the ones with the blockade. They have no place here. This is not your friend."

"That's what she said about *you*."

He stands, ignoring her. Takes aim. "For the last time. Get the fuck out of the way."

She's shaking hard, but holds fast. "Shoot me first if you gotta, but I am going nowhere."

Tony narrows his eyes. "How's your Daddy gonna feel when he finds out you're hiding a 'sickness' vector, kid? Think he's gonna figure you got 'sick,' too?"

Lexi shrinks into herself, keeping tight against Gillie, who has begun to shiver.

Stef watches them from the ground, torn. In her heart she can't truly believe that Gillie is dangerous. But what does she know? Until a few minutes ago she thought fairies were as real as the Easter Bunny. Does this mean angels exist? What about goblins? And giants? And Yeti? And what is Tony saying—they're all coming here?

See the pieces, Gillie told her. *Make 'em complete.*

Her brain isn't working right now. Words are eluding her. What she does know is that putting together that watch satisfied like nothing else—nothing except writing a song, or really good sex. It was something her body did instinctively and she trusted. If that's what folks like Gillie offer, what could be the harm?

"But it's not a sickness," she says at last, standing up and brushing off her sleeves. "That's a lie."

Tony chuckles. Lowers his weapon a hair. "Smart girl. You've always been smarter than the rest." He shakes his head. "Of course it's not a sickness. That's for the tinfoil-hat brigade. Folks who still think planes spread chemtrails or vaccines warp your brain. But a little propaganada about a 'virus' in the air no paper mask can keep out of your body? That goes a long way. 'Cause these things"—he toes Gillie—"are a disease. They're freaks and they're taking over our world. Uninvited, unwanted. They change us. I saw what happened to England when they were too nice about it. 'Oh, they're part of our traditions! Our folklore!' Well, 'scuse me, Mr. Bangers and Mash, if Paul Bunyan shows up, you bet I'll be in the first platoon to bring him down. We ain't gonna let that happen here." He lifts the barrel again. "Now, for the really last time, move off, kid."

Stef's mind clears. The whirl is gone. She understands him—at least, she thinks she does. And like a car at last getting into gear, she can think again. "Hold a sec." She stands, brushing leaves from her legs, struggling to keep her voice reasonable. Pressing the side of her watch to illuminate Gillie's face, she turns to Tony. "What you said—she's, I mean, it's—the only one in the U.S. we know of?"

"I said *North America*."

She waves that away, folding her arms over her chest, and regards Gillie coolly. "Well," she says. "If that's so, isn't it worth more alive than dead?"

Tony blinks at her just as the watch light goes out. They are again covered in shadows. "Interesting," he says.

"I mean, they'll want to talk to her. Interview her. Maybe a little, you know …." She makes scissor motions with her fingers. "Know thy enemy and all that."

Lexi makes a soft, pained noise from the ground.

Tony waves dismissively. "They've taken 'em alive before. Nothing new to know."

"Except," she presses, making it up as she goes, "like you say, first one here. New scientists. *American* scientists. Better minds. Fresh meat."

Tony runs a hand through his close-cropped hair. Gives her a considered look. "Hmph," he says at last. "Could be. But we got shit to do here first."

Of course, thinks Stef. *World might be coming to an end but T.J. has priority.* "Sure," she says. "But after that. After he gets what he wants …"

"What the hell," he says. "I can always shoot it later if it makes trouble."

Stef nods. "Sure." Her voice is strangled. "Sure."

Tony returns to Gillie on the ground. "I know you can understand me," he addresses her, though her eyes are closed and she continues to shiver under Lexi's coat. "So here's what's gonna happen. I'm gonna let you live. But you're comin' back to camp with us, and tomorrow we get out of here. 'Less, of course, you care to reacquaint me with your queen?"

Reacquaint? thinks Stef. *Queen? Queen of … the fairies?*

Gillie's eyes fly open. She shakes her head, closes them again.

"I see. Fine. Then tomorrow, we'll be getting out of here. And if you make trouble, I will use this thing to cut your limbs off one at a time. Ain't enough magic in the world to make that not hurt. Not that you have any ability to do magic right now, do ya?"

"You're the worst person I ever knew," says Lexi in a low, determined voice.

He snatches her face, stares into her eyes. "Plasma works on people, too," he hisses, and pushes her to one side. Standing, he waves the gun. "Get it up."

Lexi helps Gillie to her feet, the *sithean* allowing herself to be manipulated like a marionette as Lexi wraps her scarf around her waist, then zips the coat around her. Gillie refuses to let go of Lexi's hand, and when she opens her eyes this time, she keeps her dark gaze trained on the ground. Lexi leans to her, whispering, and Gillie nods.

"What're you going to tell T.J.? Samuel?" asks Stef as they scramble down the rise.

Moonlight streaks across his face as Tony glances over his shoulder at his prisoner, then back to the trees. "Seems like we found some lost hiker. With amnesia." He laughs.

A keening, anguished wail cuts through the night from the Ghillie Dhu, and it tears at Stef's heart.

Changing the Rules

No sleeping for me tonight. I can close my eyes but they don't stay shut 'cause there's too many bees in my head.

Nae. Aye. Wean.

I'd give anything to hear Gillie speak right now. She's here and holding my hand and where we touch it's all sweaty but she's not letting go, hasn't let go since I helped her up. We're lying down in the tent next to Daddy's and he's still making buzzy saw noises. I don't think he even woke up the whole time we were gone.

Gillie's not sleeping either. I don't know if she does sleep. She's not a person, but I don't xactly know if she's even a *sìthean* now either. When Tony showed up and waved his special gun she lost everything about her that was magic and prolly so did Stef and me but our magic was little so we just got sick in the dirt while Gillie got knocked down.

I thought about trying my abracadabra like a test when Tony was walking us back to the tents, but didn't want him to know about me just in case it worked. Still I think it's gone or at least broken, and it makes me feel empty inside. Like I lost one of my senses. If that's true for me, Gillie must be 100 times more sad-scared.

"No talking," Tony growled at me and Stef on the way back to the tents, giving us little pushes in the back. He watched Stef zip her tent closed, then tiptoed with me and Gillie to my tent. "If you two aren't in here in the morning when I check, I'm telling your father everything." He stared hard at me. "We clear?"

For a minute part of me decided I didn't care. That we'd sneak out and go back to the birch trees and disappear into The Green Place. But I looked at Gillie and realized prolly even she couldn't go to The Green Place right now, so

I yessed him. He zipped us in and I saw his shadow hunker down at the firepit. He kicked up the flames and I xpected he'd be there til sunup.

Before all that happened, when it was just me and Stef and Gillie, boy did she talk a lot. I never heard Gillie—or Gil—talk so much. I'm always a little afraid of her and what she can do. Gil maybe less. But whoever he or she is when she visits me, she's always the best thing about living here and I never wanted to do anything that might make her stop inviting me to visit. I still hope I'll get to go to The Green Place sometime, even for a little.

'Tis a place that makes most mad, if they stay long, Gil told me once. *Time measures different.*

I wonder what Stef's watch might do in The Green Place now that she fixed it. Then I wonder if Gillie's ever going to get to go back herself. What if she's like this forever? Can you live if you're an ex-*sìthean*?

There are no books in the cabin about magic. Or about the Ghillie Dhu. Or about what it means if you grow up in a forest and the first person who asks you any good questions asks the ones that make her think you're stupid or strange. Stef sees me like I don't fit in. I've been here too long. I mean, I think fairies are real.

Xcept they are.

Here's a true thing: I knew from the start reading trees wasn't normal. And I knew Daddy would be mad if he found out. But I still didn't think it was sickness. Sickness is rashes and fevers and falling over dead. Reading trees or putting broken things together isn't sick. It doesn't hurt. It's like breathing. I can stop breathing for five minutes and twenty-three seconds—Jim timed me once at the big lake. It was my Guinness World Record, he said. He could only go for three minutes and forty-two seconds. We counted with Mississippis.

So it didn't feel like being sick. Daddy might be wrong about that. Tony said something about tinfoil hats that made me think he might be. Xcept Daddy's hat never has tinfoil on it. Even when he's fulla shit, though, I never thought Daddy was *wrong* before. But if he's wrong about this maybe he's wrong about other things.

The bees in my head are pretty loud. I hear Jim telling me Daddy was always fulla. And Jim didn't laugh about it like I did.

Jim ran away. I *know* this. He always wanted to go and so he went and it just so happened he left when he and Daddy went out hunting together for the first time.

My mind is bouncing all over, trying not to think about the only thing that really matters. The thing being the *sìthean* that's holding my hand so tight it's gone all tingly.

"Gillie." I turn and whisper. "I'll fix this. I'll do whatever I have to."

At last, she turns to me. I can't see her face so good since it's dark dark in here but her hand in mine goes softer, just a bit. "Aye," she whispers. "Ye will try."

Jim never liked the woods. Not like me. Definitely not like Daddy.

Almost from the start he was stinky about it. Did everything he could think to get Daddy mad and yelling. First he stopped doing chores, then he stopped talking. When he was fourteen he started roaming. Daddy called him an *adolescent brat* and Jim yelled right back that he'd been *kidnapped*. Then he stopped talking for a while, until not talking was too hard and then he only talked to me, mostly. He always kept wandering, though.

Where d'you go? I'd ask him.

Far and wee, he'd quote this poem we both liked. *Far and wee.*

But that answer didn't tell me anything. And he kept going out on his own.

So Daddy brought out the strop. He let me hold it and it was like a belt but wider and thicker. *Shirk out here and you die*, Daddy told Jim, his last warning before he took it to Jim's backside. *Everybody eats so everybody works.*

After that first belting Jim didn't roam. He just left. He went bye-bye for whole afternoons, then overnight. Always came back scratched up and thirsty and hungry and sleeping while he stood up and had to take Daddy's angry words right in the face. His clothes would be dirty and yanked all over and his hair would stand up in places. But before he got fed or could take a drink or a sleep he got the strop. Every time.

I hid in the loft until he was ready to come up there and I was the one who put the burning red medicine on his cuts and welts. *Stay here*, I said. *Who can I talk to if you're gone?*

I didn't know Gil then.

I'm doing this for us, he insisted. *You're too little to get it.*

Thing was, he didn't know where he was going. He could only carry so much food and then he'd get out there and not find anything and have to turn around. He said every time he made back for the cabin his gut twisted 'cause he knew he had another whupping coming. Told me he had to get back to the real world.

I don't think anybody's sick, he said. *Not like he tells us.*

What if you're wrong?

Then he stopped wandering and going bye-bye. Not because of the whupping though, I don't think. He just ran out of directions to try. Told me we were in a cage. *A great big one and we can't see the bars, but we're trapped all the same. Like animals.*

Turns out Jim didn't really give up. He was just waiting for the right time.

I don't sleep but I'm not totally awake all night. I drift off and then I come back when a thought knocks in my head and then I'm awake again. I keep thinking about Jim and how it was like when there were two of us.

But I have to pee. Bad. I can't stay in here anymore. I turn to Gillie. "I'm just going out for a second," I tell her. "Okay? I'm not leaving."

Her hand slips from mine and now my palm feels cold and empty. "Go," she says and it's like a sound deep from inside a cave.

I put my boots and coat back on—I gave Gillie some of my xtra clothes, which were Jim clothes once—and slow slow unzip the tent. Stick my head out and take a breath of the almost-morning. Sky's a deep dark blue, no stars. Air's heavy, wet. Storm could be coming.

"Look who doesn't know how to listen to rules," says a deep rumbly voice from the firepit.

"I gotta whiz," I say, and step all the way out, zipping the tent behind. There he is, a shadow by the flames, all by his lonesome. I know we have a job to do today. But that's not the job I need to do. Gillie has to get home and safe again. I don't care about letting this big monster and his stupid friends go kill something, all so they can take pictures and maybe the head and call themselves tough.

Maybe not Stef. She's not like that. Or I didn't think she was.

Anyway, I'm on Gillie's side. Whatever side that is.

I walk into the darker brush and go into my crouch so I can get cleared out and it feels amazing to not have a full bladder anymore. When I'm done I start back to the tent.

"Get over here," says Tony, waving at a place by the fire.

"I don't want to talk to you," I say.

"Get over here anyway," he says. "You and I need to have words."

I think about going back to Gillie but Tony's like Daddy in some ways. Daddy tells me to do something, I do it. The way it's always been. So I walk over to the fire and toss in some kindling, get the flames up again. Tony's got his pack all ready for the day. There's a compound bow with pulleys and a sight on it resting on his pack. Compounds are for cheaters. I use a recurve.

"Anyhow," he says, handing me a mug of coffee, "I'm happy to do the talking for now."

I sniff the brew. Coffee's rare 'round here. Daddy says it's a drug, so I almost never get it. I take a sip and it's hot lightning down to my belly. All we had last night were trout fillets and potatoes and marshmallows for dessert and that all came up once Tony's gun went off and I'm crawling hungry right now.

"So let me see," he says. "You got up and found the creature and Stef followed you, am I right?"

I shrug.

"Didn't think she knew what was what," he says, almost to himself. "D'you understand why I had to shoot that thing?"

I spit a mouth of coffee in his face.

He backhands me and his ring bites into my cheek. I fall back and my face is on fire. My hand goes up over my cheek and there's some blood there. I scramble to my feet but I don't have my bow and arrow and my knife's still in the tent. Stupid.

"That's all you know how to do," I bark. "Hit things. Shoot them. Kill them."

He makes this soft little laughing sound and it's strange, coming from him. Tony isn't a guy that does a lot of laughing, I bet. But he thinks I'm pretty funny. He points at the log. "Sit."

I don't want to, but I do.

"That's a free one," he says. "Next time I hit you, you don't get back up. Got it?"

I nod. But I make him the same promise, in my head. I can do it. I just have to be ready to do the thing nobody expects. To be Offguard.

"You've been out here a long time, so I'm giving you benefit of the doubt on what happened last night," he says. "You and Stef and T.J.—you're all in the dark. So's a lot of the country. We try to keep it that way. Keeps everybody from getting panicked. But most of the rest of the world knows the truth. We're being invaded."

I look at him, cold as snow.

"You had a favorite toy, didn't ya?"

"I don't play with toys," I say, though I do still have Marches. "Stuffed dog."

"Great. What if that little dog suddenly walked and talked and turned out to be rabid? And she bit you and made you rabid, too?"

I'm frowning. Toys don't come to life.

"If that happened, you'd shoot her just like you would a real animal. Even if it was cute. Even if it did tricks." He leans into me and his breath has alcohol on it. Not beer. I've smelled that. "D'you see what I mean?"

Then I do. "Gillie's not a dog."

"Gillie," he says in a dark and hard voice. "Even sounds cute. Maybe is cute to you. But you don't know shit. You ain't seen the dangerous ones. Look, we've been safe so far here in the U-S-of-A. They mostly stay in their home countries once they get out. But you have to be ready. You never know when they're gonna try the next incursion. Or where. Your *friend* could be the first of many."

"What do they do?"

He shakes his head. "Stuff that doesn't make it into the papers. Turn people into animals, who we gotta shoot 'cause when they turn back, they're insane. Make you dance 'til your feet break and bleed. Sticks that fly outta nowhere and beat on you. That's the tame stuff. Only things we know that repel 'em are the plasma and the EMPs, strange to say. That's what the PEPs are for. EMP knocks them out, takes away what they can do. Plasma takes care of the rest. They're working on armor now that bounces whatever spell they throw at us right back on them. That'll make 'em think twice."

He takes another sip of coffee. "See, you got to take them out fast after you knock 'em over; I hear they heal pretty quick. Fact is, they're not like us and don't have any place among human people." His voice goes far away while he talks and it sounds like he's remembering things, not just telling me about them. "They should just stay on their own turf. Suck it up there."

"You fought them," I say. "In the war."

He nods. "For a time. Then I got injured and stuck in an office. Then I got back on the field and then—well, I came home. After. They let me go from the forces, and now I'm here."

"What's wrong with magic?"

He grunts. "Christ, have you drunk the Kool-Aid. Magic's this random thing that changes all the rules. They think *we're* magic, by the way. 'Cause we can build guns and clocks and cars. So we scare 'em too. If people were meant to have magic we'd have it."

"Some do," I say.

"Oh, yeah?" He leans forward. "Anybody you know?"

I shrug.

"Anybody like … *you?*"

I think about how he took it away from me. "Not anymore," I say and my throat closes up.

He sits back, thinking. "Well, now. That makes sense. The gun." He nods. "So you're cured."

My eyes fill up. It sounds like he's saying I won't get it back. Which means Gillie won't go back, either. "It's forever?" I whisper.

He sighs. "No," he says. "In the field we just kept thumpin' 'em until—" He looks at me. "Anyhow, let's just say I never saw one who got to live that long after getting thumped."

Tony still hasn't told me why magic's bad, though. He sounds like he's just angry 'cause he doesn't have any. Ones that have make the ones that don't mad, and everybody has to be the same so get rid of the weird ones. That's what I'm hearing.

He's still talking, though, doesn't matter if I'm listening. "These creatures are just walking around like this is their world right now," he says. "Like they belong here. Like they've always been here. And when we get too close, yeah, some of us get infected." Tony spits into the fire. "And there's no quid pro quo, you know. We're not supposed to go into their sacred places unless they take us. *Toirmisgte*, they call it. *Forbidden*."

We'd go mad, Gil said.

"Gil says it's green there," I say. "A forever going-on place."

"Yeah," he says, and finally goes quiet for a breath. "Who'd ever want to leave *that*."

The fire pops between us, then settles, a log falling over. "I think they have to," I whisper. "I don't think they're choosing to leave."

"Feh," he growls. "They're just greedy. Want what we've got."

"You *went*," I say, remembering what he asked Gillie back at the stand. He'd asked about her queen. "You were *there*."

He's quiet a minute longer, then makes that funny muffled laugh again. But there's no fun in the sound. "Close. But no."

"So how do you know?"

"I looked inside," he said. "Saw an air hole—an aperture, whatever—and she spoke to me."

"She?"

He stares into the fire. "Ever been in love, kid?"

My face gets hot and my stomach gets tight and I think of Gil. I shrug.

"Well," he says. "Thing about the world over there is once that window opens, you fall in love for the first time every minute. And after that window shuts, you'll do anything to get it back."

"So shooting them … helps?"

He looks at me. "It's complicated." Suddenly he grabs my chin, pinches it so I can't get away. "Here's what it boils down to. You don't want your dad to know what you were up to last night, do you? He already thinks we gotta put down anybody who's 'sick,' he told me that a couple times already. Here's our deal: You go along with whatever I say, whatever I do, and your friend won't get hurt and your dad won't know. If that thing makes a run for it, two things are gonna happen: I will kill it, and then I will tell your father it was something you cared about. And he will thank me."

His eyes slide across my face, looking for something. "You both are here to find us a deer so I can take a picture of T.J. standing next to it and we can wave it around in front of the CloudPress and he can get on with making us a fuckton of money. Then we are getting in that chopper and going home and you can stay here as long as you want. For as long as you can."

"What about Gillie?" I say but my words are mashed 'cause he's still got my face.

Tony releases me and I'm shaking. "It'll come with us, probably."

"No," I say. "No, no, no."

He leans into me and I lean back. "You wanna break our deal already?"

I think about what might happen if he tells Daddy I was sick. That I had a friend who made me sick. I don't think Daddy would hurt me. But he did hurt Jim. Stropped him good. And then Jim went away and didn't come back. My eyes get burny and I feel like such a baby but I nod at Tony.

"So we're clear," he says. "I say 'frog' and you jump."

I keep nodding. But inside I'm shaking my head. He's not leaving with Gillie. He might leave with a deer head but Gillie stays here. Whatever I have to do. I promise everybody: myself, Gillie, the world.

"Good," he says, and looks up into the clouds. He takes a big drink of his coffee, sets the mug down and claps his hands. "Well, with that out of the way: I'd like to check out that ridge up ahead where I hear the deer—if not the antelope—play. We're gonna have Stef babysit your friend, and you'll take me to the hunting spot. Now."

Guess he just said "frog."

So I take Tony to the place where it will be all right to kill something.

We Live Here Now

Jim was the one who found Artio way back when, even though we didn't know that was her true name. We were new to the forest—maybe one winter and part of one spring—when we saw her. Daddy sent us out to the Great Meadow and said we had a job: Bring home something we could eat. Jim said look for nuts so I kept bending into the grass figuring they might be hiding. I didn't know better yet.

Then I looked up and Jim was gone. I looked this way and that way and called out, *Jim, no hiding!* I figured he was doing hide-and-go-seek without telling me but then I heard it—a hoot-owl call. Daddy taught us the calls almost first thing we came out here. Way to signal without alerting anyone, people or animal. Xcept the Oscar owls, they know the difference I bet. Anyway, since it was the middle of the day and even I knew by then that owls came out at night I knew the call was really Jim.

I turned 'round and 'round but he wasn't anywhere.

Then I saw it, this wavy motion coming from high up in a tree like a leaf out of control. Jim's little white hand stood out against the green needles and he was up in an old pine. So I jogged over kind of mad he was being all secret about something. I stared up the trunk through the branches and there he was, maybe higher than four Daddys, looking down.

C'mon, he whispered.

I wasn't good at climbing but when Jim asked me for something, I wanted to do it. So I hugged that sticky sappy trunk and grabbed higher and higher until I was right next to him, and the whole time he was staring down at me and waving his hand, making me move more and more.

Once I was up on the limb with him, I started to say what kind of mad I was but he put a hand over my mouth and pulled back a branch. Back in the field where I left my basket stood a giant. I'd seen pictures of bears in books, so I knew what I was looking at, but she was big as the car Daddy drove us here in. Prolly bigger. She nosed in my basket, then stood on her hind legs and was twice the size as before.

That's beautiful, he whispered.

Barney bear, I said. Our first bear needed a name.

He shook his head.

Why?

First off, she's not a boy.

How can you—

He pointed again. Two bumbly little cubs were cutting through the meadow grass, making right for her. They were all the same color, this brownish black that made me think of those Special Dark chocolate candies only Mom would ever eat. The two cubs bumped right into the big bear and she went back down on her front paws and we watched as they nosed. Then she moved in the other direction and even though we were far off I swear I felt the ground shake.

She's only looking, said Jim in a calm, soft voice that made me feel better. *Only looking.*

My mouth was dry. Something in me wanted to go up to her and those babies and pet them. Another part of me knew this made the forest a whole lot more dangerous than we ever thought. After a long, long while she went across the meadow and out of our sight.

Jim let out a breath. *Let's call her Artio.*

The cliff fills up one long side of the meadow, and we reach the base of it after about a thousand steps. We start climbing, and Tony's almost as fast as me going up and up and up. His arms are thick and tight like ropes and he doesn't make a peep even when he slips and nearly falls on his butt halfway up the rock face. When that happens, I turn to one side and mutter some bad words, 'cause I'm sorry he kept his grip.

He follows me good, setting his hands where I do, toes where mine go and up and up and up until—leap! We're on top of Blueberry Cliff and the sky is turning gray and milky and it's starting to get light. We stand on top of the grass where the trees don't live and stare out over the long narrow field.

Daddy and me—and Jim when he was here—came out to Blueberry Cliff all the time, sometimes with clients and sometimes only us. Deer love running through the field below from one side of the forest to the other and there are fat juicy berries growing on all the bushes at the bottom of the cliff. You just have to get there before the bears do. Or about 100 other hungry little animals. It's an easy place to take folks so I know it real well. You can see the whole meadow and there's a little hill on the other side we can tell clients to hide behind so the deer don't see them til it's too late. That's where Daddy'll bring T.J. in a bit.

I didn't read Tony right when he first got here. Didn't think he was dangerous. Even when he grabbed Daddy on that first night I didn't think he was this kind of bad and mean. But that was my not wanting to see it. Before we left camp just now he unzipped my tent and hauled Gillie out and brought her over to Stef's tent and woke up Stef and shoved Gillie inside. He told Stef to make up a reason why she wasn't coming to the hunt, and to keep Gillie a secret until after T.J. had his deer. Just let T.J. and Daddy come to the meadow.

Stef didn't like being woke up like that. Her hair was standing up this way and that way and she had a squished up look on her face.

If it runs, it dies, Tony told her. *Remember it was your idea to keep it alive.*

Stef looked at Gillie and nodded. *Guess it was.*

Gillie curled up at the back of the tent and gave me a quick look with one eye open and I swear it seemed like she had a couple blades of grass in her hair but then the tent went zip zip and Tony and me were off.

So now we're here and there's no deer, not yet. I slide my eyes over at Tony. I know he's somebody I got to keep an eye on. Gil warned me. What I don't get is how sometimes I *want* to keep an eye on him. Even knowing everything. I make a list to figure out why:

1. He's tough and doesn't take shit or shine-o-la.
2. He knows what he wants.
3. And what he doesn't want.
4. I hate him for hurting Gillie but I want to be as strong as he is someday.

He's scanning the field like a machine taking in information while I watch him and I have a second to know exactly what *I* want: to push him off. I could prolly do it. Just wander behind and run up and push hard and he would fall all the way into those blueberry bushes and if he wasn't dead when he landed, he'd die soon after. Nobody would know and we could let Gillie go and nobody could tell Daddy secrets.

"Don't get any smart ideas," he says, never even turning from the field.

"Wasn't." I toe at the ground, then point off to the west. "Deer come from over there." Then I point to a chewed-up part of the ground. "Stop here, most times."

"Fish in a barrel," he says.

"Deer in a field."

He looks at me and his eyes get all squinty, even though it's still pretty dark. He's 'valuating me, I feel it. "You are a weird thing."

I take a seat and dangle my legs over the cliff edge. A minute later he sits down, bow across his legs. On the way I said I preferred my recurve bow and he said his was state of the arts or something and cost eight thousand dollars so it practically killed the animal for you. I didn't tell him it was a cheater's bow.

Now he takes a piece of paper from his pocket. "Interesting how we walked all day yesterday but we're really only about seven klicks from the original campsite," he says, showing me the paper. "Made a map."

I want to hold out my hands and say "you know shit about making maps and here's how you really make a map" but then I remember I maybe can't use Gil's words anymore and then I see the map. His paper shows just where his base is and where we slept last night and even where the chopper is going to pick them up.

I shrug like Daddy would. We weren't lying to them. It's just how we do things. Most times we walk clients from the hot water place with the flag and just wander 'em around and nobody notices but really Daddy never goes more than 10,000 steps from there. I think that's five miles. But now I can add another thing to my Tony list:

5. He's really really smart even if I don't know what klicks are.

"See, we don't get something today, I can come back here anytime," he tells me. "You know, in case we don't find what we're lookin' for."

That sounds like a promise and it makes me uncomfortable. I look out over the field, see some shifting in the trees on one side. "There."

He sits up. Two does nose their way into the field a little, then back off. "Shit," he says when they vanish. "You sure this ain't a dead spot?"

I tell him I'm sure. That we come here all the time. Only, if the deer aren't running it might be because they're hiding. And if they're hiding, that might mean T.J. is gonna get his wish. Which is not a good idea, no way. Artie could show up.

"Nobody wants to face Artie," I say.

"Artie?" He laughs. "Jesus, you got a name for every wild thing out here."

"It's not a made-up name. It's her real name. Jim just knew it." Then I hear what I just blabbed. I keep doing this when he asks me questions, and I want to stop it.

He looks sideways at me. There's a long quiet part and my face is getting red again like it did last night. I messed up. When I steal a look at him, he's got a funny half smile on his face. "Shit, I gotta know," he says, and with a flick he knocks my baseball cap off. It goes down, down, down into the bushes. My hair's kinda long right now and it waves all over the place.

"Yeah," he says, chuckling. "A girl. Somehow that's not a surprise."

I jump up and my hand's at my waist. Something's gonna die here today, might as well be him.

"Christ, please," he says, patting the ground next to him. "Get hold of yourself. You're just a kid."

"I'm not."

He gives me a long look. "Well, you're mostly a kid." He pauses. "Look, I am not here to hurt you. Unless you make me hurt you."

"Yeah," I say. "Don't even try."

It would be a long way down, but I could bring him with me.

We were here two Christmases and three summers when I heard Daddy and Jim talking. They were outside splitting wood, putting it into the shed and I was reading a book in the cabin, stretched out over Daddy's bed.

Dad, seriously, Jim was saying. *Are we?*

No. Daddy wasn't even angry, just positive. *You know my answer. We can't and we won't.*

Ever? Jim's voice cracked a lot back then. It would start normal and then go up a bit in the middle of the word. Made him mad when it happened. *Like, we'll both still be here when we're all middle-aged and you're, what, ancient? That kind of forever?*

Doubtful, Daddy allowed. *Once you're eighteen, things are different.*

Different how?

Just different. You'll be a man. Can make your own decisions.

I'm a man now. Jim was getting mad, I heard it in his voice.

That's what you think.

Jim stomped into the cabin a couple minutes later. *You heard that,* he told me. *We are never going home.*

We are home, I said, and I meant it.

But it wasn't ever home for Jim. Another year went by and I was almost twelve and he was better than me at everything in the woods. He stopped talking about leaving and just became xpert in hunting and hiding and making things and he read every book we had and I thought maybe he was okay with it now. His voice stopped making funny noises. We were always busy: Jim chopped and built and tanned hides and repaired the leaky roof. I did gardening and preserving and cooking and keeping the inside and the outside of the cabin all neat and no bugs and no holes for mice or anything.

Daddy would go away sometimes. I think he was starting to track for people but we didn't know it then. He'd go for a day, two, three sometimes and always left us jobs to do. Jim was boss while he was gone and sometimes he acted like Daddy, telling me what to do. Whenever Daddy came back it wasn't nice between them. Jim didn't go hug him, say he missed him like I did.

Then came fall and Jim told me in secret: *I'm taking off again.*

I got all scared for him. *You just want to leave me and Daddy forever.*

Not you, he said.

We live here.

No, he told me. *We survive here. Dad stole us and didn't ask what we wanted. It's been four years. I can find a way out now, I know it. And there's somebody who's gonna help me.*

Who?

Secret. Tell you once I'm sure. I want you coming with me. But we gotta pick the right time.

I like it here, I said, but a small piece of me wondered what the world looked like now.

Great. When you're older you can go camp all the hell you want. But this ain't where people should live. It's hard. There are tons of things we can't fix and Dad doesn't know about everything. He doesn't even know about ... he took a long pause. *Girl things. I'm not sure I do either.*

I didn't argue that point. I got real scared when I started bleeding between my legs that summer and my stomach hurt a lot. I didn't say anything because maybe it was sickness and Daddy would take steps. But then he figured it out I guess when he looked at the trash and I woke up with *Our Bodies Our Selves* next to me with this special rubbery cup I had to learn how to work and wash and use again. The book told me things about bodies and something called puberty but Daddy never said anything. Jim pulled me to one side and said it was normal and not a sickness and it would happen once a month but I really should read the whole book.

When Daddy left the next time, we followed him. We got our supplies together superfast and tracked him good for an hour or two and then we came to this big open field. We stood at the treeline while Daddy walked into the middle of the field, turned around and wagged a finger back and forth. *No.* He was smiling like he'd been playing a game with us.

Jim walked forward anyway, and Daddy headed back to us. They kept doing it until they were nose to nose and shouting and then—then Jim put up his fist like he was punching Daddy, but Daddy caught it and pushed him away. They shouted some more and Jim spat on the ground and turned to come back to me.

We didn't go anywhere but back to the cabin.

Daddy came home after his regular three days, late at night when we were up in the loft in our sleeping bags. I closed my eyes and tried to go back to sleep. But then a sound woke me. I wiggled my toes like I always did to alert Jim but there was nobody there. I sat up and thought he better not have run off again.

A creak on the floor made me look down. There was Jim, passing through a bit of moonbeam, holding Daddy's hunting knife by the handle with the point to the ground. He was taking his last steps to where Daddy was sleeping and looked like he was ready to gut a deer.

I yelped, then covered my mouth.

Jim froze in his moonbeam and looked up at me, unhappy. But Daddy didn't wake up. In a minute he started walking again. I couldn't breathe. I wanted to shout but my brain got stuck. Nothing would come out.

Jim stood over Daddy what felt like a long time. Eight, nine, ten breaths. His hand was shaky on the knife. Daddy's eyes opened up. He stared at Jim.

Well, son, if you're gonna try, time's a-wastin', said Daddy.

I took in a big breath and Jim's shoulders twitched. He crumpled and sagged and then in a flash Daddy had the knife and threw it against the cabin wall where it stuck and wobbled. In another second he cracked Jim in the face with the flat of his hand and it was like a piece of cooking firewood had popped. Jim didn't step back. He just stared at Daddy.

So that's how it is, said Daddy.

Yeah, said Jim, all tight and mean. *That's how it is.*

Daddy nodded slow. *Get the hell back to bed. Don't wake your sister. You and me will sort this out in the daylight.*

Xcept in the morning when I woke up, Daddy and Jim were gone. The knife was out of the cabin wall. A note told me they were coming back in a day or two.

But I never saw Jim anymore after that.

Because he ran away.

That's what Daddy said.

Betwixt and Between

"Stef, you up?"

T.J., outside her tent. Stef is very much awake; a half hour ago Tony unceremoniously unzipped her tent and thrust Gillie inside, barking orders not to let *the creature* escape and to stay mum about their discovery. After that, there was no chance of her going back to sleep.

"Mmmph," she mutters, as if just aroused. "Go without me. Got … cramps."

Gillie, wearing her blanket like a cowl, gives Stef a glance.

"Aww," says T.J. "Figures."

"Come on," growls Samuel. "Get that bow and let's get moving. You sleep in like you did yest'day and you'll miss the day."

Stef waits until their footsteps fade and the only sound in the camp is the crackle of the bonfire. Then she dresses quickly and grabs a book, slipping out. Gillie does not move, so she zips her inside and heads to the fire. After giving the low flames a poke Stef leafs through the same page of her book eight times, drinks some coffee, and chews on cereal with canned milk. Nothing has any taste. She feels electric, anticipatory, tuned in somehow—but at the same time numbed.

Magic is real, she thinks. *Or unseen. Or the soul. Whatever you want to call it. Maybe that means unicorns and dragons and witches are, too.* Her thoughts feel crazy and wild, and because she can't be sure, everything around her feels alien.

She tries the book one more time, then glances over at the tent as if it might explode. At last her eyes fix on the text and she gets through a page or two—and glances up again. Gillie is standing there, hooded by the blanket but coated in a green moss that looks like a soft velvet onesie. Her legs have grown pale, shining bark.

"Lass," says Gillie in greeting.

Stef looks her over a long while without replying. It isn't often she gets to stare at a walking, talking impossibility; seeing her in the daylight is even more startling than at night. Gillie is beautiful in an off-center manner—not like a streaming PoppyStar or a Hollywood film hero, where all that matters is an angular face and chiseled body. Instead, Gillie is breathtaking in the way a silvery still lake is, or a blossoming field of flowers, or the crystal blue sky itself. Gillie is of the forest in all ways possible, and Stef can muster no words to describe how.

She gestures for her to take a seat. Gillie folds her legs on the ground. "Coffee?" Stef asks, offering her a mug.

Gillie sniffs at the lukewarm brew, then dips her tongue into it once and drops the mug on the ground, where it spills and rolls to one side. She brushes at her tongue, then realizes she's being stared at and stops, sitting up straight.

"I say thanks but nae," she says.

Picking up the mug, Stef wonders again if what she did the night before was the right thing. She said what she had to keep Tony from burning the *sìthean* up right there and then, but in his own brutal way he had been convincing. In theory it was all well and good that little make-believe creatures were actually real and hanging out with humans, but as Stef knew from personal experience, this world had enough trouble getting along with its human inhabitants. People didn't need another thing to get worked up about, not when they got upset over basically nothing at all. Yet killing something living, something *intelligent* like Gillie, was wrong on its face.

"Want breakfast?" she asks Gillie.

"D'ye have apples?" Gillie perks up.

She roots around in Tony's backpack and comes up with two, handing them both to the *sìthean*. Gillie takes long deep smells of each and sets them on the ground in front of her, then picks up the larger of the two and makes half the fruit disappear at once. Juice dribbles down her chin.

"Why are you here?" Stef asks her.

After much chewing and swallowing, Gillie answers. "Ye knows why. Yer friend—"

"Tony's not my friend."

Gillie takes another bite.

"I mean, why are you here at all? In this world? Didn't Lexi say you have a whole other place to be? Why bother us here?"

Gillie finishes the first apple and glances longingly at the second. She is already growing fresh leaf-and-bark armor, and grass shoots unfurl like graceful dancers on her head. "Ye's in a special place," she said. "Tha woods 'round here are worn-up. So this place is more ours than yours, truly."

"Worn-up?"

"Aye. Means a thin place between here," she pats the forest floor, "an' there." Her fingers twirl into the air. "My home."

"I see. And a person can pass between if they find a worn-up place."

"Aye, mostly," she says. "But. Worn-up places are tha cause of trouble nowawhens. Becoming too big, so I hear tell. An' our home grows small in turn."

It's not making much sense to Stef, but she gets the basic idea: The apertures are widening, and for some reason that's erasing The Green Place Lexi rhapsodized about. "But you folk just come and go when you feel like it."

"When tha trees are with me I can. Time to time, others come on their ownsome. Artio, say. Morrigan maybe. I am the caretaker o' the forest, if ye will."

"Artio's one of you?"

"In a manner o' speakin', aye. She's a bear, true, but contains many."

Stef shakes her head; they're veering off course. "What's wrong with your place, though? Why leave?"

"'Tis wrong to be curious?"

"Suppose not." Stef is feeling a bit sulky about the whole matter. "But last I heard, it's not reciprocal. Not like I can go check out your—home."

"Nay, 'tis not wise."

"Why?"

Gillie picks up the second apple and strokes it, smells it. Sets it aside. "Was a time when thee and me—was from tha same tree. Same kind o' being. D'ye ken?"

Stef shook her head. No way were they related. "We don't get that particular lesson in history class. Y'all are make-believe stories for kids."

Gillie holds her hands out, palms up. "D'ye believe the make-believing to be true now?"

Stef chuckles. "Either you're a pretty excellent shared hallucination or yeah, you're real. But you're not all that … human looking."

"Nae," says Gillie, and begins storytelling.

In a time before time, humans and fey were one. Everyone had magic. Everyone created in the physical world. But over many centuries there were those who naturally gravitated toward one kind of creation—that of tools, machines, cookery (Gillie calls it "food manipulation"), construction—and those who applied magic to enhance ephemeral creations. They might take the concrete fashionings of one person and elevate them with magic—vessels that never emptied, wheels that did not break, gold that turned to leaves, bandages that healed wounds at a touch. Then they went further—trees could whisper, songs could hold a listener in thrall, souls might be transferred into animals when the body died, a warrior who could warp into an unstoppable beast-man.

Over time there came a split—a divide beyond which one half could only make with their hands, and the other half only could make with their magic … and as the divide grew, the fear of the other increased. Battles broke out. In the end an invisible barrier became necessary to separate the fey from the humans. On one side, fey might live in their forever green country of magic and maybes and semi-immortality; on the other, humans would exist in a more substantial world of absolutes, constants, and rules. Each had magic, but only one used it. The other feared it.

In time, each became the other's myth.

"We cannae do tha clockworks and fashioning," says Gillie, "tho' we dae know how to make a shoe, funny thing. An' ye's people rarely access tha true unseen, save for a few. We have come an' gone betwixt an' between for ever and ever, an' some of times ye have come our way through tha worn-up places of tha world. But. Nae without price."

At last, something tweaks in Stef's memory—a story she read of a handsome musician, taken to the fairy world, brought back many years later. "Time bends on your side; for us, doesn't it," she says slowly.

"Aye," says Gillie. "So, 'tis not good for travel an' visits an' the like for yer kind. Ye lose time an' desire only to stay. Too long over here, my folk have a loss of mind—of remembering."

"You forget?"

She nods. "The longer we remain on this side, the harder to recall why to return. Or who we are. Or the things we do. An' so we are lost."

Stef pictures it, a lonely endless displacement—to know you don't fit but also not know where you are supposed to be. Or even who you once were. "So is that what has everybody so worked up? Y'all are curious, so you come over and forget to go back?"

"Nae," says Gillie. "My home turns dark an' cold, an' we fear 'tis maybe the barrier is dying. 'Tis a mystery why. My world is narrow. Trees fare terrible in war, so we stay clear. But—we need help, from some such as yerself. An' Lexi. An' even … T.J." She sighs. "But things move so fast in this world, lass. A blink to us, an' all changes."

Stef thinks about this. They know something is going wrong, but time on their side moves so slowly that the answer is always out of their reach. "Don't know how I can help."

Gillie nods. "Aye. But. Answers will come soonest. Clíodhna has plans."

"Klee-nah?"

The *sìthean* doesn't answer, jumping to her feet. Her blanket falls to the ground as she cocks her head, listening in the direction of the hunt.

"I must away," she says. "Come with, if ye like."

Don't run, Stef wants to say. Instead she asks, "What's happening?"

"Artio has come."

Living in a Box

Tony and me sit up on that ledge and wait out the morning, not talking. Sun is coming up but it's hiding good behind these clouds. Storm for sure on the way. If rain, not a problem. Snow—well. It's early for big snow, but not too early.

At last we watch the others trickle into the field. Daddy first, then T.J. They stop where the trees end. No Stef. She's babysitting. I think of Gillie and my heart falls into my stomach and I feel sick. Daddy points up at us and they wave. We wave back.

"Come on up!" Tony shouts but they just wave harder.

"Too far," I say. "Can't hear us."

"Hmph," he says, so we watch as Daddy takes T.J. to that grassy low hill at the far end of the field where you can be invisible until you want to shoot. A berm. Daddy sets up T.J.'s bow—another one of those complicated eight-million-dollar ones like Tony has with wires and pulleys, and they settle in for a wait.

Thing is, the deer should be here by now. Something's spooking 'em, keeping' 'em out of the field. I keep my eyes on the grass but sometimes I feel Tony looking at me, studying up and down. Then when he's not looking at me I turn just a bit. His arms are soft orange-brown like tree bark and look like branches, the thick ones down below that hold everything else up, and when he moves them, cords stand up and muscles move. It's like watching something grow.

"Fuck me," he mutters after another bit of time. "You two ain't exactly earning your keep today."

"Bears," I say. "Artie, maybe. Not hibernating yet, maybe. Deer know."

"Jesus," he says. "When did you decide this? That kid can't shoot a bear. Thinks he can, but he's just gonna get hurt if he tries."

"Daddy can handle it," I say. "He'll be okay." I don't really think this, though. Fact is, I need to protect Artio, not T.J.—and I don't know how I can keep the bear from getting shot if I'm all the way up here. If she's roaming, I should try to get everyone out of her way.

"Y'know," he tells me, "it's giving me the hives you calling him Daddy."

"He is."

"For fuck's sake, ain't you old enough to say 'Dad'?"

I don't answer. I see it now—and I can hardly breathe.

Tony makes a swear and we both stand up.

The buck comes out of the west and is the most beautiful thing I've ever seen. His chest is thick with pelt, getting shaggy for the winter, and his head curves up like he's royalty. He has a rack of antlers big as tree branches. He's a king. His eyes are half open, xamining the field and even from here I see his wet nose twitch, testing. He's here to make sure it's safe for the others; they've been waiting for him to show up. He's in charge of this part of the forest; he's doing what Gil would do if Gil could be here.

I know Gil gave me the okay to grab a deer but he couldn't mean this one. It's wrong to want to kill this beast. He's the kind of animal Daddy avoids on a hunt out of principle, like he told me once. He only takes folks to animals that we can cut up and carry away in one go—smaller ones, ones who limp. Anything so young it has spots are no-goes, same as does carrying babies. This one has to be on that list.

"Wait," I say, resting a hand on Tony's tree limb arm. It's solid and unmoving.

He shrugs me off. "Do not fucking interfere with this," he hisses. "It's what he's paying you for. And if he misses, that's what I'm here for." He lines up his arrows and places them into the contraption.

Down on the ground, T.J. has his bow in hand, but it looks like Daddy's giving him the same warning I tried with Tony. T.J. turns his back on him and holds up his bow, arrow nocked.

I think of Daddy, from one time a couple years ago. We were at the cave and he was gone a long time down inside it. When he came back he was talking to himself and his hair was all over the place and his beard had cobwebs in it. His face was dirty and it was a couple minutes before he saw me. I sat him down and gave him water and used a little comb to get those silky strings out.

"Sorry, kiddo," he said after a while. His eyes were unfocused and looked not at me, but into the cave. "It's a box, y'see. It's a box I put myself in and turns out I brought you with me. Didn't see it at first. Wasn't a box then. Don't know the way out, now. We're in this box and the future's in it and the past's in it and I just wish to Christ I knew where the exit was."

Daddy fell asleep sitting up. Was normal the next day.

Cage or box, it's the same thing, isn't it?

I feel like I'm in another box right now. I can't change anything even though I know I have to. I'm stuck in place. See, what I figure is Daddy didn't think about the what comes next part when he brought us to the forest. He wanted to keep us safe even if he was wrong about sickness and he brought food and clothes but he forgot about the last part. That part where you say "the end" and we all live happily ever after. 'Cause sometimes you don't know when the end is coming until it pops up and surprises you.

T.J. has the deer in his sights. Tony also takes aim but holds it, ridges in his arms shaking from the pull of the string. Down on the ground, T.J. releases and his first arrow goes wild. The King Stag starts and his eye rolls. He's going to run. T.J. lets another fly and it hits his rump. The King Stag makes a half turn—and that's when Tony lets fly a single arrow. It lands perfect, deep in what Daddy calls the "boiler room"—right over the king's front leg. The buck totters this way, that way, like he's dancing, then goes to his knees. He leans forward like he might rise up once more and then—falls to his side.

My heart stops for a breath, then two.

Tony whoops and he's already scrambling down the rocky slope before I can even clear my eyes.

It's done now and we have to take care of business so I scurry after him. We run over to the buck and stand over him while his breaths get shorter and shorter. His shaggy chest pumps up and down, and life twitches out of him. I meet Daddy's eyes and they're wet too. He hasn't moved from the grassy patch next to T.J. He shakes his head at me once, just a little, and I nod back. We feel the same right in this one minute.

A crow caws in the distance and I look up at the whitening sky.

"Jesus, that's beautiful," says Tony and he gestures at T.J., who scrambles over. They kneel in front of the deer. Tony grabs T.J.'s hand and presses it on the shaggy neck. "Feel there."

T.J.'s pale face stills and his mouth hangs open.

"That's it," says Tony. "Last ebb in the artery."

Daddy showed me that first time we killed a deer. Put my hand on its neck. It was like feeling a river going to sleep. My heart's all fluttery and I can't see for a minute.

"You piece of shit," comes a voice from the treeline. "Y'all can go to hell."

Stef. She's here. And if she's here—where is Gillie? I'm staring hard as I can into the trees but I don't see the *sithean* at all.

"Who said you could come?" Tony glares at her.

"I did," says Stef, staring right at me while she taps on her watch face.

"C'mon, Stef," T.J. says, his voice going up high at the end. "You knew what we were coming out for."

Her look at him is so pointed I feel it. But she doesn't cross the treeline. Doesn't come out here with us.

Daddy jogs over to the carcass, gives me a wave of his hand. Wants me to go with Stef. But I have to stay, in case Artie comes.

"I'll help cut," I say and start bending down over the deer.

"Get outta here," Daddy hisses at me.

"No," I say and we lock eyes. "Won't."

I hear Stef clear her throat but I don't look away.

"You will do what I say, boy," says Daddy. "This is not the hill you want to die on."

I lean over the stag's neck with my knife and draw it across and steaming blood spills out. "Too late," I say.

We stand up together and both have a knife in our hands. I don't know what's happening here but I also feel like I can't back down. Part of it is my promise. But a bigger part is I'm tired of everybody telling me what to do all the time. Daddy 'specially.

"Hey, I don't care," says T.J. "Let him stay. More hands, goes faster. Right?"

Daddy and I are still eye to eye to eye to eye. I know this means the strop later on. But inside I'm crumbling. I don't like Daddy being mad at me.

Tony hisses quietly, "Frog."

I lower my knife. "Frog you," I mutter and my shoulders go slump. I turn toward Stef and head her way.

"That's right," says Tony. "G'wan. Let the men do the work from here."

I flinch at that and then I flinch again when Daddy chuckles at him. The backpack is already on the ground and Daddy's dumping the organ containers all around.

"Tupperware?" I hear T.J. laugh. "That's hilarious."

Daddy starts showing him how they'll 'viscerate the beast, then plunges his knife in the chest. The three of them hunch over the dead king and there's a whiff of metal in the air. Blood. Blood smell carries.

I reach the edge of the forest and join Stef, wiping the knife blade on the grassy ground. "Where is she?" I whisper.

"Gone," says Stef. "Back to her trees."

What Needs Protecting

"Burt Reynolds FTW!" T.J. grins, now wearing smears of blood across his cheeks and forehead left behind by Samuel as part of what he called an "initiation" a few minutes back. Fresh blood from a first kill, you mark the hunter. Or the supposed hunter. Tony's never seen the kid so unabashedly wild and happy; he really thinks he brought down the deer and all of his worries are solved.

Mission accomplished, thinks Tony. *We can go home now.* "You do know what that stands for, right?"

" 'Fuck the world,' " says T.J.

Tony laughs. " 'For the win,' you goof. But yours ain't bad either."

He does like T.J. He's not just a paycheck. The kid has layers. Top part is the classic brat, spoiled by too much attention and money for too little effort too early in life. That happens; Tony saw it even when he was overseas fighting and upper ranks promoted a shining star fast—only to see that particular star flame out. Give a man too much too soon and the best will try real hard but most fail to keep an even keel. What the financial guys say: Past performance is no guarantee of future results. Tony gets that on a personal level now. He knows what it's like to be out of your depth.

But beneath T.J. there's more, a little kid still who wants to play and beneath even that there's an almost-man who has a good heart and is far from stupid. It's like watching a fledgling take to the skies, seeing T.J. go from nobody to somebody to being the only one who matters to millions, and it's up to Tony to make sure he always soars and never falls. It's almost like having a younger brother, just one who pays your bills and bosses *you* around.

Right now Tony feels particularly close with him, elbow-deep in slick deer viscera, the coppery scent of hot blood sending his own racing. This was a particularly magnificent beast, and while he'll let T.J. take the credit—they already took about a dozen pictures Tony can upload to the Cloud once they get home—he'll always know it was his own arrow that really took the stag, and from up on a cliff at distance. Tony's shot from tree stands and cliffsides before, and getting up on the ridge early meant he could test for wind, so he was more than ready. He even had an edge, having tipped his arrows with paralytics so they wouldn't have to track the wounded son of a bitch for hours or days once he got hit. Down for the count, and out.

Samuel extracts the heart from the deer, holding it up for examination. It's a dark red, triangular shape outlined in pink and white stripes. "We get back, this gets eaten first," he says. "It's the trophy nobody sees."

"People used to consume it raw," Tony tells T.J. "Not so smart now. Heartworm and shit."

"We'll cook it," says Samuel in his flat tone, and hands it to T.J. to put in one of the containers. Tony can still feel his anger radiating after the tête-à-tête with Jim—or whatever her real name is—it rises off of the old man the way their bloody hands steam. It was a strange, unexpected confrontation, and he wonders a moment why it was so important for the kid to remain in the field.

"It's heavy," says T.J., weighing the heart in his hands. He looks at it a long while, turns it over, and then places it gently in the Tupperware. "That which you kill, you own," he muses.

"Read that someplace?" Tony asks.

"Just made it up. Maybe Stef can use it."

Stef. Jesus, Tony almost forgot about the other shit that's been stirred up since the night before. But he's not concerned: Either of those two crazy girls let that thing escape, he's got them by the short hairs. Samuel will freak out, and he's pretty sure T.J. will find it disturbing in the extreme. Imagination has never been one of T.J.'s finer qualities.

Something the girl Jim said earlier: *It's forever?* has been rolling around in his head. She meant, does the PEP strip these creatures of their magic forever. Well, no. Eventually that thing he shot will get its powers back. Tony makes a mental note to attend to it once they get back to camp. In this moment, though, his mind drifts to an open plain in Brittany. To when he was running. When they were all running together, fleeing the stench and the curdling music of the pits. Running to nowhere.

T.J. coughs and Tony starts. Right. T.J. is the unit now. They have their deer and their photos and that's a job well done. When they get back to the site he'll thump the thing and then announce they found this lost camper who needs to be taken to safety. So they'll cut the trip short, and hey, T.J. got his deer anyway so let's ride back home in triumph.

That's the the plan.

T.J. finishes putting the heart away and burps the Tupperware like he was taught back at home, laughing. "I'm never gonna see leftovers the same way again," he says, covering his face with his hand and coating it with more blood in the process.

"You look like you escaped from a horror movie," says Tony.

"Six hands," urges Samuel. "We can finish fast. Need to."

"How come?" asks T.J.

"Weather's gonna turn."

Tony cocks his head at the sky. "Y'think?"

Samuel nods, gently extracting the stomach and intestines. He places the liver in a separate container. Tony knows they don't want to taint the meat, so the bowel has to be handled carefully. "Gonna snow for sure," says the tracker.

"Tasty," says T.J. "Don't think I've built a snowman since I moved out of Maryland. This trip just gets better and better."

They fall to the job, cutting and peeling back the hide, exposing the innards and ribcage and muscle. Meat comes away from the stag in pieces that must be hacked down to fit in the containers, and as they turn to the task, the world around them all but vanishes.

But when the forest goes silent, Tony notices. The birdsong stops. Doesn't fade, just cuts out. He lifts his chin, surveying the meadow.

The ground shakes.

Samuel pauses, breathing heavily; T.J. just keeps cutting. The earth unsteadies again and there's a rustle of branches and leaves, a crackling just above the thudding, like lightning before thunder.

"Hey, what—" says T.J., looking up, and freezes.

Tony follows his gaze and his mouth dries. Perhaps three yards away, over by the western treeline, looms the largest black bear he's ever seen. She's standing erect like a human, loosely dangling gigantic forepaws tapering into shining spears. She's about the size of a truck's tractor unit, covered in shining ragged fur that's even darker on her belly and legs. Her squarish head is topped off by curiously small ears, one of which appears chewed, and her eyes are equally as absurd: small yellow circles focused directly on the mutilated stag.

"Artie," whispers Tony, without even thinking about it. "Artio."

Then he makes the connection. *Artio*. A name from his boot camp classes. A name even more weighted than the Ghillie Dhu and even more magically dangerous. The blood cools on his arms and knees and he wants to shiver but holds steady. Thinks about his training. Thinks about what he needs to protect, what can be sacrificed, and where the exit is.

"Do not move," whispers Samuel, crouching. "Get low." He presses his belly to the ground, gripping his knife. Never takes his eyes from the bear. Tony does the same, and T.J. follows suit, hand scraping against Samuel's bow. He lets out a little yelp, startled.

The yellow circles come to rest on the three men in the grass. The bear's ears flatten against its head, taking them in. Tony's heart pounds in his ears, blood surging. The answers to his evaluation arrive in this order: Protect T.J. Sacrifice Samuel. Exit into the woods.

I don't have to run the fastest, he thinks. *I only have to run faster than you.*

"Shh," Samuel shushes T.J., and between his teeth he says, "back up slow. Slow."

Tony breaks away from the giant bear long enough to meet T.J.'s gaze. And to his astonishment, the kid is grinning. He mouths three words at Tony.

Burt. Fucking. Reynolds.

With that, T.J. leaps off to the side, landing and rolling behind the grassy berm where he left his bow and arrows.

Things happen quickly then.

T.J. reaches his weapon with ease, but his bloody-handed grip is slick. He wipes his fingers on the grass and quickly nocks one arrow, then a second … and drops the bow. Grabs again. But he's lost his advantage; before he can look up again the berm explodes when the bear smashes into it, and he's soaring, flying. He falls hard against a tree with a sickening crack and crumples forward, going still. The bear shoves her nose in T.J.'s unconscious form and prods him with her muzzle. She opens her jaws wide and clamps down on the boy's jacket, lifting him off the ground as if preparing to take him with her.

Horrified, Tony swipes his own hands clean on his chest and nocks his bow, taking aim. He releases once, twice, and the arrows land on the bear. Both bounce off the tough hide as if he'd tossed rocks.

Fuckin' magic, he thinks, and reaches for the PEP. But before he can touch his pocket something crashes against him and knocks him to the side. He lands hard, and one of the cords in his bow snaps. Flushed with fury he whirls on his attacker.

Jim. The girl called Jim.

Only she's not near him anymore; in the moment it took him to recover, she's up and standing just a few feet from the bear, blocking its advance. The bear has gone back up on its hind paws again, T.J. dangling from its jaws like a stuffed animal. The bear and Jim stare at each other, transfixed. Without her hat on, Jim's wavy hair blows in a gathering breeze, and it's as if a spectral aura has encircled her body. The wind billows her shirt and she seems to double in size, as if trying to match the bear for intimidation. Tony imagines he sees her lift a few inches off the ground, hovering.

"Put him down," says the girl. "Leave him here and we'll leave you alone."

The bear stares at her, dark muzzle quivering, and there is no sound except for Tony's breaths.

Then Jim calls out nonsense words at the bear, as if she's trying to speak its language. She places the palms of her hands together, forcing her arms out straight and repeating the words as she draws her hands apart. Behind the bear the trees seem to vibrate and the woods begin to … hum. Tony squints directly into the source of the sound, and it's as if he can see for miles down a sunken lane that has just appeared in the forest, an open avenue to someplace else that wasn't there a moment before—and isn't really there now. It's just the *suggestion* of what is there.

The bear makes a growling sound deep in its throat, but there is no fury in it. It drops down to all four paws and deposits T.J. in the grass, giving a big, wet snort. Then it half turns, as if it's considering walking right back into the forest.

Fucking fuck, thinks Tony. *So that's what she can do. She's as dangerous as that Gillie thing.*

Part of him wants to let it go. There are other fish to fry, as it were. T.J.'s still unconscious, and he is the only thing that matters here. But Tony's wired differently than he was before the war, and letting it go when it comes to these creatures is not as easy a thing to turn off and on as it once was. It's not even as easy as it was before he went running across the Brittany plain with a whole group of creatures. They reeducated him but good after that. Something inside him shifts when that conditioning kicks into place, same way a third eyelid slides down before a shark attacks. It's involuntary. It's inside him. And watching that bear—which is as magic as that thing he took down the night before, no question—just slouch off is not what he is trained to permit.

Leaping back into action, Tony draws his PEP, skipping the pulse and reaching directly for the plasma, setting his thumb over the ID pad and sending out a long stream at the bear. The magenta ray hits her in the hindquarters, and she whirls again with the grace of an animal half her size, a searing fiery line drawn through fur and flesh. She bounds over T.J., leaping at Tony and swiping at him. Her claws rake across his chest, slicing through his coat, his clothes, his skin. He falls hard against the ground, the gun flying high and far away into the grass. She comes down on all four paws and looms over him, her breath a wet, oddly floral moisture.

"No!" He hears Jim as though from a very long distance. "Artie, go!"

Until now, Tony hasn't been afraid. The adrenaline coupled with his extensive field experience means that won't happen until much later. But as he stares into the yellow eyes of the bear, that all changes. What he expects to see—the raging, alien glare of an injured animal—is absent. Instead, those eyes are almost human; they hold a soul that's both intelligent and aware. Seeing a person inside the animal has him ready to scream.

Lips pulled back in a teeth-baring grimace, the bear goes up again. Tony fully expects it to land on him, stomp the air right out of his lungs. He can no longer move—terror has him locked tight. But a deep-throated "Hi-ya!" comes from nowhere, and there's Samuel, running at top speed and jumping on the bear's back. His long beard flies in all directions, and he grips the bear's fur with one hand while brandishing his knife in the other, plunging it into one of those yellow, human eyes.

Artio makes an earth-shaking roar and paws at the blade, then at its owner, but Samuel won't let go. Tony goggles at him as he holds on atop the bear like he's riding a bronco. Artio jumps and pounds against the ground, and it's the most astounding thing Tony has ever seen. But then Artio stands as tall and straight as she can, tottering and finally falling backward on the deer carcass. Meat and blood spray in all directions as her body crashes into the ground, the impact so profound Tony's fillings rattle. As she lands, there's a terrible cracking followed by a wet squashing sound as Samuel is crushed beneath the giant beast, which immediately rolls from side to side, pawing at its eye, the blade having slid out in Samuel's hand. At last she flips over and shakes her massive shaggy head, sniffing at the tracker as Samuel's hand twitches reflexively.

Jim is unmoving, frozen in a half crouch, her face a mask of horror. She's normal-sized again, just another punk kid who can't take orders. She's not glowing, not doing magic. She's watching the place where her father landed and is now in his final throes—if he isn't dead already.

Tony staggers to his feet, gouged chest starting to burn like hell. A quick glance and he can't make out what is his and what is the deer's blood. He races over to where T.J. was dropped and slings him across his shoulders, then dashes back to Jim and scoops up her hand.

"Move!" he shouts. She listens to him for once and they are running, not looking anywhere but straight into the trees. Jim's tear-streaked, dirty face holds no expression as they disappear behind the trunks, making their escape before Artio has second thoughts.

What Can Be Sacrificed

Tony wakes to near-total darkness and a familiar, yeasty scent. Blinking, he perceives a weak and filtered daylight some distance away and tries sitting up. White-hot agony wraps around his abdomen as if fiery fingers are squeezing his body. He falls against a stone wall and rests his head there, taking long, deep breaths.

Slow, he thinks. *Go slow.*

Thirst has made his throat raw, but he sees no water. Can barely make out anything of his surroundings—he's on a cot of some sort, and there's a second of the same on the other side of a narrow dirt floor, also set up against a ragged rock wall. Someone's in it, probably T.J. Tony's eyes adjust to the dark, and he can now make out shapes of a table, two chairs. A stack of interlocking boxes.

Gently propping himself up on his elbows, he jostles his torso again and winces. More deep breaths help him manage the pain. His fingers brush layers of gauze encasing his torso, and where they graze the hottest, wettest section just an inch from his navel, it's like touching a raw nerve. He groans. Fucking bear nearly disemboweled him, and he knows he's not out of the woods yet.

He chuckles darkly. *Live the metaphor.*

Then: *Why does it smell like bread in here?*

Squinting toward the light he perceives an exit to his room, and memories begin to slide together. They were running like hell away from Artio, and he had T.J. slumped over his shoulders in a fireman's carry. He was shouting at Stef to follow, but she didn't need urging as she pounded away alongside them. They blasted past the campsite from the night before, leaving their belongings behind, and kept running until Jim released Tony's hand and they came to a halt.

Behind them, no bear.

Ahead of them, a wall of leaves. Jim, beckoning.

The memories fade after that. Tony sure has no recollection of them finding a cave, much less a furnished cave, yet that is clearly what he's in. He's wearing a shirt he didn't start the day off in. Like the bandages, it's something that happened that he can't recall.

A burning wood scent and a fire crackle drift toward him from the light, and he makes out the image of Stef walking past the cave entrance, peering in, and then ducking out again. Taking everything with agonizing slowness, Tony raises himself to a seated position, dangling his legs over the side of the cot. His boots touch ground and he wants to spring into action but considers the blazing pain that will snatch him back if he does.

A walking stick propped up on the table seems left there for him, so he takes the long carved limb and leans on its padded end, shuffling to T.J.'s cot. Holding a shaking hand over the boy's mouth, parts of him unknot once he confirms the gentle, slumbering breath—but the fact that the kid's still out cold is not a good sign. Of all the memories Tony recalls from that morning, the image of his employer soaring through the air and landing hard against that tree and the whip-snap back of his head colliding with the wood is the clearest.

T.J. seems almost unmarked, though it's hard to tell in the dim light. In any case, it seems relatively certain the bear didn't bite him—it must have mouthed him like a lion with a cub.

But ... why?

A breeze drifts across his neck like warm, gentle breaths and he straightens, eyes narrowed. It's coming from the back of the cave, not the front, and while he's got virtually no experience with spelunking, everything he knows about caves is that they are wet and cold. The breeze comes again and he sniffs deeply. That's where the yeasty smell is coming from.

Could the kid have a propane stove back there?

Makes no sense, but he can't not know. Half-bent, Tony shuffles toward the rear of the cave, his walking stick making tapping, echoing sounds. He follows the tiny breeze, holding out one free hand so that it tickles his fingers, but the darkness is too much: He can't see anything and winces when his fingers jam up against a rock wall. He runs the fingers along the wall until they reach a loose stone, which rolls out of place and thumps against the floor. The breeze is a shade stronger now.

Aaaaaaaaannnnnnttttthonnnnny.

Tony stands and nearly cracks his head against the low roof. Singing. But a sour sound all the same. Not kind. Wheedling. Wanting.

Aaaaaaaaannnnnnttttthonnnnny.

Behind him comes a shushing of blankets and he whirls, grateful for a reason to retreat. He backs away from the rear of the cave and returns to T.J.'s cot, but the boy has only shifted slightly, his blanket tumbling to the ground. He's still out cold.

Bad news, this cave, he thinks, then shuts his eyes. *Put it in a corner. Don't focus on what you can't take care of in the right now.*

Inhaling deeply again, Tony calms and tries to assess. They can't hang around here long. Mobilization is the next item on the list, and he'll have to put his own pain to the side for now. Pawing through T.J.'s pockets, he locates the plastic bag of prerolled smokes, expecting they can get him through 'til the chopper arrives. Now all he needs is something to light one up with.

Tony sets his hand on T.J.'s forehead gently. "Gonna get you out of this," he murmurs. "You're my territory."

Hobbling toward the cave's entrance, Tony blinks into the early afternoon gray light and finds Stef alone as she's adding wood to a healthy, blazing fire. She meets his eyes when he lights up a thin piece of kindling and brings it to one of the joints, now clamped between his teeth. He tosses the wood into the fire and lowers himself onto a log on the ground.

"He's still out," she affirms.

"Yup," he says, drawing down. He'll need to watch out not to get too stoned, but already the pain in his gut is starting to dissociate.

Scanning their enclosed area, he tries to figure out where the hell they are. The trees here look different than the ones at base camp, which were weedy and stark, bare of leaves and closed down for winter. Here stands a profusion of pines, conifers, larch, oak, ash, hemlock—every one is as full-leafed as if it were high summer. He even catches a faint, sweet scent of wildflowers that reminds him of bluebells and primrose. Of battlefields. Of burning.

The same flowers they saw when they first hopped off the chopper.

It's not just that the trees are in full leaf; it's that they're old growth and towering higher overhead than any he's ever seen. It's like being protected in a cathedral, with branches arching a hundred yards or more in the air. Lower down he can make out the brush that surrounds the yard outside the cave—but he can't seem to find a visual path through the wall of leaves and vine. Standing, he hops to one edge and brushes his fingers against the greenery, a tightly woven barrier of plants that someone has trained meticulously to grow together so it blocks the outside. The wall arcs around the enclosed area and meets up with the limestone rock of the cave exterior on both sides. He suspects they are perfectly, naturally camouflaged.

We probably walked right by this yesterday, he thinks. *And didn't even see it. Wonder how long it stands if I thump it.* His fingers dangle to his pants pocket, then curl into a fist as he remembers the PEP gun soaring out of his hands. He feels naked without it.

"Lexi brought us here," says Stef as he returns to the fire. "This is where she lives in the summer."

"Lexi?" He frowns.

"The former Jim. She's a girl. Disguised."

"Yeah," he says. "Figured that out this morning. Didn't get a name, though." *She's camouflaged, too,* he thinks. *Just like her summer home. Nothing in this forest is what it appears to be.* A fresh lance of pain lights up his stomach and he winces, pulling on the joint. "I'm at a fuckin' eight or nine here. Ten and I might pass out. Fill me in, willya?"

"You were cut up pretty bad. Did what I could with what we had, but you need real stitches."

"Could've lost my intestines." Gratitude sticks in his throat but finally he coughs it out. "Thanks."

"Yeah." She's got a smug smile on her face. "Seems I know how to put things back together, if I got all the pieces."

"And T.J."

"Nothing I can do," she says, looking away and putting a thumb against one eye. "I checked him out but except for a couple bruises, he's fine. I was sure she bit him."

He nods. "I'd say that's the weirdest fuckin' thing of all, except I'm not sure I can even rank all the bizarre shit we've seen in the last few hours. Speaking of which—"

"I let Gillie go."

"Fuck."

"I know you're heartbroken. She's also fine. Grass came back, whole outfit."

He waves the joint in the air, thinks about getting home and coming back. He could get some fellow vets back here, light the place up. Figure out what's in that cave. Later, though. "Not the priority right now. Maybe later, not now."

"So what is the priority? You got a big plan?"

"Well, first off—where's our tracker?"

"You don't remember?" Stef pushes her glasses higher up on her face. "Guess you were pretty out of it by then. We got you two in the cots and then she took off. Went back, I figure."

Tony stares at her. "Crazy girl."

"You'd do different?" Stef tilts her head. "That's her dad out there."

"Was," says Tony half to himself, and he settles down to think. He reaches into his pocket and pulls out the small map he drew and showed to Jim—Lexi—earlier, along with his compass, and does some rough calculations. They're likely halfway back to camp. Could be there before dark if they really put some muscle into it. If T.J. were mobile, no question. But Tony's not sure if he can handle a multi-klick hike in his condition, even if Stef and he shared T.J.'s weight.

"Depending how close we are to camp, we've got a couple hours' walk ahead," he says. "We gotta get to camp, set off the emergency beacon. It'll take 'round an hour, two for the copter to scramble and pick us up. Then it's another hour to the pickup site in that meadow and we are out of here." He squints at the sky, which has turned a solid shade of white and does not bode well. "How soon can you get moving?"

She goggles at him. "We can't leave—Lexi—"

"Is not our concern," he says. "I'd think you'd understand that getting T.J. to medical treatment is the only thing that matters right now."

"It is, but she's—"

"She's nothing to us."

"She's not *nothing*." Stef's voice is pathetically strangled. "She's some seventeen-year-old kid who just lost her father and you'd let her come back to an abandoned campsite?"

"*If* she's coming back. That hasn't been determined."

"Of course she is," says Stef. "Anyway, it's going to snow."

"It *is* snowing." He gestures at the sky as scattered flakes tumble down. "Besides, she's no kid. She can take care of herself. And she's not the priority."

"I can't—just—"

Tony leans in close, wincing. "You fail to grasp the severity of the situation, chiquita. T.J. got a knock on the head. For all we know he's bleeding inside his skull. He might never wake up. Every minute we waste gabbing about this is a minute less he may have. You're going to tell me your best friend since you were kids isn't more important than some nobody we just met forty-eight hours ago who *lives* out here? What are you going to say to her once she comes back? What could you possibly tell her that may be worth sacrificing Tom?"

Stef's eyes are wet, but she stares at the sky, then back down, and the tears are gone. "Jesus, you don't sugarcoat it, do you?"

"How long have you known me?"

"She could come with us, if we wait. Just a few minutes."

Tony rolls his eyes. "Fuck that noise." He spits. "She's not our problem. Our problem is right here in front of us. Open your goddamned eyes." He bores his gaze into her until she quails. "Say it with me: 'T.J. is the priority. T.J. is family.'"

"Yes," she whispers. "Of course."

He starts to make a torch with a stick and a piece of cloth, but Stef pushes the side of her watch and the light that shines out is so bright he's momentarily blinded. Keeping the watch lit, they return to the cave, and Tony gives T.J. a quick look over, then runs his hands down the cot's legs. As expected, they fold inward.

"Gotta find some rope, or string, or twine," he says. If they can tie the legs to the bottom of the cot, it'll be a stretcher and they can carry him. It'll be a shit-slow walk, and it might be dark before they set off the beacon and get to the meadow, but at least things will be underway.

But when no rope or string or twine appears, Tony launches into a round of cursing. Stef dashes out of the cave, leaving him to consider Plan B. Or C, at this stage.

"Jesus, Tom," he mutters. "Couldn't you just wake the hell up?"

"Tony," calls Stef. "A hand out here."

He hops outside the cave in time to see her yanking vines from the camouflage wall and stripping leaves from the tendrils. *Smart girl*, he thinks in admiration. *Too sentimental. But never an idiot.*

They're busy at work when a rustling in the leaves catches their attention. Tony and Stef freeze and he turns, gripping the walking stick as a weapon. The camouflage fence parts only slightly as Lexi, hair mussed and clumped with dirt and blood, backs in through a hidden opening. She drags a sodden mess wrapped in tent silks and acknowledges no one. She pulls and pulls until her fingers slip from the silk and it drops to the ground with a soft whoomphing sound.

Lexi melts to her knees, head bent, back quaking, and Stef covers her mouth before running over.

Snow falls.

No Unnecessary Deaths

Daddy had a story.
Daddy always had a story.
Sometimes it was fulla shit, and sometimes it was fulla shine-o-la.
Now, all his stories are done.

I go back all the steps I need to go back, not even counting, 'cause I got to. 'Cause if I don't go back right at the very second we are out of danger I will never go back and something not Artie will come and Daddy will be that something's dinner and I can't think about that happening.

So I go back. Alone. I'm all alone in the forest for the first real time. There's no alive Daddy I'm going home to or walking toward, it's just me and the thing I have to do. When Jim left it was like somebody took a big chunk out of my insides but it wasn't like this. Half of everything I know about me is gone. Daddy knew everything.

Xcept how to get out of his box. Xcept when *the end* was coming. Xcept when to let me go.

I storm back to Blueberry Cliff fast as I can go, breath pulling like thorns out of my throat but I go fast, fast. My head's loud and rushing and one minute I'm seeing Stef and Gillie at the treeline and the next minute I'm feeling the world bounce and the next minute I'm doing what I promised Gil I would and I knock Tony down to save Artie and the next minute Artie has T.J. in her mouth—where was she going to *go* with him?—and the minute after that I see Daddy jumping up on Artie's back and the last minute she's falling over and I don't want to think about that so I stare up at the white sky and blink and blink until I trip and fall over right into the dirt, the leaves, the rocky ground.

I stay there a while.

§

Morning after the knife ended up in the cabin wall, Daddy and Jim headed out hunting. Was the first time I ever heard of where two of them went off together. I got left behind and not told anything.

Five days later when Daddy was back and xplaining, he said he took Jim to a place by the big lake where there was special hunting and a little shack the ice fishers used. He wanted to make things up to Jim. Get on the better foot, something like that. Then Daddy went to sleep at night and woke up in the morning and Jim was gone—took all the xtra food and water and even his tent. Daddy searched high and Daddy searched low, he found nothing and came home with nothing.

That boy will return back when he's ready, Daddy said. *Always does.*

Xcept I wasn't sure. Jim usually told me when he was running someplace.

Then Daddy said he had a surprise in his mind. This time when Jim came back we just wouldn't be at the cabin. *We'll go camping*, he said.

We are camping, I said.

No, we're not, said Daddy. *We live in a cabin. Camping is with tents. Closer to nature.*

Seemed to me we were pretty close already. And leaving without telling Jim was mean. I didn't say so to Daddy, though. He had a funny look on his face, like he didn't believe in the world anymore.

When he comes back, he'll worry about us for once, said Daddy. *Then we'll come home and it'll be okay again.*

Daddy made sense, least when he talked right to your face. So we packed up sacks and tents and xtra blankets. I put a note upstairs on the loft where Daddy didn't need to know it xisted but Jim would find and read it. My little secret thing.

On the walk out Daddy talked a lot about stuff he taught me years ago—eat what you kill, keep clean and dry, leave no trace. That last one was so important to him. When we came to the woods first day he said some people who were sick might follow us so we had to pass through the woods the way deer did. We couldn't throw anything away. We couldn't leave footprints. We had to bury the things we couldn't carry.

Leave no trace. We weren't ever here. We didn't xist.

Jim usually asked questions for us both. Without him I didn't know what to ask. Also, I was getting mad at Jim—he said he would take me with him and we would get ice cream once we were Outside and found nobody was really sick. But then he left.

Daddy and me went a whole day and a half, more than 21,736 steps. After that I lost count. Since I wasn't talking and since Daddy ran out of things to talk about we got silent and that was okay. I went up into my head and lived there, just moving and not thinking. It was quiet and peaceful. Daddy roamed like he was looking for something, and then—we found it.

We were about to set down for lunch near a big thick bush and he was like, "Hey, what's this?"

We pushed back some tree branches that waved in the breeze but on the other side of them waving was just rock. Then an opening, a little one we made bigger. We cleared the mouth of the cave and shone a flashlight inside and some bugs and bats zoomed out. A Bertha bat landed in my hair and when I stopped screaming Daddy plucked her out and let her flap away. We walked inside the cave and it just got bigger and bigger the deeper we went. Room for Daddy to stand up straight, and it was dry. It was also warmer than I xpected. I always thought caves were cold and wet but this one was—different. Special. Back outside Daddy counted out paces and held up a wetted finger to check wind direction.

Whole time Daddy acted like he was totally surprised, but he just reminded me of Xmas morning. When Jim and me were supposed to think Santa brought us presents but it was really Daddy after all. I decided pretty early on that Santa couldn't find us in the woods, 'cause we were too good at leaving no trace. So I knew forever what Daddy looked like when he was just pretending about something. And with the cave, he was being Santa again.

Well, he said. *What do you think?*

It's a cave.

So it is.

How'd you find it?

He went quiet. *We found it, chicken. You and me. Just now.*

There was a funny minute between us where it was almost out of me to ask why he was lying—and then my knowing it wasn't smart to ask at all. He'd been here. I could tell. You don't live in the forest long as I have and don't know how people change things. Was like someone wrote on a piece of paper in pencil then erased it. I could see the lines, and the eraser bits. But Daddy didn't want me to think that way. So, I decided.

Right, I said. *It's a neat place. Someone could live in here if they wanted.*

You, he told me, *are a very astute young woman.*

It was nice not being called a kid and my face got all hot and the funny minute passed.

We can use this place, he said. *We can have a summer retreat.*

Next morning we started creating the cammyflage wall round it with vines and branches and replanted tree saplings. We swept the inside and made it a place you could live, but I didn't really think we'd come back. Who lived in a cave? Anyway we had the cabin. But then we did use the cave in later years. Became a place we went during the hot days. It was a funny place full of ... well, *unseen*. Trees were always leafy, even in winter. Vine wall we made grew like it was on fire and pretty soon it blocked out the rest of the forest. It was special. And inside the cave was always warm in the winter, cool in the summer. A backup home.

Daddy spent a lot of time in the cave, more'n me. I went out wandering and hunting and swimming and xploring but he'd go deep in the cave—there was this nice little breeze inside that kept it warm and sometimes I'd even imagine it was whistling my name—and spend hours way in the deep deep parts.

"Don't follow me," he told me once. "Too dangerous."

So I didn't. Didn't want to go in the way way back anyhow. But he made me, sometimes. We spent a whole lot of time on our Sissy Fuss project, trying to block the hole with the whistle and the breeze but it always fell back down, no matter how good we built it. And I couldn't stay way back there too long. After an hour my head would get all swimmy and my heart would feel squeezed so I'd go into the sunshine and take long deep breaths until he called me back for more repairs.

Anyway, that first time we didn't build anything. We spent a week at the cave and I even got a few days to myself, since Daddy was way back in the cave most of the time and even was gone for two whole nights. I loved having the world to myself, even for a little bit.

'Ventually Daddy said it was time to go home. He meant the cabin, of course. And that made me so happy 'cause returning meant seeing Jim and he would be surprised—but not too much because of my note—and we would all be a family again. It was a long walk but Daddy was talking again, all xcited about our new summer place.

'Bout 100 steps from the cabin, Daddy had another joke he wanted to play on Jim. *He's inside pining for us*, he said. We would be slow and quiet and not loud and cheery so we could surprise him when we burst inside. That was kind of funny so we tiptoed around the whole cabin and the shack before poking open the door—but the surprise was for us 'cause Jim wasn't there. Never had been. Dust was on my note, which hadn't moved from the loft where I left it.

My insides felt like they were splitting apart.

Daddy set down his bag and shook his head. *Sorry, chicken*, he said. *Just you and me now. He got away from us. Guess that's what he wanted all along.*

Every night since, the only person in that loft wiggling her toes has been me.

'Ventually, I get up from where I fell. I brush myself off and feel thirsty. Been crying, losing water but I don't have anything to drink on me. I am just me with my knife and my bow and arrows. That is all.

Don't know when I was last just me, alone. Nobody xpecting me at home or at the kill site or in the meadow or anywhere. My head feels spinny and I close my eyes a second before going on.

I stop at the place where we slept last night and pull one tent two tents down and tie them at the corners and ball them up and head out to Blueberry Cliff. It's darker there now, and quiet. So quiet I'm not hearing birds or bugs or anything, it's like a big empty spot in the world.

Or maybe it's just 'cause my ears are ringing and my head is still full.

Artie is gone. She's left a trail of broken branches in the trees from where she pushed through and disappeared. There are marks where her long claws and big paws touched the ground.

This is not the hill you want to die on.

Last thing he said to me.

Daddy is there, all of him, but he's split open in places and there are flies over his cut open parts. A big antler sticks through his chest from where he fell on the dead King Stag and his eyes are open and dry and not blinking. I pull down the lids so they don't look at me while I try to figure out how to get him off the antler but once I touch his face I don't move for a long while and my brain feels froze up. I just look at him. He's all still, blood crusting where he got pierced, his mouth hanging open, and his beard going this way and that way. He's not making any zzz's. He's dead. I've seen dead and I've made dead and this is what dead looks like. Like something that was there but is now empty.

I scream at him, loud as I can, and no sound comes out. Just me and my mouth hanging open wide.

Jim once told me how there are two parts to a person:

1. Your body
2. Your soul

The body is easy. We see the body every day. The soul is something we don't get to see. It's the hiding part inside, the piece that makes us human. Makes us different. Makes us ourselves. You take one away and maybe the other half lives but it's not the same. I asked him where the soul goes when there is no more body.

He squirmed and asked if I remembered church. I kind of did but mostly that it was quiet and boring. He said some people who go to church believe the soul goes to a nice house called heaven or an ugly house called hell. All depends if the person was bad or good. He said some people think it gets reborn inside someone or something else and starts all over again.

But he also said a lot of people don't believe it goes anywhere. They don't even believe it xists. That we are just pieces of meat and bone and brain and once we're dead we're just like a stag on the ground, we're a shell and we get eaten—if not by other animals then by worms.

I don't know if Daddy had a soul. What I do know is he has a body and that body is empty. It needs to be taken care of. I think about all this while it starts to get colder in the forest and I know I can't sleep here no way no how so I wipe off my eyes and clean off my face. Part of me isn't sure why I'm even crying. He's Daddy. He's the man who built our cage.

He's the man Jim ran from.

So maybe he didn't have a soul.

I sit on the ground behind where he fell and brace myself and I push and push with my legs on his back and the whole time I'm not seeing too good, it's all blurry but finally there's a soft noise and he rolls over and he's free from the antler. I roll him one more time with my feet so he's not face down in the dirt.

I stand up over him. His beard is sticky with blood, his hands all bent and twisty. I want to think he jumped into the whole horrible mess with Artie to save me; but that's not how it happened. Daddy saw Artie maybe going after me but he didn't do nothing until the bear turned on Tony. I'm glad he didn't do anything while I was trying to send Artie away—but why not? Didn't he think Artie was gonna jump on me and chomp chomp and I'd be dead?

I'm not going to know that now. All I know is it didn't have to be this way.

No unnecessary deaths, Gil promised me all those years ago.

But neither Gil nor Gillie are here to help. Not this time. Gil was the one who gave me orders to do what I did—keep Artie safe. I did what I knew how to do. And it still ended up this way. No more Daddy, no more Jim.

D'ye ken if yer brother had unseen? Gillie asked me last night. Which was her way of asking if he was magic.

But Jim is gone. I don't know if he had magic. What true I do know now is this: Daddy was why Jim didn't come back. Maybe he hurt him, maybe he ran him off, I don't know. I bet Gil knows, though. Gil knows everything that happens in this forest. And he never told me. 'Course I never asked. I should have. Maybe I didn't want to know the answer. Easier to never know. Easier to never xist than to know that answer.

I kneel down next to Daddy's body and have a funny moment where I see him like he's the King Stag. I almost reach for the Tupperware containers. I would know just where to cut. What to take out. What to eat first. My heart's making noise in my chest and it's hard to breathe and something bad is bubbling inside me. I look at Daddy and think about how he didn't save me this time and he didn't really save me the first time—I didn't need saving. I had some magic and Mom had some magic and maybe the baby had some magic and he said no to all of that and this has to go his way or no way at all.

He really was fulla shit.

Now I am a stranger to everyone I meet. Now I have nobody. I have nothing. And I don't love him. Here is why:

1. He lied about bringing me here.
2. He lied to me about sickness.
3. He lied about not believing in magic.
4. He didn't let Jim and me xcape.
5. He was never true about what really happened to Jim.

I lean back and scream loud as I know how into the sky and this time the noise comes out of me, all of it. I want to shake the world with my screaming. Make the trees hear me and the animals hide and the sky fall. Make sure everyone who ever lived hears me. Sees me.

When I finish I throw the tents over Daddy and tie him up tight. Last thing is his face. I look at it and think about how much he taught me. How much I only had to learn 'cause he brought me here. But I also think about the way he would light up when he was shine-o-la. Half of everything I know is 'cause of him. Prolly half of everything I am is 'cause of him, too. And I think you don't finish loving somebody all in one day.

I cover up his face and look around the meadow. It's getting darker but I see Tony's popper gun and I don't think it should be in the field like this so I grab it and tuck it into the tarp. Maybe I'll bury it with Daddy. He can have protection wherever he is now, tho my guess is he's just prolly worm food.

Then I tie everything tight and make loops for my hands to pull him up. I stand up to go for one more time into the trees.

And that is xactly the moment when Gil appears.

"Ye are full o' noise," says Gil, leaning up against a tree. I don't even know he's there until he moves like a shadow peeling himself away from the trunk. "An' for who d'ye cry out?"

For just a minute everything I'm sad and angry about disappears: Gil is here and he's looking almost like himself again. I only had a few seconds to see Gillie with Stef this morning before Tony dragged me out of camp, but even then I could see she wouldn't be stuck without magic forever. Mossy fuzz was running up her arms and legs and her skin was starting to shift colors again and a tough white bark was all over her chest and it made me think of the way skin comes back after a scab falls off. Her hair looked like she rolled around in the grass for a while and it made her pretty.

Now she's become Gil again and the bark is darker and like clothes and the hat is small but in three points and I throw myself at him and hug him tight. Gil stands there like a big old birch tree and lets me but I figure out pretty quick that he either doesn't want to get hugged or doesn't know what to do if he's hugged. We never touch like that. I'm surprised to feel how warm he is. It's cold out and getting colder.

"Aye, lass; that's me together again," he says when I step away. "Or nearly so. I'm nae so easily put down."

"Is it—all back yet?"

"Most," he says, voice soft. "But I cannae dae much." He blinks up at me. "D'ye have an apple?"

Real things come back to me and I feel tired. "Nae, Gil, not this time."

His mouth twists and he shifts from side to side. He looks over my shoulder. "So," he says. "For what are ye taking yer father?"

"I have to bury him, Gil. He died." And my throat closes again.

He makes a scoffy sound. "Ach, makes nae sense. Leave him to the forest. He's nae good to ye now. Nae use to anyfolk but the animals. If I'd known—"

My head whips up. "Known what?"

"Time to time, a dyin' person can have a second home," he says. "W'us. But. Is a tricky thing. Too late now."

I squint at him and start walking. Gil knows everything there is to know about the forest and about being a *sìthean* but he doesn't know people things. And the more he talks the more I'm feeling rotten inside and the sad-angry is coming back. Daddy is dead and nobody cares but me and the reason he's dead is Artio and the reason Artio didn't get shot first thing is *me* and the reason I did that with Artio is 'cause of Gil. And pretty soon I'm sweating because pulling Daddy is hard work and I'm breathing hard because the last person I want to be mad at is Gil.

So I think about being mad at Artio, instead.

"Ye failed," he says, bouncing along aside me after I don't talk for a while. "Ye failed to protect Artio, ye know."

My head spins and I stop hard, gasping. "She's alive, isn't she?"

"She's hurt. I asked ye for one thing an ye failed."

"Yeah," I say, my teeth tight. "I'm awful. I'm a bad person. My Daddy died, though. So how about acting like that matters for maybe five seconds?"

Gil shakes his head. "Man Samuel was ye's captor, lass. D'ye not see that? 'Tis what Jim was tellin' ye all the time an ye did not see. Ye's free now. Take it and be blessed."

My breath sticks in my throat. "You talked … to Jim?"

His eyes go shifty. "Oh, aye. Many moons back. He was gonnae leave the trees w'ye, an' asked my help. An' then … it changed."

"What changed?"

Gil's eyes shift this way and that. "I said I would help him go away but he said he must get his sister first. Then it was nae possible as Daddy Samuel took steps. So I helped ye stay, until such a time as ye may ask to leave. But."

"But what?"

He toes at the ground. "But I wish ye to stay, now."

I think about throwing my hands in the air and running around in circles until I fall down and then once I'm down not getting up. I stare at the ground. "Jim's dead, isn't he."

Gil doesn't answer at first. Then, "Aye. Nae."

He talks like he's telling a joke and it's like every part of me is on fire and every emotion I have is going all at once. I can't listen, not right now. I need to do one thing and one thing only. I get my feet going.

Gil jogsteps with me. "Ye are pulling again."

"Shut up," I tell him. "For once, either help or go away. But stop talking."

The ground goes silent and his feet do not whisper in the leaves. But I can't stop. My face is hot and the world is blurry again but I can't stop now. And then—then I have no weight to pull. My arms behind me go loose and I look behind and there's Gil, standing at Daddy's feet, his hands holding the silks like they are air. He nods at me and we walk on in silence and all I have to listen to is the song of the forest settling in around me.

It is going to snow.

§

We reach the outer rim of the cave vines and I stop. Gil lowers my father's legs to the ground. I can hear the crackle of fire on the other side of the wall, but no voices. I wonder if everyone is resting or asleep.

While we were walking in silence, I tried not to think about too many things. Just very specific ones. Like what I'm going to do next. I thought 'bout how Daddy didn't know when to say *the end* and I thought 'bout the way he built us a cage, or a box, and didn't know how to xcape when it was time. I don't want to do that to myself. And I might do that if I don't think things through careful. What I decided, finally, was that I need to be alone for a while. Alone to figure things out. Really, really alone.

I half turn to look at Gil, who I know isn't coming in. Not with Tony so near. There is business unfinished everywhere and I don't know what's going to happen to Tony or T.J. but I know it won't be good if Gil has a say. He looks at me, eyes wide and shining.

"Okay, you can speak," I say.

He smiles a little and sets a hand on my shoulder. "Yer father is gone," he says. "An' I dinnae understand why it pains ye but I feel it does so I am sorry for it."

There's a sinking inside me, as if all my insides are being drawn to the ground. "You said I failed," I say to him and my voice is flat. "You said it was my fault Artio got hurt."

"Aye," he says, nodding.

"Then whose fault is it my father is dead?"

His mouth opens, then closes. "We didnae see it coming," he says. "We couldnae know. But. Are ye truly sorry?"

Am I? I'm scared, that's what I am. And I'm angry at Daddy. And I keep thinking there's prolly 100 other things I don't know about that are going to have to be learned about in the coming days, whether I stay in the forest or I try to leave. But all of this is tangled together like the vines that wrap around our cave yard and I can't even start to untwist them. The one clear thing I have in mind is this: I know xactly whose fault it is that Daddy is dead, and I know xactly what I have to do to make it right.

It is the one thing Gil has ever told me not to do.

So we have to be done.

"Gil," I say, not realizing what I'm going to say until it happens.

"Aye?"

I stare at him a good long time. I try to memorize his skin, how it pulses with the colors of the forest the way sun dapples on leaves and branches. I replay his voice in my head so I can memorize that, too. "Don't come see me anymore," I say.

Then I turn from him and push my way through the wall, to the cave.

My face is wet. My chest hurts.

Daddy and I are home.

The Bear Chooses You

"This ... is ... not ... good," mutters Stef, but she is speaking to no one. Instead her words are scooped up by the wind and join the snowflakes swirling before her eyes, and her voice seems to only accentuate the forest's dead emptiness.

Tony was clear, she reminds herself: Follow the compass south for around four thousand steps. Two miles. Three-point-two-one klicks. If she's done her job right, the campsite is only a few more steps away, on the other side of the stand of trees before her.

But as she's walked alone all this time, she's expected she would smell or hear the campsite long before she arrived, and there is no scent of wood fire or lunch, no music booming from speakers, no crunching of footsteps, no barked conversation. Ahead of her the quiet seems so vast it's as if it is leaching all the noise from the world around it, an aural black hole.

I told him to go, she thinks in a gush of panic. *What if they already left?*

She and Tony parted about an hour ago, after Tony insisted he needed a breather. They'd been on a fast march since leaving the cave site, unburdened by packs but weighed down by the cot and T.J., moving through increasing precipitation and a noticeable temperature drop. By the time they set T.J. on the ground for a brief rest, Stef's arms were dead and unmoving, stiff wooden rods. She wiped sweat from her face.

Open up yer damn jacket, Tony growled. *Sweat when it's cold and it'll freeze on your skin and you can drop into hypothermia faster than a fat kid eats candy.*

She unzipped and yanked off her hat, full of questions: How much further to the campsite, and whether Tony felt anything when he unceremoniously fired Lexi after she stopped sobbing—but she held her tongue. The man's face was positively gray, his light eyes sunken into his head. He was not getting better. Tony was losing ground, fast.

He took the measure of their location by consulting a small old-fashioned compass and turned to her. Even without his hat and gloves he was dripping sweat, too, his dark cropped hair frozen into wild punk spikes. *Here's how it goes from here,* he said.

There was no discussion. He showed her where to go, reminded her to count steps, and pressed the compass into her hand.

You'll get to the beacon faster than if you struggle with us, he said. *We'll wait on the meadow edge. Just hit that signal and track out to the meadow when you're done and we'll all be there when the chopper arrives.* He lobbed a few more directions for the second leg of her hike, and she made notes in her lyric notebook. Without ceremony he hefted T.J. from the bed over his shoulders and groaned, then cut east through the trees, never looking back.

Stef felt like saluting, half sarcastically, half in admiration.

Now, according to her steps—4,392, give or take—the camp is ahead. But the quiet is wrong.

Shouldn't have left Lexi, she thinks, then breaks into a run, pushing through the trees and into exactly what she feared—a deserted campsite. She turns around twice, shouting for anyone who might still be around—and only then realizes it's not just that the site is deserted.

The site is also destroyed.

It's as if a hurricane of knives has whirred through the clearing, uprooting and shredding everything in sight. Each tent is ripped through, long canvas strips flapping in the breeze. Tent support poles, snapped in two, jut up from the earth like teeth. The dirt around the site is littered with clothing, bottles, food containers, toilet paper, hangers, bedsheets, linens, cookware. Not one item in camp seems to be in the place where it was when they left, the devastation is so complete.

Daryl is the biggest asshole who ever lived, she thinks. *Wrecked the place, then took off. Guess Ian helped him. And Martinique, the cook? Suppose ...*

But that makes no sense. At his most wound up and furious, Daryl is too lazy to pull off something this total. Stef runs her fingers over one of the broken tent poles, and shakes her head. Even if Daryl had found some reserve of energy he wanted to expend on something other than his guitar or weed, he physically couldn't have done this. Nor Ian. Nor Martinique. The wreckage is from a mightier hand, a very localized storm.

An unseen, magic storm. She thinks of Gillie, who surely did not do this. Then she thinks of others coming through apertures who might have.

A chill that has nothing to do with the weather steals down her spine, and Stef shivers. Her throat is tight, and she's doing her best to keep focused and rational.

Beacon's in my footlocker, Tony said earlier, so she runs over to where the cooking area had been and finds the splintered sign that once stood outside his tent flap: *Anthony Garcia.* Lifting up a large swath of collapsed canvas, she slips into the darkened, partially collapsed tent lit on the inside only by gray light streaming in from the great rents in the fabric.

She tosses items left and right, digging randomly, and rips a nail on something too heavy for her to lift easily. Rocking back on her heels, she tilts her head back and swallows a scream of frustration.

Find the pieces, comes Gillie's voice in her mind.

Slowly, she relaxes. Takes a deep breath, releases. Her fingers tingle.

First, light. She presses the side of her watch and the damaged room is immediately less frightening. The bed is intact but the sheets are askew; the side table and armoire split and mangled. But the footlocker is metal. It's upended, dented—and already pried open. She sweeps off some random snow and undoes the latch, pushing aside clothes, a spare pair of boots, and a strange gray-and-black box. She flips it over and spots a small switch next to a single, flashing red light.

The beacon has already been set off.

Stef thinks about sobbing, but refuses. She knows why everyone's gone: She told Daryl to get out of there before they returned, and then the snow came. He wouldn't have needed another excuse. The question is—how long ago?

A piece of paper flutters from one corner of the beacon, and she unfolds it to find a note in Daryl's jagged handwriting.

"Dearest friends," it begins, sarcasm radiating from it like toxic waste. "Snow showed up so we decided to hightail it early. Thrilled you let us know you'd be hiking out solo at your own pace. Will tell everyone at home not to circle back for you, or expect you early. Ta-ta!"

Stef has to read the note a couple of times to understand the lies in it. She pounds her fist on the ground, feeling sick in her gut and muzzy in her head. Daryl wasn't just an asshole—he was trying to get them all killed.

But even that is not the most important thing right now. So much seems urgent, impossible, life-threatening that she can hardly get a grip on what to do next.

We have to go, she told Lexi a few hours earlier. *I am so, so sorry.*

Lexi did not look at her.

T.J.—he's really—he's really bad off.

Thanks for the walk. Tony's voice cut through Stef's softness. *You're discharged.*

Stef shot daggers at him. To his credit, he seemed more tired than gleeful.

You can come with us if you hurry, Stef said to Lexi.

That bought her the young woman's attention. *Can't,* she said, and sniffed once, deeply. There was no trace of sadness in her words. *Burying comes first. In the cave. And then I have to find Artio.*

Time! Tony shouted. *Exit through the leafy door.*

You don't have to do either, Stef said, offering her hand.

Stephanie Holliday, Tony had bellowed. *Now.*

I'll come back, Stef promised Lexi, who wasn't responding. *I'll find you.*

Don't, Lexi shook her head.

The last image Stef had of the broken woman was of her down on the ground, surrounded by swirling snow, with the hardest project of her life ahead of her.

And we just ... left, thinks Stef now. *But we had to go.* It could have happened no other way. But in this moment, she feels like Daryl—not caring about what mess he leaves behind, thinking only of himself.

The flashing red light of the beacon calls to her from the bashed-open footlocker. Stef glances around with fresh eyes. Daryl and the others can't have left here very long ago. He must have seen the snow, set off the beacon, and made up a story to convince Martinique to come with them. Probably the lie of how the rest of them would find their own way to town.

But how long ago? An hour? Two? Could they have just missed their ride home?

Stef grits her teeth. She hardly realizes she's chattering with cold until she goes to zip her jacket again and fumbles several times before the metal piece slides up. She must get to the Great Meadow before the helicopter arrives. If it lands while she is still unaccounted for, Tony may not wait. After all, he would not wait for Lexi. Why should Stef matter if T.J. needs help? Has she ever mattered?

Standing, she steps outside the tent and squints at the wind and snow. A frozen fear steals in and she begins quaking. "I can't do this," she says aloud. "It's too far."

A single tear trickles down one cheek and T.J.'s face comes to mind. She thinks about how her heart once fluttered when he looked at her a certain way. She will see that look again. She takes one awkward step forward, then another as the snow picks up and flakes of ice cut into her face. It will be at least an hour to the meadow, if not more, in this weather. She barely remembers.

The wind drops to a low whistle and then she hears it: a regular, thick huffing behind her, as if a steam train is arriving in the station. Halting, her heart threatens to break out of her chest. She turns slowly to find Artio walking directly at her, muzzle twitching, breath steaming. The bear is a giant dark shadow shifting against the growing whiteness of the forest, coming inexorably closer.

Don't move, Stef tells herself, even as every inch of her cries out to flee. You can't outrun a bear; she knows this from a guidebook. Bears are faster. They will chase. They can climb. They will tear you up. But would Artio? The bear protected by the Ghillie Dhu? The one responsible for crushing Samuel earlier that day—an event that seems so long ago it's as if it happened in another lifetime?

The bear stops so close that her hot, meaty breath brushes up against Stef's face and fogs her glasses. Her mind stills, the aural black hole in the world claiming her. Stef stands in a vast empty space, head awhirl with its own silent storm, echoing—but clear.

Raise your hands, the guidebook said. *Be big. Sing.*

As if her empty brain has any songs in it at this moment.

She prepares to raise her arms, to try and appear larger than the giant creature before her, this mass of fur and musk and paws the size of dinner plates, of moist breath and one ragged, destroyed eye encrusted with blood. But then she meets the gaze of that keen second eye, that tiny yellow thing—

Stef removes her fogged-over glasses. She grew up with two dogs, three cats, and a hamster. She rode horses for three years, until the expense of equipment and dress and rentals went beyond her parents' ability to pay. She loved every animal that came across her path and spent hours staring into their faces in the hope that one day one might speak to her—that there might be some communication beyond adoration or wide-eyed confusion. It never came.

Artio's good eye is different. It gleams like glowing sea glass or a moon of Jupiter, filled with an uncommon depth and perception that Stef knows is beyond any animal recognition she has ever witnessed. Gasping, cheeks aflame, Stef sees it now: something beyond instinct in that eye—a gleam, focus, recognition.

"Artie—Artio—" she stammers, fitting her glasses back on. "I have—" she takes a step backward. "I have to—to go. Please let me go."

A low growl from the back of the bear's throat begins, followed by a muffled whoofing sound that fans out its muzzle. A flicker in the bear's eye like the shadow of a person walking across a darkened stage makes Stef momentarily fearful, but then the incredible depth in the gaze returns. Slowly, the bear bends one front leg under itself, then a second, going down before Stef in a bow.

Artio twitches her head briefly to one side.

Had the bear been a horse, there would be no question. The offer is being made. But Artio can't be asking Stef to go for a *ride*, can she?

Stef scans the campsite for Gillie or a stand of birches but sees nothing. Just the wind bending the trees, picking up speed again. She shivers.

Artio's growl is like a steely purr. Definitely an invitation.

Stef places her hand on the beast's enormous head. If this is real, she can be at the meadow in a matter of minutes, not an hour. Unable to believe she's really doing it, Stef runs her hand around to the animal's broad back.

"The meadow," she says. "We have to go there." Her voice is halting and stiff. "You can't take me anywhere else."

Another whoofing noise.

She grasps one hank of the coarse fur, surprised by how it feels like caressing a very large dog, one that badly needs a bath. Artio's body is a vast warm pelt that calls to her, and she's grateful for the warmth. Sliding one leg across her back, Stef grips another fistful of fur with a free hand and sits up straight.

Artio rises up on four paws and begins trotting.

Stef instantly loses her balance, sliding to one side and scrabbling at the fur before slamming into the ground. Artio stops and doubles back, nosing at her.

"Yeah, yeah, I'm an idiot," she says, climbing up again. It's been a long time since she rode a horse, and she forgot one of the basic premises of riding: to hold on with your whole body. Rider and ridden are one beast in these moments. Squeezing with her thighs and holding tight to the fur, she leans down into the pelt. "I'm ready now," she whispers.

This time the bear does not hesitate, and they fly through the late afternoon like an arrow shot across the forest.

Rebalancing the Scales

Tony is in a circle of hell.

Sweat coats his face and neck, despite his coat hanging unzipped to the elements. His shoulders are leaden from the weight he's perched across them for the past hour or so. They're close to the Great Meadow now, he can feel it, but he won't make it without at least a short breather.

His gaze falls on a thick pine tree with a wide, spreading base that's relatively snow-free, and he lays T.J. down on the pine needles and forest detritus. He makes a pillow of T.J.'s blue scarf and sets it under the kid's head, then bends down to listen for a heartbeat and steady breathing. He gets both.

He's all right. For now, Tony assures himself. *Help is on the way.*

He hopes.

Half collapsing next to T.J., Tony struggles to get his wind back, but his breaths scrape against his dried-out throat like a line of strung needles that reaches from his gut to his mouth. Each step this morning has rung like a gong through his body, sending ripples out from under the bandages to his fingers, his toes, the small hairs on the back of his neck. He bites off his gloves and with trembling fingers unbuttons the strange shirt he woke up in, not surprised and yet horrified to see what is lurking beneath.

Stef's homemade stitches have torn open, and the gouges from Artio's claws are expanding. It's as if he's slowly being turned inside out. He's not cold; the freezing temperatures should have seeped into his bones by now, but instead he feels as if he's home in New Miami. He should have known a swipe from Artio would be like no other. Artio, as he learned in training: bear goddess, protector, and defender. High Payoff Target, Level C. Recommendation: Approach with extreme caution, never solo.

Tony allows himself a third joint once his breaths normalize. The sweet, pungent aroma of the fine drug courses through his system, and he concentrates on the soughing of the wind in the trees, the scraping of the snow and ice, and closes his eyes.

He thinks of her face. Clíodhna. The banshee queen. Back in Brittany she appeared to him through an air hole—that's the jokey word they used for it in the field, but it was an aperture, a way to see a whole other perfect green world—and spoke with him. Asked for his help. And he saw her and he saw the emerald perfection behind her and the crystal blue of the sky above her, and who could say no?

I love you, he told her, and said yes to whatever she asked.

And so, was damned.

Not then. Not in that moment. But as soon as he told his superiors about the request for help, he was yanked from the field. Given a debriefing. Eventually returned to the field, but transferred to the pits. That was where he made his greatest mistake: sympathizing with the doomed enemy.

I tried, he thinks. *I tried to help.* He opened the cages, let the fey go free, helped them escape. He even ran with them as far as the Channel. But of course they were tracked. Recaptured. Incinerated. It broke his heart. And when they took him in for reprogramming a second time, it broke his soul. Now he has nothing left but contempt for the fey and all their diseased magic.

Or, almost nothing. There is an ignored corner of his heart that burns like the last ember in a firepit to see her again. To visit Clíodhna's Green Place. To be welcomed there, despite his sins. Perhaps because of them. To prove he is not the monster they believe him to be.

Or to prove to himself that he is.

Thup thup thup.

The sound of flying heartbeats rouses him, and he starts from his doze. The joint has burned out, hanging from his bottom lip. He reorients, trying to hear the rotor again. How long has it been coming? Has the chopper arrived? Is it waiting for him in the field right now with Stef and the others?

Tony leaps to his feet, his back an agony, his gashes bleeding freely again. He can't see the field from here, but in that short time since he fell asleep under the pine tree he realizes he can't see a whole lot of anything: The wind has picked up mightily and the snow is coming down in sheets. They have a very small window of time in which they can be carried out of the mountains safely, and that window is closing.

Hefting T.J. against his chest in a bridal carry, he lurches toward the field and the noise. The chopper is closer now, but the sound is different. There's a pause and a slow whine. It whistles metallically and then cuts out. Then the heartbeats return. And then they stop. There is a long moment of pausing, and Tony tries to put on speed but knows he's not close enough. The copter must have arrived while he was out and is now taking off—for whatever reason—without them. Weather? Still, it can't leave. They can't be left behind here.

Tony bursts into the field and skids down a small embankment, wobbling. The field is empty, dotted with orange sacks and empty food wrappers dancing in the wind. He squints into the snow blow and can't see the other side of the field—there's too much of it. Turning his back to the wind, he sets T.J. down and grabs the blue scarf, waving it like a signal flag, staring up into the sky where the copter is rising higher and higher.

"Hey! Jesus, hey!" he shouts, knowing it's useless. He reaches the middle of the field and halts just in time to see the wind pick up the copter like an invisible hand and turn it three-hundred-sixty degrees. It sways, trying to regain control, but the southerly gale is too strong for it, and it blows it hard and fast toward a high cliffside.

Almost before it happens, Tony knows what will occur. It's like dropping a paper boat into a typhoon. Perhaps it wasn't snowing back in Eagle where the copter originated; perhaps they came simply because the world-famous T.J. Furey appeared to have called. But whatever reason the pilot might have had to take off two hours ago, it would be the last trip he would ever take.

Time hangs for a long breath, and the beats of the helicopter match the beats in Tony's chest. Then everything happens: The helicopter ceases to fly, and starts being flown. It soars high and nearly clears the cliffside, but its rotor halts, and a few seconds later the chopper collides with the rock face. There's a sickening, awful crunch and several small explosions, then one giant one. The last one radiates out at Tony, and he stumbles in the snow, agog and staring. Hot burning metal chunks begin raining into the field like giant black snowflakes, and something not metal spears into the snow near where he stands. He steps over to the smoking, raw thing and understands it is a hand and a wrist, the latter painted with a temporary tattoo of one of T.J.'s lyrics. There's a sweet, burnt odor to it and his stomach turns over, but he has nothing inside that can come out.

He's smelled burnt flesh before. He's smelled all kinds of burned things.

Get a grip, soldier, he tells himself. *Focus.*

Tony bolts back to the meadow's edge, bending down to scoop up T.J. and preparing to return him to the safety of the trees.

Anthony.

Tony halts in place at the voice, which exists in his head—not in the whirling snow around him.

We have unfinished business, do we not?

It's a voice he hasn't heard in years, but it lights something inside him he thought had been seared away long ago.

"Clíodhna," he murmurs, heart thudding. A white pain slices into his gut, and he sets his hand over the wound, fingers coming away wet and slick with blood. His head spins, and he believes for a moment he will faint. Biting down hard on his tongue, he tastes salt and iron. It rouses him again.

Look at me, Anthony.

He faces the field again. The swirling white gale that destroyed the chopper moments ago—killing anyone riding in it—has coalesced into a tremendous crystalline tornado of snow and ice. It hovers in place several feet above the ground, tremendous, terrible, beautiful. Then it takes true shape.

The fae queen fashioned from ice and snow before him is as breathtaking as he remembers from their first meeting on a field in France. But she is not as she appeared through that aperture. Now she is a projection of the weather around them, eyes empty shells and with a flat, unreadable, unearthly visage. She watches him as expanding, crackling icicles fashion her hair from frozen rivers and flowing snow crystals quilt a gown around her body. Her cloak billows and sweeps behind her like a peacock's tail, The Green Place shimmering within her transparency, faint and pulsing in the space where her heart should be.

Four gone, she says, words that form in his mind. *Yet the scales remain unbalanced.*

"You remember me," he whispers. A part of his mind begins counting: Daryl, Ian, the pilot—the cook, Martinique—not five? What of Stef? Was she not on the copter already?

I forget nothing.

He scans the field's edges, looking for the girl. Where would she be? Did she never get to camp? If not, who set off the beacon?

To me, she orders, and he whips around to the fae queen, mind racing.

"Help," he pleads. "Unless you're hanging out to add to your total. Won't be long now. Your bear did a pretty good number on us."

Artio does as her unseen bids her. An icy smile creeps across the fey queen's head. *Are you asking for a boon?*

He knows what this means. He knows he will owe her. But what choice is there? "I don't figure you flew all the way out here just for the hell of it," he says. "Help us."

So I shall, she says in a voice of absolute cold, and then she is on them.

The Truth of a Blue Knit Scarf

The Great Meadow stands empty. Whispering and wailing with the winter wind, jagged pellets of snow swirl and soar amid the open plain, scraping across a landscape freshly pockmarked with smoking bits of black, gray, red.

But it doesn't stay empty. From the distance comes a galloping approach of heavy footsteps. Pawsteps. Artio emerges from the treeline, slowing to a stop at the meadow's edge, her gallop ceasing so abruptly that Stef nearly tumbles off.

Artio goes low to the ground, giving her passenger time to recover.

Stef lifts her face from the creature's musky, oily fur and blinks ice from her lashes. The beast moved as fast as she seemed capable of, and there were times the passing forest trees were just brown blurs.

Here, Stef thinks excitedly. *I'm here. They're here.* She takes in the smoking wreckage, the smell of death, the blood-sprinkled snow: *Not here. Can't be here.*

Because no one is here. And there is no sound but the shrieking and swirling and crackling of ice that bites against her exposed cheeks like tiny mouths. Her heartbeat thuds in her ears. Shivering without her protective bear pelt, Stef steps into the vast whiteness, nose wrinkling from the high, acrid scent of metal and burned rubber. She breaks into a run—or an approximation of one—and beelines to a twisted piece of metal. Touches it, jerks away: Despite the freezing temperatures, it is still warm. There are numbers painted on one side and twisted rivets protruding from the other.

There should be a helicopter here. A T.J. A Tony. Maybe a Daryl and an Ian and a cook named Martinique. All that is here, though, is evidence of disaster. Scanning the field, Stef spies another blackened piece of metal, then a torn leather seat cushion and a dented first aid kit. Half a piece of hoverluggage. Her fingers tremble as she brushes against each one in its turn.

Her heart won't let her believe what her mind insists is so.

A blue knit scarf scampers across the snow like a playful animal wanting attention. She catches it in one hand and brings it to her nose. It still smells like him. Like T.J.

She buries her face in the weave and bursts into tears.

The wind swirls on.

And Artio waits.

PART 2

"A watch is not a world.
A voice is not a cure.
A direction is not destiny."
 — *Clíodhna*

Forest Dreams

Winter comes fast, stays long in the forest. Everything goes to sleep under the snow blanket, but down there, it's dreaming. Come spring—any day now—and it'll wake up again.

Jim said I mumbled and twisted when I was deep in my zzz's, like there was still all kinds of stories going on in my head. That's true of the dreamy forest. It kinda looks like it's resting and waiting for the warm to return. But you look closer, stand with a quilt wrapped 'round your shoulders, stare out your cabin window and go all still, you know different.

Hey Fox showed me how to watch the forest dreaming.

It's just about time for us both to wake up.

Morning's still the time to get things done. Even if it's freezy and stiff and smoking-breath cold, even if the only sounds I hear in the cabin are my breaths and the sometimes creak of the boards—morning's still when I gotta get up.

So I get up. Throw the quilts aside, hop out of Samuel's bed, feet in boots and rush to the cookstove where I load it up and poke the fire alive. That fire goes out entire one night, I might not ever wake up so I learned pretty quick to drink a big mug of water before bed. That makes me get up in the center of the night to pee and then I poke the coals and get it going for another few hours.

I have to think of those things now. It's only me here in the cabin. Daddy—Samuel, I call him now in my head—he's gone. Almost a whole season on my own.

Today's different. Today, things change. Two days ago came Sign No. 1: mountain bluebirds dipping into the trees like pieces of sky. Yesterday the aspen buds came out, pointed like arrows. *Telling you things are wakin' up*, Samuel would say. Sign No. 2.

Sign No. 3 is waiting for me outside. If I see it, then I know winter is ready to be over. Then I know it's a special day. Decision Day. Change Day. Everything Starts Day.

Packed into my coat and scarf and boots and socks and gloves and hat I'm like a big puffy snowman but this is winter in the mountains and *you do not fuck around with it*, Samuel always said. I take my usual path, cutting through the snow and taking off my layers when I get hot and putting them on when I get cold. On the way I pick up the frozen caught animals I snared in the traps. Winter's good that way: keeps food fresh and froze 'til you can scoop it up, so I come home with at least a little meat any time I go out looking.

I wonder once I'm on the Outside if it'll be easier to catch food. I remember going into stores to shop, a whole aisle that was brr chilly and you opened up special cases and the icy smoke spilled out and you grabbed boxes fast as you could. There were big hallways of boxes of food and fresh piles of fruit and vegetables but I might've dreamed that. Seems like something a person would make up.

I'm leaving, see. It is going to happen.

A few minutes on the path and I pass by a group of white birch trees and I count 'em: seven. Always seven. Gil's number. But they're minus Gil. I told him to go, and he went and it was that easy and it was that hard. Past months, I've seen his trees showing up here and there and everywhere and usually there are even those little blue and yellow flowers poking heads out of the snow. Harebells. Primrose. First, it scared me a little, like he was following me. But since he wasn't with the trees I actually felt like he was sending me a signal. A ring-ring phone call. I'll have a phone again Outside. I might even have two. And when someone calls I can pick up or I can ignore it. I don't pick up Gil's calls. I don't say, *Hello*. I don't say, *I miss you, too*. He's not my friend anymore. I'm not sure he ever was.

I'm almost at my next line of snares when I spot a funny splash of orange-red sitting on top of the snow crust. The fox sits, small black paws pressed together in front of her.

"Hey, Fox," I say.

Hey Fox shows up a lot, too, ever since winter hit and I came back from the cave to the cabin. First time I saw her my brain went to a goofy name—Frances Fox—but I stopped there. That's a game you play with your brother so the scary new place you landed in feels just a little bit friendly. I don't play games anymore. I'm not a kid. She's not Frances Fox. She's just an animal, prolly a hungry one. I've seen foxes before but she's the first one who seems to see *me*, with her fire-colored sleek face and topaz eyes.

It's good to be seen. Makes me remember I'm real.

Hey Fox screams at me, a big high-pitched yowl that sounds like a woman in pain. Then she goes low against the snow, nose pointed at the ice. She goes this way and that way and then she makes a giant bounce (*leap!*) like I used to do up on the cliff ridges and (*wham!*) she's headfirst into the icy snow, buried up to her shoulders. Her back half wobbles.

I laugh.

When she comes up out of the ice there's a mouse in her teeth, squiggling around. She bites hard and it stops. A drop of blood hits the cracked snow and she looks at me again, that fire-and-snow fur waving in the breeze, her fat fluffy tail out straight.

"Have a good breakfast," I say, and wave.

With a flick of her tail she's gone into the trees like I made her up.

My next line of snares is clear so I wipe away the snow and set them up all hidden again, and then my glove catches on something. It's an old snare, one I never put out. Prolly neither did Daddy or even Jim: It's rusty and barbed and twisted. I pull it out of the ground and wrap it in a cloth in my pocket. Prolly I'll bury it back home.

I'm 'bout to stand up again when just off to the side I see it: a burst of green. A small tuft of grass, poking out of a melty bit in the snow. I put a hand over my mouth and I grin and grin and grin.

Sign No. 3.

"Happy birthday to me," I say, and I hurry back home.

I forgot when my birthday was a long while back. Daddy—Samuel, I mean— didn't do birthdays with us, not really. He just made up shit, and it sounded like shine-o-la. Jim's birthday was the first snow of the year. Samuel's was the first day we went swimming when it was hot. And mine was the first day we knew for sure that spring was on the way—birds, buds, and grass.

I spend the day making cake. There's a whole treasure trove of things in the root cellar under the bed, and I dug into that weeks ago. I pushed the bed to one side and climbed into the freezing dark underground and picked through all the things we weren't ever allowed to touch. Underground was Samuel's Just In Case place of things he earned from tracking—cans and jars and preserves, boxed mixes and dry milk and powdered eggs. Well, Just In Case came and she looks like me and I take what I want. It's all mine now.

I have so much.

There was more than food down there, too. There were trunks of clothes all labeled with names and ages on them, for all three of us. There were grown-up books. And there was a metal locked box that had no name or anything on it, just looked like something you'd put tools in. I picked it up and shook it and the insides made swishing noises, not banging ones. I brought it upstairs and left it on the counter.

Samuel was so good about pretending there was no Before for us in the woods. That we came here and were born all over again. But when I finally opened that box I saw it wasn't true.

The cake comes out of the woodstove burny on the edges and soft and gooey in the middle but I don't care: This is my cake. I leave it by a cracked window and find a recipe for frosting in a book and slather it all on so there's almost as much frosting as cake. Then I take a bag of M&Ms and make a big "18" on the frosting and wedge a thick candle in the middle and light it. The cabin smells like happiness.

I hum the happy birthday song to me since nobody's here to sing it xcept me. I listen to the cabin shifting and the boards rubbing against each other and I want to make a wish and blow out the light, xcept something goes dark inside me. It feels very empty in here and I wonder—not for the first time—if I really even xist. If Hey Fox didn't look at me sometimes, I wouldn't know for sure. My eyes get blurry so I quick blow out the candle before I get all weepy. I get weepy a lot these days.

I eat some cake and I take down the metal box again. It's been opened; I know what's in it now. But I like to look at what's inside every once in a while. I sit at the table and pull out the contents and touch each one carefully, like Gil once did with my backpack things. There's a journal and a wallet with a California driver's license for Samuel R. Jacobs that xpired the year we came here and twenty-five bills with a 50 on them that are old and wrinkly and a little soggy. And a photo, a square picture with funny scalloped edges of a boy and a girl and a man and a woman standing 'round a car on a street in a sunny neighborhood. I know who they are, or I know who they were. Half of them are dead. Prolly most of them.

I don't look at it too long. I never do.

But the night I read the journal I did it all in one sitting, on a day that was the coldest ever and the snow was piling up so hard it took an hour to clear the front door when I went out. I made me some tea and ate some stale cookies and read Daddy Samuel's journal like it was a book about other people.

Samuel didn't say much. Most of the entries in the front were long and all about how he found this place and made his plans, but then got shorter after we'd been here a while. Then they got real short and had a lot of questions, like he was having a conversation with the book. A couple stood out: *Now we're here, can we ever leave? J asked if we'd be here when he's 40 today & I had no reply. Came here for safety, but nothing changes. War drags on.*

I wondered if that was the same war Tony fought in.

There was another, later: *L getting big. Needs her mother. Not* her *mother, but a mother. No advice for her. Left the book. Hope it helps.*

Then his writings changed.

Found a cave. Strange sounds, smells. Needs exploring. Will investigate this summer. Leave J, L at cabin, say I'm hunting.

Knew I was right. Samuel found the cave before we "found" it. Lied to us about where he was when he was checking it out. Not the first lie Samuel ever told me, but it's the first one I nearly figured out myself right at the time it happened.

After that page things stopped being normal. The journal dates got further apart. Weeks or months between one and the next. Then when he did come back his writing wasn't flowy and normal; it was like someone else was scratching out the letters. I had to read the jagged, shaky words a couple of times to figure out what he was saying.

Saw cave again: Unnatural. I hear my name again and again. Makes me tired inside, weak. Strange smells come from deep inside. Why so warm?

Later: Flashlight tells me the cave goes quite a ways back. Never gets cold. Just that breeze. The bread smell. Had to turn back, felt sick.

Across one whole page: *HUNGRY*

Another page: *Spent whole weekend in cave. There's something back there but no light reveals it. Calls to me. It wants something. Got sick twice but kept going. Had to. Warm breeze all over me, needing. Wanting. Pulling—like sipping from my insides. Draining me. Tripped and fell and when I woke up hardly could walk. Disoriented. Found my way out by sheer luck. Don't want to go back but I must. Will bring J, wall it off.*

Then across two whole pages: *THE WAY IS CLEAR.*

That froze me up. That's what I was told to say, to make my abracadabras. Words Gil gave me. I raced ahead to the next page.

We are all damned now.

A big space, then more: *Took J to cave to help. Always fighting me. Won't listen. Never listened. Went inside but it pulled at me—needing. J pecking at me, little bastard, always wanted to know when we're leaving. Knew we never were. Wanted me to say it. "The way is clear," I told him and shoved him deep inside. "Go."*

Swore at me. I pushed him in further and he turned on me and—

So many rocks.

The wind changed after that. Like a sigh. Grateful. Swirled all around and pinned me on the wall and took from me. No sipping this time. Drinking. Pissed myself. Felt like my mind would turn inside out. Screamed and screamed and then—it stopped.

Ran outside. Waited by fire for J to follow but—no. He won't. Too many rocks.

Very tired now. Not myself.

I flipped the pages, came to the next one and it was stained and wrinkly. Smelled a little like the whiskey Samuel sometimes drank. *Showed L the cave. L listens. She will obey.*

And I did.

I started to put pieces in my head together, the way Stef did with pieces of her watch.

Samuel found the cave.

Samuel found something bad in the cave.

Samuel brought Jim to the cave and they had a fight.

& Samuel waited for Jim but Jim never came out of the cave again.
So prolly Jim is dead. But maybe he isn't.
Samuel took me & we started trying to patch that cave up. Every summer.
& every time the cave made me a little sick.
But it would not stay closed up.
I am never going to know all of Samuel's story.
But now I know some.
What is in that cave?
I don't think I'm brave enough to find out.

I flipped to the end of the journal but it was all blank after. He didn't put down dates and I guess I don't really know what date it is anyway.

I went to bed after reading that and didn't get up for three days. Xcept to feed the fire. 'Cause I didn't want to die. I wanted to live. I had all these questions and the one person who could answer me was dead and he was dead because of Artio. More than ever before, I wanted to kill a bear and xcape the woods and finally, finally go Outside.

Because Inside was crazypants.

Now I'm standing in front of our window with the quilt wrapped 'round me, shoving pieces of cake into my mouth when Hey Fox shows up again. She sits in her formal way, black feet out front, head turning this way and that way like she's showed up to take me out somewhere.

I grab a chunk of cake and toss it into the yard. She walks over to it with gentle, tiny steps, so light she barely makes a noise in the snow, tail out straight and ready to flee.

She's beautiful. Once after watching her in the yard I ran into the cabin and tried drawing her with pen and paper. I'm no artist. But I was trying to capture a little piece of her that I could look at and touch any time I liked. The real fox was out of reach, but this one I hung on the wall and talked to, from time to time.

Hey Fox, I would say to the drawing. *Think the stove needs fixing?* Or, *Hey Fox, I might be getting a cold. Can I have one of our apples?*

She always agreed with me.

Hey Fox is nearly to the piece of cake and has her jaw opened to take it when she sees me looking at her. Our eyes meet. "Hey Fox," I say. "Glad you came to my party."

When I wasn't doing every chore possible all by myself every day for the last months, I would lie back on Samuel's old bed that's now my bed and stare up at the cabin roof and make plans. I looked at how the beams crossed one another like lines on a map, dividing things into parts. I put different ideas into different parts of the ceiling.

It was like playing the "what-if" game, but for real. Jim used to want to play that: What if … you were ten feet tall right now? What if … a swimming pool showed up in our front yard? What if … Daddy wasn't here anymore?

He always brought it 'round to that last one and I'd get squirmy and go quiet. Samuel was like the forest. He was always there. What-iffing over Samuel being gone was like what-iffing the trees vanishing and us being in a desert.

I spent hours what-iffing into the cabin ceiling. *What if... I decide to leave? What if... I decide to stay?* I walked through all the what-ifs and left them up there to think about for later. I had bigger unknowns in my life: how I was going to get through the winter, and how I was going to kill Artio. Because even if Samuel wasn't a very good father, I don't think it was Artio's right to kill him. Jim should have done it. Or I should have. But not a bear.

The day Samuel died, Stef and Tony took T.J. and went home and left me behind, and part of me was sad but part of me wasn't because I had a plan. I stayed at the cave another day and made two decisions:

1) I'd get Artio after hibernation. She'd be weak. I'd be strong.
2) I'd raid the base campsite after the snow went away. Too much to carry in & bad weather right now.

After that I went back to the cabin and here's where I've been ever since. Truth: I don't think about the cave most days. I don't think about Blueberry Cliff much either. I don't even think of Jim and Gil and all my questions. I am doing one thing right now and after that I can think about another thing. And another. These days, I am focusing on that big base campsite, with all of its tools and machines and supplies and tents. It's all mine; I just have to go get it.

So after my birthday party I lay back once more on the bed and I think about what I'm doing next.

How do you kill an Artio? First you have to find her. I don't worry much about that. She finds me a lot. Also, I have my abracadabras—I can find anyone I want. And I have Tony's special gun—I took it from the meadow when I went to get Daddy. I think it might knock Artio flat. But what I mostly need is a really good bow and some really good arrows to finish her off. Metal-tipped arrows. A cheater's bow that costs eight-thousand dollars and practically kills the animal for you.

I know I can get most of those things at the Glampsite, which Stef called it once. There's all sorts of things there, including cheater bows and arrows. Those other two who came with Stef and T.J.—they never went hunting. So they never used them. They're brand new. And they're mine. I earned everything there.

I have so much.

Also, I have nothing.

So that is where my plan begins: With me having nothing but what-ifs, and my plans to make every one of them happen-nows.

I leave at sunup the day after my birthday. Want to catch the whole world Offguard. Should take me four days to get there, depending on snow. Got my daypack, my bow, my arrows, my book. Tony's PEP. Some leftover cake. Just in case.

As I walk, Stef comes to mind. She's been inside it a couple times over the winter, when I wonder how she's doing back in her world. If she's writing more songs for T.J. or if she's learning more about her fix-the-watch unseen. If she has to hide it from everybody else or if now the world is safe for special abilities. It should be. I mean, if most everybody has a little unseen in them, how can it be bad? If everyone has the same sickness, what does it mean to be well?

After I have some lunch, I think of Artio. I hope I'm ready. She's a big animal, bigger than anything I ever killed before. She could kill me. I'm not so afraid of the dying part, but I am afraid of the pain. Do you hurt a lot just before you're dead? Did Samuel feel all the pain he had inside him when Artio crushed him? Part of me hopes so. How long did he feel it? Did it all go away when his soul left his body?

Still, even if the actual being dead part doesn't bother me, that doesn't mean I want to die. I have a lot of things I want to do still—like get out of the woods and see the world and eat more ice cream and maybe kiss a boy who looks like a combination of Tony and Gil. If I die, I don't get to do those things.

But I'm not scared of dying. I'm not.

I take my usual paths, leaping over this, climbing over that, hands and feets and—well, it's just walking. I go mostly where the snow is soft and the grass peeps through, crunching through the crumbly ice and scattering it with my boots. Helping spring come faster. Soon it'll be barefeet season again and I can't wait. My toes feel like they can't breathe in boots.

A woman screams.

I stop so fast I skid in some leftover snow and my arms go 'round and 'round—but I stay up. Then I crouch in case I'm spotted.

The high-pitched yowl comes again. But it's not a woman. It's like someone faking a woman.

Gillie?

Could be, xcept when she got hit by the PEP she didn't make a sound. Not until later, and that howl knifed into me like nothing ever has. It wasn't a sound people could make.

This one's like that.

I lift out of my crouch 'cause I'm not scared of being seen like I once was, but part of me is jangly and worried. I run around searching for the source of the yowl, and while I look it comes once more from my left. Past a big brushy area that's usually green and leafy but is now just buds and spindly twigs. Xactly the kind of place Jim always told me to place a snare. Animals couldn't see it, he promised.

This time the sound's fainter but when I reach the brushy area, I don't see anything. So I do what I haven't done in months: I start to say Gil's words, the ones he gave me to find the way—but I only get a couple out before they stick in my throat.

I see it now.

There's a red splash on the green-brown-white ground, twisted and bent like an acrobat. A real old snare, like the one I dug up the other day, has caught Hey Fox by the neck and left more red in her fur, streaks of blood. Her head is fluffed out and swollen against the metal as she pulls and tries to xcape.

"Hey Fox," I call soft to her. "It's just me."

She tries to bolt, topaz eyes wild and not seeing me. She screams, but a different yowl than the one I just heard. It's choked and thin, but she fights 'cause it's all she knows how to do.

I hold my hands up and go into a crouch, pulling out my xtra piece of cake. "Hey Fox," I whisper. "Let me help you."

'Ventually her hungry overcomes her fear and she calms down. She takes a little step at me, then another. I hear her breathing, see the smoke come out of her nose. There's some blood at her mouth and now I can see—that snare is not ours. We don't use barbs. But she's barbed up well and good and the sharp bits are prolly deep in her neck now. Maybe in her throat.

"Oh, Fox," I say and get chokey.

She dips her mouth down to pick up the cake and that's when I grab her, fast and not thinking and my glove is over her muzzle so she can't bite and I'm pushing her under my arm and she's like trying to catch a fish with your hands, all muscle and moving and I guess I did this wrong but too late now.

I try to fit my fingers under the snare at her neck and loosen it up but then the barbs cut through my glove and even when I get one out there's a gush of blood from her neck. She slips from my grasp and dashes away as far and as fast as she can—and the snare goes taut, yanks her right off her feet and against the ground. She lies there, panting.

We're both splashes of red in the snow now, her with her fur and me with her blood and I don't know what to do. I could cut the snare at the base but it'll be like a necklace on her forever. She'll prolly bleed to death. I could leave her here but that's worse. She'll die slow and starve.

I have a little idea what it means right now to be both shit and shine-o-la. I know what I want to happen, what I wish would happen, and I know what isn't going to happen.

Then I know what is going to happen.

Jim once stepped on a baby bird that fell out or was tossed out of mama's nest. It was still alive when he picked up his big foot and we stared at it, broken and peeping. It hardly had any feathers and its eye was round and swollen and not even open. Jim looked at me a second, then stepped down hard on it one more time.

I shrieked.

It's called the mercy kill, he said. *Sometimes you have to help a suffering thing die.*

I clear my eyes with the back of my hand and stare up into the trees. I look at the wild broken thing before me, a wild thing made less wild because of me—I fed it and talked to it and didn't know how to warn it that the forest was full of bad things people made—and I feel like this is my fault. The snare isn't mine, but it's ours. *People* ours.

Sometimes, the best answer is also the worst answer.

Hey Fox is still breathing hard, tongue lolling out of her mouth. Her eyes are dull but watching me. I unsheathe my knife and stand up, and in one flash I'm on the end of the snare with my boot and the next I'm pinning her down with my knee and the third there's a bright flash of the sun on the knife blade and I draw it across her neck just like I've done with a hundred deer before.

I wait until her kicking stops and then I ease back. Her topaz eyes are open and staring, but there's nothing in them. I try to see her soul escaping, the one Jim told me about, but it's too fast for me. And the world is all blurry anyhow.

I sit down hard in the snow and let the tears fall. All of them, as long as they need. Just like back at the cave. I've been saving them up all winter, and didn't even know it. Makes me tired, all of this weepy sobby slobbery crying, but I just let it go and after a minute it's hard to stop. But finally, it fades until I'm only hiccupping. I'm done.

Then I promise myself: No more crying. Not for anything. Or anyone.

I make a little bed in the leftover snow and pile leaves and rocks on my fox because the ground's still too hard to dig into. I could take Hey Fox with me and put her in the back of the cave like I did Samuel. But that was before I read what Samuel wrote about that cave. So I don't. She stays here.

I stick the snare in my pocket, then stand up, hiccupping and breathing fast. But my eyes are dry. The world is clear.

"Hey Fox," I say to the little mound at my feet. "Thanks for seeing me."

An Unholy Mess

A rustling in the campsite rouses Stef from a chilled half sleep, and she bolts up in bed, listening. More rustling. Shuffling. No voices—but no growling. She fits on socks, boots, and as many layers as she can lay hands on, then grabs her hunting knife.

Probably a raccoon. Maybe a fox, she thinks.

Or rescue.

But she knows it's not rescue. Couldn't be. Rescue, if it were coming, would have landed as soon as the snowstorms abated last September after the crash. Five months later, she knows no one is coming to save her. When they come, if they come, it will only be to confirm what they already know: that everyone is dead.

Artio? Gillie?

Also unlikely. She's seen neither bear nor *sìthean* since the day everything went to hell. Since she went to hell. The bear ferried her back to the Glampsite after she'd finished her meltdown amid the crash fragments in the meadow. Since then, everything magic, or unseen, about the forest has abandoned her.

Well, nearly everything.

The meandering, exploring noise comes again. Stef threads through the cooking tent, which she grafted onto Tony's old sleeping quarters while making repairs. She'd stitched the mangled canvas into protective walls and a roof with woven vine branches, stuffed leftover clothing in the cracks. She's had a lot of time to mod the Glampsite. Quite a lot.

Peeping outside she spies fresh footprints in the snow and smells burning wood—whoever's here has started up the firepit. She grabs a cast iron pan, more confident with both sword and shield, and slips through the tent flaps, picking her way through the newcomer's footsteps.

No one. Just the Glampsite with one newly healthy fire in the pit. The other wrecked tents flap in the breeze. No need to fix everything, even with five months of free time on her hands. Instead she's tackled other repairs: the generator, the solar panels, the water tank. It only needs to be a Glampsite for a party of one. And it needs a party of only one if that party knows how to put the pieces together.

Crossing one foot over the other like she's seen in the movies, Stef advances in a half crouch. A shift in the snow—and she whips to the left, coming face-to-face with a stranger bundled in a thick parka and ragged fur-ringed hood.

"Ha!" she shouts, trying to be terrifying. Only then does she comprehend the nocked bow and arrow in her face.

Stef wiggles her knife but tilts her head. She knows those eyes.

The person lowers the bow and arrow and pulls the scarf down from her mouth. "Oh, *wow*," says Lexi. "You came back."

"Actually, I never left," croaks Stef.

Lexi touches everything as Stef gives her a quick tour of the revamped campsite. "It was all just an unholy mess," Stef says. "I was an unholy mess." *I still am.*

She explains how she fixed what needed fixing, rationed her meals based on what was left from Martinique's extensive stocks, and waited the winter out. "At least I had the generator," she said. "Kept the heat going, most of the time."

Lexi's eyebrows rise. "It didn't break?"

"Did," she says. "But I'm pretty good at taking things apart and putting them back together again. If you recall."

That's only part of the story. The fact is, since she tinkered with the generator, it no longer requires fuel. When it runs it can chug along for hours; when it doesn't run there's nothing that'll get it going except time. When she gets home Stef will either be locked up for magic or win the Nobel Prize.

Lexi runs her hands gently over the stitches holding the canvas together, smiling but not commenting. But quiet is all Stef has had for months and words are bubbling up in her, wanting to spill out. Singing with her music pod has not been enough.

She's about to say something more when Lexi asks, "Why are you here?"

Stef deflates. "Why are *you* here?"

Lexi shrugs. "This is my stuff now. Tony gave it to me. 'Cause I tracked for you. I came for supplies, since I can go find Artio now." She waits a moment. "Your turn."

Stef's lip quivers and she tries to hold it together. All this time, Lexi was just on the other side of the forest. She didn't have to be alone. She didn't have to wait here. There was always a way out. Lexi could take her now: They could be in a warm, safe place in just a day or two. It's on the tip of her tongue to ask.

Instead she says, "Because I can't bear to leave." And bursts into tears.

Lexi watches her a moment, then sets a hand on her shoulder. "We can have cake for breakfast."

Food is a neutral matter they can both get behind, so after Stef dries her face, neither woman brings up any tricky subjects as they bustle around the cook's tent. Stef has rationed Martinique's food caches carefully—just two meals per day—and while she's running low on supplies, there's enough to share for at least one meal.

Soon they're sitting on chairs around the cookstove, spooning warm oatmeal with cinnamon and tough pebbly raisins into their mouths, finishing the meal off with a side of Lexi's half-cooked, frosted birthday cake. Stef wears T.J.'s scarf loosely around her neck and has calmed down. She almost feels normal again, then feels guilty about being anything other than in mourning.

Lexi goes on about her own isolated months at the cabin, how Gil kept away when she ordered him to—and how he sort of listened but sometimes sent trees. She talks about a fox and fixing the roof and all kinds of mundane details. It sounds like a grand adventure she's had, with small stumbles but no real problems.

But Stef is also reading between the lines: Lexi never mentions her father or Jim. And she recognizes the other woman's sudden pauses, the moments when Lexi goes silent and stares into the distance, then comes back to where she left off as if there had been no break at all. Stef recognizes all of that. It's the feeling of being strange to oneself, of nearly—but not completely—being crushed by aloneness.

"Wish I knew you were out there," she tells Lexi during one pause.

Lexi nods, pushing her spoon around in the empty bowl. "I needed … I *wanted* to be alone. For a while." She looks up. "I never was alone before."

Stef meets her gaze. "Guess I never was either."

"It wasn't … bad," says Lexi. "It was right. Until the day I didn't have new thoughts in my head. I woke up one morning and it was like I'd dried up inside." She picks a raisin from the bowl. "Like this." She pops it in her mouth and they look at one another for a long beat, hearing the breeze rustling in the branches around them.

Stef holds out her hand, and Lexi holds it back, just for a minute. They smile.

"So," says Lexi, releasing. "Your turn. Where's everybody else? What went wrong?"

Stef's smile fades and her eyes burn. "Everything."

As Stef tells Lexi, it was her grandmother's watch that saved her. Stef doubts she'd have lived through those first weeks of grief and fear and cold, darkness and worry and hunger without it. That first night she shivered for hours buried under blankets on Tony's old bed, but the watch's light burned bright and warm, like a tiny animal she could hold to her heart. Clutched in her hands, the heat from the watch and the steady tick of its heart reminded her that she was alive and that she would get through all of this. The next day, she wound the watch afresh and located a pen, making a single slash mark on the canvas tent: day one.

She could do a day two. Then she could do a day three. Beyond that, Stef did not think.

In time, the panic receded. It never went far, but she started to be able to think rationally, and the watch reminded her that she had the power to make the Glampsite whatever she wanted it to be. She'd repaired a watch and a tent, so maybe she could try out more comforts of the site. Her days filled with to-do lists and fix-it projects, and that allowed her not to face the darkness she felt brewing in her soul.

She missed T.J. fiercely. At first all she wanted was to hear his voice. He could be speaking or singing or bitching or moaning, it didn't matter. Then she missed the personhood of him—they'd always been together, so close, and it was strange not to have her shadow just steps away. But in time even that began to fade, and the more distant it became, the more guilt-ridden she felt. Mere months, and her best friend and brother was nothing but a memory to her.

Yet when she examined it closely, that wasn't precisely true. Sometime at the turn of the year—after she had almost ninety days marked in pen on the wall of Tony's tent—she discovered something new: She did not *need* him every minute, every day. She was doing just fine without him, without Tony—and without music.

It was a strange, nerve-racking concept. *Without him, who am I?* she wondered more than once. *Who is—what is—Stephanie Holliday? What does she want?*

She wasn't sure. Not yet.

When she finishes telling Lexi all of this, her oatmeal is cold and congealed in its bowl, but she eats it up anyway. Lexi's wide eyes blink, and she straightens in her seat. "Well," she says.

"Well, what?"

Lexi tilts her head. "Do you want to know what I think?"

"Lexi, I haven't had a chance to talk to *anybody* for months. Please, for the love of everything, give me an opinion that's not my own."

The young woman grins. "Nobody ever wanted my opinion before."

"Trust me. I do." Stef nods. "Spit it out."

"T.J.'s not dead."

The small piece of hope inside, the part that's been in denial all this time, turns wary. "Wait, what? Do you know something?"

Lexi shrugs. "Nothing for sure." She zips her coat and steps into the frigid afternoon. "C'mon, follow me."

The breeze has died and the world is still. Lexi stands there, breathing deeply. Three birds streak through the sky above, dark dots against an azure sky. Stef and

Lexi amble to the firepit, which has gone low. "Look 'round," says Lexi, holding her arm out.

Stef sees nothing out of the ordinary. Most of the campsite is still in shambles, broken poles standing up into the air, flaps of canvas peeled back like skin. It's tidier than when she first arrived after the crash, but mostly she's only made it expedient.

"What did this?" Lexi asks, eyes narrow.

"Storm," she says, vocalizing what she's always assumed. But saying it aloud sounds ridiculous.

"Mmm," says Lexi.

"Artio?" Stef has not told her that the bear showed up to give her a ride to the meadow and back—and does not offer it now. She does not believe the bear destroyed the camp, even if it physically could.

"That's closer," says Lexi.

"But not correct," says Stef.

Lexi shakes her head, running her hands over one of the wrecked tents thoughtfully. She turns, and her eyes survey the site again. She stares over Stef's shoulder into the far distance, and part of her mouth cocks upward. "Close as in—"

"Magic," says Stef, realizing. "Gil. But Gil didn't do this. I'm sure of it."

"But he might *know* things." Lexi lifts her chin toward a clutch of birch trees with glowing bark that has emerged from nowhere. A snow-free patch of pine needles encircles their base. Stef is positive they were not there last night. Or even ten minutes ago.

They walk to the trees and Lexi reaches out to one trunk with a bare, flat hand, caressing it the way she touched the tents a moment ago. "These are Gil's," she says. "His trees. He's left them for me everywhere I've gone, all winter. He's never there. But it feels like he's calling to me. Like a phone is ringing."

"Well," says Stef, "maybe it's time to pick up the call."

For All That Bodes Well

I'm pretty sure I don't want to see Gil or Gillie, but something about this Glampsite makes me quivery in my stomach, the way I used to feel when the Ghillie Dhu would show up out of nowhere. The whole site hums without me saying abracadabras, glowing and fading, glowing and fading. I think that means there's been magic—unseen, I mean—here.

Gil once told me about traveling between my home and The Green Place. Said there were these *worn-up* places you could slip between, if you knew how to look. If you were invited. I don't know what one looks like xactly, but the way the Glampsite now pulses as if it's here and not here at the same time, I'm starting to think this might be a worn-up place. It wasn't special when Stef and her friends first arrived, but she's spent the last months doing magic all over it.

There's something about this forest that changes people. No reason it can't change places, too.

Gil will know. That is why we have to find him. And I want to help Stef. I've actually got this funny new jumping-around-inside-my-body feeling of xcitement now that I know she's here. I'm happy to see her big smile, the one that makes me feel like I just got wrapped up in a hug. She gave it to me after I pulled down my scarf earlier and it was like the sun coming out.

I still have my important plans. I need to:

1) Get the bows and arrows.
2) Use my words to find Artio.
3) Use all the arrows and bows and maybe the PEP to finish Artio off.
4) Use my words to xcape the forest. Finally.

I want to get started *now*. But it's not yet full spring. Artio is probably deep in her zzz's and a lot harder to find. I could grab what I need and go home and make more plans in the cabin but—I also look at Stef and see how worried she is about her friends. They might be all dead in the meadow. But I think that's not so. Gil wouldn't let that happen. Not if he could help it.

Now that I've read Samuel's journal, maybe I have a question or two for Gil myself. There are things I am in the dark about. Maybe those are things I need to dig into before I go out hunting again.

I take a seat on the pine needles inside Gil's C-shape of trees and Stef joins me. Nothing happens. I don't know how you're supposed to answer a call from a *sìthean*.

"Gil? Gillie?" I say. "You there?"

Nothing.

Stef's watching me with big round eyes. I wonder how long we'll have to sit here. 'Course, what if Gil has no answers? And if he does show up—can I even look him in the face?

"Well?" asks Stef when a few minutes go by and nothing happens xcept we start getting cold again. "What next?"

I play with some pine needles. "I have no idea."

"You're a terrible detective," she says. "Sure-outta-luck Holmes."

My jaw gets tight for a second but I hear playing in her voice. She can be like Hey Fox was sometimes, dancing around something even when it's all serious. "I'm kind of new at this," I say. "I'm kind of new at a lot of things."

She goes quiet, then springs up with a question. "When was the last time you saw Gil, anyway?"

"When Samuel died."

"Samuel—oh, right. Hmm."

"I told him to go away. He—he knows things he's never told me. About Jim. About Dad—Samuel. We're not friends now." My voice goes wobbly and she puts her hand over mine and I stop tearing up pine needles.

"Tell me how you met," she says after a bit. "I never heard that story."

So I do.

Like I tell Stef, I was prolly twelve when I first met the Ghillie Dhu. It was the winter after Jim left us, and I was working xtra hard to be xtra helpful with Daddy. With Samuel. I worked more around the cabin, laid more traps, made sure everything was ready when the snow came.

I had one goal before I turned thirteen: to bag my own deer. I was getting to be a woman, sort of. I could carry more and do more and I wanted to help. I spent hours what-iffing into the ceiling from my spot in the loft, trying to figure out how to take down a deer solo. I pictured myself running home one day from a kill carrying its heart in my hands.

I was fast and sure and true, I would tell Daddy then.

I love you even more now, he would say.

Finally I was ready and one morning in the late of the year I slipped out before sunup. The snow was hard-packed and icy, and the day promised more. I sniffed at the air and figured I had a few hours. So I ran off into the inky dark and tramped over the white ground with my knapsack that just had a cold small lunch, my flint-and-steel for a fire, and the Tupperware for the organs to tote home. I could come back with Daddy to carve up the full kill later.

Usually we got to the Great Meadow and struck out for game to the right, but I decided that morning to hook left and lit out for unxplored areas. An hour, then two went by and I realized I was pushing my luck if I kept trying for quarry. Snow was coming.

Then a twig went crack! I went into my deep crouch. I sniffed the air and caught the musky tang of a deer, so I slipped between tree trunks, hunching over. I thought of myself as bark, as ivy, as the forest itself. The earthy odor got stronger but there were no sounds. My hand was red with cold from holding the bow, but my palm was sweaty.

A soft white light flickered off the main path.

I darted between some pine trees and came to a hard stop: There was a stand of bright birch trees, and the pine-needle floor at their base. No snow, just a cleared-out area like the one me and Stef were sitting on at that very moment.

Behind me, I heard a stirring sound, so I whipped around with my bow up and arrow nocked. The deer was bounding away from me in that zig-zag hop-skip that made aiming hard, but this was my only chance so I drew the string back.

Dinnae, came a voice and I was so startled I released. The arrow flew wild and vanished into the night.

My hands were shaking and for a minute I couldn't move. I nocked another arrow and pulled, turning to the birch trees—but then I saw him. This young man in the center of the trees, arms wrapped round his knees.

Ye won't shoot me? he asked, cocking his head. *Wouldnae be sportin'.*

I didn't lower the bow. *We can't eat you.*

How d'ye ken that, wean? All his words sounded pushed together. *I might be tasty as an apple.*

I laughed, forgetting I was supposed to be mad, and a flake of snow landed on my nose.

Come and be welcome, lass, he said. *Set.* He waved me in with his long fingers. *'Tis near to snowing, an' ye won't be home before it covers all. Best be safe here.*

That was so: The sky was now grayish white and more flakes were hitting me. *Who're you?*

Ghillie Dhu. He thumped his chest once. *But ye can call me Gil if ye like.*

He was warm, not like a fire but like—well, it made me think of when my mom hugged me. I missed that. So I took a step forward but Gil held up a hand.

The weapon stays, he said.

I was crushed. My bow and arrows would get ruined if they ended up buried in snow, and it took a week to make a good bow—even longer to get it seasoned right. "Really?" I asked.

He nodded, and blades of green grass you never could see in the forest in winter fell from his cap. *'Tis the price ye must pay*, he said. *For all that bodes well always an exchange must be had. Ye ken?*

So I sighed and wrapped my jacket round the bow and arrows and put them near an oak trunk. The wind slashed into me so I reached out for Gil's hand and—

—was yanked inside.

It felt mossy and earthy inside there, smelled like we were sitting in a hole, but that was Gil. He handed me a leaf filled with tea and I took a sniff, then drank it all down. It was so warm and smelled like flowers, and I was all heated up in a second.

Ye came to hunt, he told me and we sat on the ground. I put my knapsack to one side and took off my sweater. *But ken that isnae how 'tis done in this part of the woods.*

What isn't done?

Death, he said. *Willful an' unnecessary death.*

We have to eat, I told him. *I wasn't doing it for fun.*

Didnae yer Da bring home a stag not a week past?

I stared at him, wondering how he'd known. Meanwhile, Gil reached for my knapsack and plucked at the zipper.

What are you? I asked.

I havenae said? Gil thumped at his chest again. *Let ye be satisfied that I keep watch in this part o' the woods.*

What's special about this part of the woods?

He flipped the zipper pull back and forth. *An' for what is this toy? I should like to know what ye carry in your sack.*

He was strange, but he made me giggle. *I'll tell if you tell.*

'Tis a bargain then, he said, and held the pack out.

Gil waited patiently while I pulled out the sandwich, the flint, the cookies, the apple. He picked up each thing and gave it a good look-over, then set it on the ground again. When he was done, he had a row organized from smallest to largest.

He leaned back on his hands and explained: He was of the woods. Visiting for a short time from what he called the bright and green place. His true home. He had many in-between spaces in many birch groves all over the world, and all he need do was step into a tree back in the green, bright place and out of another wherever he wished to be. This day he had only planned to watch the snow—until I came along. Now I was in his keeping and would remain safe.

So nothing dies in this part of the woods without your say-so.

Nae, wean. I care for what I can, else is up to the way of the woods. Trees guide me where to go next. Trees speak to me. He patted one of the birch trunks.

Something about his bumpy voice made me feel sleepy, and my eyes kept trying to close.

Now, he asked. *Will ye share the apple?*

I didn't want to. I was still a kid and didn't share anything well and apples especially were pretty rare. I wanted to bite into the red-and-yellow skin like eating the last bit of autumn.

You can have some.

Aye, he said, and ate half with one bite—core and seeds and everything. *'Tis very fine, an' very long since I have had such a fruit.*

He seemed to love it so much, his face all bright oranges and yellows, that when he offered the second half back I pushed it at him. *G'wan,* I said and curled up on the needles and went to sleep. Snow fell around us but nothing ever touched our bodies.

I was there in that small magic place for three nights as snow fell. It made a wall around us, it went so high. I slept a lot—Gil said that was usual when he met people. I could stay awake with him maybe two hours before I had to nap again, but when I woke up he always had my food for me, even if I already had eaten it. I always gave him the apple.

When I was awake, Gil told me of his green bright place inside the trees. How it was a forever-going-on place, a place where all a newcomer might see was a field of bright soft grass. But then there would be a great tree, and then another. Or a mountain or a lake. Whatever the visitor imagined would appear, eventually. Mostly. In that place time took great deep breaths and released them only slowly—a moment in that world was a long while in this.

'Tis a world separate from this one, though we are joined, he said. *Yet there is a crumbling in the wall between. May not bode well.*

So there'll be an exchange? I asked.

Gil nodded, but did not smile. *Aye, without a doubt.*

On the afternoon of the fourth day, he tapped my forehead until I blinked my eyes open. The snow was finished and the bright blue sky peeked through the branches. *Time, wean,* he said, handing me my backpack. *For me an' for ye.* He reached his hand forward and drew back an invisible door, revealing a four-foot-high notch cut out. Just my size.

How do I get back? I asked.

He patted the apple I just gave him. *Put into yer remembering these words,* he said, and gave me my abracadabras. *'Tis our exchange for now. P'haps one day I shall ask a thing of ye.*

So I spoke the words and the trees round me started humming, and a trench opened in the snow to show me the way. I turned round to thank him, but he wasn't watching me anymore. Gil touched one of the trees and curled round it like he was a piece of bark, and was gone.

"He saved your life," says Stef, but I'm almost not listening to her. I'm staring at those birch trees, remembering. I feel like pieces are coming together in my head, as if Stef is making me into a new thing.

She's looking at me like she thinks I'm going to cry, but I'm not. I'm absolutely not.

So many mysteries. If only I could get Gil to show up. Or I could go to The Green Place myself and track him down. Then I could ask about my missing brother. Then Stef would know about her missing brother. And Tony. Then we would all know everything. We could decide what we wanted to do next. And not be stuck. We've both been stuck a long time.

Gil owes us.

I stand and think about Gil leaving me that first time, folding around the tree. It comes to me that I don't have to wait for him to find me. *I* know the way. I reach out and place my hands on the trunks, one at a time. They hum against my palms. When I reach the fifth one, I stand up straight—it's like touching a song. It sings to me, all these voices on top of one another. It's not messy, either, it's beautiful. It's the way in.

Stef is by my side and I toss my other hand to her. She slips hers into it.

"Hold on," I say, my ears all filled up with music, and think about T.J.

I say my abracadabras.

And we are gone, falling, falling.

The Country of the Young

Tony first caught sight of The Green Place when he was on reconnaissance. He and his squad were scoping out a group of farms east of Saint-Pol-de-Léon where locals had spotted individuals wandering randomly in fields, pointing at the sky and snatching clothes off of wash lines. The paths the strangers walked along sprouted vibrant tufts of grass—despite spring still being many weeks away—and they were easy to track until they changed shoes. Tony's patrol split up to cover more territory, with orders to report back in an hour.

In those early days in Brittany, Tony was happier than he'd been in his life. He was where he was supposed to be: doing good work on behalf of his and other countries, as the Peacekeepers were a multinational force. And he was being rewarded for his diligence, moving up the chain of command quickly. That fact pleased his ex-Captain father back home in Tennessee and would have pleased his grandfather too, if old Corporal Garcia hadn't died two years earlier. Soldiering was in the family blood. Tony was honored to carry it into the next generation.

Detouring down a back road, Tony ducked behind a set of birch trees to take a leak. Yeah, he was in the middle of a war zone, but the enemy rarely struck first unless provoked, so he didn't anticipate an ambush. He'd just zipped up when he caught sight of a shimmer in the air, like heat rising from a summer tarmac. Only there was no road here, and it was February in Northern France.

Squinting, he caught a light at the center of the shimmer and stepped forward to get a bead on it. His compass was swinging wildly, and the GPS chip behind his ear emitted crazy lat and long numbers. He buzzed his remote mic and got static. His legs felt wobbly and his heart seized up as he took careful steps toward the light. It called to him.

It was an aperture; he knew that immediately. Or, as some wag in the field had dubbed the strange partings, an air hole. It was how fey traveled into the real world. Tony saw them all the time; he had a talent for locating them. But he'd never been there when a fey came through directly. They were always stationary, illusory things, as if someone had painted on the air.

In that moment he should have marked the closest tree with paint they all carried for such purposes and doubled back for an assist; instead, when he looked a third time, it seemed the phenomenon was expanding and contracting like a mouth.

Come to me, it seemed to sing. *Aaaaaannnnntttttthonnnnny.*

He peered closer, and there she was, on the other side. The *sìthean* stood in the middle of a great field of waving green grass beneath a sky bluer than a baby's eyes. She did not pop into existence like the culmination of a child's trick; nor did she materialize from thin air. It was as if she had always been there, just waiting for him to turn his mind in the right direction. His heart stilled.

Tony was no poet, but seeing her he wished he could be. Wherever his eyes fell—on those high cheekbones and narrow chin, the almond-shaped eyes of piercing green that shifted hue from moment to moment, to her unruly wavy flame-colored hair that seemed to come with its own gentle breeze riffling through it—he had to shift his gaze a moment later, as if staring into the sun. His eyes settled on the long red dress that flowed around her curves, blossoming into a bell shape near the ground, and he envisioned what it would be like to trace those curves with his fingers. Then he couldn't resist and was taking her all in, her ears jeweled with glittering raindrops that never fell; her hands, long and tapered into pointed nails; her feet, covered in embroidered satin slippers with images of horses, rabbits, and foxes dancing across them. Three iridescent birds—one cobalt blue, one sunshine yellow, the other hunter green—circled the air around her head, sometimes settling on a shoulder only to dart away a moment later.

Greetings, Anthony Garcia, she said to him, approaching the opening. Her voice was in his head, not in the air between them. *Your face pleases me.*

He nearly threw himself through the air hole, checked only by his Peacekeeper training. This was the enemy. Their home was poison to humans. Their food was an entrapment. They were never as they seemed. They lied as easily as they breathed. All the lines drilled into him from training flitted through his mind, and all held the substance of cobwebs.

He also knew specifically who she was—his handbook had been thorough. No one was precisely sure what fey leaders should look like—folklore documents might be highly specific but they contradicted one another on nearly everything—but the presence of her birds solidified it for him: Clíodhna, one of the banshee queens. Goddess of love and beauty. Basically, Venus with the ability to scream you into death if she so chose. Ultimate Payoff Target, Level A. Recommendation: Do not approach without highest level clearance and dedicated armor. He knew he should aim his PEP through the hole and fire, then follow through with plasma. *Shoot when the target presents* were his orders.

But he didn't shoot. It was unimaginable to hurt a thing of such beauty, regardless of orders. There were rules. She was not trespassing on his land. She was on her own, speaking to him on his own soil. His pack felt heavy, his PEP a lead weight in its holster.

"I love you," he said out loud, which was absolutely not what he meant to say. It was not a phrase he was accustomed to saying to anyone. A hot flush spread through his body.

She laughed a chiming sound. *That is a good start, Anthony, but perhaps we can speak of it later. Time is passing for us both, and we must address important things first.* She blinked prettily at him. *Would you come visit me?*

His throat blocked. *I would like nothing more on earth*, he thought in that moment. But he was rooted in place. The rest of his unit would be along any minute. "Not now," he said, the biggest lie he had ever told.

Then I will explain, she continued, words sliding smoothly across his mind. He was looking into a place many called Tír nan Óg, she explained. The Country of the Young. The Other Place. The Green Place. The Land of Promise. It had as many names as a person could dream up, and all were correct but none fully accurate. And slowly, it was being eaten alive by a force they did not understand—like paper being burned through. Once it had been endless. Now it was finite. So her kind were leaving, leaking into a world on the other side that at first also seemed infinite, but which was proving deadly.

"We thought you were invading," he said.

She was silent a while. *Some of our kind delight in the idea of invading the world of men; they feel we could rule your kind if we chose. We disavow such troublemakers. Invasion is not my desire. Preservation of the divide between our worlds is.*

"My higher-ups would agree." He blinked. "Did I mention that I love you?"

She smiled briefly. *Please concentrate, Anthony. Our world is dying, and we know not why. Our lands and our powers recede daily—leaving only your world behind. Some of our folk have panicked and departed; others are vowing to start a true war with humans if the assaults on those of us who flee continue. Speak to your leaders. Tell them to speak with me. Most of us do not want a battle; that course does not turn out well.*

"Come on over here," he said. "I'll give you safe passage."

Best if we find a neutral ground, she said. *Tell your lords. Then find me.*

"How?"

She smiled and his heart raced. *Peer inside,* she whispered. *Find your unseen. You have a way of locating our worn-up places. You will succeed, when you are ready.*

"But I'm nobody," he said. "I'm not some kind of hero."

No, she thought at him. *But you will do for now. And you are not our first effort at such contact. This decision took us far too long to come upon. We do not—we do not rule as you do. And our time is so different from yours.*

He was aware of that; the ratio, some said, was that a full hour spent in The Green Place equaled a day in the real world. Or it might be closer to a day equaling a month. What he was not aware of until now was that fey bureaucracy existed.

"No one's gonna listen to me," he said. "Gimme something to prove you're serious. That you're you."

She produced a scroll bound in a leafy vine from her sleeve and passed it to him through the air hole. *Your words are difficult for me, but I hope they will be understood. There is a spell within the parchment and may only be read by your leaders. It is not for you.*

"Why should I do this?"

Because I wish it. That is all anyone needs. She blew him a kiss, and the aroma of roses enveloped him in an embrace soft as petals. *Should you succeed, understand there are rewards.*

"I'll try," he said, his insides on fire. "For you."

In the end, Tony would attempt whatever she wished.

And he would fail spectacularly.

After the helicopter disaster, Clíodhna brings Tony and T.J. through to the other side this time amid a whirl of ice and wind, across a barrier Tony can't breach on his own. Burning with fear and fever, the rents in his skin threatening to eviscerate him, Tony has no say in their taking but wonders: *Where is the green? Where is the blue?*

There are no colors here, just an endless world of white, or nothing. The banshee queen deposits his body on a floating bed of the white nothingness. "You will be cared for here," she says. "You are in my palace."

Her voice is no longer in his mind; it rings like a bell amid all the empty blankness. She hoists T.J. in her arms.

"Where—" asks Tony, forcing the word out. "Don't—"

"He is no longer your concern," she says with a royal hauteur he remembers from their previous conversation. Then her features soften. "He will be made well," she adds, and is gone in a flurry of cape and snow.

Dozens of smaller fey swarm Tony and hold him down as he flails, trying to follow. He feels like Gulliver, as helpless before them as that traveler was with the Lilliputians. He expects at any moment they will show him burning pits full of bodies and toss him inside.

"G'wan," he shouts at them, bracing himself, knowing he deserves whatever they will throw at him. "Do your worst."

Instead of killing him, the minions flutter around and cover his wounds with a mélange of aromatic oils and pungent herbs redolent of primrose and pine. They murmur words he can't decipher, running their small hands over his skin, smoothing it into place with whispers and caresses. He sips what is offered and shifts his body as requested. He passes out, revives, and passes out again. He loses time. He loses himself. As his fever abates, he focuses on being the most obedient patient they have ever treated. He needs his strength—and their trust—to find T.J. and to get them the hell out of here.

Through all of it, Clíodhna stays away. He can only wonder what she may be thinking. Does she know what he went through once her aperture closed and he returned to his unit? Does she know what he did … after that? He racks his brain, trying to interpret the seconds they had together. All he can be sure of now is that she is aware he failed to complete the mission she set before him. Whether she knows more—he can't be certain.

In time the small fey attending him trickle to just one or two, then none. He sleeps again, lulled by a blissful silence. It is a relief to have no pain from his abdomen or tickling tiny fingers doing their repair work. He relaxes into the comfortable, cushioned no-space he has been left in—a place without walls or ceiling or even floor, just this cloudlike mattress that moves as he does and supports his every twist and turn. For a long time, though, he is too weak to move much.

Yet everything he wants—or nearly everything—is there at a thought. When he wants some grub or a drink, he only has to think of it and something appears. When he wants a book, one pops up on a small table next to his bed, though it's usually in a language he can't read. Or it's blank. Or it doesn't open at all.

Time passes. Tony sleeps. Tony heals.

And Tony remembers.

After agreeing to Clíodhna's boon, Tony watched as the air hole shrunk and vanished, tucking the scroll away in his vest pocket. It gave off a faint, fluttery heat as if it were a living thing.

Boots raced up behind him and he turned, oddly lightheaded and startled to find himself in near darkness, lit only by the moon. It had been just an hour or so before lunch break when he found the aperture, yet as they spoke it had become night.

Garcia! a soldier called out. Suddenly he was surrounded by helmeted Peacekeepers. One tapped a receiver at his ear and spoke into it: *Located him, sir. Bringing him in.*

As he discovered later, Tony had gone into those birch trees to take a whiz, had a brief chat with a supernatural being, and emerged some twelve hours later. He was ravenous and thirsty and disoriented and had nearly been declared AWOL.

The next morning he reported to his commanding officers to explain what had actually happened, but the accounting was not received as he and Clíodhna had hoped. As he told the story again and again to every CO who asked, he was greeted with snickers and derision—it was a likely tale, clearly invented to cover up his real absence. Everyone thought he had snuck into the nearby village and sat around in the pub getting drunk.

Tony ate the shit they doled out and kept trying. The faster he completed this task, the faster he could hand off the scroll and receive his rewards—which he fervently hoped involved being able to see Clíodhna again. He barely knew her but he loved her, he loved everything about her, and every day without her around was a form of torment. Food had no taste, people were like gray cardboard cutouts.

What baffled Tony was why there was so much disbelief. Fey were part of their everyday life: They rounded up dozens each day and transported them either back to an open air hole or to a holding cell until one opened. Troublemakers were dealt with differently. They had places to … discard them in. But this was an international peacekeeping force stationed in the ass-end of nowhere for this very specific, particular reason. Why was it so difficult to believe that he had been designated as a messenger?

Show the scroll, something nagged at him every time a new person showed up to talk. But every time he held back. He was waiting. The scroll in his vest went dormant whenever he spoke with another officer, and when they left the room it would begin to vibrate again. He believed it would let him know when the right officer came along. He'd received it from a queen. Why would he ever hand it over to a mere captain? A mere colonel?

But as the days passed and they kept him out of the field, under observation in the medical tent, he began to wonder: What if he handed it over and it exploded? What if the "spell" on it was harmful? He could be waiting to place the equivalent of a magic bomb in the hands of a general.

So one night, he pulled the small rolled paper from his inside vest pocket. It was still curled tight and held in place by its knotted vine. He examined it on all sides, peering through the tube, weighing it in his palms. Whatever magic it held could not be seen; it was just a piece of paper and some grass.

Tony toyed with the knot. Then he undid it. He unrolled the scroll, feeling like a town crier about to announce "hear ye, hear ye"—and froze once it was fully unfurled.

There was nothing on the paper. A complete blank. He ran his fingers over the parchment's expanse, feeling not even the impressions a pen might leave.

A trick.

Stunned, he dropped the scroll to the ground, where it dissolved into a small pile of sand.

Trust none of them, he remembered from his training. *They do not think as we do. They are different.*

Something he had not fully realized until that very moment.

The next morning he woke his guard early and summoned the closest commanding officer, giving a full account: He'd been drinking while on patrol, got drunk, made up the whole story to explain away his dereliction of duty. He was very sorry for having wasted everyone's time. *Just please*, he begged. *Don't court-martial me.*

He embraced his own lie the way a drowning man embraces a life buoy, and his false honesty kept him from being booted out entirely. But they did not trust him in the field again and sent him to the pits.

Tony had heard of the pits. As Clíodhna had suggested, not every fey was a willing traveler to their lands, and some were pure troublemakers. Those ones got the EMP and the plasma. Some had to be put down, like rabid animals. That was the purpose of the pits, as he understood it: Fey regenerated quickly, and if they could not be trusted to go back home and stay there, they were killed and tossed into the pits to be burned.

But understanding the pits and experiencing them were two different things, and in the end, the pits were Tony's undoing. Facing the stench and the smell was bad enough—at least they were given earbuds and nose plugs—but seeing the fey in person, held packed in small holding cells, weakened from multiple EMP pulses, made him ill. Thanks to Clíodhna, he knew their story. He could no longer see them as the enemy—not when one spoke to him and asked how his efforts on behalf of the queen were proceeding.

I'm not your hero, he told them.

But he couldn't get the image of those packed cages out of his head. *She asked for my help*, he thought. *And now I'm making things worse.*

So Tony went to the cages one night and made his second and final error: He released the fey and led them into the night. They ran all evening, through into the morning, going blindly in the direction of the English Channel. He reached out for what Clíodhna had called his unseen, doing everything he could to find an aperture that would send the fey back home, but no such escape hatch appeared. In the end—inevitably—they were recaptured. Exhausted and broken, Tony was given two choices: reeducation or dishonorable discharge.

He took the former.

Reeducation had nothing to do with school. The brutal, invasive medical procedure was becoming more common for soldiers in the field: a complete rewiring of the thought process by way of a surgically implanted chip. It was known as a conscience lobotomy by some, a reverse-Clockwork Orange by others. Yet the alternative of a court-martial—a dishonorable discharge and prison time—was far worse. Tony would arrive home with the ultimate stain on his record if he took that route. He would be unemployable.

Worse, he would have to face his father. Better to let the doctors into his skull.

After the procedure Tony was different. Numb. He could stand for hours in front of the massive pits that had begun pockmarking the cleared-out countryside, scooped hollow indentations filled with fey bodies, which they doused in gasoline and set alight. His hate was clean and pure and completely involuntary. It felt instinctual. In time, his body no longer rebelled at the swirling, sickly-sweet aroma rising from the pits; he hardly vomited at all after a week or two.

He could even listen to the discordant, grating music that arose from the dying fey in the pits without the earbuds.

He was a perfect pit master.

If a diminished human being.

When Tony opens his eyes in the vast white room, she is there.

Clíodhna is again accompanied by her iridescent birds, and she's wearing the same red dress he first met her in so long ago. It pools prettily on the edge of his floating cloud-bed. Seeing her there is like being welcomed home but greeted by a hostess whose mood he can't anticipate.

"You are a difficult one to be rid of, Anthony Garcia," she says to him in a silken voice with a foundation of steel.

"Good to see you again, too," he says, wondering at his calm around her. Ever since the indoctrination procedure, just the sight of a fey has made his hands twitchy for a gun. For years, even the mention of magic has been enough to get Tony to go to mental battle stations—he could no more have ignored Gillie in the forest the other night than have turned off his heart. But here is one of their queens, within inches of his hands, and all he feels is calm quiet. The raging anger the witch doctors had implanted in him is gone.

Maybe he's just weak. Probably as he heals, it'll all return and he'll have no choice but to hunt her down again.

Clíodhna flicks a dismissive hand at him, and her birds whirl above her head. "I believe we can dispense with the niceties," she says.

"Fine. But first things first. Where is he?"

"Thomas is with some of my courtiers," she says. "He is well and has been up for some time. As you know, he has the loveliest of voices, full of the most astounding virtues."

Relief surges through him; T.J. is all right. "I want to see him."

"In time."

"We don't have time." Abruptly, he wonders: *Just how long have we been here?*

"No," she sighs. "Nor do we. Your failure has cost us more ground. More lives."

Tony grinds his teeth. "You set me up. That scroll—"

"Was not for you, Anthony."

"It wasn't for anybody, you fraud. It was blank."

Her eyes darken. He feels slapped, though her fingers never move. His neck feels stiff, and it's as if someone is caressing the inside of his body. He wants to squirm—and can't move. His eyes go wide. *Mercy*, he pleads in his mind. *Mercy*.

"I told you the scroll was not for you," she says. "You only *thought* it had no words. It only had no words for *you*."

His face flames; he has suspected he was the victim of his own stupidity for some time, but hearing it from her is worse. "It was never going to work even if the right person read it. It was a shit idea."

She flattens him with an imperious look. "We are unaccustomed to diplomacy, Anthony." Her voice is full steel now, the silk vanished. "Humans typically do what we wish without negotiation. That is not working in this instance. So we must try other methods, with other humans. This process is very slow. It must be, if it is to be done correctly. There are—missteps."

"Like me," he growls.

She stares into the no-space and her birds settle on the bed, looking up at her. It is the first time he has seen them still. He tries to find the rage he accessed so easily on the battlefield. But in her presence it doesn't exist. "I am sorry," he says. "I can try again."

She waves her hand. "We are exploring other avenues. Other possibilities."

He waits for more, then tries to refocus her. "Look, thanks for fixing me. And T.J. But—we gotta go. We gotta get home."

Clíodhna nods once. "No one need stay that does not wish to remain." She blinks at him. "How do you ... feel, Anthony?"

Tony's heart revs. Absent the need to destroy that had been programmed in him, the painful love he felt for her surges again. All he has wanted was to get back here. To live and stay forever. "Better in here." He taps his chest, then moves his fingers to his head. "And up here."

"Good," she says. "You have been made well in more ways than one. Consider that my kindness for your attempt at doing the right thing, once."

"Not the scroll," he says.

"No," she says. "For the other."

He thinks again of what it was like to run with the fey, the tireless escapees, as his chest constricted and the wind burned his throat. He was fit and well trained, but after twenty miles at a decent clip without a real break he was falling over, and they'd had to carry him. "Another failed shot," he said.

"You attempted to carry a greater load than you could support," she says. "But that itself is not a failure."

Tony closes his eyes a moment. It is the closest thing to a kindness she has shared with him, and he wants to remember it. "But—T.J and I can't stay. He's got a life he needs to get back to."

She chuckles. "Such as it is. He may go if he wishes. But he will be reluctant to depart."

He sits up, too fast, and winces. "You're gonna keep him a prisoner?"

Her birds rise up again and sit on her shoulders. "Anthony, you are dull at times. Thomas is a favorite with us all. He has expressed a desire to stay. We have ... given him things. Opened his eyes. He will have to leave his gifts behind if he goes, and that will pain him."

"Bullshit," he growls, but he also knows better. Of course the kid wants to stay. Having all of fairyland shining down on you—that must be like being drunk with no hangover, the spotlight without the heat or exhaustion. "Let him tell me that to my face."

Clíodhna tips her head back and glances skyward as if considering. "I think not."

Tony lunges at her, then freezes in place, every muscle like solid rock. The birds raise their wings collectively and form a shield around their queen. Clíodhna fixes her emerald gaze on him, and gradually his rush to choke her fades. He sinks back into the pillows and realizes: That was not the conditioning. That was him being furious all on his own.

"Your time here is at an end, Anthony," she says. "We are releasing you to your cold world. Thomas will make his own decisions, in his own time."

"Why did you bring me here?" he growls.

"Had we not, you would be dead. You would both be dead. Remember that well."

"We were about to be picked up." It comes back to him—the helicopter. The crash. Fire and black snowflakes. "That was you," he said. "If you'd stayed away—"

"I did not smash your airborne conveyance," she said. "That was no concern of mine. I do not refer to that." She reaches forward, long tapering fingers fluttering like wings at his linen shirt, and rolls it up. Her faint caress and nearness to him light a fire inside he has not felt in years, and his eyes burn as he realizes the truth: She has mended him. Undone what the doctors did. He owes her now, and that is both terrifying and thrilling.

"I love you," he says. It seems the only thing he knows how to truly say to her.

She ignores him, holding him immobile with one hand. He watches her fingers trail down the long pink scars that now stripe his belly. Each touch sends tremors through his body, and he aches in a way that has nothing to do with his injury.

"These were a gift from Artio," she says, releasing his shirt. "A gift to us."

"How?"

"They make you ours now."

Part of him wants nothing more than that—to be hers. But that's not what she means. "How? Can we maybe start over—" He reaches for her arm, trying to caress that luminescent skin.

"*No.*" Her voice a physical force. "That door is closed to you, Anthony. You ensured that some time ago. No. You have been placed under a *geas*. Your healing is conditional. Should you move to injure one of our kind again—if you take steps to hurt any of us in any way, the healing will vanish. All of it. Your scars will split like seams in a coat and you will be exactly as you were when I came to you in the field. There will be no respite a second time, and your own healers will fail to close the claw marks. Consider your scars as a—"

"Leash," he says, fists clenching. "Everything with your kind is a trade. Nothing comes without strings."

She straightens and seems to grow in size. As always she remains breathtakingly beautiful, but there is a terribleness in that beauty now. "We asked you to help," she said. "Instead you turned your failure into fury upon us. Asking that you cease menacing and killing our kind hardly seems an outsize request."

"I didn't have a choice," he says.

She gives him a level gaze and straightens. "There is always a choice," she says. "Consider this your final opportunity to do good. Look for other chances to help us and take them. We shall notice."

"And how do I know when I pass your test?" he growls, leaning forward on the mattress.

"Mostly, you will know when you fail," she says. "Farewell, Anthony."

"What about—" he starts to say, but she snaps her fingers.

"—T.J.?" He finishes his sentence in a wide, green, empty space. He is sitting in a meadow beneath a sky the color of a baby's eyes.

There is no sign of T.J.

All the same, Tony is not alone.

A Dark, Worn-Up Place

We splat down hard on a patch of grass and dirt.
My ears whoosh like I've been underwater. The sound swirls inside me for a few seconds, then fades. I'm on my side, staring at a thick high wall of leaves and when I flop on my back the trees above me tower so high they nearly block out the sun.

I make fists and squirm against the ground. My face is hot and I'm grinning even though I'm tired. I usually am after I say the abracadabras. But I'm so excited right now, I hardly feel it. We made it to The Green Place. I took us here.

"What the hell?" Stef is standing above me, a birch branch caught in her hair. It sticks up like a flag. Her mouth is turning this way and that.

"We're here," I say, scrambling to my feet. "We're on the other side!"

But I'm wrong. I look 'round and there's the firepit and the compost pile and the cammyflage green leaves Daddy—Samuel—and I built. I asked for T.J. and it took me to the cave.

"Oh," I say.

Stef is running 'round the campsite but there's nothing xtra that we can't already see by standing still, 'less we decide to check out the cave and I'm pretty sure T.J. is not in the cave.

Least, he better not be.

So many rocks.

Finally Stef comes over to me, breathing hard and quivery, like somebody plugged her in. "Do it again," she says and it's not an ask. It's a must.

I fold my arms. Samuel was ordery 'round me all the time and these days I give myself the orders. It's like Stef poked me in a soft spot. "Do what?" I ask. Knowing.

Her hands come up like she wants to grab me—but she doesn't. "Use your abra—use your magic. Your unseen. Now."

I wait. She stares at me hard. I'm about to say maybe there are snacks in the cave and la la la when she goes all limp. "Please, Lexi," she says. "Please."

One day I should tell Gil that humans have abracadabras, too. " 'Course," I say. " 'Course I will."

And the way is clear.

Straight into the cave.

Stef pokes the side of her grandma's watch and it bursts with so much light I can't really even look straight at it. She wraps the watch 'round one hand so she can aim it better and we start into the darkness.

There's nothing to see at first. Just our storage boxes and the one remaining cot. We go deeper and deeper and the cave narrows, but there's nobody in here xcept us. Definitely no T.J. I start wondering if my abracadabras are broken. The thought makes me a little sick inside.

A warm breeze reaches out and brushes on my face and I reach up to wipe it away. Last time I was in this cave was when I dragged Samuel's body into the way way back, behind where we always tried to wall things off, and buried him under a big pile of rocks. If the cave sang to me on that day I didn't hear it. My head was so full of bees and anger and sadness I couldn't hear anything.

Today is different. Today I am the person who buried Samuel and the person who read his journal and the person who no longer thinks this is just some funny cave we stumbled across one day. This is a cave that Jim once went into—and never came out. I did not plan to come here again, and I don't want to be here right now. My feet drag over the rocks the deeper we walk in, and my head feels sweaty from all the abracadabras I've done, and it's like I'm trying to breathe underwater.

Leeeexxxxi, the cave sings at me.

I wake up, all bright and quivery.

Leeeexxxxi, it comes again.

"You hear that?"

Stef turns, blinks at me. "Wha?" It's like she's in a dream.

"This cave sings," I say. "This cave is not a normal cave."

"I didn't hear anything." She keeps going forward. Past our Sissy Fuss wall. Into the dark dark part. There is nothing here. No light. No plants. Only rocks.

So many rocks.

"Stef," I say. "This—maybe—we shouldn't go."

She swings 'round and her light flashes into my face. "Why not," she says and it's not a question.

"There's nothing to find," I say. The real answer is too big to xplain.

"According to you, T.J. is in here," she says. The light bounces as she wipes sweat from her face. "That's not nothing."

"But he *can't* be," I say.

"He *could* be," she says. "I have to know. You'd search if you thought Jim was in here, wouldn't you?"

Hearing his name twangs my heart. I never looked for Jim, not once. Samuel said he disappeared and I believed it. We came back here every year and I never tried to look. My cheeks are hot and my heart is going so fast it's in my ears. "This is a bad place," I say. "It's not—safe." I don't know how, xactly. Only from what Samuel wrote. But that was shine-o-la, what I read. He wouldn't put shit into his own journal.

Her breathing is soft in the solid stillness of the cave. "Bail if you want, Lexi. I know you'd rather be out looking for Artio. I get that T.J. doesn't matter to you. But he matters to me."

My insides feel sour. I want to say: *He matters to me because he matters to you* but the words don't come fast enough.

"Still," she continues, "I'd much rather do this together." She holds up her hand so the light reflects on both of us. "I'm pretty much scared shitless. You get that, right?"

I laugh. I don't mean to but it just pops out of me and echoes off the walls. "Me too," I say. "Okay."

The cave goes on, winding and twisting and confusing, deeper and deeper. I wonder if maybe it goes into the center of the entire Earth. Stef picks her way through the thin passage and I keep my eyes on her feet best I can. There are broken rocks all over the ground; I used plenty to bury Samuel but there's more here than anybody could count.

While we walk it gets warmer. I picture how when we landed in the campsite we hit grass, not snow. How the trees were full and the wall of leaves was full of cammyflage. The whole campsite outside this cave was like stepping into summer—not the tail end of winter. The cave breathes, I think. Breathes out and in and keeps everything 'round it warm forever.

I unzip my coat, tie it 'round my waist. I'm finally understanding that these woods I've grown up in aren't *normal* woods. Normal woods apparently don't have Ghillie Dhus and Artios and trees that stay leafy and green even in the deep snowy winter or caves that inhale and xhale. It's like the whole woods is this enormous living thing, and this cave is its beating heart. Or thinking mind.

That doesn't actually make me feel better.

We keep stepping over loose rocks, ducking our heads under the low ceilings. Pretty soon when I glance over a shoulder the light from the cave entrance is just a tiny pinprick in the far, far distance. Then it winks out.

We get to a loose mound of rocks on the floor.

"Walk 'round this," I say 'cause I don't like the idea of stepping over Daddy. We shuffle to one side and my eyes get a little sore and my throat gets thick. I stumble and Stef catches my hand and lifts me up.

"You okay?" she asks.

I nod, and I shake my head. The glow from the watch light paints shadows on her face and her dark eyes are glowy and have bits of gold in them. She's looking at me and I'm looking at her and I reach up and take the birch branch from her hair. I give it to her and she twirls it in her fingers, then tosses it aside.

"I'm sorry about your father," she says. "Don't think I said that before."

Here's what I like about Stef:

1) She says what she's thinking.
2) She's pretty and her hair bounces. Well, it used to bounce more.
3) She listens to me.
4) Her heart is still warm and beating. Mine feels like it's buried under a big pile of rocks. Or ice. Or both.

She puts her arm 'round me and side hugs me. We're both in this tight dark space and I want to squeeze her back in a real hug 'cause I'm thinking: A minute ago the only person in her head was T.J. and it's like he doesn't even xist right now. She put him aside for me. In this minute we're the only two people that xist in any of the worlds we know about. I don't know how she does that, but it makes me feel important. Like I matter.

Like I xist.

"Samuel came back here," I say before we start walking again. "I read his journals. He came here and it scared him and he brought Jim to wall it all off with rocks. But something happened."

I hear her breathing. The light makes shadows on her face. Her eyes are on me.

"Jim didn't walk out of here, Daddy wrote," I say. The words stick in my mouth as I say them. Reading it was one thing. Thinking it another. Saying it makes it real. "He didn't say why. Just—he waited for him and he didn't come."

"Oh, Lexi," says Stef and her voice is soft. "I wish I—"

Stttttteeeeeepppphaaaaaaanniiiieeee, the cave sings.

We're both quiet.

"That wasn't you, was it," she says.

"No."

"It sounded like you." Her voice is tight. Scared.

"I'm right here," I say. "It sings my name, too."

"But—how?"

I shake my head. "It scared Samuel."

"I'm not going back," she says, turning. "It can sing all it wants. Let's go."

She's ordery again but I understand why. She's scared. We both are.

We start going forward once more. I'm feeling strange. There's something in this cave, something that knows our names and calls to us. But it's not a friendly calling. It's like someone who wants you to do them a favor. Asking, but the way a little kid asks.

Leeeexxxxi comes next, and a tired blanket falls over me. I just want to sleep right here, right now.

"Stef," I whisper. "You okay?"

The light stops bobbing. She turns 'round and her face is flat and empty, like it forgot how to smile. "No," she says and her jaw doesn't move. "This place is wrong." Her eyes flash on me and they're suspicious. "Why did you bring me here?"

"We—followed—" but I stop talking. She's the one who wanted to come. It's her fault we're in the dark and starting to feel strangled. "You wanted to find T.J."

"Yeah," she says. "But *you* brought us here."

Suddenly the ground shakes and there's a scraping, tearing sound and we both jump back against the rock walls. It's like everything is shifting around and the roof is gonna fall. Like something is pulling apart. I grab a piece of the wall and think about how Samuel wrote about noises he couldn't understand. But these noises are so much worse and bigger when you're in the dark. Things stop shaking, but after we start walking again Stef keeps looking over her shoulder at me, like she doesn't get why I'm following her. Or who I am.

The cave smell changes. For a while it was just dank and warm and maybe a little bit like bread but that's all gone. This is worse than mildew; it gets into my nose and makes it itch. I sneeze once, twice. Stef coughs. Then comes that ripping sound again—a grinding and a growling—and it's everywhere: behind, in front, above, below, all sides. Like it's part of the rock itself. We hold tight to our walls but not to each other and wait until all is quiet again.

The warm is uncomfortable now; I'm actually sweating. And I'm having a harder time breathing. It's like I've been running for miles and now my breath won't come in. I take long, deep inhales and put my hand on the side of the cave to keep from falling over. I close my eyes and two hot tears trickle out the edges. There is no turning back. We are never leaving this cave, least not the way we came in it.

When I open my eyes again, it's completely dark.

Stef's light is gone.

I'm alone.

"Stef!" I shout and the noise fills up the space, echoing. "Stef!"

Stttteeeeefffffff, the cave sings. Asking. Pulling on me. *Leeeexxxxi.*

There's a cluttery sound of small rocks falling on each other, tumbling and crackling. I reach down and my fingers close on a jagged stone that's as big as my fist. I grab it and stand, ready to strike out at whatever comes for me.

Then the watch flashes on and it's so bright I wince but in that second I see Stef, just a few footsteps from me. She's got a rock in her hand and it's up in the air like a baseball she's gonna throw into a glove, only my head is the glove.

"Drop it," she tells me.

"Drop yours," I say but my hand's shaking. What's happening? I don't want to hit her with a rock. But it's like something got into me and is scraping my insides, whispering *throw it throw it smash her head open and scoop out the insides. Lexi do it for meeeeee.*

My eyes go wide and I take a deep breath. I see Stef's face and realize she's hearing it, too, on the inside. "I don't want to hurt you," I say and I mean it so hard my eyes get burny again. "Not you not ever."

Her eyes go wide and blink. She lets the stone tumble from her fingers. Then she whirls away from me, dashes deeper into the cave, leaping over a low stone wall, and disappears. There's a yelp and I hear rocks crumbling.

So many rocks.

I drop my rock and race over to where I saw the low wall but the only thing I can see now is dark, dark—and a bobbing, swaying light. Stef's watch. It's down below me, wavering. It comes closer and then I see her, one hand grabbing a pointed stone, her hand scratched and bleeding. Her other hand is loose, flailing over a big open empty space. A floor that is not there.

Throwing my hands forward I go onto my belly and grab at her watch hand, bringing it close to the fingers she has gripping the edge of the world. We are four hands together now and I try to pull her up out of the chasm but I'm tired from the abracadabras, tired from walking, tired from being scared. Tired from feeling like something I can't see is draining me, pulling pieces out from my insides every second I'm here in this cave. My hands slip and she grips me tighter, nails digging into my skin.

"I'm sorry," she whimpers. "I didn't want to hit you either."

What is happening to us? I think. There are bees in my head again and my arms are getting sore trying to pull on her but she's not moving. It's like there's something yanking down on her feet.

"Pull," she says. "Pull and we'll go back. We'll leave the cave. I promise."

I try. I try with everything inside me and my arms stretch and burn and I brace my feet on the stones but she doesn't move, she doesn't come to me. My head is aching and I want to sleep and I feel awful in this dark, terrible place I didn't even want to come to. A place that calls your name and makes you want to hit another person with rocks.

A person you really like.

A person you care about.

Maybe even a person you love.

So many rocks, Samuel wrote and I understand now.

"Ah," I sigh and my knees go soft and instead of me pulling on her she's pulling on me and I am rolling forward and we are falling down, our hands tight together, into a world that smells like old, rotting things, where the only light we can see is Stef's grandmother's watch, bobbing and swirling alongside us like a shooting star.

The Unseen

Tony lies flat against the grass in a bright green empty place, deposited there by Clíodhna. The same green bright empty place he saw her standing in years ago when he first spied her through the air hole. It could even be the same spot; the whole place looks the same. Everywhere he looks the grass is the same. The sky is the same. The smell is the same. And she's sent him back here without T.J.

Stay if you wish, leave if you like, he hears her in his mind. *But you will do it alone.*

He gets to his feet carefully, testing the limits on his newly healed scars, and gazes around. This place isn't quite as empty as he'd thought. There's a large spreading tree in the far distance, almost at the horizon, too far to make out details. As expected, a shimmery aperture hangs in midair a few feet from where she landed him, along with a neatly folded package of clothing bound up in a leather strap. Once he steps through, he'll be back in the frozen winter of Colorado and he'll need all the layers of clothing he can muster.

If he leaves.

Instinctively he thinks, *Have to find T.J. first.* But then—*what if T.J. really doesn't* want *to leave?*

Something small moves in the near distance.

A figure is tossing a ball in the air and catching it deftly, just taking one step to the left or right before letting it sink back into its hands. A small backpack rests nearby in the grass. Tony walks toward him and the figure tilts his head and squints. It's not a *sìthean*; it's human. A few more steps forward and the person resolves into a young man, long hair ruffling in the breeze. He's slender, actually closer to gaunt, dressed in a white linen shirt and dark pants, soft handmade shoes. There is a strange shape to his head, an asymmetry that feels wrong. The young man catches the tossed ball behind his back and turns, revealing his entire face. He wears a patch of brown leather over his right eye, and it's held to his head with string.

"Hello," says Tony cautiously. The white ball is sewn together with red stitches and reads "Rawlings" in stylized script on one flap. It's a baseball. A baseball in fairyland.

"'Lo right back," says the young man, and smiles. His teeth are crooked and there's a scar across his forehead, and in that half-second before he speaks again Tony knows exactly who he is, though they've never met and he's supposed to be dead. "How's my sister?"

Jim—the real Jim, not a girl pretending to be her brother—tosses the ball. Tony's barely able to think straight but his hand reaches up and snatches it from the air anyway.

"Nice reflexes," says Jim. "Coulda used those a couple years ago."

Tony's mind slowly unlocks. Of all the places he might have expected to see Lexi's long-lost brother—and truly, that list was pretty short—The Green Place is the least of them. "All due respect, but … aren't you dead?" he asks.

"Rumor would have it," says Jim, cupping his hands for the ball's return. Tony underhands it at him. "Guess I am, for all intensive purposes." He chuckles. "That's what Lexi used to say. Instead of 'intents and purposes.' She came up with her own way of talking, and I quit trying to fix it. I mean, who cares how you talk in the middle of nowhere, right?" He loses the crooked, boyish smile, looks up. "Y'didn't answer me."

"She's fine," says Tony in an automatic tone, still processing. "Least, as fine as somebody can be after her father dies in a gory accident."

"Yeah." Jim adjusts his eye patch. "Not exactly an accident. He was always fulla shit."

The dime drops and Tony flashes back on that last heroic move Samuel made, leaping atop Artio and plunging his knife into the beast's— "Wait." He holds up his hands. "What the fuck's going on here?"

Jim's baseball has turned into an acorn, and he lobs it at Tony. It smacks him in the forehead and feels like a bullet.

"Jesus Christ," says Tony, furious. "What the hell—"

Another acorn.

"I'm gonna bust you—"

"No, you're not." Jim squares his shoulders. Tony figures he could take him but—maybe this isn't the time or place. Maybe Jim falls under the "do no harm" edict from Clíodhna; he can't know. "Act civil and quit thinking you're in charge. Let me show you a thing or two. 'Cause you don't know anything about this place and it's 'bout time you saw it with your eyes wide open."

"I see things clear enough."

"Bullshit," says Jim. "You see what you wanna see. Like everybody who comes over here. They get here and see grass and think, 'Gee, we could use some trees.

Where are the trees?' So suddenly they get the biggest, lushest trees to grow anyplace. You think about a cloud, you get what you think a cloud should look like, but the prettiest one ever. Hungry? You get food and it tastes like nothing you ever ate. But it's not real. It's all a fucking mirage. Or a glamour, that's the right word for it. Underneath ain't so pretty. Especially not recently."

Tony bends down and pulls up a fistful of grass. Each blade is precisely like the other. "Looks real to me."

"They do a good job," says Jim. "Unseen is made for this. But fact is these are beings that are thousands of years old, and they don't eat and they don't sleep and they don't shit and they don't play by any rules we understand. We sent rockets into space looking for alien life, and it turns out we got aliens right here and we still think they're made-up kid stories. Or, at least, we did think that. And what's funny is they think *we're* the aliens."

His eyes are blazing and his cheeks have flushed. His not-so-latent fury is familiar to Tony; it's the same thing his sister contains, this subcutaneous anger. Cut them and they will make you bleed.

"Look," says Tony. "I don't know what your beef is, but I've got my own problem."

"Getting your child-boss back from his new owners?"

That stops Tony cold. "Man, you don't mince words."

"I'm dead, remember?" says Jim. "I don't need to play nice." He pauses, closes his eyes a moment, and lets out a long breath before opening them again. "We've both got a problem right now."

"Hit me," says Tony. "Oh, wait, you already did that."

"Ha, ha." Jim's voice has no tone. "You think you need to talk to your boy. You think you're gonna be able to talk him out of wanting to stay here, but you also know that's pretty futile. I mean, he knows now what you've known since Brittany—you'd give your left arm to live here. With her. Clio, I mean."

"This is a waste of time," says Tony, wanting away from wherever this conversation is heading.

Jim barrels on. "Lemme just dish it out. Gillie owns me. Same way Clio owns you. Same way she owns your boy. The way they all end up owning us, if we stick around long enough. That's the power of unseen."

"Unseen?" He's heard that word but never fully grasped it. The fey he freed from the cages tried to make him understand, but he wasn't ready to hear them.

He chuckles. "Magic. Unseen. Same thing. Invisible. *Dofheicthe.* Things that have no shape or image; they just happen. It's the way they describe the soul." He puts his hand on his forehead. "I'm getting away from the point."

"I was wondering," says Tony. "How about starting by explaining how for all 'intensive purposes' you're alive and dead. What are you, Schrödinger's *sìthean?*"

The ball is back in Jim's hand and he throws it as far as it can go. It travels and travels and eventually disappears into the horizon. It is an impossible place, full of impossible things. Jim sits in the grass; Tony joins him, setting down the pack of clothing he discovered when Clíodhna snapped him back.

"That's amusing," says Jim. The buoyancy is gone from his voice. "See, over here either they charm you into loving this place or they find a way to make you owe them so you can't really ever leave. Right now your boy T.J. is in the charm stage. You were there once. So was I. But break past that and suddenly there's a favor you need that only they can deliver."

"And what was your favor?"

Jim's silent a long moment, then: "I'll try giving you the short version. You know my father kidnapped me and Lexi when we were kids, dragged us into the forest. Or you figured that out by now, right?"

Tony nods. If he didn't before, he does now.

"So, I get old enough, I know this is wrong. We have to escape. Lexi's harder to convince—she's younger; this felt normal to her. We just moved from the suburbs to the woods. Makes sense to an eight-year-old. Anyhow."

Things went downhill fast between Jim—who wanted to leave the woods—and his father—who was equally as adamant that they were going nowhere. Jim would leave but never could find the way out. Every time he returned to the cabin, Samuel made his life hell. Jim went after his father with a knife one night but couldn't do the deed. The next day, Samuel took him out hunting. "We never went hunting together," says Jim. "I shoulda seen that it wasn't about repairing a bond. It was about snipping off a loose end."

Something changed about Samuel after they came to the woods. "He'd always been a little … off with his thinking. He started going away for a few days or a week at a time, and when he came back it was like … there was a little less of him in there. More hollow. He got mad more. Especially at me. Especially because I'd seen through his plans, which were no plans at all. The milk had curdled in his cereal, if you know what I mean."

Tony nods. "But did you see it coming? Did you know he was going to—kill you that day?"

Jim spits at the ground. "Shit. No. Who thinks your *father* is going to do that? Who would ever believe it? Even if he was insane, I didn't think he was crazy."

"So you went hunting."

"We did, but there was a detour," says Jim. "He brought me to this cave. He said we were going to wall off the back, because there was a bad draft, and then we'd use it in the summers for vacation. We went all the way in the back, through this crevice, and I heard—I heard my name. 'James.' Not 'Jim.' Very formal. It sounded like Samuel, but same time I knew it wasn't him. There was something—strange in the cave. I told Samuel he could get his own damn rocks and then—"

Jim swivels his head to one side, and now the misshapen skull reveals itself. His hair has grown over a deep indentation.

"He brained you?"

"Sure did," says Jim. "You ever get hit in the head with something heavy? Not like in the cartoons, that's for sure—though I did see stars. Worst pain I'd ever felt. I went down, hard. Expected to feel it once more before my lights went out for good. But—it didn't come. I passed out. And when I woke up …"

Tony takes a deep breath. He's seen and done some terrible things in his time. He shouldn't be surprised by what bad shit people can do to one another. But to your own *son*? He tries to picture his father, never was an easy man to live with, attacking him. With a rock. In the head. The image just won't come. It's not something a sane person would do.

"So—you died in there?"

Jim chuckles. "Funny thing: I didn't. I woke up and it was pitch black and I had, like, three matches on me. Made a torch with a stick and my shirt and shined it all around and saw—well, a lot of rocks. A whole lot of rocks. I started walking. The cave started singing at me again. I got really weak—maybe 'cause my head was all bloody, maybe from something else, but it came on pretty fast. Last thing I remember was falling on this rock wall and going down, into a pit. I fell pretty much forever."

"And ended up—here?"

Jim nods. "Opened my eyes in this sterile, perfect place with a woman standing over me who looked like she was made of moss."

Gillie, thinks Tony. He has not really thought of the green creature since coming here, and thinking of her now brings on a wave of guilt, not rage.

Jim nods, guessing at Tony's expression. "You two have met. She got me stitched up but I was pretty far gone. ''Tis only fairy thread we have after all,' she said. 'Will fall apart in yer world.' They did what they could but they couldn't send me back. Fairy medicine fixes magic wounds. Not heads bashed in with real-world rocks. She stayed with me for—I don't know how long. Hours? Days? I told her everything, about Lexi and Samuel and the whole business. I drank a lot of tea. And then one day my legs wouldn't work. I could feel myself dying by inches; the rot was creeping up through my legs. So I said to her: 'Please look after my sister.' She promised she would. But she asked me for one thing first."

Tony waits.

"My unseen," says Jim after a moment.

"For what?"

"So that after I died," he says, "I could become Artio."

The Places That I Hide

Stef has never fallen so long or so far before. There's no bottom to this gap in the world. She's not screaming. Sure, she yelped when she first jumped into the nothing and barely caught herself on the tip edge of the world—but now that she and Lexi have tumbled into this great crevasse, there's no voice left inside her to make a noise.

Minutes go by. Maybe hours. She loses track.

Alice fell, she thinks. *Alice fell into Wonderland by chasing the White Rabbit down a great hole, and we're following right behind.*

Or maybe they are falling to their deaths.

There was a stench when they first began falling, a fermenting pungency of rotted weeds and dead things that made Stef's stomach lurch. But that has faded, and as it has the falling has begun to change. There's less absolute dark. More gray. Even a bit of faint washed-out blue, like the side of a barn that needs painting or the sky after a storm.

Stef looks over at Lexi, who has her eyes closed. There are strange marks on her cheeks, charred, evenly parallel lines that resemble burns.

Lexi opens her eyes, stares at Stef. "Your hair," she says, pointing.

"What?" says Stef, unable to fully comprehend that they're falling at what must be terminal velocity and having a conversation. "Bet it's pretty vertical right now."

"No," says Lexi. "It's white. There's a stripe in it."

Well, thinks Stef. *Ain't that a thing.* She declines to tell Lexi about her face. The girl will learn soon enough. "I'm—tired," she says instead. But that's such a pale word. She feels emptied out, exhausted. *Weak as a kitten,* her mother said after Stef battled the latest pandemic virus. It was like that, not an ounce of energy left in her. She's not even strong enough to hold Lexi's fingers, and they drift apart.

"I know." Lexi's whisper is rough. "I know it."

The blue of the sky is resolving and they are falling into it, shifting from pale to rich to the brightest, sharpest cobalt, cornflower, sapphire blues Stef has ever seen and she gasps. They're so much *more* than she could ever have imagined, as if she's been living in a world of only grays and now here they are in vibrant Technicolor.

"We're going to die," she tells Lexi. "When we land. They call it terminal velocity for a reason."

Lexi shakes her head. "Won't."

"That's optimistic of you," she says.

"Think," says Lexi. "Think how you want to land. It's The Green Place we're going to. Gil always says it gives you what you want, when you need it." She closes her eyes again.

There isn't time to chew on that, so Stef surrenders to the falling and thinks about a ground below covered by the thickest, most cushioned grass that ever grew, feathery leaves on which they might land like dew drops on the frond of a fern. Grass that catches what falls and lets it roll to safety.

The ground rushes up beneath her and she arrives.

Stef opens her eyes to shadows and light dappling her arms and clothes and a soft breeze tickling at her skin. She doesn't remember landing, exactly—just *being here* abruptly. In her head she is still falling. Staring into the sky, she gathers herself, watching thousands of leaves riffle among one another, hiding then revealing a brilliant yellow sun behind them like ladies doing a fan dance.

This is a quiet place. The only sound Stef makes out is the whisper of the breeze in the leaves above and through silky grasses, which shift and fall back in place like little soldiers. Each one is precisely like its neighbor, and when she finds the energy to roll over she discovers there are no weeds, no flowers, no bugs. It's like wandering into the first level of a complex Holo Game: the basic template for a perfect world, ready to be built on.

Except there is this tree she is under.

Except she is alone.

Where am I? Where is Lexi?

Sitting up, she gawps at the mammoth oak tree before her as if she has never seen such a thing before. And in a way, she hasn't—this is the largest living creation she has ever encountered, the sort of tree that comes from a dream, with a trunk at least as wide as the Glampsite's footprint. Its muscular branches spread like mighty arms, supporting all the fan dancers of leaves. Three beautiful birds of hunter green, cobalt blue, and sunshine yellow settle on the lower branches and cock their heads at her, watching.

Music ripples from the tree, and a voice croons: "Come. Seek me in the places I hide."

This is not the singing cave. This is the kind of singing that revs her heart. Singing words she wrote—wrote for just one person. Stef's stomach knots and she instinctively finishes the lyric. "You're the one knows I'm alive," she sings back to the tree, voice shaking and weak.

Jesus, he's a tree he's a tree, she thinks wildly—and then there he is, peeping out from behind the expansive trunk.

T.J.

Stef scrambles to her feet, tottering like a newborn colt, and stares. His hair is loose and long at the ears, his eyes are shining. She can't move for a long moment, then hurls herself forward and they catch one another. She hugs him so hard the air whoofs from his mouth.

"Hey, Peps," he says, holding on tightly. "Miss me?"

"You jerk," she tells him back. "Of course I did."

"Well," he says. "Glad you finally got here, too."

Tears prick at her eyes and she swipes them away, then pulls back to get a better look. He looks very, very physically well but they've dressed him like he's got a leading role in a well-financed Renaissance fair, a wide-sleeved green velvet robe edged in tiny shining white gems. He is a prince in it. She suppresses an urge to hug him again and swipes at his hair instead.

Lexi was right, Lexi led them to the right place—and while Stef gives her a brief mental thanks, wherever Lexi is at this moment just isn't as important as the fact that she's back with her best friend. Her brother. The relief checks her for a second: His singing, something she hasn't heard in months, resonated like a gong inside her heart the moment she heard it. Yes, she was happy to know he was present and healthy—but there was more to it. Her stomach did a funny *flip* at the sound of that voice.

"Hungry?" He waves at the base of the tree. A full picnic has appeared, complete with basket and checkered blanket. "The food here is amazing. The people—okay, they're not people but still—are amazing. This whole place is like—"

"A dream," Stef whispers, and pinches her arm. It's a cliché she's only ever read about in books, but if it's got any validity, it should wake her up. It doesn't. They're both really here. Her stomach rumbles. "Yeah," she says. "Let's eat."

"Race you there!" he cries, and takes off to the blanket. Stef stumbles after, and they collapse around the cloth's edges, taking long, deep breaths. Neither touches the spread of sandwiches, turkey legs, wine, and fruit.

"Hey," she says, still emotional.

"Hey back," he says with crisp delight, and grabs an apple. "Okay, so you have *got* to hear about this place!" Without taking a breath, he starts rattling out what his time here has entailed: coming out of his coma with a totally healed head, discovering that there truly is magic in the world, and that part of it resides in him. He even uses the word "unseen."

"Wait," she says, trying to interrupt. "Where *are* we?"

The Green Place. That's what Lexi said, before they landed.

"Fairyland!" He grins. "It's totally real, and if it's not, then these are really good drugs I'm on." He holds out some fruit. "You have some, too."

Stef picks at a grape and rolls it around in her fingers. Everything is *too much*; going from the dark terrifying cave to this bright sparkling hyper-reality is giving her mental whiplash. Then she hears what he just said: T.J. understands about possessing real magic—and he's not afraid of it.

"About that 'unseen,'" she says. "I think I've got some of it in me, too."

He grins, juice from a mango running down his chin. "'Course! No surprise there."

"What do they say you can do?"

With a shrug, he wipes off his mouth and launches into the song he was singing earlier, full-throated and with perfect pitch. He gives her a verse and chorus, clearly eager for her to join in, but Stef can't catch her breath. For five months she's been without that voice. It hits her now with the weight of a hammer and makes her squirm. Finally she gets how it affects people—it turns them the fuck on.

No wonder all the girls love him. It's like he *charms* them.

Stef pinches herself again. She does *not* want to be charmed by T.J. Not in that way. The pain jerks her out of whatever spell his voice weaves, and she watches him return to eating. She rolls her one grape between her fingers and looks into her heart. *Am I in love with this total goofball?* she dares to wonder for the first time.

The answer comes back: *No*. He's her bestie, he's Old Salty—and he's her brother. Anything else she might have thought would crop up between them is gone. A small part of her feels the loss, but a bigger one realizes the world is much wider now than it once seemed.

I'm gonna have to ask Tony about some earplugs when we get— she starts. Tony. She's assumed he's also dead all this time. But if T.J.'s here, is Tony? Not Daryl, not Ian. They're definitely dead from the copter crash. But Tony would never have left T.J.

He might still be alive.

She shakes her head. "Hey, stop singing. I can't—I can't hear it now."

"Hold on a sec, that's not the best part." He tugs her hand toward his. Only now does she see where she sliced it open while grabbing the cliff's edge. It's not actively bleeding now, but she's still got an open, ugly wound. He turns her palm skyward. "Try not to freak out."

"I do *not* freak out."

He shrugs. Then gently, softly, he sings.

Again her stomach flips and butterflies alight in her chest, but the real happening is on her hand. He sings, and the skin knits together. He sings some more and it becomes soft pink welts. In another moment they color over and—are gone. Stef holds up her hand, unmarked and undamaged.

T.J. looks up at her with a shy, impish grin. "*That's* what my unseen does," he says. "The locals love it."

"Jesus Christ," murmurs Stef.

"Not exactly." He leans back on his hands. "Only works over here, least that's what they tell me."

Stef blinks at him in wonder. The ladies already love him because he charms the literal pants off them at home. Here, he's a bona fide healer. "You are going to be completely impossible to live with now."

T.J. shrugs. "What can I say. I'm me."

"You sure are." She tilts her head at him. "So that's what they're having you do these days?"

He nods. "They just wanted me to … sing. See, they have this queen, and according to her a big war is going on. A lot of them get hurt and can't heal so fast if they get fired on by this Peppie gun that takes away their magic. Their unseen, I mean. And they'll die if they can't heal back before the unseen gets strong again. So that's why they need me."

He takes a deep breath. "I *heal* them, Stef. All I have to do is sing at 'em and then sometimes they sing with me and—then they're all better. And if you haven't heard them sing—" His eyes well up. "It's not sad, but it still makes me want to cry. So we sing together. They really, really love that."

"I see," says Stef, trying to imagine it. T.J. would certainly be very valuable to a group of creatures fighting a war if he could just sing them back to health. No wonder they kept him so long. She wonders if they would ever have let him go if she had not arrived.

"But that's not what you were gonna say," he says. "You felt something else."

"Well," she says, "you change people when you sing. At home. You must know some of this already. You make them—different. You made me—different."

Their eyes meet. "Different … how?" he asks.

"Like—like not brother and sister," she says. Any words sound awkward, and those might have been the most awkward she could have come up with. "I thought for a while I was … in love with you. Your songs did that to me."

Silence. Just some bird twittering in the branches. It's not a good sign; T.J. is not known for shutting up and listening. "Right," he says in a flat tone. "Then I guess … it's good you lost me."

"Not forever," she says, putting her hand over his. "We're family. We'll always be family."

T.J. draws his knees up and leans his head on them.

"Please don't tell me this is upsetting," says Stef. "I love you, you dope. But—"

"Like a sister, I get it," he says. "I guess I just liked knowing you were my No. 1 fan."

"Who says I'm not?" she shoots back. But that freedom she feels in her heart, knowing where she stands with him now, is glorious. He might have a face that launches millions of crushes at home, from his dimpled chin to his wide brown eyes and guileless expression—and voice that is wanted in two separate worlds—but he's not for her. She doesn't know who is, but it's definitely not Thomas J. Furey. "Okay?"

He nods slightly, "Guess so."

"Now," she says. "Please tell me one more thing."

"Yeah?"

"Where the hell is Lexi?"

Fixer, Finder, Healer

It's not a green place at all. It's a world of nothing.

Where I am right now, it's the xact opposite of that horrible black hole we fell through and even though it's open and bright and clean it scares everything in me and I'm thinking *I'm dead. This is what dying looks like.*

The walls are the same as the ground, which is the same as the ceiling, and there are no corners, no doors, no windows, no nothing. I'm too tired to move much so I'm just sitting—or maybe floating, I don't know—inside the nothing. There isn't even any sound, it's just—blank.

Then the air turns a different color and it's the shape of a person and then it's the shape of a Gil, carrying a cup of something. He *blends* through the nothing and stands, looking at me.

"Didnae move too swift." He kneels next to me, settling on the nothing. "Ye havenae come here afore. Can take some … gettin' used to, so I ken."

My heart leaps to see him. Then I remember I'm supposed to be keeping away from him and then I remember I'm also mad at him over the whole Artio thing but then none of that matters and I am lurching forward and wrapping my arms round him.

"Nae, nae," he says. "The drink, it—" He totters, trying to keep his hands aloft. He doesn't hug back, but that's okay. He never does.

I sit back and he is all smiles, his dark eyes shining, his skin reddish. " 'Tis good to see ye again," he says, handing me what he brought into the nothing—a cup made of twigs and leaves, filled with a dark, steaming liquid. "A little somethin' to help ye ease in."

It doesn't smell like the tea he's given me before; there's something sweet and also tangy about the aroma so I take a sip, then another, and then I'm thirstier than I've ever been so I drink it all down to the last drops. Fire rushes down my throat and blossoms in my stomach, but then it fades and I'm licking my lips, wanting more. I blink a few times and—everything is normal.

Least, as normal as anything can be in a world full of nothing.

"Where is this?" I ask. "Where is Stef? Why are we here? What was that drink?"

He chuckles at me. "Ye always are full o' questions, an' nae the right ones." He turns serious. "Yer pal Stef is communin' with her brother again, an' is well. Ye are in the queen's palace since Clíodhna has asked for ye, and one does not ignore the summon of the queen."

"The *queen* wants to see me?"

"Aye. But I see ye first." He is looking at me, tilting his head this way and that. "Ye have changed," he says and brings his fingers to my cheek. It burns and I pull back. He xamines me close.

"What's on my face?"

"Mmm," he says. "Ye have been marked. D'ye ken how?"

"Of course not," I say, wishing I knew what I looked like. "Maybe when I fell."

"That is of which we may speak," he says. "But when ye see Thomas, ask him to sing to ye. Will help."

I look into the empty cup, and it's half full again so I drink some more and lick my lips. Now I feel light in my head and very, very calm. "That is delicious," I say.

Gil takes the cup from my fingers and unfolds it against his shoulder, where it blends with his jacket. "'Twill be enough," he says.

I look around the endless space. "This is a palace? I thought I was coming to The Green Place."

"'Tis both," he says, and falls back into the nothing, which captures and cushions him as if he's tumbled into a broad sofa. "Come."

"There's nothing there," I say. He looks like he's floating. He holds up his hand and when I take it, he tugs me so that I tumble into the same soft emptiness next to him. It's like collapsing into a cloud.

"Ye will see more the longer ye are here," he says. "But *how* long that may be depends, Lexi. So before ye see Clíodhna, I must ask: How did ye come to arrive here?"

Part of the answer is *I have no idea* but the real answer is: "I told you. I fell. In the cave. It went on and on and on until it stopped—and the world ended." I tell him about using my abracadabras since the only thing Stef wanted was to see T.J., and how it wasn't very kind at all that Gil took T.J. away from her for five months and then I'm offtrack so I try to tell more about why we went into the cave.

Gil doesn't say much but as soon as I say "cave" he leans forward and goes deep, dark colors and I know him enough by now to understand this means he's thinking—and is scared. This is new. When Gillie got hit with Tony's PEP, that was one thing; she was hurt and mad and quiet. But I've never seen fear in a Ghillie Dhu.

"Tell more o' the cave," he says, quiet and focused right on me. " 'Twas dark, I ken. 'Twas deep, I ken also. But. What else?"

So I xplain more, about the sounds. The tearing. The singing. Our names.

"Ye lived in the cave an' this didnae happen?" he asks.

He knows we spent our summers there. "But I never went so far," I say. "We stayed up front."

"Yet, somethin' is different," he says. "Like *ye* changed."

"I buried Samuel deep inside," I say. "And I found out he took Jim there once. That was new."

Gil straightens when I mention my brother. He is silent a long moment. "I am tellin' ye things now I have not spoke of before," he says at last. "Things ye need to ken and ken well. Aye?"

I nod.

"Ye know I watch the forests. I go between certain forests—not all o'them, but just some special ones. Ones that are marked. I watch what goes on in them all an' I help when I can. But in some there are places that are *toirmisgte*. Forbidden. None of our kind can go, an' I cannae see inside. They are—"

"Blind spots," I realize, thinking of when we go hunting, how some animals can't see you even when you're close by.

"Aye." He tugs on his hat. "So much to say, so much serious. I dinnae care for it." Grass tumbles down.

I reach over and take his hand. He's stiff like a tree at first, then softens up and holds my hand back. I never used to touch people but I'm starting to do it a lot. It feels right. And it's like more of our kind of abracadabras—it makes people feel better. Maybe it makes *sìthiche* feel better, too.

"Ye ken of worn-up places," he goes on. "They are born, made in places of great feeling, great passion. They appear to us as bright places where light charges through an' we see them like stars in the sky. But. The worn-up places we use are born of good an' pleasant things. We shun ones of despair an' anger. To pass through a dark one steals from the traveler—steals unseen. The essence. The meaning o' a creature. When ye came through the dark one in the cave, ye lost some unseen an' we dinnae ken how it will change ye. Nae much, likely. 'Twas one time. But a creature coming close to the darkness twice, three times, more—would change. 'Twould take more of him than he could give. He might lose himself."

I don't know if I've ever heard him speak so much at once. "Why is there a worn-up place in the cave?" I ask. "How did it start?"

Gil shakes his head and grass tumbles down. " 'Tis beyond my ken." He cocks his ear, as if he hears something, but all is silence to me. "What I mean to say is—to have a dark worn-up place in our forest is wrong. To have one in our—blind spot—is disaster."

"Why?"

"Means the Ghillie Dhu is failing to keep things safe. Means Artio is failing. Our forest is full o' unseen, an' we work to keep it so. Keep it special. If we fail, if Artio fails—'twill be nothin' to hold back the darkness in the cave. An' if 'tis truly tearin' apart, growin'—the battles may—" He falters and shoots a look over his shoulder.

We are no longer alone.

Three birds of the shiniest green, yellow, and blue flutter in and swirl round our heads, then dip back to settle on the shoulders of a woman who—like Gil—must have *blended* through the nothing and is now with us.

She's a goddess. She's a queen. Her face is so pale it's like she's never even thought about the sun, and she is so beautiful I can't speak. I stare like I'm stupid at her flowing red dress and delicate red curly hair that's floating off her shoulders like she's got her own personal breeze.

"Ah, my Ghillie Dhu," she says, fluttering her fingers over his hat. Gil jumps to his feet and gives a little bow. "Please do not allow me to interrupt." She sends a smile my way, but it's not very warm. Her birds circle her head, settling on her shoulders.

"Was only tellin' Lexi 'bout watchin' over the forest, mistress," he says, and his eyes won't meet hers. " 'Tis but a tricky task. At least we have Artio."

"At least we do," she says and now that smile turns friendly. "So this is your Lexi. Our very own *lorgaire*." She xtends a hand to me and I don't know if I'm supposed to shake it or kiss it so I jump up and do a bow just like Gil. She laughs and it sounds like bells.

"Gil calls me a 'wean' usually," I tell her. "Mistress."

More bells. "I am Clíodhna, queen of the banshee," she tells me. "You may address me as such; you are not my subject. And you are clearly no 'wean.'"

"Nae," says Gil in a soft voice.

"So what am I?"

"You are our finder," she says, touching my chin and I feel a rush of—well, I don't know what it is, it's like how I felt eating ice cream—running through me. I smile with my whole face, my whole body. "Your friend Stephanie is our *fuasglaiche*, our fixer; Thomas is turning into a fine *lighiche*, a healer. They shall join us shortly."

Hearing her say it is a funny thing. She sounds like we're already part of a story we never signed up for. "Our? Us?"

"Indeed," she says. "We have a need of your abilities, dear Lexi. We have need of your friends' as well. For our world is running down and running out, and we are losing time to save it. You will both come with me, and I shall show you what I mean."

"Is this about the war?" I ask in a small voice. She is not much taller than me but every time I look her direct in the face she seems like a giant and I'm starting to do what Gil does, look past her, not at her.

"So it is," she says. "But before I explain further, is there anything you need to tell me, my Ghillie Dhu?"

Gil's hands reach up for his hat, but he checks them. "Nae," he says, words rushed. "All's well, so it is."

That is the first lie I have ever known Gil to tell.

Today is a day of firsts.

The Invitation

We are riding a giant white horse with a silver star on its face and a back so broad that all three of us fit and it is the finest thing I have ever done. Clíodhna's up front, with me behind her and Gil behind me, all holding each other's waists though really, I bet if we let go we'd never fall. Things like that just don't happen here.

Clíodhna is taking us to the war. She didn't say that xactly, but I understand. Over here that is the thing most important to them, the way finding Artio is to me. I also get that they think me and T.J. and Stef can help them, but how that's supposed to happen, I don't know. How can a person help save one world when she hardly knows anything about her own?

The horse just appeared in the white space the way everything else did—by kind of fading into it—and once we were onboard it made a mighty leap! into more nothing and then we were through the empty nothing and surrounded by instant blue-and-green Spring that made me stop breathing for a bit.

It was The Green Place. Finally. Finally. Finally.

So we're speeding through it now and I want to jump down and run 'round like a wild person in that softly waving grass, grass that makes me think of the Great Meadow but is superior to all the grass I ever saw or walked on before. Even though it is empty. I didn't imagine The Green Place wouldn't have hills or cliffs or trees, just be made up of grass and sky forever.

"Is this all of it?" I turn and ask Gil.

"Nae," he tells me. I feel his hands at my waist and get a little wiggle of happiness. "'Tis like a place-before."

Clíodhna doesn't turn but calls to us. "He means an 'antechamber.' It is but an introduction to our home. Few visitors come this far, and even fewer are permitted beyond to places like the palace. You are in rare company, Lexi."

"But the palace—"

"Requires a depth of stay," she continued. "The longer you remain, the more you see. Perhaps another time."

Sìthiche seem to have a lot of requirements, I decide. Not always ones that make sense. I turn back to Gil and say, "We have more to talk about."

"Aye," he says, darting his eyes to the side. "But. Later. 'Twill be time, ken?"

I want to talk now. I want to discuss Jim. I'm not dumb: Jim went into the cave and didn't come out, if I believe Samuel was shine-o-la in his journal and I do. That means Jim either died in the cave or he kept going and fell into a hole and *landed here in The Green Place* which means he's not dead at all and I bet Gil knows the answer to all of it. I will ask him. And he will tell me.

I also want to know why Gil kept the blind spot place from his queen. It scared him, hearing about it. Maybe I should be the one to tell her. But—I'll wait.

"Look 'round," he says. "Observe the world about ye."

Truth: I do want to see this world, this empty, color-bursting world that makes my heart sing. Our ride is so smooth—no bounces, no thuds. It's like we're floating above the grass. I settle in and put my hands back on Clíodhna's waist and touching her is like having a waking dream. I look out into the fields and see my mother tying up my shoes before school. I see me climbing a tree with Jim, scramble-racing to the top. I see myself finishing a book in the cabin and looking up in time to see Daddy whack a log outside and the sun come out from the clouds and light him all up. Small things. Life things. But it's like I'm *there* again and tears are rolling down my face. The real shine-o-la.

So much for never crying again.

I start noticing something on the horizon, something far away that is getting bigger, then larger, then the biggest thing ever. It's an oak the size of ten trees tied together. Maybe twenty. The white horse with the silver star slows without being told to and trots toward the trunk. Shade falls on us cool like rain but not wet.

On a branch a few feet off the ground sit Stef and T.J.

I slide down and leap off the horse before it even comes to a stop and run over to them. Stef jumps off her own perch and runs to me and we give each other big hugs. "Shit," she tells me. "I woke up and you were *gone*, girl."

"They took me to a room full of nothing," I say. "Gil was there. So was Clíodhna."

Gil waves at her from the horse, while Clíodhna just nods. The white horse paws the ground like he has someplace to be.

"You saw the palace!" T.J. cries. He looks hardly different at all and definitely not frayed like an old blanket like me and Stef seem after a winter in the woods. He's dressed like he ought to be Clíodhna's son, not a singer with a voice that makes you like him a lot. *Lighiche*, that's what she called him. But what does he heal?

Then I remember. "T.J.," I say and he looks at me right on. I touch my cheek.

"Will you sing to me?"

He doesn't even wait. There's music on his lips and words coming out and I close my eyes and it's like he's reaching inside me and putting me back together again. I get a funny feeling in my gut and lower and my heart starts pounding but I feel it mostly in my face, the skin pulling and touching and knitting back together again. He stops after a few seconds and I open my eyes.

Stef is crying but also laughing. "How's that shit?" she asks me.

I reach up and my face is—my face. No burning places. Just smooth lines in my smooth cheek. Better, like Gil promised. "Oh," I say. "Oh." And I jump forward and kiss T.J. right on his lips and he kisses me back and I wish for just a minute that no one else was anywhere around because then I might want to do things besides kissing—

"Lexi," says the queen, and I stop what I'm doing.

"Sorry," I say and my face is all hot. So is T.J.'s. I look at him and think: *Why did I want to do that?* "Thanks," I tell him. I shoot a look at Stef. She's biting her lip and I can't tell if she's mad or laughing at me.

"No problem," mumbles T.J.

"Come to, now," says Gil. The horse gets on his knees and now there are *five* of us on its back and I can't imagine how this works—but the back is still wide and long enough for us all. I make sure I'm up near the queen. I want to keep my waking dreams going. It's like I'm in them—I can smell Jim's sweat, my cooking in the cabin—and I can do things I never could in the real world. Dreaming, I can hold a living Hey Fox and tell her again how sorry I am. Dreaming, I don't have to think about kissing T.J. again.

'Ventually the horse stops again and we slide off; it runs away across the endless grass and I wish for a minute I could run like that, never getting tired, pounding the ground and going places.

"We walk," says Clíodhna.

"How come?" asks T.J. with a whine in his voice.

Stef rolls her eyes and whispers to me, "That boy would hire a palanquin and get himself carried everywhere if he could." I have no idea what that is, but I can imagine what she means: T.J. hasn't changed at all in five months. I grin behind my hand.

The queen drapes her arm round T.J.'s shoulders as we strike out across the field, and after only a few steps it's not so green anymore. It gets tufty and the tufts are yellow and brown. Then the ground starts bumping up with rocks, then whole patches of nothing but bare ground.

"The unseen is thin here," Clíodhna explains when we start up a steep rise. "We dare not work magic as we grow closer."

"Closer to what?" asks Stef.

"To the border."

The rise ends as a drop-off, and we stop right before the edge. It's a much higher cliff than any I've ever climbed with my monkey toes and fingers, way higher than Blueberry Cliff. The sky here is ash-gray and smells like burning meat and smoke and crispy electricity. We stand in a loose semicircle, looking over the cliff edge, which winds far away in both directions as far as I can see. I look down, to the ground.

It's a flat, empty plain that's mostly brown and only some green, and any trees are just blackened sticks. It looks like the whole ground has been used for target practice and is all torn up and messy. There's a smoking, dark wavy line that shimmers and I think it's moving—but so slow you almost might miss it. On the other side of that burn mark things aren't so empty: Dots of people run here and there and I think I hear some pops and sizzles that make me think of the PEP Tony used on Gillie.

For the first time I touch the coat that's been tied round my waist since it got hot in the cave. I feel for the pocket and yep, it's still there. The PEP. I haven't lost it.

"That's the—war?" asks Stef.

"A portion of it," says Clíodhna.

"Where?" I wonder. "Here?"

"Breizh," says the queen. "In a land you call France; some know it as Brittany."

"France?" Stef gasps. "Can't be."

"But it is," says Clíodhna. "Were you down in the midst of it, you would not be able to see us here. You would gaze out over the waters, to England in the distance, perhaps." She pauses. "There was a divide, once. We passed through into your worlds only rarely—certainly not as often as we were given credit for—and peace reigned between our folk. But in recent years that has changed. The worn-up areas—our apertures—have begun widening, joining to one another. This is the largest and shows no signs of slowing."

The high, light quality in her voice is gone, and she sounds angry and afraid. "Think of it as a bubble that stretches and tears but does not rupture. As this bubble expands, it erases this world—and is replaced by your world. Not expanded. Not made better. Our land simply vanishes."

"How?" I whisper. "Why?"

Clíodhna shakes her head. "We sense a *uilebheist* is behind it. A creature half made like we are and half like you are, raging and obsessed. Someone who finds a sensitive area and pours all of his unseen into it out of fear, or hatred."

I turn to look at her. She knows more than she says. She knows more than any of us, and that includes Gil.

"This isnae in your country yet—just here," Gil says quickly. "But. W'out Artio an' her unseen, the forest is helpless. Ken?"

I can't look at him. He's telling me I'm sentencing the forest to what's down there if I kill that killer bear.

"Alas, we are without true understanding and time is not our friend," says Clíodhna. "None of us have the strength we once did; you may see many wondrous things when you visit us here, but we are drained and fading. This has been going on for at least twenty-five of your years, but for us it is so much faster. We are unable to react with alacrity. We need humans who are willing to help."

I bite my lip, much sadder than I realized I might be. The Green Place is like nowhere else and I can't imagine it not being there. What happens to Gil? To Clíodhna? To all their snow white horses wearing silver stars?

"We were like you once, and you were like us once," says Stef. "So—maybe it's time that it came down. Maybe we should reunite."

"Alas, we are very different; your kind fear and distrust the very air we breathe," says Clíodhna. "And we have lost the skills of crafting things; what you did with your grandmother's timepiece is unseen even I must marvel at. If we cannot use our native skills among your kind, we are without purpose. Vestigial."

"Why are *sìthiche* leaving?" I ask. "Why would anyone leave?"

"Some believe the destruction of our land is inevitable," she says. "Some are curious. Many wish to make trouble. Some who no longer are under my sight believe they could take over and rule humans. There are as many reasons as there are stars in the sky."

"Yeah, but what can *we* do?" asks T.J. There's a crack in his voice. "We're not special."

Stef looks at him with wonder.

Clíodhna begins walking down the rocky rise and we follow. When she gets to the bottom, she turns. "This war has thus far been contained because the border between our world and yours has only parted in places where we have long residence—lands you call England. Ireland. Scotland. Wales." She is speaking with all of us but looking direct at me. "We have had lesser presence in Brittany, but there is still a strong connection. Lexi, your forest is a form of—outpost for us. A place of your world that we have made our own. Gil visits at my request to watch over it and the creatures who reside in it. Artio holds all the unseen we can give her and provides protection. Should a rift like the one you just saw begin in one of our outposts, we would need to know immediately. It is very important."

She knows already about the cave's worn-up place. Samuel would do this to me from time to time, speak a little about something he knew a lot about—then wait for me to fill in the gaps. But I don't want to get Gil in trouble.

Stef does it for me. "You tell her about the cave?" she asks, looking at me. "The dark hole and the scratching and the big empty pit that brought us here?"

Around us the air grows cold and light fades from Clíodhna's face.

Gil steps to one side. "I must away," he says, and begins to make a small turn—but Clíodhna raises a hand and he stands fast.

"You and I will speak in time," says Clíodhna to him in a deep, angry voice. She looks at me and tempers her tone. "Yes, I am aware of that aperture, though it has not been seen by our kind in thousands of years. I believe it has always been there, waiting, but that its discovery by your father made it powerful, Lexi.

He fed it his unseen and has let it grow. Expand. Perhaps—create a new tear in your own world. We cannot know as yet."

"He sent Jim inside," I say. "And—I think he hurt him there."

She takes in a long breath and when she breathes out, I smell flowers. Bluebells, maybe. "Your brother came to us, badly done in. We were unable to mend him, and he did not survive." She looks at Gil, who looks away. "I believe it was your father's doing, to strike him, and I believe that act has only fed the darkness inside the cave."

My eyes are burning.

Clíodhna turns to Gil. "Artio is weakening," she says. "She should have prevented their entering that cave. You swore she would be enough over there."

Gil dances to one side. "'Twould be best to speak of … at a very other time," he says, but I'm hardly hearing him. I'm picturing me with a rock in my hand and Stef with a rock in her hand and then we are Jim and Samuel and—Samuel's aim is faster and stronger than Jim's. Jim goes down. Jim is … gone.

Clíodhna adjusts Gil's hat on his head. "Go," she says. "We will speak."

And with a slight twist in his step, Gil vanishes completely.

"Wait—" I call, but he's gone. And we have so much more to say.

The queen folds her arms. "We have fought wars on many occasions, against many races and creatures. This one—is different. This is the one that threatens our actual existence, and the one we seem to be the least equipped to wage. We must find a way to recapture our own borders while at the same time look for a way to live with your people—in case we are unable to do so. Both are intolerable, and both appear to have just become much worse. We have tried many things, and none have succeeded."

"Tony," I say. "He was a thing you tried."

T.J. stares at me. "He was?"

"Yes," says Clíodhna. "I gave him a task, but he did not—complete it. Clearly, we erred in choosing him. But we believe we have what we need right now, right here."

"Me?" says T.J., perking up.

Stef rolls her eyes. "I think she means the three of us."

Clíodhna nods. "Yes: We need one who can find the way, one who understands how to make the pieces into a whole, and one who can heal. These talents you have are freshly awoken. Stay here and refine them. In time, help us repair the breach."

In time, I think. "How much … time?"

"I cannot know," says Clíodhna.

"But—Gil always said people lose time here," I say. "And your kind lose your memories in our world."

"True," she says. "The longer you are here, the more time passes at home. This is not a small sacrifice."

T.J. chuckles. "I've got a spare couple of days," he says. "Already been here a week, so why not. Make a bigger splash once we walk out of the woods finally."

Stef frowns. "T.J., it's March," she says, and the date lands like a rock tossed into a lake.

T.J. frowns. "Cute," he says. "It's October."

"They speak the truth," says Clíodhna. "Each day here is far longer in your world. That is what I mean by asking much of you. Your time runs so quickly for us, it is difficult to catch hold of a moment or a person at the right time. We glance away for an instant and then everything has changed. This war has sprung upon us with virtually no warning; one moment things were as they always have been and then the next we began losing hold. We cannot keep up. This is why we need your help, your insight." She takes his hand. "But I will not keep the truth from you: To stay with us is to return to a world that may have forgotten you."

T.J. runs his hands through his hair, stands up, and paces. "Everyone at home is gonna think we died," he says.

"Probably," says Stef.

"Where is Tony?" T.J. whirls on Clíodhna, upset and looking around. "We need Tony here."

"Anthony has been made well and dispatched," she says. "There is no place for him here anymore. He is not the hero we are looking for."

"So we stay, and he can't. We stay and lose everything out there, and it's all to help you?"

Clíodhna nods. "That is the essence of it."

T.J.'s jaw clenches, unclenches. If he was like Gil I bet his skin would be shifting colors, he's thinking so hard. He wants to stay; I can feel it. I mean, I've only been here a couple hours and I can't imagine not wanting to stay.

And I would stay, xcept I have one thing left to do. Even though I don't know that I can even do it anymore. My last thing is killing Artio—and it's not something that can happen. Not if I love The Green Place. Not if I love … Gil. My one last thing—if I do it right—means the woods are unprotected.

"Wow," says T.J. finally. "That's not really a choice. Tony should be here."

"He cannot be," says Clíodhna.

"Tell me why."

"Do not make demands of me," she says, eyes fierce. "Let him tell you."

T.J. flinches at her anger. He knots his hands, stares at the ground. Finally Stef puts a hand on his shoulder. "It's okay," she says. "We'll go."

Well, if they're both going and I have my own plan, looks like none of us are staying. But my stomach hurts; this is not what should be happening. We've been asked for help, and 'cause T.J. wants to stick up for Tony, we're *all* running away. "I'll come back," I tell the queen. "I just have something to do first."

"Take heed of that notion," Clíodhna warns me. "I know what is in your heart, Lexi, and I can only say that you should listen to the Ghillie Dhu in this matter. Should you complete your task, we cannot allow you back here. You will be to us as Anthony now is."

All or nothing, then.

"We understand that we ask things of you that are difficult to give. But if you will not help us, you will never find ways to use your talents beyond mere parlor-room tricks. A watch is not a world; a voice is not a cure." She looks at me. "A direction is not destiny."

My head is starting to hurt; I have so much to think about.

"So—if we leave, we can't do … the things we can do?" T.J. asks.

"Yeah," says Stef. "I thought—these were things inside of us. That you all woke up."

"They are," she says. "But the three of you have mere seedlings of ability. Without the proper light, or water, or food, seedlings wither. We feel it is a worthy exchange."

Suddenly this is all feeling sour and wrong, like we've fallen into that black hole again. I spent so many years wanting to come to The Green Place—and now I can't wait to leave.

"For all that bodes well, a price must be paid," I say. "I hear that a lot."

"It is fair," she tells me.

"Well," I say. "Sometimes a person does something just *because*. Not to get a gift. But because you *care* enough." I look at Stef and T.J. "I care about them. I want to be here more than anything but *they* didn't ask for help. And they need it if they're gonna leave the woods. So I'm *giving* it to them. Then I'll do what I have to. Or not."

Clíodhna sighs and takes my face in her hands. She kisses me on the forehead and glances at all of us. "This loss of time together saddens me," she says. "But … I suspect you will return."

I can almost hear the queen's voice in my head: *It is inevitable.*

"Don't kidnap me again," says T.J., but his tone indicates he wouldn't mind it a bit. I get it: It's impossible to come here once and not want to come back the whole rest of your life.

Clíodhna smiles at me.

"Follow me," I say, holding up my hands to say the abracadabras again. I cut a glance at her. "You haven't taken this one away from me yet, have you?"

No, she hasn't.

Bear Necessities

Tony's mouth has gone bone dry while listening to Jim. He'd like nothing more right now than a drink of cold water.

As if on cue, a small brook begins babbling nearby. At its edge a bowl-shaped rock sits waiting for Tony to scoop up his drink before sipping it. It's so clear, cold, and pure it even puts the water he drank out of an Icelandic glacier stream to shame.

He turns back to Jim, wiping the back of his mouth with his hand. "You're … Artio." He shakes his head. "Can't be."

"Well, I'm part of her, let's say," says Jim. "What Gillie wanted was what was inside me—that unseen they keep talking about. I was dying and she put her mouth to my lips and did something to me that pulled me out of my body. My … soul, if you believe we have those. Spirit if you don't."

"Sounds like she did CPR on you and told you a funny tale," growls Tony. "You've been hoodwinked."

"The body—my body—died. She took it back to the surface and sank it in a lake." Jim is nearly as cool as the water Tony just drank. "I've gone swimming in the lake while inside the bear. I've seen … me. My body is still down there, just bones and rotted clothes. There is no corporeal me now."

They are silent for a long beat. Tony envisions, as best he can, what it must be like to feel your essence inside another creature—like a suit—swimming weightlessly past the discarded remnants of your old casing. Is it what a snake feels like, seeing the skin it shed? Or is it like seeing your twin, unreachable and lost?

"So she put your—*soul*—into the bear?"

"Artio needs a human soul to anchor her in the real world; without one she's just a bear, a bear that can die easy as any creature," he goes on. "The last unseen inside her was crumbling away; had been in there centuries, I got the impression."

"And if you said no?"

"Then she said she'd let me go. When the soul escapes—she said—it appears as a butterfly that finishes the journey to the next world, whatever that next world is. I didn't think long. I told her that was fine by me."

Tony frowns. Who could make that decision so quickly?

"It wasn't hard to decide. I was pissed at my father and terrified for my sister. Gillie told me if I was Artio, I could keep an eye on Lexi, make sure he didn't go after her with a rock one day."

"So that was it."

Jim takes a deep breath. "I had a condition—that she release me for good once the old man was dead. I didn't want to end up crumbling after centuries being a half bear, half person. It seemed—indecent. She was okay with that. But you know how they operate here—"

"There are no free lunches."

"I kept up my end. Lexi has no idea I've been around all this time, and that's okay by me. Better if she doesn't remember me like *this*. Better to let her think—"

"That you ran off."

"The problem is that Samuel is dead. Five months now. And Gillie isn't making any moves to let me go. She needs another unseen, something she's not able to get at the drop of a hat. Samuel would have been perfect, but she wasn't prepared. She didn't see that one coming. Truth is, neither did I. Considering what that old man did to his kids, he deserved a lot worse than getting impaled on a stag's antler." Jim's jaw is tight. "It all happened pretty fast."

Tony leans back on his hands, mind on fire. He thought he understood how this other world could be dangerous and attractive and irresistible and capricious and completely out of his control. He understood nothing, it seems. "Why tell me all this?"

"When it first happened, being Artio was the greatest thing ever—like tasting the world again for the first time. But I've learned that it doesn't take centuries to start crumbling. Lately, every time I become the bear I lose more of me. I'm mostly bear when I'm in there these days, and that's like being trapped inside a costume that's wearing you, instead of the other way around. I've thought about trying to talk to Lexi—to explain—but aside from the fact that she doesn't exactly speak bear I worry if I do say anything to her I'll violate some kind of *geas* and end up stuck for good."

Geas, thinks Tony. *Like the one I have. We're both trapped—iron fist in a velvet glove, is that how it goes?*

"You want something, then."

"Lexi's already planning to kill Artio. She has your PEP. So … let her find me and take her shot. I think that'll do it. She'll feel like she did something good and right and avenged our father and then she can leave. Which she should do. She should go and see the real world before this fairy one gets its hooks in her. Once she does it, she'll be shut out of this place for good, and that's how things ought to be."

Jim's face softens. "And, you know, if you feel like seeing to it that she doesn't end up alone and destitute on the street, I'll take that as a personal favor." He hikes up his shirt to reveal a long, ropy plasma burn. "After all, you owe me for this one."

Tony grimaces. "Sorry, man. About shooting at you. About your sister—well—" he pauses. When they return to the woods it's still going to be tough to walk to civilization, particularly if there's a lot of heavy snow. They will need Lexi's guidance. All he has to do is make sure she gets the bear and gets out. Throwing her a couple of bucks once they're safe in town should be easy.

"You gonna promise me something in return?" He narrows his eyes.

Jim's face darkens. "I'm not one of them. Never was. If you can't do this with an open hand—because it's the right thing to do—well, there's not a lot of help for you. Neither one of us asked for a lot over the years. We were trapped in a place we didn't ask to come to and made the best of it. At least one of us should get to see what's on the other side of the exit door. What if she were your sister?"

Tony is already nodding. "Yeah," he says, sorry that he never got to know Jim in the real world. Sure, he's a pain in the ass the way Lexi is, but they might have been able to hoist a few cold ones together. And when Tony thinks about it, he's happier that Jim has nothing to offer him. It's a move the fey make—to give and take at the same time. Tony doesn't want to be like that.

"What if she hesitates, though?" he asks. "Can't pull the trigger at the right moment?"

"Then you should do it—only, shit, I guess you can't. And neither of your charges are exactly mighty hunters." He thinks a moment. "If it looks like she can't do it—then tell her about a baby bird we found on the ground once. She'll understand."

Even Tony thinks he knows what that means. "Got it. But one last question."

"I got nothing but time."

"Isn't Artio in hibernation right now?"

"Yeah, but it'll be spring in a couple days."

A bell goes off inside Tony. "We only landed in the woods about a week ago," he says, but his words come out like toffee. He knows that to be true, but in this moment he also knows it to be false. He and T.J. have been in The Green Place for nearly a week.

Jim raises his one good eye's brow. "You sure about that, man? Time's a funny thing here. Winter is almost done."

A Wild Test

When we were small, Jim and me used to wait until Daddy was asleep and then we'd zip our sleeping bags together into one big bag and then we'd be warm enough to zzz on the really cold nights. I don't remember not being cold in wintertime but Jim said our first house, the one with mom and the baby in it, had heat where all you had to do was push a button and it came out of the floors and the walls.

I'm not sure how they do it. A big fire under the house? How come it doesn't burn down? Anyway, it sounds like something you'd make up. Or something close to magic. *Dofheicthe.* Unseen. When I think about that, and what Gil taught me to do, and what Gillie showed Stef she could do, and what T.J. can do without anybody ever teaching him about it one way or the other, I think magic's prolly about the way you see the world. Perception, that's the word.

Which means my world is just as magic as The Green Place. In its own way.

"That makes a crazy kind of sense," says T.J. when I xplain it.

"That's how Gillie said it was to me," says Stef. "We all came from the same source. But now we do our own kinds of magic."

We sleep.

We are back in the real world, one that returned to winter while we were gone. Not sure how long passed here while we were in The Green Place, but it was enough time to snow hard again. Winter's like that. Doesn't want to give up. We come from The Green Place into the white place and all I can say is I'm glad it's the repaired Glampsite because I am never going in that cave again, ever.

We get the genny grinding and make it warmish and we wrap blankets round ourselves and look at our hurts. The place on Stef's hand where she cut it falling into the dark space started bleeding and my face turned burny and raw once we returned to the Glampsite. Whatever T.J. did to help in The Green Place doesn't last too long in the woods, I guess.

So we pile snow on everything and that helps some but then we're hurt *and* cold. T.J. tries singing to us but it doesn't help the hurts this time, just makes Stef and me both feel funny so we tell him to quit it and he turns over in bed and won't talk to us. Guess the queen was right: We only have little magics right now, right here. We're just seedlings.

'Ventually we snooze together and I think of fox kits with their mama. It's nice: T.J. is on one side of me and Stef on the other and they're like bonfires, blazing with heat.

Morning comes and we eat all the oatmeal we can and its quiet with everybody thinking all kind of things. I'm thinking about Artio. But I'm pretty sure they're not. So finally I speak up.

"I'm going hunting," I say.

They both look at me. "We have to find Tony," says T.J.

Same time, Stef says, "We gotta get out of the woods already."

Almost makes me want to laugh, we're thinking so different. The only things they want have zero to do with where we just were—almost like they don't care anymore there's a whole world on the other side of things that's being eaten alive. I listened to Clíodhna and looked at the burned land in France on the other side of the cliff and I didn't have any words. My heart hurt. I can't stand the idea that things are vanishing for no reason. We could help, all of us.

After I find Artio, that is.

And see if I can do what needs doing.

But I'm thinking about Gil and how he and I didn't get to have our talk. I suppose I will have to deal with him and what he knows 'ventually. But first, there is Artio, who will be un-hibernating any day now and needs to be found at the right time.

I have a very long list of things to do. I am so busy. I have so much. Xcept sometimes I don't think I do.

"Well," I say. "You can do what you want but I'm going hunting."

"Lexi," says Stef and she's got a mom-sound in her voice. "Don't do it. It won't bring your dad back."

"Don't want him back," I say. "But it wasn't up to her to take him." Still, saying that makes me wonder: Why am I all on fire to go shoot a bear? Why does Samuel need avenging? Sometimes, the answer is just *because*. It's been my plan. It's something I hold on to. 'Cause if you don't have a plan you don't have anything.

I get up and start making a pack of things I should take. Grab one of the special bows and arrows with metal tips while they just sit there watching me.

"So nobody cares where Tony went?" T.J. asks.

We both look at him. "Tony can take care of Tony just fine," says Stef, then tells him all about how she first met Gillie the day before the hunt and how he shot Gillie all up and hid her in the tents. "He's a little hard to look in the face these days for me."

T.J.'s face has turned red. "I don't believe any of that."

"True thing," I say. "He was in the war. He shot a lot of *sìthiche*. Why do you think they don't want him there?" I take the PEP out of my coat and slam it on the bed. "He used *this* and she *screamed*."

His face is hard and angry and his mouth is this thin line. He stomps out of the tent into the Glampsite and Stef follows.

I finish packing. When I am done, I stick my head out of the tent. Storm's done, but the sky's still low hard white. Could be only a breather between blows. Spring comes late, but I try to mark it the minute I can. Makes winter feel shorter.

I think about what's coming next, about tracking down Artio, about finishing my plan. About disappointing Gil, about maybe never seeing him again. Seeing that whole world again.

The wild always tests you, Daddy liked to say. Samuel, I mean. *Never a test you xpect, either.*

I hear him in my head, Samuel. Not new things. He's not a ghost. I just hear him saying all the old things he used to tell us. Wish I wasn't so done with loving him. Still would like to have a Daddy who was more shine-o-la. Who I could hug hard and tell *I don't know what I'm doing.*

Stef and T.J. are huddled together and she's got her hand on his back. I say in a strong voice, "I'm going now. If you come with me I will walk you to the Outside, and if Outside shows up before we find Artio I will take you there first. But right now, I am going hunting."

I hold out my hands and think of the bear and say, "*Tha an t-slighe soilleir.*" The snow parts like someone has a giant spoon and has scooped out a trench. It'll still be hard slogging, but at least we have a start.

I start walking.

Soon, I hear them follow.

Where Is the Exit

We stop at the edge of the lake, about 3,245 steps from the Glampsite. It spreads out ahead of us all white and still on the top but—as I know anyway—dark and cold beneath. I swam in this lake all the time. It doesn't have a bottom, least not one I ever found.

We tie each other together with a cord from one of the wrecked tents and now we're one person, stepping careful over the snowy empty plain. The new snow'll cover any cracks or holes in the ice so we have to watch it, 'cause nobody wants to go swimming now.

Go down and you prolly won't ever come up again.

"It's like Clíodhna's palace," says T.J., first thing I heard him say since lunch. Whenever I look over my shoulder he's staring off into the distance, like he's half here with us and half someplace else.

I know where that someplace else is. The Green Place is in my mind, too. Not at the front but it hides and then pops out the minute I'm not focused on something in partic'lar. Like the way water seeps into every crack or how ivy winds 'round a tree until it swallows it up, The Green Place is in me—and I bet it's in him. I bet it's in Stef.

Clíodhna told me, *I suspect you will return*, but it wasn't like she was asking. She knows it has us. We're not the same since being over there. And T.J.—he was there for days. Or months. However you want to see it.

"You were in the palace, too," says T.J., wistful.

"I woke up in a big empty space with no corners. No roof. No walls," I say.

"Sounds horrible," says Stef. "Empty."

"It's not empty once you color it in," says T.J., but doesn't xplain.

Under our feetsteps the ice is talking to us, shifting and groaning and popping. Not actual cracks—that would be bad—but we step up our pace. The world is unsteady right now.

At last my path leads us off the lake and up on the opposite bank and since it's starting to get dim out, we figure we should rest up for the night. Stef swears she can figure out how to make a lean-to and T.J. promises he can go round up lots of wood to keep a fire going, so after we get things lit and cut down and the building starts, it goes quiet round us. All we hear is the whispery sound of snow skittering across the lake ice.

That's when Artio comes back to mind.

I eye the trench my abracadabras carved out, squinting into it. The path keeps going on and on, sweeping back into the forest, and then it disappears into the trees. I watch it for a few minutes, and the more I watch it the more I want to get up and follow it. It's like somebody tied me to the path with a tent cord and it's pulling me along. Makes me wonder if Artio's just 'round the corner. I could find out. I could see.

I know this lake. This is where Jim and me and Samuel came on hot days and went swimming and practiced holding our breath. Those days were easy. We caught fish for dinner and swam in the daytime and built a fire and slept under the stars. When it rained, we all bunched up into this one abandoned ice shack that smelled like socks and mildew.

The fire's leaping and hot and now I'm starting to think of bad things so I jump up and brush snow off my pants and decide to walk ahead. Just to see.

"Be back," I say to Stef and T.J., who are working on the lean-to, and grab my bow and arrows, following the snow.

It's soft and quiet and soon I can't even hear them chattering behind me. I start thinking about what it means to live here all the time by myself. When I was at the cabin all those weeks and months I was free—but I was also empty. Sad. Like the snow was burying me and I couldn't breathe and I didn't know how to count Mississippis so I might never come up again. I don't want to feel like I'm drowning every day. But when I think about Outside my throat closes up and when I think about staying in the woods my face starts hurting again and it's like I'm back in the cave again, in the dark.

The trench ends.

I jogstep the last twenty or so paces and come up to a rise of thick rugged stone, dark and patched with snow. Icicles hang off small ledges like rows of teeth. The black rock curves off to one side, then inward and I realize this is another cave. The trench has taken me to Artio's home, and it's a cave.

Step one step two step three and I'm inside the cave. Smelling that musky thick blood scent that means an animal lives here, a big one. I strain to hear any sounds, feel any sense of a giant unseen bear inside the cave. But I can't hear anything but the *drip drip* of water deep in the dark and my heart is pounding in my ears—this cave is way too close to that other cave and I can't be here right now.

I jump back out of the cave and paste myself against the outside wall, breathing hard. Maybe she's in there. This could be it. I could just go in and shoot her with the arrows while she's in her *zzzz*'s and then we could all leave the woods together and la la la we'd be happy ever after. That is my plan.

Xcept I'd prolly never hear from Gillie or Gil anymore. No more white horses with stars or palaces that need coloring in. They'd never let me back into The Green Place. Clíodhna said so, mostly.

When I made my plans while staring up at the roof of the cabin over the winter I hadn't been to The Green Place yet. It was somewhere that sounded wonderful and somewhere I knew I wanted to go—but I hadn't been. It was all in my head. Now I've been there. I've seen and tasted and smelled and felt fairyland. Curled its grasses up in my toes. Rode on its horse and climbed its tree and met its queen. It is a real place. More real than anywhere I ever lived before.

My throat is tight. It is hard to give up plans sometimes. Plans are the things that get us from one day to the next. Sometimes you don't even have to think, you just remember the plan and you move to it and you don't ask any questions. But The Green Place has me asking all the questions. Including ones 'bout myself.

I take a long, deep breath and decide … that I will wait. For a bit. I will see what morning brings. I will go to bed and when I wake up I will have my answer. I will know then what to do about Artio.

I turn to head back to the lake edge.

I'm a few minutes away from lakeside when I hear them: feetsteps. Bootsteps. Not quick like Hey Fox, not heavy like Artio. Somewhere between. To one side.

I jump out of the trench and slide under a pine tree bough and snow goes snowing down all over me and the ground but I don't move. I just keep crouched, breathing heavy.

"Hey," comes a voice. "Your tree camouflage is for shit."

I step out from under and shake all the snow off me. It's Tony. 'Course.

"You're back," I say and I'm actually kind of glad about it.

He looks magic. The three of us are just wearing old clothes from the Glampsite—T.J. changed out of his fancy robe once we got back 'cause it didn't keep him warm—but Tony is dressed like a prince. He's got on a heavy black velvet coat with gold thread designs on the edges, and his feet are covered with soft furry boots that match his big thick mittens. He lowers the hood on his coat and puts his walking stick into the snow, where it stands up all by itself. He looks like he just stepped out of a fairy tale. I guess he kind of did.

"Where are the others?" he demands.

I point to the lake. "That's Artio's cave," I say, turning the other way.

He makes a little jerky motion, starts to say something. "Your face—" he says, then stops.

"I fell," I say, and it's true. But I don't say more.

"Right." Closed subject. "Well. I want to show you something that I found a minute ago." He waves at me and I follow him into the trees. "Been tracking you guys most of the afternoon, trying to catch up," he xplains. "Went a little off course toward the end."

We push through the pine boughs. The tangy sap mixed with the dry cold gets into my nose and the smell makes me feel like a little kid again.

"Check this out," he says, holding back one more tree branch to reveal our old, gray wood shack.

It's like a cabin, but much smaller. I think Samuel said it moved if you pulled it with a horse or motor or something out on the lake, then used a hole in the floor for ice fishing. In not-winter seasons people park their shacks on the lake edge for safety. But this shack hasn't had an owner in all the time I've known about it—there's even some brownish bushes on one side and a tree sapling shooting out of the pipe in the roof. There's a thin door and a small window on each narrow side.

"Yeah," I say. "Thought this might be 'round here."

"You've been to this place before, then."

"Other years."

"Well," he says, "let's peek inside."

Door's not locked. Nothing's locked 'round here. *Forest eddy-kitt,* Samuel called it once. I push inside and look around. There's some shelves with rusty cans and a tiny woodstove that's supposed to connect to the pipe in the ceiling. There's a skinny mattress on top of a long shelf with hinges and under that is a big storage space. The whole place smells cold and the air is stale.

"If Stef can't finish the lean-to we could all prolly stay here tonight—" I start, turning 'round but I stop when I see Tony pulling the door shut and coming up behind me. Only light is the gray white that comes through the windows and for a minute the only sound is us breathing and all I can see is the smoke coming out of our mouths, mixing it up and making clouds.

I feel like there's electricity all over my body. Something is going to happen.

Tony slides past me and shrugs out of his coat. I've been wondering why he seemed so humpy, but once the big black furry thing is lying on the mattress, I can tell he's got a pack on underneath, one he slides off his shoulder. It's an old tired looking canvas backpack with one broken shoulder strap and when he hoists it on the mattress I see someone's written a name in marker across it: *James*.

"G'wan," he says.

I can't move for a second. I know this pack. Jim took it everywhere. 'Course it's his. I glare at Tony but I'm too interested in the pack so I reach for it and pull it open. Inside is a can of beans and a box of matches and a scout knife and a book that says *Huckleberry Finn* on the cover.

I hold the book in both hands and stare at the picture on the cover. "Open it," he says in a soft voice so I curl the cover 'round the rest of the book the way Gil wraps 'round trees. On the first page over the title it reads: *Property of James Henry Jacobs.* The last word is smeary but I know what it means to say 'cause it's the last name on Daddy's driver's license in the cabin. It's the last name I had when I came to the woods when I was a Brownie. When Jim was my brother.

I think about the morning after the knife ended up in the wall. I imagine Samuel saying, *Let us go hunting, my son.*

Okay, Dad, but I am still mad at you, Jim might have said. Then he would have grabbed his backpack and he would have walked out of the cabin and into the cave and out of my life.

And if I could, I would break into their trip and I would say: *Don't go, Jim, he's going to take steps with you and that means you're going to be dead.*

But I'm too late. I was asleep when it happened and I was asleep after it happened and I've been asleep for a long, long time. I looked and looked and looked at this story for so long and I never wanted to believe anything xcept that Jim was gone from the woods. That Jim forgot about me.

"He wanted you to have it," says Tony. "He left it in The Green Place so you could have it someday. So you'd know."

"Ah," I say and it's thick and wet and my legs go soft.

Tony catches me as I fall and I sink into him and then he's moving me to the mattress and I sit on his coat and I don't make a sound. One, two tears roll over my burned face and the salt gets in my mouth. I sniff hard since I don't want to cry about anything anymore, but it's hard. Really hard.

I put the book next to me and my hands go into my lap.

"I'm sorry," he says but I'm hardly hearing him.

Steps. No more pretending. No other words. When Daddy *killed* my brother. When Samuel Jacobs decided James Henry Jacobs was too much trouble and probably had a sickness and pulled him into that dark place that eats your unseen and lifted a rock and—well. I've known for a long time Jim didn't go away. He's dead. Not out of the woods leaving me behind. Not hiding. Dead. I knew it. I just didn't look for it. I didn't point my hands and ask for the way inside me. I had to wait for someone to make me see it.

Then I cry. Again.

'Ventually, I stop.

"Look," says Tony once my hiccups go down. "I'm gonna tell you a couple of things about what I saw over in The Green Place."

I remember I'm not supposed to like Tony—he shot Gillie, he took Stef away, he made the queen banshee so mad she kicked him out of The Green Place—but it's been a long time since I saw him. Five months. And I like looking at him, even though everything else is true. So I nod. "I was there," I say. "Me and Stef got T.J. out."

"I know. Thanks for doing that. Really."

Anything's easier than talking about what I know now so I just keep going. "He wants to go back. Back there, I mean. Not home."

"I'm sure he does," he says. "They have everything they could ever need there. But they still come and take things from us."

"Like what?"

"People," he says. "People go over and don't come back."

"You came back," I tell him. "T.J. came back. We came back."

"I'm not really back," he says. "And I don't imagine he is, either."

I look at him, confused.

"In here," he touches his chest, "I'm over there. Been there from the minute I went the first time. But know what? I learned a few things this visit. Like maybe it's all just an illusion. Maybe everything we see over there isn't even real."

It's not empty after you color it in. That's what T.J. said.

Tony stares at the door of the shack. "They're not human," he says, but it's not xactly to me. "May look a little like people but they're not. Don't think like people, either. Anything that lives for a thousand years is not people." He sighs. "But whatever they are—" His voice catches. "They are beautiful. Jesus, it's blinding to look at them for too long. You lose yourself."

My stomach clenches. I already feel like my hair's standing on end xcept I'm wearing a hat so it can't be. Don't know why I should listen to Tony; he is not xactly a good guy like they have in books. He's not a hero.

But maybe we don't need a hero here.

"Are you still set on killing Artio?"

Funny question to ask. I didn't even know he heard of my plan. "I don't know," I say. I was at Artio's cave. I could have done it then. But I'm waiting. I'm deciding. I'm still, always, deciding.

He makes a half smile at me and my face gets warm. I forgot he could do that to me. "What I have to tell you isn't easy to hear. I don't even know if you should hear it, but it might help you decide about taking down that bear."

"It killed Samuel."

"Yes, it did," he says. "Now tell me: Was that entirely a crime?"

He's up to something. He knows things. He's reminding me of Gil right now. I narrow my eyes and suddenly I'm thinking about how it all went down out by Blueberry Cliff. How mad I was after, and how sad I was, too. How it all got piled together into a heap of emotion.

"Who are you really mad at here?" he asks. "The bear? Or your father? Didn't he just steal you and your brother away and keep you both out here for years, even though at least one of you wanted to go home? Seems to me that having that bear come along when it did was pretty much the best thing that could have happened to you."

I don't say anything. Now he *really* sounds like Gil. Once again I wonder: *Just how does he know all of this?*

"My guess is you're so fixed on this bear because you feel guilty as hell that you listened to one of the *sìthean* and not to your own father, and he ended up dead. That you chose and your choice changed your whole life." He takes a deep breath. "That's how life works, though. It's a bunch of choices. We try to make the right ones. And sometimes even then there's a roadblock that says, 'Nope, go this way instead,' or 'You are definitely not getting that thing you had your heart set on, so deal with it.' I promise, I know. I was gonna be a soldier and then an officer and run the army. Then I fucked up bad. At some point, you gotta be responsible for your own shit. The bad and the good."

"The shit and the shine-o-la," I say softly.

That sinks in on him and he almost smiles but doesn't. "If you kill Artio you'll get locked out of The Green Place, and it sucks. Having that window open to the other side—it's like falling in love the first time. If somebody slams that window shut on you and says 'never again,' it hurts worse than anything you've ever known. You're gonna miss it. I miss it, and it made me a little crazy for a while. But that doesn't mean I think you should leave Artio alone. It just means … make sure you've thought it through."

I put the book aside and sniff in the rest of my tears. "It's not just about me and Samuel, though," I say. "Without Artio the forest might turn into like it is in France. On the battlefield. The world might split open."

"Clíodhna tell you that?"

I nod.

"Hmm," he says. "That's not anything I ever heard. Might be a big fat lie. You're gonna have to decide if that matters." He stares out the tiny window of the shack. "In training, they taught us a shit ton of things. But one that sticks best for me is finding ways to make a really tough decision easier. You ask yourself three questions: What do you need to protect, what can you sacrifice, and where is the exit? That's cleared a lot of things up for me over the years."

I think about his questions, and he's right, it works. My heart quiets and I hear my answer: I'm protecting the woods. I'm sacrificing the truth. And the exit will come to me, when I ask. I make my choice, but it's so hard to let things go. To let Artio go. There are too many reasons not to hurt her, and only one really good one to do it—one that doesn't mean as much anymore.

"Okay," I say. "What else?"

He's very serious, almost like he was back 'round the campfire that first morning, when he asked, "what else don't we know about you" and I thought, *everything*.

He knows just about everything now.

"It's about your brother," he says. "He's the one who gave me the pack. He's … Artio."

With that, Tony puts Jim back into the world for me.

Then comes the roar.

I know the sound right away. *It's her*, I think. *Artio is here*.

We stand up at the same time and both of us know there's more to be said here—but we can't wait. Tony busts out of the shack first. I'm right behind, about to dash to the lake—though I have no plan for what I'll do when I get there.

"Lass," calls Gillie. She's sitting on the ground with her back against the shack, pulling a piece of braided grass through her fingers. The space around her is lush and green and spring. "Dinnae rush 'way yet."

I stop hard in the snow but Tony barely pauses. He looks over his shoulder. "Can't stay," he tells me. "Gotta make sure they're not getting mauled." He glares at Gillie, then looks at me. "And don't you listen to anything this one has to say."

'Xcept I do have questions. Lots of questions. "Tony—" I grab for him but he's already heading to the lake. I turn 'round and look at Gillie. "I have to get to Artio."

"To kill him, nae?"

I lean forward. I want to get away so fast, but something about her makes me stay.

"Even though I tell ye nae time and again? Even though ye ken what will happen?"

"You lied to me," I say. "Gil—lied to me."

She flashes bright red, then goes orange. "Aye," she says. "So we did. D'ye not see why?"

"I don't care about the whys," I say. "You should have said something."

She kicks at some snow, which melts and reveals a green patch. "Mebbe," she says.

I want to pound on her; she's like a little kid sometimes. So is Gil. So are they all.

"I will say it once more," says Gillie. "Harm Artio an' the forest here will be as if ye had never known any o' us. 'Tis a hard weight to bear. Anthony kens. An' Thomas—he will waste away w'out returning soon. So choose wisely."

"I have," I say and make my legs move. I get five steps.

"'Tis yer brother in there," calls Gillie. "Ye want to kill him?"

I stop and my eyes burn. "He's already gone," I say, and know it to be true. "But you won't let him leave."

"Nae choice, wean," she says to me. "He is needful to us."

I whirl. "I'm nobody's wean anymore," I say. "I am the *lorgaire* and you can't stop me."

Another howl. My throat is tight and my head is singing. *Jim. Artio.* Then my feet are moving swift and sure through the snow.

Chateau Artio

"She's been gone a long time," says T.J.

Stef lays another layer of branches on the lean-to and tamps down the snow on the side. She stands back, examining her handiwork. It was mostly her doing, this shelter they're going to sleep in tonight—T.J. did some chopping and helped her lug some of the bigger branches, but mostly he's spent the last few hours staring off into the near distance, shivering and quiet.

Apparently being worshipped by mythical beings in an alternate world where there's no such thing as cold or hunger or work ethic is pretty attractive, she thinks sourly. But when she looks at him she's overcome anew by the fact that he's here with her and breathing. Living. Alive.

"You listening?"

"Yeah, yeah," she says. "She's fine, I'm sure." She stands back and gestures at the structure, which looks like half a roof angling out of the ground. Having felled and trimmed multiple saplings and pine boughs, they were able to create a sturdy, thick-roofed layer to protect against the elements, and she used snow to build walls on the shorter sides so the wind won't get to them. This is a new way to find the pieces and make them fit, and she'd like a little credit for creatively interpreting Gillie's words.

"C'mon, be impressed." She waves at him.

T.J. leaves off half-heartedly digging a trench and gives the lean-to a quick eye. "A long way from the Presidential Suite at Chateau Marmont," he says.

She throws a handful of snow at him, then bursts out laughing. Stef knows better than to expect an attaboy from T.J. "Well, consider it the Presidential Suite of Chateau Artio, and that's all you get tonight, buster."

"Last thing I want is a *bear* inside with us. I got close enough once already."

"But it'd be so warm." Stef clasps her hands under her chin and bats her eyelashes.

T.J. turns serious. "Okay, okay, you are pretty incredible. I never say it, but you are."

She swats at him and dances away. That would have melted her heart a few years ago; hell, even recently. But now it stirs nothing in her but affection. *It's happened,* she thinks. *We're real siblings.*

"Know how you can amaze me back?" she asks with a tilt of her head.

"What?"

"Get digging." She points at the trench. "We gotta move the fire in there before it gets full dark. We've got maybe an hour, if we're lucky."

"Think dinner's happening anytime soon?"

"Seriously, Salty." There's an edge in her voice. "We're all cold. We're all hungry. We're all dying to get out of here. You not putting your shoulder in is really not cute at all."

"Why do you sound pissed at me?"

She sighs. "I'm not. But you're staring into space like you don't get that we're all in trouble until we walk out of this forest. Like everybody should be doing stuff for you."

"I keep thinking about being back there," he says. "It was the greatest experience of my life. Like a present I didn't even know I wanted."

She snaps her fingers in front of his face. "Hey. I thought you were pretty happy with being the king of the world back home," she says. "So you didn't get to be Burt Fucking Reynolds here. So what? You have millions of people who love you out there. Including two parents who probably think they lost both their kids five months ago. Going on six."

"I know," he says. "I know. It's just—maybe she was right."

"Maybe who was right?" This is starting to concern her.

"Clíodhna. She said I'd want to come back. And I do. Singing in this world is—well, it doesn't *mean* a whole lot," he says. "Back there I was making people better. Making *sìthiche* better, I mean. It wasn't just about fun and games."

Stef crouches in front of him. "Thomas," she says, and he focuses. Using his first name usually works. "It's cool that you've decided your life should have meaning. So maybe that means you go home and go to medical school and become a doctor. Be the first pop-star doctor ever. But understand—you're charmed by them right now. Hell, I kind of am, too. That doesn't mean we get to just throw our whole lives away because we got sprinkled with pixie dust."

He's nodding slowly. "I guess."

"You want to do good, maybe try and help Lexi when she walks out with us. 'Cause it's gonna be a shitstorm when we leave—and it's gonna be even harder on her, walking into it."

That's something that's been worrying Stef ever since they came back from The Green Place. The last thing a woman who hasn't hung around with more than a few people at a time since she was eight probably needs is to dive into the maelstrom of modern-day superstardom. That's an average day for T.J. Add to it that he's about to emerge from the forest after five months of likely being considered dead—and that's going to become a hurricane. Tony'll be a help, but Stef remains uneasy on all of their behalfs.

Straightening, Stef leans backward, giving her spine a good bend. She'll sleep just fine tonight. But there is one more task she wants to take care of before they settle in for the night. Lexi pulled out Tony's PEP back at the Glampsite, and Stef's mind has been going to it all afternoon, waiting for a chance to get her hands on it. Taking it from Lexi's backpack, she holds up the weapon, looking at it from all sides—then pulls it apart, laying the pieces on a rolled-out blanket under the lean-to in order of size. Absently, she gives her wrist a gentle rub and flips on the watch light to see better.

T.J. sticks his head into the lean-to. "Gonna go for a walk. There's a new path leading out of camp, not the one we came in on. I'm gonna explore, think about some things."

"Good, good." Her eyes and attention are on the task at hand. "Don't get lost."

She's aware of T.J.'s footsteps as they fade from the campsite, and they fade from her memory just as quickly. She's getting into her zone.

Suspending the glowing watch from a stick above her head, Stef illuminates the disassembled PEP's pieces, her mind slipping into a new gear. The pieces glow and faintly vibrate, the more fluttery ones seeming to insist that they be selected for recombination first.

But Stef waits. She could just put the PEP back together the way it had been when Tony used it. It could once again be the same weapon he turned on Gillie, Artio, and probably countless others when he was in the field. Tony knows how to recognize unseen; he's been doing it for years—and that's why he knew instinctively to use it on Artio. He knew the animal was magic long before any of them did.

Now it's Lexi's turn to want to use it against the bear, and Stef's mind balks at that. Turning it on Artio seems wrong: She attacked everyone because she was attacked first. Maybe there's a way to just ... disable Artio. Make Lexi believe she's dead. Stef concentrates harder: The first use of the PEP knocks the special out of everyone around; the second use is for more final applications. Tony would have turned that pulsing beam on the *sìthiche* next if Stef hadn't found a way to stay his hand. The gun has so far only been an instrument of pain and death.

But it doesn't have to be that way.

One option is to scoop up all these loose pieces and toss them into a hole in the lake ice. She's spotted a few out there in the snow. Yet Stef is sure the gun is with them for a reason. Closing her eyes, she turns her thoughts to the pieces themselves and imagines them to have new purpose. Images of Gillie, Artio, and Lexi come to mind, and she feels as if she's showing a problem to the pieces, then asking them to rise to the challenge. When she opens her eyes again, she gasps.

The pieces are hovering in front of her, still separated but now stacked in a new configuration. She reaches up for one and slides it in mid-air onto the other, then brings that combination around to a third. Her fingers become a blur as she places the hovering, vibrating parts together when they call to her. It takes seconds but feels much longer, more intense. When she stops, the finished PEP slides into its casing and rests on the ground; if it were an animal she could imagine its sides heaving with effort.

There is one piece left over. It looks like a washer, but when she picks it up it resembles a silver eye.

A faint trickle of sweat runs down her spine and her heart is pounding. Her hands are dead weights and she shakes them up and down to get the circulation going again. She is inordinately rejuvenated and pleased. *I did a thing*, she thinks, feeling happier about this creation than the lean-to—which was also something she assembled without questioning how.

What else can this unseen do? she wonders. *Could it even—*

Is someone calling her name?

Stef peers outside the lean-to. T.J. is still out on his walk; all she can hear is the silence of the lake and the trees and the world.

She returns to the finished PEP and sandwiches it between both hands. It emits a hum of satisfaction, as if the pieces are pleased to be reunited. Yet now it no longer feels like a weapon. It feels like … a tool. A tool fashioned with magic. A hybrid made for a task she does not yet understand. But the Peppie knows.

Peppie. It's changed. It's got a new name. She's Peps. She's made a Peppie.

Stef sets it aside and releases a long, deep breath. She's tired. A lean-to and a weapon-tool all in one afternoon; that can wear on a person. She starts daydreaming of pizza. Hot chocolate. Grapes.

"Stef!"

No question—that's her name. And … where is T.J., anyway? Stef crawls outside of the lean-to, scanning the lake. Then she spots it—a large, dark smudge emerging from the trees, moving in her direction. A large smudge in the exact shape of a bear. Artio.

"*Stephanie!*" T.J. calls again. "*STEPHANIE!*"

But I don't need a ride this time, she thinks. Grabbing at Tony's binoculars, she focuses on the bear—and instinctively feels that this is not the same Artio who helped her before. There's a snarl in its mouth and its one good eye is flat and wild. It is approaching in a straight line, with a very specific intent.

Scrabbling at the woodpile they amassed earlier she snatches up a long stick and winds a scarf on one end, making a fast knot. She pours cooking oil on it, then dips it into their starter fire. The scarf comes alight and she steps carefully to the ice line, waving it as if expecting to land a plane. There's T.J. steering a wide berth on the far side of the oncoming bear, which lets out a howling roar as it crosses onto the lake ice and continues plodding to their camp.

T.J. nearly barrels into her, then catches himself and snatches up one of their remaining bow and arrows. His hands are shaking as he nocks an arrow, and when he pulls back, the string snaps against his arm and he drops everything. "Shit, shit, shit," he mutters with a high spiral of panic in his tone. Stef jams the end of her stick into the snow and grabs him by the shoulders.

"Think," she says, bringing her forehead to his. "Take a deep breath, and think."

His eyes meet hers and she feels great satisfaction when the crazed glint in them submerges. He turns away and grabs one of the leftover pointed branches they fashioned for the lean-to, holding it out before him. Grabbing her torch, Stef regrets some of the shaming she's thrown his way before; in this moment of need he's doing the opposite of running away.

"Be big!" she calls to him. "Be big so she'll go away!"

"I don't think any of us can be that big," he tells her, teeth chattering. "I can't kill it. I don't want to kill it. I just want it to go away."

"I know, Salty," she says. "I get it." Calm steals over her as the bear nears. By the light of the fire she can see her in detail now, that one yellow eye trained directly on them and the other a scarred-over mess. Artio's rubbery lips peel back as she roars, spittle flying, jagged teeth on display. Together they hold their ground, and once she reaches the snowbank at the edge of the lake they take a step forward.

"Get!" shouts T.J., slipping his jacket off and using it like a matador waving a cape at a bull. "G'wan!"

Artio halts, then backs up. Emboldened, T.J. takes a big step her way, then a second, and she's forced back onto the white expanse of the snow-covered lake. Stef cocks her head; even as her heart is pounding, she can't figure out why the bear seems to want to maul them one minute, then the next is backing away. It's like she's toying with them.

"C'mon" T.J. jabs his stick. "Let's do this."

They take a step, then another. Artio retreats and with each thudding footfall Stef hears a muffled splintering beneath the snow. The pop-pop-pop underfoot grows in frequency and intensity until she actually feels the ground shift. There's a hole out there, she bets. Either that or a very soft place in the ice.

"On three," she tells T.J., teeth gritted.

"No!" says T.J. "She'll—"

There's a blood rush in her mind, yet everything around her is sharp and clear. "One, two, *three*."

Together, they lunge at the beast. Artio tries to stand up, but wobbles unsteadily. T.J. grabs Stef's hand and together they hold both torch and stick together and drive them at the matted brown pelt, narrowly avoiding a swiping paw. Artio's fur catches fire and she roars again, this time a sound of terror and pain. The ice crumbles beneath her hind paws and she tumbles backward into the lake. There's a soft sizzle as her pelt hits the frigid water, and the bear goes under howling with rage, clawing at the shards of ice swallowing her.

T.J. and Stef fling themselves against the banks of the lake and scramble toward the lean-to, gasping for breath, dragging the icy air into their throats.

Stef giggles softly. "We done kilt ourselves a bar," she drawls.

T.J. plants an enormous kiss on her forehead. They have just a moment to look at one another when the ground erupts.

Artio bursts from the depths of the lake sopping and roaring. Stef screams in surprise as ice shards spray into the air and skitter across the frozen lake. One thick chunk slams into her leg and a sharp pain slices through her, shattering the mind-freezing terror of seeing the bear emerge again.

With a mighty leap, Artio is back atop the lake, water stiffening her pelt. She claws at the ice, roaring, and gallops toward Stef and T.J. They cringe together, expecting the worst.

And then—Gillie is there. The fae springs from the lakeside bushes, landing on the ice and deftly skating on her boots toward the bear. She halts next to Artio, holding up her hand.

"Stand down, all o'ye," she orders, looking up at Artio. "All is well," she says. "Ye will be fine nowwhens."

If anyone can be a bear whisperer it's Gillie, but the bear doesn't relax. Her one yellow eye glints to life like a light going on inside a dark house. She raises a thick paw and bats Gillie away like a doll. The *sìthean* tumbles against the ice, rolling into the bushes, and disappears into the snow. A moment later, Gillie pops back out, shaking her head, and rises to her hands and knees.

That would have been the end of one of us, Stef thinks. *Those fey are tough.*

A throaty shout from the trees reaches Stef, and she and T.J. whirl to see Lexi barreling their way, jumping down the bank and breathing hard. She tosses aside her bow and arrows from the Glampsite. Her hat has toppled off and her hair is loose and wild in the growing breeze. She takes slow, careful steps toward Artio, blinking briefly at Stef. "The PEP," she mouths.

Stef races over to the lean-to and grabs it, tossing it at Lexi.

"Works?" she asks in a low voice.

Stef makes a seesaw motion with her hand and shrugs, two responses that are as true as she knows them to be. Lexi resumes her careful walk to the bear as Gillie watches her, narrow-eyed, from the ground. "Lass," she says.

Lexi ignores her.

Stef catches a swift flash of shadow over the snow, coming from the edge of the bushes. To her surprise it's Tony, decked out like some kind of royal huntsman, long black coat trailing on the lake ice. T.J. spots him and starts to wave, but Tony sets a finger over his lips and approaches Gillie from behind with careful steps. He is, of course, trained for military missions. To sneak behind enemy lines and remain stealthy. To be ... well, *unseen*.

He closes in on Gillie as Lexi strides forward, Peppie gun low at her side.

"My turn," says Lexi, and stops directly in front of Artio.

Shoot When the Target Presents

She should have been in that cave. We should've heard her coming. But no. I messed up. Artio, she's a better tracker than me and she's found us and she's maybe going to try and get to us before I can get to her.

Xcept: She's not just Artio. She's Jim. She's got my brother inside her—or at least what's left of his unseen—and while that's not totally stuck into my mind as something that can really be true I feel it in my heart. It makes sense that a crazy person would understand and so, I think, I might be crazy.

But not yet. I don't get to be crazy. Artio is here and she's got a passenger who wants *out* and of course the two of them won't wait for winter to be over. That might actually be a good thing. Might mean Jim has control. Tony didn't have a lot of time to tell me things and in places I just blanked out, staring at the broken wood of the shack, thinking, *Of course* and *never* and *how* over and over before snapping back.

I run so hard to the lake but while Gillie and Tony and Jim and Artio all pass through my head, the person I'm really thinking of while I pound through the snow, gasping for breath, is Stef. She and T.J. are totally unprotected down there and I keep thinking with every step *don't hurt them Artio don't hurt them Jim*. But I'm sure *he* can't hear me, and I'm sure *she* doesn't care.

Everything happens so fast once I get to the lake but here I am now and I have a PEP Stef has fixed and I Artio in front of me and there's Tony, hiding in the bushes. Being a secret weapon. At least nobody's been hurt. Not yet.

"My turn," I say and step in front of Artio, who comes down on her front paws and turns her head, growling at Gillie.

How much is Jim?

How much is Artio?

That one yellow, shining eye glares up at me and I try to see him, I stare right back and I say, "Jim. I didn't know. I'm sorry."

Artio tilts her head, shaking it. Ice crystals spray.

"Is it you in there?" I ask.

"'Course it is," says Gillie, who's back up on her feet. " 'Twill change nothing, but ye should ken 'twas done with yer brother Jim's say-so."

"But he's failing," I say. "The forest used him up. That's why the cave has a dark heart. He's not helping you anymore, Gillie. Let him go." I look to one side and wipe my eyes. Stef and T.J. are standing like heroes on the edge of the lake, sticks held up and ready for battle. Stef gives me a nod and that helps in ways she can't know. They are scared but not afraid. So I will be, too.

"The story is the truth," says Tony, who's finished sneaking up behind Gillie. She turns 'round and her eyes go wide. "But she's leaving one part out. She promised once Samuel was dead that he could be free. That hasn't happened."

Gillie bares her teeth at him.

I stand up straight. More lies that were never told, just ignored. "D'you want out, Jim?"

The yellow eye blinks at me.

"How dae ye ken if this one has been true?" says Gillie. "For what does he deserve yer faith? Our kind trusted him once, and our kind burned for it."

It's cold out here but my face feels hot and I'm not breathing too good. Guess I never knew everybody could lie to me so easy, and now I don't know how to tell truth from not truth. I look between Gillie and Tony and truth is, he's not a good man. Gil, and Gillie, have been my only friends. Until recently.

Gillie strolls my way. "Or," she says. "P'haps ye should take care o' the problem yerself, Anthony Garcia. Take yer gun, an' use it."

Tony gives her the angriest look I've ever seen. Suppose he could. He knows the PEP, and he can't go back to The Green Place anyway. So he could do it. But—it's my job. Jim's *my* brother. I'm his keeper, like he was mine. I turn back to the bear. To Artio. Her eye is less yellow. Flickering brown. More like … Jim's eye. I lower the PEP and take a step forward. I just want to touch Jim one more time, give him a hug. Then I'll know what he really wants. I don't know how I'll know but I'll know.

Gillie smiles. " 'Twas his wish, Lexi. Artio must have some human in her to walk this world, ye ken? An' this world needs protecting. So, a good trade."

It's always a trade with them. Never a kindness. I take another step and the PEP goes loose in my hands. "I can't," I mutter. "I can't. I can't *know* so I can't …"

The weapon makes a soft crunch sound when it falls in the snowy ice and in that second Gillie is a piece of lightning and she snaps it up. "Aye," she says to herself.

"That's not for you," calls Stef.

Gillie smiles at her.

I can reach out and touch the fur, the stiff frozen fur on Artio and the instant I do the brown of the eye flickers away. She stops being Jim and starts being Artio again. Her lips quiver back and her haunches go up. She's not going to let me do it. She's going to kill me first. I flinch, my shoulders going down. Maybe I can get away before—

"The baby bird," Tony calls to me. "Jim said 'Remember the baby bird.'"

My throat gets tight and I make a gasp sound and I think of Hey Fox. And now I know who is being true. But—I have no gun. I have nothing.

What do you need to protect?
What can you sacrifice?
Where is the exit?

I hear all Tony's list of questions in my head again and without saying any abracadabras I know the way. I meet Tony's eyes and we move at the same time, two pieces of lightning hurled at Gillie. He goes for her body as I go for her hand and I twist in time to snatch the PEP from her fingers just as Tony hits her hard from behind. They both go down against the ice and out of the corner of my eye I see Gillie slide right into an ice hole.

Tony groans.

I do my own sliding on the ice but land on my back. I smell winter in the air and spy stars in the sky. Then they are gone as Artio rears up and comes at me. She swipes a claw my way that scrapes my coat and tears it open.

I point the PEP up at her and pull the trigger and—

Whomp.

The push rebounds on me just like it did when Tony shot it five months ago, like an echo you can feel, and under my back the ice makes a cracking sound but holds. But I hardly feel it 'cause Artio—a bear twice any our sizes, a monster, a goddess, my brother—goes *flying* across the ice, like she's been punched with an invisible fist. She goes up and over and lands hard on the ice, making a little bounce before rolling on her back and going still.

"Shit," murmurs Tony from where he fell on the ice.

Nobody moves, nobody says anything.

Artio's mouth falls open.

A brilliant blue butterfly that reminds me of one of Clíodhna's birds crawls out and perches on the tip of the bear's muzzle, fluttering its wings. He's delicate and impossible and is there only a second, just long enough to be noticed. Then he jumps into the sky and comes to me, circling over my head once, twice—like saying hellogoodbye, then darts high into the sky, swirling and diving and rising until he's just another piece of the night.

I never knew tears could freeze on my face.

I roll over. There's Tony, face down on the ice, up on his elbows. My eyes are burning and wet and cold and I drop the PEP. Then I remember Gillie. She went down, down. Past the ice, into the water.

Wiping my face on my sleeve I wave at Stef and T.J. and they don't ask questions, they just come running over. "Hold my legs," I say, and take one of their sticks. Then I go Ghillie Dhu fishing, sticking one end as far as I can down the hole while the two of them make a chain behind me.

"Won't do any good," mumbles Tony. "She's gone by now."

At first he's right. Seconds go by and I can feel the ice getting into me, freezing me up—I've been cold but never this cold—but then the stick jerks and a dark hand with long fingers reaches into the sky. I let the stick go and grab Gillie's hand with my free ones, shouting, "Pull!"

It takes forever but Gillie's head, shoulders, and finally her whole body slides out of the water and we drag her onto the snowbank. I flip her over; she's covered in beautiful clear crystals like a tree after an ice storm, but her eyes are wide and she sees me. With a big shake she sits upright, the ice cracking like glass. Big chunks fall off her and she blinks at me.

"Ye pulled me out," she says. Her skin is turning from slate gray to its usual dark forest shades. "Ye brought me back."

"Nobody should be at the bottom of a lake forever," I say.

Gillie reaches over with fingers that are shaky and very slowly touches my face, then brings her hand to mine. "We did right, helpin' ye yesterwhen," she says softly, and pulls me to her. She's wet and cold but she's also hugging me for the first time ever. I'm the one who always does the hugs. "Thankee," she says. "I cannae swim."

Her eyes flick to the rest of the lake, where Artio lies still, and she pulls away. "Nae! Nae!" Gillie pushes away from me and dashes toward the bear, who has collapsed on her back with paws splayed out. Stef follow her with Stef to the bear's side.

Gillie buries her hands in Artio's fur and rests her head on the bear's chest, which is rising and falling gently as if she's just taking a nap. "'Tis empty," says Gillie in a whisper, and slides down onto the ice next to Artio. "What have ye done, ye two?"

"Why me?" says Stef. "I didn't shoot it."

"Ye remade the gun, aye?"

Stef nods. "I did what the Peppie wanted. Artio is alive. Right? Just not—without—"

"Not without my brother inside," I say, and I'm getting angry again. Artio will live. Stef made sure that I didn't kill her. What more does Gillie *need*?

"W'out a human soul the forest is in danger," says Gillie. "Artio is but a bear, now. An yer cave is—a dark heart, as ye say. Maybe a month, a year. But now our forest is doomed." She looks at me and she's sad, not angry. "'T'was a bigger story than yers and Jim's, ken?"

"I'm not sorry," I say. "You didn't have the right to keep him."

Gillie shakes her head, and frozen strands of grass clink on the ground. "'Tis nae fight to have now." She sighs. "Ye are set to leave the forest. Ye will be with yer kind. Go, then. Find out that yer kind are nae friends of me and mine. Be like them. Forget us all."

"Clíodhna said she wanted us to help," says Stef. "And we want to help—but we also have lives outside. Family. Friends."

"Aye," says Gillie. "So is the choice. This isnae yer fight, I ken. But."

She doesn't say it, but I hear the missing words: *It will be.*

I set my hand on Gillie's shoulder. "My whole life someone's been telling me what to think and what to do," I tell her. "I can't let you be the next person in charge of me. *I* need to be in charge of me." I look over at Stef, who's biting her lip. "It had to happen this way. You see that, right?"

Gillie doesn't answer, just looks at the ice. Artio's breaths are so hot and heavy she's making a small patch in the ice melt by breathing on it, and that's the only sound we hear.

"I want to still be friends," I tell her.

Silence.

And then the world is full of T.J., who's been with Tony this whole time, and he's shouting louder than anything else "Jesus," he's yell-crying. "He's bleeding. He's bleeding everywhere."

The Mercy Kill

Tony can hardly feel anything as they roll him over and pack his newly slashed-open stomach with snow, binding it tight with a blanket and carrying him off the ice. He didn't think. Didn't think at all, just gave Gillie a shove and that's why she fell into the water—but it doesn't matter. Not anymore.

This was going to happen sometime, he thinks. *I never had a chance.*

T.J.'s yelling is starting to get to him—the kid is alternating crying and yelling with singing, and who knows why the kid has to *sing* right now but it is not helping one bit—when Gillie and the others arrive. The creature gives him something to sip that blunts the edge from the burning, but it's not enough. They can't stanch the blood fast enough, and he senses he's going into shock.

Meanwhile, T.J. keeps keening, and Tony can't help but wonder how much of that is sympathy and how much of it is that the kid is now realizing he'll be without his own protector pretty soon.

That's me, he thinks. *He's had his own Artio all this time.*

"What the fuck is going on?" Stef barks once they have Tony stabilized.

"Clíodhna," murmurs Gillie. "Cursed him, so she did."

Lexi grips Tony's hand and it feels good; she's warm and strong and he holds her back. "Why is this happening?" she asks. "Can't you do something?"

"I could sing some more," sniffs T.J. through a clogged nose.

"Nae for this," says Gillie. "Will nae work against the queen's *geas*."

Gillie offers more of the cure-all that cures very little: tea from a cupped leaf. They bring it to Tony's lips and some dribbles in but much falls to one side. He forces his eyes open and takes a shallow breath; more and the searing returns. "Christ," he murmurs, gritting his teeth. "That unholy witch."

"Nae," says Gillie, sitting back in the snow, which disappears around her and becomes grass. "Ye knew the rules, Anthony: Hurt us an' the wounds from Artio return. 'Tis what makes a *geas*—that it can never be ignored forever. A raking from Artio 'tis a fatal thing. Eventually."

"So because he stopped Lexi from getting eaten by your bear—he's—he's going to die?" Stef stands and grabs at her hair. Tony knows that she doesn't like him much, but it's nice to hear she isn't actively rejoicing right now.

The cold is seeping into him, so cold it's almost warm.

"Get her here!" cries T.J. "Tell her it's a mistake! Tell her I won't ever, ever come back if she doesn't fix him!"

Tony wants to rail at this. If he had the energy, he might. But trapped in his own mind, hardly able to concentrate anymore, he feels the truth of it in his heart. It isn't a mistake. He has taken his own steps—steps not so different from Samuel's—and they have walked him right to this place, this moment. He has listened to the wrong sort of people and believed them, on both sides of this war.

But everything he did was voluntary. He wanted something so badly he would do anything to get it, and that was always his choice. He only wishes he had another chance to see The Green Place. Jim might not have been able to stand it, but Tony knows he's made of sterner stuff. He could do just fine over there.

Something turns in his mind.

T.J. is still wailing.

"Shut it," Tony whispers to him. "It's okay. I—I knew this might happen. But that wasn't Jim. Jim didn't go after you, Lexi. The bear took control." He winces. "Ah, shit."

"Can you at least make him not in pain?" Stef snaps. "Think you can be useful for once?"

Gillie glowers at her and grass falls in large clumps from her hat. "I can go, if ye like. Go entire."

"Stop it," says Lexi, voice thick and furious and full of tears. She leans closer to Tony. "You didn't need to die. Not for me."

"Didn't do it ... for you," he says. "I've done ... monstrous things. One good thing can't negate that. I've killed so many *sìthiche*, they—they owe me." He glances up at Gillie. "I'm sorry for shooting you."

"Didnae hurt," says Gillie, puffing her chest. "Much."

Tony looks around at all of them. He wants this in the open. "Over in Brittany, I did ... horrors. I shot every *sìthiche* I could come on. I've killed dozens. Maybe hundreds."

Lexi makes a soft noise and Stef's breath catches. T.J. is finally, blessedly, quiet.

"And," prompts Gillie softly. "Tell of the pits."

His breathing feels sharper now, more ragged. He wants to confess. He wants them to know what this war is like. What fear can do when it has a weapon in its hand. "You saw the battlefield," he says. "You didn't see the holes in the earth where they put the bodies. Once they're shot we put them in the holes and cover them up. We light them on fire so they can't reanimate with magic." His voice weakens and trails off. "That's—I can't." The queen fixed him inside and out, she said, and he understands what that means. The brainwashing his superiors put him through is gone, and that leaves him naked and aware of all of it. The memories burn worse than his injuries.

"Then I will tell," says Gillie with no joy in her voice, just a flat, hard tone. "This one here put those of us that wisnae dead yet on the piles. An' they couldnae escape. They were weak from the thumps. Then they started the fires. An' the screams from the pits, they were music, aye?"

"The most terrible music I ever heard," sighs Tony, opening his eyes. "We heard it in our bodies." He remembers coming home from those days in the field covered in misshapen bruises; the music of the dying fae had left marks on him.

T.J. stares at him blankly. Stef is wiping her hands on her pants almost abstractedly, as if she has been coated in something unspeakable.

Tony feels lightness in his mind. He is thinking of trains, of journeys, of places without snow. "I tried," he said. "To be better."

"Aye," says Gillie. "So ye did." She looks around at Stef, T.J., and Lexi. "Set some of us free an' tried to find the way home. But. 'Tis nae as easily done as that. All were found. All went to the pits."

A tear rolls down Tony's face. "There aren't words for how sorry I am. Once, I wanted to help."

Gillie stands, rubbing at her mouth, and walks in a circle. Her footsteps leave green paths in her wake. Even on ice, she makes things grow. After a moment, she returns to the ground. "Ye can say sorry, if ye like," she says. "Or ye may be of help."

Tony's eyes go wide and he trembles inside.

"Ye have only ever wanted to live in my hame," says Gillie. " 'Tis true?"

"Always," Tony whispers, thinking of the aperture that opened and showed him a new world.

"Will ye then yield? Artio's an empty bear now an' needs one like ye."

Lexi gasps and holds Tony's hand tighter.

"You don't waste any time," says T.J, his voice full of angry tears.

Tony nods. "Ah! Oh. Yes. Jesus, yes." It is more than he expected and more than he deserves. He has been wrong all this time and that will sit on him until the day he, too, is released.

"Aye, then," says Gillie, and removes a green wooden box from a pocket in her jacket. " 'Tis agreed."

Tony turns to T.J. "Will miss you, kid." He looks at Stef. "Keep an eye on him. Or—don't. Maybe he needs fewer eyes than we've put on him. Maybe he needs a chance to make some mistakes."

Stef nods, and T.J. takes Tony's free hand. "Be a better man than I've been," he tells him, flicking his eyes over the others. "Not that it'll be too tough." He coughs once and opens his eyes to see Lexi bending over him.

"I'll see you again," she says. "You know how hard it is to stay away from The Green Place forever. I'll find a way in."

"Aye," he says, and coughs long and hard; blood fills his mouth and he feels as if he's drowning. His vision grays.

Gillie's face hovers over him and is the last thing he sees. There is a tugging, a tearing and then something small and wispy drifts from Tony's mouth into the small green box.

What is left of him lies quiet and still against the red snow for a time, until his heart finishes beating.

Natural Magic

The torch won't catch fire.

The bear is coming and the pieces of what to do have assembled in Stef's mind, but when she takes the branch meant for the fire and dips it in flame she keeps missing. She even jabs directly into the heart of the coals and it still won't catch. She makes one last stabbing gesture, trying desperately to turn this useless piece of wood into a tool, a weapon—something that will save all of them—and then Artio is upon her.

She wakes, head buzzy. It takes a moment to realize none of that is true. There is no bear, no fire. She is surrounded by thin wooden walls in a structure that shakes gently from the wind outside.

Today, she thinks. They'll be out of the woods today. Going home. Facing the music.

Wincing, she gets up on her knees and rolls down her pants to examine her thigh. An ice chunk struck her in the leg the night before when Artio leapt from the water and it has left a bit of swelling and a bruise. She set snow against the joint before falling asleep last night, so it could be worse. It also reminds her that unlike in the dream, there was a bear and a fire and a death last night. *None of us escape unscathed*, she thinks and quickly locates her notepad. She scribbles the lyric down. More pieces of an invisible puzzle assembling themselves.

My natural magic, she thinks, and writes that down too. Closing her eyes, she sees pictures and words and music intertwining. Wonders if they will fit in a song; people don't sing much about magic anymore, even if they're just being fanciful. It feels almost transgressive. If she can write lyrics, then for five more minutes she can hold back the memory of what happened to Tony. That is not a place she is ready to visit again, and she's still unsure what really happened.

Last night after Gillie left with Artio, Lexi guided them to the ice shack where they piled together under a blanket. Stef was completely out of spoons for the day, to quote her mom's favorite old memephrase. But sleep did not come immediately, and her mind refused to shut off.

"Love you," T.J. murmured in his near sleep, and she took his hand.

She repeated the phrase back to him a few seconds later, out of habit. By then he was already unconscious. It is oddly freeing, and terrifying, to feel unbound to her heart this way. Imagining that she and T.J. were inevitable for so long made it easy to ignore everything the rest of the world offered her.

And now, what an entire other world offers them both.

We need one who can find the way, one who understands how to make the pieces into a whole, and one who can heal.

Three people. On a whole new hunt. A hunt for something called a *uilebheist*. The thing that is causing so much suffering. There's a lot Stef doesn't know, but it's the not knowing that makes her tingle inside.

Stef sits in the quiet and writes more words for the man she loves but is not in love with to sing someday, and hears a muffled hacking cut through the morning air. It goes on, pauses, turns into a noise she cannot define, then resumes. For the first time, she glances around the tiny interior of the shack and realizes she is alone. Piling on another layer of clothing and her coat, Stef steps into the world, following recent footprints in the snow. Down by the lakeside Lexi and T.J. are pulling apart the lean-to and lashing together thick tree branches with the tent cord they used while walking across the lake yesterday.

Stef rubs her eyes in surprise: T.J. is doing manual labor.

She looks closer. Between the tree branch frame they have stretched a blanket and several pine boughs, tying them on securely. Then she gets it.

"A sled," she says, walking up to them. "You're making a sled."

T.J. blinks up at her. "Hey," he says absently. "We have to carry him out somehow."

Stef swallows. The other thing they did before collapsing into sleep after Gillie departed was to use Tony's sleeping bag as a shroud, zipping him in and covering his face. Overnight, his body rested outside of the shack and could probably remain there for some time, preserved by the cold.

She isn't sure how to feel about Tony, or the loss of him. He gave them the world, but only under his conditions. He kept them sheltered—but also protected. He was their shield against danger, but ultimately he was the most dangerous person she'd ever met. The things he said before succumbing are going to stick in her head forever. Terrible things from someone who, in the end, recognized his own terribleness.

"We can send someone back," suggests Stef. "Won't it really …." She knows how it sounds and is too tired to care anymore. "Won't it really slow us up?"

"We'll pull if you don't want to," says Lexi. Wind ruffles her hair, sending it spiraling in several directions. She looks like a witch of the lake, intense and pale, jewels of snow encrusting her eyelashes and brows. T.J. is also changed, face pink and shining, hair frozen into strange points and directions. Stef hasn't seen it herself, but she now knows she has a streak of white in her hair, a bit of snow embedded into her person. In this moment, they are all otherworldly beings folded out of winter, breathing steam into the chill air.

"No," says Stef. "We'll all pull."

T.J. nods, and she joins them in finishing the sled.

"And ... then what?" she asks after a while.

"We walk," says Lexi. " I get you to the road and—"

"And?"

Lexi doesn't finish the sentence.

"What do you want to happen next, Lexi?"

She continues tying off the ends of the stretcher. "Don't know what I want anymore."

"I'll tell you what's going to happen," says Stef, and waits until she meets her gaze. "We take one day, then the next day. We get into whatever bumfuck little town you're walking us to. We rent rooms. We take baths. We eat dinner. We call our parents, maybe the lawyer."

"But that's not what *has* to happen," says T.J.

Stef thinks about the Peppie she remade the night before. How it seemed destined to be one thing forever, then showed her how it could be another.

They fall into silence again as the forest groans around them, snow sliding from branches, ice settling. The noises are clear to her in ways she could not have expected five months ago. She is ready to leave the forest—she has a crusty, itchy feeling all over and has been dreaming of a hot bath and getting her hair looked at and a gooey slice of pizza—but those things feel like they belong to another person. She finds herself looking over her shoulder more than once, searching the trees, looking for a stand of birches. The fact is, the adventure she has been seeking is here, with T.J., with Lexi, with Gil and Gillie. With The Green Place and the battles that are to come.

Lexi pauses, wipes her upper lip. "Can you—be shine-o-la with me?"

"Shinola?" She remembers a thing a friend's grandpa used to say: *He don't know shit from Shinola*, and when Stef thinks a little harder she recalls how Shinola was some kind of shoe cleaner or something.

"Jim always said Daddy was sometimes fulla shit, and sometimes full of shine-o-la," says Lexi. "He was always fulla somethin'."

"I bet he was," says Stef. "So you want me to be ... honest with you, is that it?"

"Yes. Be true."

She nods. "What do you want to know?"

Lexi sticks her hatchet down in the snow. "You and T.J. keep telling me about what happens when I walk out with you. You always say how great it is. But you also make it sound like it's the scariest place in the world. So. Tell me if I can make it out there."

Stef hears the young woman's fear. She thinks about being a person who has grown up with the sounds of the forest and the voices of her father and brother and Gil—and how all of them are gone now, except the magical being most people wouldn't even believe existed. About what it might be like to step from a quiet, knowable place into a typhoon. T.J.'s world is extraordinary even for those who live it; tossing a person like Lexi into that chaos with no warning feels wrong.

Behind that, Stef thinks for the first time about what it means to promise safety and protection to Lexi. She's a grown person but she's also a child. She knows how to start a fire but not a stove. She can sleep on the snow but doesn't know what a box spring is. To her, clouds aren't storage space; they're just weather. She hasn't been around more than a handful of people at a time for nearly ten years. The awesome responsibility settles on Stef's shoulders like snow.

We are so not the right people to do this.

Yet another part of her wants to try. With money and time and insistence on privacy—*she can be my personal assistant! Nobody pays attention to those folks*—they can make this work. Stef can make it work. She wants to believe this. So the best she can do for Lexi is to say what's in her heart with the limited knowledge she has, and believe it can be enough.

"Yes," says Stef, hoping it is not a lie she's telling herself. "You will. 'Cause you'll have us. And 'cause you're you. You know the way. And I know how to make things work."

T.J. has been watching them quietly; there's a sadness in his eyes Stef has not seen before. "But why would you want to?"

The day has a dreamlike quality that reminds Stef of her first step into the wilderness, bouncing out of that helicopter, unable to catch her breath. Everything is sharp and absolute and clear to her now: There is magic in the world, they have seen death, they have lived among the wild things of the forest, they have lost friends. Or at least cohorts.

Her thoughts bounce between concern for T.J., who is quiet and interior in a way she has never known as he pulls the sled with Tony in it, and anticipation for Lexi. She feels as if she has taken on a hard, welcome burden. It is real, at least—unlike their life of celebrity. That has been the strangest thing of all, to discover that she is capable of expansion, of becoming new all over again. She is not afraid. The hyperawareness she felt on arriving in the woods feels permanent. She has never been so awake.

The day comes full-on and they trudge through it. They come to a point where the trees are spaced further apart, and the forest becomes merely a wood, with a thicket here and there. It is a different place they have walked to now, a foreign place. The quality of light thins and wanes; the steady chill in the air grows harsher. It will be a cold, wicked night if they spend it outside.

"Can't be much further," says T.J.

Stef nods. "Man, I'm ready for a hot bath. And real food."

No one contradicts her.

Abruptly, Lexi comes to life, halting and scanning the brush and trees.

High above them, a bird circles and catches the breeze, a dark spot gliding against the indigo sky. They set Tony down and Lexi ventures a few feet into the brush, holds out her hands and waits. The trees appear to vibrate and Stef hears a low, musical hum. Lexi jerks around and gestures forward, rubbing at her temples. "This way."

They can't run with the sled but they go as fast as their burden and the terrain allows. The wind bites into Stef's lungs, the absolute power of the moment holding them fast. And then—suddenly—there it is. A trail. Not the faint spaces they have hacked and trod through over the past several days but a true two-person-wide trail.

"We are found," says Stef.

They stand side by side, glancing down the snow-covered path. A slight hint of tarmac peeps through the trees.

"Well, I'm gonna say it," says T.J. "Since nobody else will." He looks at both of them. "Lexi, we want you to come with us. But you should also get that it's really not a good idea."

"Why would you say that?" says Stef. "Why now?"

Lexi tilts her head at T.J.

"Think about it," he tells them both. "Walk it through. First, we're not gonna get a ride if we have a dead body. A cop car, maybe. So that's No. 1 bad idea. We roll up as missing hikers with a dead body, that's a cop call before anything else. Then the press shows up because T.J. Furey is actually alive and there's a huge story they want. Somebody might start asking about who Lexi is. And Lexi doesn't exist—at least, not on the outside. Lexi, you have no ID, right? And no tracking device? So, a lot of questions."

T.J. pauses, and now Stef is twisting her mouth from side to side.

"If Tony was still—here, we probably coulda slid back in," he goes on. "Let him get security and lawyers. But without him we're naked. Asking for trouble."

Now nobody looks happy. "We can park Tony under some leaves and send the authorities back when we're ready," says Stef. "I know, I know. But—think he'd want us walking into a shitstorm if we could avoid it?"

T.J. sighs. "Suppose. But that's only half of it."

"I'm the other half," says Lexi, who has turned her back to them and is holding her arms out straight. Ahead of her, the trees vibrate and a distinct hum rises. The snow begins to part, then opens wide, leading back into the forest. She's a little out of breath and Stef's chest is tight.

You sure you wanna leave magic land? Stef asks herself. *It sure doesn't look like she does.*

Lexi lowers her arms, expression unreadable. "This is not my way," she says. "That is."

Stef takes a deep breath. "Lexi, come on. I know you're scared. But look where you are. It's not a place for people to live. It's just a place where people survive. As scary as the outside may seem to you—it's even more terrifying for me to imagine you living here alone. It's like you said last night. This life was chosen for you. You didn't pick it."

"Well," she says. "I'm choosing it now. I want to see."

"See what?"

"See if they let me back in. See if I can help. That's my choice."

T.J. is staring at Lexi with a look of longing Stef can't interpret.

Inside, she feels her heart tearing. Have any of them chosen their lives? Can you just drop one existence and pick up another? Is it that simple?

"Well?" says T.J.

He will do as she does. He always has. Just as she does what he does.

"We're going out," she says. "We *have* to." She launches herself forward and hugs Lexi until she gets a hug back. "You can always leave," she tells her. "You can always come and find us. Ken?"

"Ken," says Lexi and there's a hitch in her throat.

And she lets them walk off without her.

I'll come back, thinks Stef, because she can't speak right now. Her throat has closed. *I will.*

But she isn't sure if she's saying that for Lexi or for herself.

The Way Is Clear

I follow.
   Least, I follow once my legs start working again. Takes a minute, funny thing. When I was saying it to Stef I knew xactly what I wanted: Go back, find Gil. See about the doors that are open to me. Now I'm not sure. It's so hard to watch them just … go. I feel like I'm falling again, falling into a black hole that has no end this time.
   Path's mostly clear so I dodge into the trees and duck and make no real sound. Once again I'm alone and I'm the fastest quietest thing in the forest. Being Offguard. Doing the thing nobody else xpects. Including me, sometimes.
   I eyeball them. Up ahead Stef's upset. T.J. has his arm on her shoulders. Wind stills and I hear a big sniff and my heart stops a minute. Why did I do that? Stef's the only friend I have. Only human friend I have. And I still don't know 'bout Gil.
   Changed my mind once about what I wanted, then changed it back. Shot Artio, but also let her live. Not used to this, making my own choices. Even after a winter in the cabin, I don't always know what it means to do the right thing. Wonder when that happens. When I know for sure.
   Right now it doesn't feel right.
   But it also doesn't feel like there's another choice to make.
   I turn away when I watch them put Tony aside, under the leaves. Something inside me tears when they do and I get mad because it's like Tony turned into a tick and burrowed inside me and I can't get him out. But the same's true for Stef. Even T.J. They were even more Offguard than I was. Totally un-xpected.
   "Ah," I say to the trees and it's a wet sound. Didn't know I was going to make a noise until there it was, made. I swallow it down but it keeps wanting to come back out and my face is all hot and sweaty suddenly.

I keep following them 'til I see road ahead. Actual road. Road cars drive on, dark and shiny with yellow lines down the middle. Last time I saw road like this was just after Daddy picked me up and gave me grape soda. Jim was in the back seat. He was sleeping hard.

I've been sleeping, too.

Thing is, I'm not ready for the road yet. I might get out there but I'm only ever gonna be trouble. I have no place on the Outside. My place is here, on the Inside. T.J. and Stef will forget about me being here and 'ventually they will decide I didn't xist and they'll tell their stories the way they want to. Without me.

Other things for me to do here, anyway.

Yesterday after everything happened, I was the one walking with Gillie back to her trees. We left a long green trail of grass behind us. Went back to the shack and there were the birches right behind it. Gillie put her hand on my shoulder. *Well, lass,* she said. *Ye ken the whys and wherefores now?*

Aye, I whispered.

'Twas what must happen, she said. *What we did together, isnae wrong, isnae right.*
You should have told me, I said. *I could have understood.*
Maybe, she said. *An if ye didnae? Then what. I loved yer Jim, too, ye ken.*

My eyes must have been real big 'cause she laughed and it was like spring came out a minute.

As ye love Gil, so ye dae. As ye were beginnin' to feel for Anthony. 'Tis fine to love whosoever ye choose, with body, with dofheicthe.

Now what happens? I asked.

Well, she said. *We will be here. Long as we can be. Artio is herself again, thanks to Anthony, and Anthony has what he wanted, of a sort. So. I believe the forest is safe for the nowawhens, though I cannae ken about yer cave. That is trouble, Artio or no.*

I handed her the Peppie. Knew she wanted it.

I cannae use it to harm, she said, tucking it into her mossy coat. *But. 'Tis transformed now. 'Tis both magic and a tool. We will see to its power.*

I understand, I said and I think I finally did. *I'll try to come back. If you let me in.*

Aye, she said. *If ye come, we will find a way together. We need such as ye.* She leaned over and hugged me and it was like that first time on the ice, all fast and sudden and warm.

You're getting better at that, I said over her shoulder. Feeling her arms round me was like being embraced by the whole forest.

She pulled back and had become Gil. *D'ye know the way?* he asked.

I looked at him with a raised eyebrow. 'Course. I always know the way.

He turned to his birches and slipped 'round them. And was gone.

Now I find a tree and scale it though it's slow going 'cause I keep having to wipe my eyes and remember to breathe. T.J. stands in the middle of the road, waves his arms at a big boxy car that looks like it's gliding. So quiet, this car. I remember Daddy's car making noise, coughing and smelling like gas but now maybe they make cars silent and clean. Stef leans in the boxy car's window. T.J. pulls something out of his pocket and waves it at the driver. Door opens and they crawl inside. I think of driveways, of parking lots, of home. Of air coming out of vents in the car and warming us up. Magic. Unseen. *Dofheicthe.*

"Wait," I say, but I don't yell it. I only say.

The car speeds off, the road taking them away.

They are outside. I am inside.

I descend the tree. Turn 'round. Go back to where we split off. They left their packs behind so I rifle through and make one big bag and leave what I don't need behind. Don't care anymore if someone knows I'm here. I can hide. I can run. They don't have to find me. There are whole other worlds where I can go now. And I will always know the way.

I stand there for a couple minutes and let it wash over me, all the sounds of the forest. The silence of being alone. Things I haven't really listened to for months. This is the sound of life. "Wait," I say again but it's only to myself.

It'll be a long walk back but we started the path already and there's some tents just a few hours back and then a whole campsite of things to dig up and raid. It'll be spring soon, and I know xactly what to do. Plow forward. Don't think too much. Wait for the way to open up to me again.

I turn to head back and there is Artio, down the path. She is looking right at me, brown and black and shiny and big and healthy. There are no arrows in her. Her ears are smooth and new. Also: She has two healthy, bright, yellow-green eyes.

Artio, the endless.

I hold up my hand and she gives her head a mighty shake. I think about walking over there. About touching her fur. Seeing if *he* is inside for true. But I don't need to. I keep my hand up until she sneezes once, twice, then turns and lumbers into the thickest part of the trees. I hear her saunter away, breaking new trails, and stand there in one place until I hear her no more.

I look back over my shoulder. The road is still there. I could go. I could walk it, easy.

Not today. Not tomorrow. But someday.

It's good to know it's there.

I choose for me, now.

Start Where You End

Each bed comes with four feather pillows. The mattress is firm, luxurious, and covered with a down duvet which itself is encased in a beige cover, clasped together with wooden buttons. The room has central heating, which at this moment is bathing Stef with invisible warmth. It is a womb.

To some, she thinks, *it's magic.*

The clock reads 4:12 p.m.

Stef can't think of putting herself on such a clean bed in her state, so she shucks off every inch of her filthy, torn clothes and makes a puddle of them in the middle of the room. Eventually she piles everything into a plastic bag and leaves it outside the door. Ginny, their host, said she would come by and do laundry that evening. Stef isn't sure she can bear to put those clothes back on again.

From the other side of the wall she expects to hear T.J. snoring—but it is quiet. Maybe he can't figure out what to do with himself right now, either.

She wanders into the bathroom and stares in the mirror. She has to touch her face to make it seem real. There are hollows around her eyes she never had before, and her chin is sharper than when she left home. Her eyes seem tremendous, wet and clear, the cleanest part about her. She pulls a twig from one of her grown-out locs and twirls it between her fingers, thinking about the cave and Lexi before tossing it into the waste bin. Her fingers travel the length of the white stripe in her hair and she has to admit, it does look pretty cool.

She takes stock of the rest of her body. The bruise from last night is shining and dark and when she pokes it, she winces. Odd scratches and lines draw crosses around her body, as if she has rolled in briars. Her fingernails are jagged and blackened.

The blasting shower heat is glorious, and she scrubs for a long time, which opens up some of the marks on her so they bleed again. She lets the water gush over her until it runs clear, then cleans out the muck in the drain and runs a bath, settling in for a soak. The soft drip of the tap soothes her as she leans back, resting her head on a towel. This is normal. This is good. Knots in her system loosen.

Natural magic, she recalls one of the lyrics she wrote down this morning. Words that are carved into her notebook by her pen as sure as a knife into a tree. She tries to hold on to the feeling that came over her when she wrote them, but it's slipping away like drops from the faucet. A wave of sadness that Lexi is not with them passes over her, then retreats.

She chose not to be a part of our outside. We are terrifying.

She admires Lexi's decision. Standing on your own and living an independent life is a form of magic, too. By choice, Lexi has become unseen by the rest of the world, and that takes bravery.

The driver of the car that picked them up suggested a B&B her sister-in-law ran and dropped her silent passengers off in front of a gingerbread house with wood-paneled walls and flower-print décor. T.J. channeled Tony's authority and laid out dollar bill after bill until they had the whole place rented for two nights. Then he promised more if they went undisturbed during their stay. They requested sandwiches, fruit, and lots of water. And Full Stuff Oreos, if they could find any. The owner—a retiree named Ginny—brought what was asked for and asked nothing in return. If she recognized T.J., she did a good job of acting as if he were just another customer.

Stef phoned their parents, who did not believe what they were hearing at first, but after a few moments of convincing were sobbing on the other end of the line. T.J. came on for a few minutes but was surprisingly uncommunicative and after a minute or two hung up his extension. Stef insisted that her parents tell no one that they were alive and safe. It was too risky. They promised, but also said they were getting on the first flight to Denver and would drive out to … what was the small town Stef and T.J. had wandered into?

"Leadville," she said, sent her love and hung up the phone as quickly as possible.

Now Stef opens her eyes, shrouded in bath fog like a dream. She touches the porcelain tub with wrinkled fingers, running them over the soap, the tiles, the rubber duck, the gash on her hand. Everything feels alien. Everything belongs in another place, another time. Her perspective is struggling to readjust, and in a way, she doesn't want it to.

Once again she thinks of that strange, unknowable creature named Lexi and then of the entire other world that opened up to them briefly. It's a world where she has real purpose, a world where she can make a difference.

Does that make it better? she wonders, knowing there is no equivalency between writing pop tunes and helping to stop a war.

Stef feels a question has been asked and no answer given. The absence of that answer is like an itch she can't scratch. Pieces slide together like song lyrics trying to send her a message. Or like magic words that help show you the way.

When the water grows cold Stef steps out of the tub, towels off, and tumbles into bed, wrapped in feathers and cloth and dreams.

Their parents arrive the following afternoon, and there is a great joyous reunion between them all. But after things calm down and they are sitting in the common living room before a fire, coffee and cocoa in hand, everyone goes silent.

It's our cue, thinks Stef. *Now is when we tell them everything.*

She looks at T.J., who hasn't said much. He seems weighed down by unseen hands, and she wonders where his spark has gone. "Well?" she asks him.

He nods.

So Stef tells their story. She doesn't preface it with *you'll never believe this* and *I know what the news says about "sickness."* She just spells it out. Acts as if people living in the woods and fey are commonplace and normal. She talks for a long time, and as she does, T.J. brightens, hanging on every word and only adding a few of his own from his days—months—in The Green Place. Together, they are formidably convincing, and by the end their parents are sitting in their chairs, stiff-backed and unreadable.

Stef falls silent and waits for some reaction. Mom and Dad look at each other, then away. They say nothing.

So she takes it a step further, telling her father, "Give me your music clip."

"No," he says.

"Oh, Malik, hand it to her." Her mother's voice is curious but stern.

Her father unclips his small ancient music player from his waist, and Stef quickly tears it apart. Neither one of her parents move, just watch her as if she's an exhibit at an old-fashioned zoo. She lays the pieces out in front of her, hoping everything didn't vanish once she left the woods, then focuses on the pieces. Her father's favorite music is early-last-century jazz and more recent speechrap dub combos. She thinks of his face and what he will listen to. She thinks of the songs she knows are important to him—the song he and her mother danced at during their wedding, the tunes that always get him up and moving, holiday songs, and—of course—anything his daughter has written. She waits until the pieces begin vibrating, then closes her eyes and clears her mind, asking them: *Help me help him understand.*

There's an audible gasp from her mother and she opens her eyes. The pieces are hovering before her, shifting themselves around, laid out and waiting for her hands. She reaches up to grab this one and that, moving the tiniest of chips and wires together as if she's done this all her life, and in what feels like an hour but is in fact just a few seconds, the player is reassembled. She presses it between her hands and it feels *right*. It is happy.

She offers it to Dad, numb palm aloft.

"Play it," she says.

"I won't touch it," he says. "You need help."

"No, I don't," she says. "Play it."

"She's fine," says T.J. "This is what she can do."

Her mother reaches forward and her father takes her wrist. "Don't, Valerie."

"Psh," says her mother, picking up the device. "Now what?"

"Think of a song Dad likes," she says.

Her mother closes her eyes briefly. The device starts to sing a long-ago tune about farewells and goodbyes, of new beginnings and love. It's the song Dad always says was playing the first time he asked her mother out on a date.

Dad turns and eyes the device, and the tune changes—this time it's Louis Armstrong and his brassy ways. "Stop," he says, and the device quiets. He reaches out to Stef. "Let me see my mother's watch."

She slides it from her wrist. He knows the story now; she told him about Gillie and the rebirth of the watch. He presses the side and light bursts into the room—only there's more to it here than in the woods. Here, the light reaches the ceiling and draws designs, words in a language Stef does not know, sentences and concepts all made of pure light. They weave together and form the image of a woman's head, then her body, on the ceiling. She is sitting astride a motorcycle, a scarf at her neck and the wind in her hair.

Stef knows this woman. She's Grandma. Or, she was.

"Yumma," her father whispers. And as he says it the woman guns the motorcycle and it shoots off into the light. They all turn away from the ceiling and he stares at his lap. He hands Stef the watch and walks out of the room and out of the house.

Stef jumps up to follow.

"I'll go," says T.J. "Let me." He jogs after their father and soon Stef can see them walking past the big bay window of the B&B.

She slips the watch back on her wrist and meets her mother's eyes. "Mom," Stef says.

"Shh," says her mother. "Of course I believe you. And so will he."

"There is one more thing," she says, then explains what they have to do next. What she has only just now decided.

Their parents leave the next day. Stef slips a letter into her mother's luggage that she will find once they reach Maryland again. It is much of what they spoke about when T.J. was out with Dad, but she felt she had to underscore it: *We'll come back when we can. Please don't tell anyone.* But that wasn't all. Stef also wrote in the note where Tony's body was located, so they could anonymously inform the authorities later on.

T.J. finishes a talk with their father outside, after which Dad seems to be, if not entirely on board with their story, at least believing that they believe it. Something extraordinary happened to his kids out in the forest, something that will take everyone time to digest, but their father no longer believes it is imminently dangerous.

Back upstairs, T.J. disappears into his room. Stef gives him some time, then goes down the hall, pausing outside the door. *I'm taking steps*, she thinks. *Just different ones than Samuel did.* Rapping quietly, her knocks push the door open a crack. "I'm here," he says, and she slips inside, prepared for anything.

But she's not surprised at all to find him packed and ready to leave.

There are many things Stephanie Holliday and Thomas Furey have not thought through clearly. They have food. They have a tent. They have matches. Beyond that are question marks. They don't know where they're going, only where they have to start.

You start where you ended, Stef thinks, and gives Ginny instructions on where to drop them off, about twenty minutes outside of town.

It's not about being awake, T.J. said when Stef came into his room. *It's about being alive.*

She can't agree more.

It is simply what has to be done, and done now. If they wait, their old life will envelop them again. Today's memories will be the experiences of different people. Everything will fade and become an anecdote, then a feeling, then ancient history. It will be a thing that once happened—not a thing that is still happening.

Neither of them want to lose everything they have discovered.

Ginny drives until Stef pokes at the car window and says, "There." She recognizes the trailhead immediately; you don't forget such things. It's possible any trailhead will do, but she wants to pick up the thread exactly where they dropped it. Ginny swerves the car around to make a U-turn back into town, then pulls off the road. The woman has been quiet through the entire ride, but now as they prepare to hop out, she speaks up.

"'Gonna snow tonight, I reckon," says Ginny, idling the truck.

"That time of year," says T.J., squinting at the heavens.

"You'll be okay out there?" Ginny wonders.

Stef stares out the window, eyes tracing the path back in. It has flurried here recently and a light dusty layer of snow marks where they emerged. "Don't know," she says, and thinks of Lexi. "Prolly." She smiles.

"Not good 'prolly' weather."

"It'll do," says T.J.

They climb out of the cab, hoisting spare backpacks Ginny turned up in her attic. "We're meeting someone, anyway," she says.

"Here," says Ginny, handing her a flashlight. "Think y'll be needin' this, though the batteries are gonna be dead soon, I reckon."

Stef turns over the heavy thing in her hands, then gives it back. She'll have all the light she needs now from grandma's "fixed" watch. "Thanks anyway, Ginny."

"Don't mention," says the older woman, holding up a hand. T.J. and Stef give back the same signal and turn to face the trees. There's a low bank of fog rolling out of the forest that gives it a haunted quality. A moment later, tires on the gravel shoulder start up and the car drives off.

Silence scoops them up again.

"We'll find Lexi," says Stef. "Or maybe she'll find us. "

"I'm counting on Artio," says T.J. "I'd like to see what it's like to ride a bear."

"As if Tony would ever let you do that."

He looks at her with a half smile. He's still got that sadness in his eyes, but apparently knowing a part of Tony still lives is comforting.

"We got this," says T.J. "We totally got this."

They begin ascending the path. One foot forward, then the next. Keep moving, keep an eye on the horizon. Step by step, they crunch through the snow. The image of Artio breaching the lake surface comes to Stef, and in retrospect it is a glorious memory to have. She thinks about the bear falling under the surface and imagines she has an inkling of what it is like to die just enough to do anything to keep on living.

T.J. points far ahead. "Are those birch trees?"

They keep walking as Stef counts: One, two, three …

Soon, the forest wraps them in its embrace, and they are gone from sight.

Without a trace.

Glossary

Tha an t-slighe soilleir
The way is clear

Toirmisgte
Forbidden

Sìthiche (plural), *sìthean* (singular)
One of many versions of "folk of the fairy mounds." In Irish, it's *sídhe*.

Dofheicthe
Invisible, unseen (Irish)

Lorgaire
Tracker, seeker, finder

Fuasglaiche
Fixer

Lighiche
Healer

Uilebheist
Great monster

Geas
Unusual restriction or taboo in folklore

Tír nan Óg
The country of the young, home of the sìthean. In Irish, spelled Tír-na-nÓg.

Acknowledgements

For a long time, camping was traumatizing to me. When I was about ten, our entire sixth grade class went on the annual "outdoor bound" trip in which we spent multiple days living in cabins by a lake and doing camp type things. But to start everything off, the school bus dropped us off by a trailhead on the side of a road, drove off with our packed suitcases, and we were given our marching orders. As in, *march*.

At ten, you have no sense of anything, especially distance or time. That hike felt like the Bataan Death March to me: endless, hard, uphill and did I say endless? Also, we had no cell phones or internet—this was the before times. It must have ended, because I eventually came home after the whole ordeal.

(To be fair, I had a great time during my visit. I got a lot of reading done, made crafts, learned to read trail signs, ate Rice Krispies and met the boy I'd eventually get my first kiss from. Hi, Danny!)

Hiking and camping have become more ... enjoyable to me these days, but the thing is, everything in the woods wants a piece of me. If there's a mosquito in the vicinity, I am dinner. Don't even get me started about waking up in the middle of the night and having to find the latrine in the dark and the cold with little rocks and dirt under your feet.

Despite all that, I managed to go all in on *wanting* to be good at The Woods. I camped with the Girl Scouts, spent time in a sleep away camp in the woods on Maryland's border with Pennsylvania. We had our privations, but I learned what the quiet of the woods sounded like, and that sun streaming through trees towering into the sky got my heart racing. I wanted to be self-sufficient so badly in those adolescent years, and the woods tossed up every challenge imaginable.

The Woods stayed with me. It's primeval. It taps into our uncivilized selves. Trees hide secrets even as they reveal sunlight. The forest knows what time really means, and how humans are just another animal briefly passing through.

Leave No Trace is a book that also understands time. It's always been about the woods and a version of me (though definitely not me) who was forced to live there. Lexi began as a classic "what if" character, born after I watched (at a too-young age) Roger Donaldson's 1980s indie film *Smash Palace*. Amid a New Zealand couple's disintegrating marriage, the father kidnaps his daughter and plans to hide out with her in the bush. ("Bush" in New Zealand terms meaning a lush near jungle of trees, plants and breathtaking scenery.) Spoiler alert: This part of the movie doesn't last long. Daughter gets a cold, father leaves to get her medicine, and they're caught at the pharmacy. But I saw that movie and asked, *What would've happened if they never left?*

That question started the story and decades of research about what it meant to survive in the forest, to live without people, and then to face the incursion of the outside world—by musicians, no less. I didn't start with a fantasy element, but once I learned of the Ghillie Dhu (the Green Man of the forest), I knew everything was going to head in a new, more exciting, direction. Lexi would no longer be a victim of her father's terrible decisions—she'd be a survivor, and find her own way out. If she chose to.

It amazes me how many elements are the same in this finished version from the one I originally dreamed up in middle school. *Leave No Trace* has been a long journey, and undergone as many trials and challenges as Lexi herself. So let me at least attempt to remember everyone who's had a hand in helping make it all happen. Undying thanks and love to Alexis, Rebecca, Valerie and Julia, all of whom were my earliest readers. I passed handwritten chapters of the first drafts to them between classes, and sometimes they even tolerated me reading a chapter over the phone to them in the evenings.

Julia especially (who I've dedicated the book to) helped me choose "Alexa" from a list she had of what names went. We went through the alphabet in this book she owned—pre-internet days, that's how you did this!—and settled on Alexa, which comes from Alexander (as in, The Great) and means "leader of men." Lexi leads people. She knows the way. She takes them where they need to go, and then she finds out where she herself needs to go.

Muchas gracias to Señora Brown, who never noticed me writing the first drafts in my notebooks in Spanish class. To the generous high school librarian who let me transcribe the hand-written pages onto her Macintosh. To the librarian's husband who rescued the document after the computer crashed, and gave me a chewed-up version that required another rewrite. To everyone who volunteered to read these versions over the years and offer feedback, including my agent Bridget Smith at JABberwocky, Lezli Robyn and Shahid Mahmud at Arc Manor. Thank you to Fiverr's Marsaili, who helped me with my Scots Gaelic translations (though all errors are mine). I mix Scots and Irish folklore and the occasional word in this story intentionally, and hope to cause no offense in doing so.

More thanks to Roger Donaldson, whose *Smash Palace* short-circuited and then rebooted my imagination. To the musicians whose lives I paid very, very close attention to at a remove and then, later as a music journalist, up close. To all the survival experts out there who I also paid very, very close attention to, reading their books and making notes about how a person might survive or even thrive in the woods, which is so much harder to do than anyone imagines. And a big special extra thanks to fellow author and total mensch L.J. Cohen, who brainstormed with me over a weekend how to make the second half of the story come together. I couldn't have done this without any of you, and you have my heart.

Many thanks and so much love as well to my brilliant, funny husband Maury, who supports me in every way possible and insists he's ready to be known as "Mr. Randee Dawn." He has enjoyed my other books but thinks *Leave No Trace* is my best work, which is yet another reason I love him. To my mom, my brother Craig, and all of my families—found and otherwise. The way hasn't always been clear, but that doesn't mean we stop looking. If you can't find the path, you make it for yourself. But to learn a lesson from the forest, it's best to take the long view about time. Have patience. The trees wait for you.

Be sure to let me know what you think! Find me at RandeeDawn.com, and I hope you'll join my mailing list.

www.ingramcontent.com/pod-product-compliance
Lightning Source LLC
Jackson TN
JSHW021908160825
89473JS00001B/1